Synchrony

Cindy Ray Hale

Book Two of the Destiny Trilogy

Alissa,
Happy Reading
Cindy Ray Hale

Synchrony

First Edition: 2014

destinybycindyhale.blogspot.com

ISBN 978-0-9910374-3-8

Cover design by Steven Novak

Cover photography by Virginia Rose Hodges Photography

Cover Models: Christian Lopez and Selena Renteria

For my grandpa, William T. Allen, who loved the woods as much as I do. I'm sure he's smiling down from heaven to know that the cover photo of this book was shot in his home state of West Virginia.

Synchrony: n. a state in which things happen, move, or exist at the same time.

Chapter 1

Missing Screen

Destiny

"I hate saying goodbye," I whispered, holding Isaac's hand tighter. I glanced back toward Michael's bedroom window. If he found me out here with the forbidden Baptist boy at three o'clock in the morning, it wouldn't be pretty.

"I know the feeling." Isaac turned to me with a rueful grin.

I reached up and cupped a hand around the back of his neck. Immediately, he leaned his face down and kissed me tenderly. I never got tired of kissing him, running my hands through his lush, dark hair, smelling his sandalwood cologne, or listening to him serenade me with his delectable voice.

Reluctantly, I strained to lift my bedroom window. It was a little high for me, so Isaac reached up and helped me push it into place. He laced his fingers together and held them down like a stirrup. I stepped into his hands and grasped his broad shoulder for stability before climbing into my bedroom. Once I was inside, I leaned out the window to give him a final hug and kiss.

"Goodnight, beautiful." Isaac's mahogany eyes gleamed in the moonlight.

"Goodnight," I whispered. Although Olivia was gone on an overnight school trip, I still had to avoid waking Michael from where he slept across the hall.

A few days later, after finishing the dishes with Olivia, I was about to retreat to my room to finish my homework when Dad called me into the formal living room. That was never a good sign. The living room was where Mom and Dad summoned us when we needed to be raked over the coals.

Mom was there, too, a grim expression on her face.

"Destiny," Dad began. "Have a seat."

I sunk into the same armchair I'd squirmed in after Homecoming when they'd found out I was dating Isaac. I was so panicked that night. I thought for sure that they'd ground me for life, publicly humiliate me, or have an embarrassing confrontation with Isaac's parents. In the end, the only punishment I received was a stern lecture on the dangers associated with dating nonmembers. Sure, Dad was furious and Mom was appalled that I was dating the forbidden Baptist boy, but they hadn't done anything to punish me and had not demanded that we stop dating. They'd just expressed their displeasure. Their deep displeasure. Then there was the time when they'd gotten a phone call from Hannah's mom saying that we'd been using her house to meet. But even then they didn't ground me.

Isaac had had it much worse. His dad had taken the keys to his truck and his new iPhone. That was why he'd come to see me that night. We had no other option.

I should have known this was coming. Dread crept in from the shadows of my mind where I'd pushed it away for the past few weeks since we'd begun dating. I took one look at Dad's face, and I knew this meeting wasn't going to go so smoothly.

"Earlier today, your mother discovered something that concerned me," Dad continued.

What could they have possibly found? Isaac and I had been so careful to cover our tracks.

"When she was out doing some yard work this morning, she noticed your screen was missing."

I felt the blood rush to my face. We'd forgotten to replace the screen? I could have sworn I'd put it back. Isaac wouldn't have left it off, would he?

Mom got straight to the point. "You snuck out with him, didn't you?" she accused.

The stricken look on my face must have given me away because Dad sucked in a disbelieving breath, a quick sound that sickened me as the guilt settled deep in my stomach. What must they think of me? That I was the black sheep of the family? I'd never wanted to be that person. I'd only ever wanted to please them. The disappointment in Dad's eyes cut through me like a knife, and I couldn't even look at Mom.

"What are we going to do with you, Destiny? We can't even trust that you're safe in your own bed anymore," Mom said. "We've been more than understanding about your relationship with Isaac. I don't think you have a clue how hard this has been for us."

Understanding? They hadn't been. Understanding would have been welcoming Isaac into their home as my boyfriend with open arms. At the very least, Dad could have reached out to Isaac when he stepped out of his comfort zone and came to church with me against his parents' wishes. Isaac had sacrificed a lot by doing that, and Dad hadn't even acknowledged his presence.

I should have said all this to them, but I didn't have it in me. Instead, I caved. "I was perfectly safe. I promise. Isaac would never do anything to hurt me. He's a complete gentleman." It sounded lame and whiney in my ears, like I didn't believe it, even when I knew it to be the absolute truth. There was something so intimidating about Dad's commanding presence that sucked all the fight out of me.

"You admit you were with him?!" Dad's voice boomed.

Great. Why'd I have to open my big mouth? "Honestly, I wish y'all would trust me more. Then Isaac and I wouldn't have any reason to sneak out at night together." I could tell from the furious expression on Dad's face that he wasn't buying my argument.

"You think we're going to encourage you to date a nonmember?" Mom said incredulously. "Destiny, we want what's best for you. How many times have we told you, 'You marry who you date?' What kind of life would you have with him?"

A beautiful one.

Those were the first words that popped into my head, and despite everything I knew, I couldn't help but believe it. I imagined living with Isaac up on top of Walnut Ridge, in the beautiful white house of my dreams, with a few kids running around, and goose bumps ran down my arms. He could make me so happy, but they couldn't see it like I could.

"Where would you take your kids to church? What religion would they be?" Mom asked.

"Mormon, of course," I said with a forced smile.

"Oh yeah, sure," Dad said with a sarcastic bite to his voice. "You think that just because he came to church with you once he's just going to magically convert. It's true. Sometimes that works out, but I've been around, and usually, in these situations, the Church member either falls away or is forced to bring her kids to church alone every Sunday. Just look at Sister Whittaker."

As much as I didn't want to admit it, he had a point. Sister Whittaker was this lady from church who'd been raised by good Mormon parents but had turned wild as a teenager and ended up marrying a nonmember. Now, three kids later, she'd reformed and come back, but her husband didn't want anything to do with the Church. So there she sat, every Sunday, alone with her kids. And now her oldest son, Ryan, who was fifteen, was starting to follow in his father's footsteps. Megan told me at church a few weeks ago that she'd seen him smoking weed out by the dumpsters at Acorn Creek High School.

"But I wouldn't marry Isaac unless he was a good Mormon." That was true, wasn't it?

"Destiny, once you're in love with someone, it's too late," Mom said gently. "When you get to that point, you'd do anything for that person, even if it meant marrying outside your faith."

For some reason this bugged me. Who were they to tell me what I would and wouldn't do? I was only sixteen. I had years before I had to think about marriage. How could dating Isaac hurt me? He was graduating this spring, and then he'd probably leave for college.

As much as I loved and respected Mom and Dad, sometimes there was no reasoning with them. So I did the only rational thing left to do. I nodded and put on my repentant face. "I see what you mean."

Dad let out an audible sigh. "Promise me that you'll stay away from him."

I smiled faintly. He didn't get it, did he? "That's going to be hard, Dad."

"Ben, she can't just stay away from him. They're in *Les Misérables* together."

Dad's face darkened. "Oh, that's right." I had a flashback of the day we'd all watched *Les Mis* together as a family. He'd muttered through the entire movie, grumbling his displeasure about the fact that a Baptist boy would be putting his hands on me. Now he opened his mouth to say something else, but then shut it, clenching his jaw tightly.

"And what if he wants to come to church with me again? Am I supposed to just turn him away?"

"Of course not," Mom said soothingly. "But you can let Michael be the one to talk to him about the Church." She continued on and on, and I refrained from rolling my eyes, keeping my face as neutral as I could. There was no way I was breaking up with Isaac just because they wanted me to. Isaac had stood by me, even when his truck and phone were taken away. But that didn't mean I had to be so openly rebellious about it, either. What they didn't know wouldn't hurt them, right?

Chapter 2

Doodles

Preston

"Hey, Preston, can I borrow a pen?" Destiny asked. We were in seminary, the church class we attended every morning before school.

I gave her a tight smile. Ever since she'd been dating that Baptist guy, things had been strained between us. It wasn't that there weren't any girls who liked me; it was that Destiny didn't. I'd thought I had a chance with her. I'd thought I was good enough. Apparently I was wrong. Just look at her. She was nice and beautiful with long, dark hair and she enjoyed camping and the outdoors. What wasn't to like? It was no wonder Isaac wanted her. I'd wanted her for as long as I could remember.

After handing her my spare pen, I turned my gaze away, pretending I didn't notice the way the light caught the highlights in her hair.

I'd never forget the horrible Sunday he'd come to church with her, and she'd admitted they were dating. The wrenching in my gut was like that sick feeling you get when you suddenly remember a test you forgot to study for. Or when, six hours into the drive home, you realize that you left your favorite stuffed animal from when you were a little kid in the hotel room.

What could I have done differently to win her over? I'd gone over it in my head repeatedly. Had I been too bold at the paintball game when I'd put my arm around her? My cheeks burned in humiliation as I remembered the way she'd twisted away from me. Should I have fought harder for her? I'd considered beating the crap out of Isaac more times than I could count, but what would that achieve? It would just make her pull further away from me.

What did she see in him? That's what I could never understand. Sure, he was a pretty boy, but Destiny should be able to see past that. Even if she never picked me, she should at least find a guy worthy of her. He wasn't even remotely close to worthy. He seemed to think he was better than the rest of the world, like we should all bow down to him. How could a guy like that make Destiny happy?

She was the bravest, strongest, most beautiful girl I'd ever known. She tackled life just as fearlessly as she conquered the toughest cliffs when rock climbing. If she gave me a chance, I would make it my goal in life to bring a smile to her face every day.

But today wasn't that day.

A small sigh escaped her lips, and I glanced over at her open notebook to see her doodle his name in a curly feminine script.

With my pen.

Chapter 3

Some People

Isaac

The halls of Bethel Baptist Academy were full as I headed to Mr. Byrd's for homeroom. It was a chilly, gray November morning and my first day back at school since Dad's idiotic attempt to manipulate me while driving landed me in the hospital with a concussion. And people say *teenagers* are reckless drivers. I couldn't believe he was being such a jerk about me dating Destiny. Actually, I could. He was just like that. Most of the time he was a pretty cool dad, but sometimes he could be so stubborn. And my relationship with Destiny Clark was one of those things that set him off. I'd spent the weekend debating whether or not I should tell Mom that he'd lied about the cause of our accident. On one hand, I didn't want to upset her. On the other hand, I felt like she deserved to know what a jerk he really was. I was still undecided.

Some people aren't what they seem to be. The thought popped into my head as I pushed my way to my locker before homeroom. It was something that I'd seen too much of lately. On the surface, Dad was a perfect Christian. He'd spent the majority of his life studying and teaching God's Word, and most of the students seemed to think that he was doing an excellent job as headmaster, so far. Of course, that wasn't including anyone who knew how he'd been treating Destiny and her family.

Honestly, back at the beginning of the school year, I hadn't been much different. At the time, I'd felt that my bigotry was justified. Dad had had me convinced that Destiny was on the pathway to hell.

I'd been so stupid.

In the hallway, I slipped past a group of girls clustered together outside the choir room.

"Welcome back, Isaac!" Evelyn Cooper, the junior class president, waved as I passed.

"Thanks." I smiled. I was about to turn into the doorway to the choir room when Hannah called out to me from down the hall. I raised a hand in greeting, and she rushed toward me.

"Hey, I have something for you," she said, handing me a folded piece of notebook paper.

I raised my eyebrows, but she just smiled and waved before turning away and darting behind the clustered girls.

As I stepped into the choir room, I wrapped my fingers around the small rectangle of folded paper and took a seat on the front row. Looking around to make sure no one was watching me, I unfolded the paper and read: *Meet me under the southwest stairwell at 10. –D*

Was everything okay with her, or did she just want to see me? It wasn't her style to randomly skip class for a make-out session, but if that was what she was up for, who was I to argue?

Sydney Carter, my ex-girlfriend Aspen's best friend, plopped down into the seat next to me. "Hey. You're back! How are you feeling?" She ran a hand through her long, dark hair.

I refolded the paper casually. No need to arouse suspicion.

"Fine." My tone was slightly aloof. So, she was going to be all nice to me now? Sure, plenty of my old friends had come to see me in the hospital, but I thought that was out of curiosity. Well, better her than Aspen.

A high-pitched laugh caught my attention in the doorway as Aspen herself came into the room with Will. I clenched my jaw and averted my eyes. Even after everything I'd been through with Destiny, it still hurt to see them together. It just didn't seem fair that they were so happy. Whatever happened to "you reap what you sow?" Aspen and Will were lying, cheating hypocrites. It wasn't until I discovered them making out in the parking lot of her favorite sandwich shop that I realized she'd been cheating on me with my best friend. Shouldn't they be reaping the whirlwind?

At 9:58, I stepped out of Honors English with a hall pass, so I could "go to the bathroom." When I arrived at the staircase on the southwest corner of the building, Destiny was already there.

"Hey," I said, smiling. She looked beautiful in her white oxford and plaid skirt. Some girls couldn't pull off the uniform thing very well, but Destiny was definitely not one of those girls. I moved deeper into the shadows, pulled her close to me, and kissed her gently. If I was going to skip class, I might as well make the most of it.

She pulled away. "As nice as this is, I didn't ask you to meet me here just for a kiss."

An uneasy feeling came over me. She wasn't breaking up with me, was she? No she wouldn't have kissed me if that were the case. Still, something in her tone put me on my guard. "What's going on?"

"My parents found out I snuck out with you. They gave me this long speech about it last night." A pained expression moved across her face, like she was stopping herself from elaborating too much on the subject.

My brows knit together in a mix of confusion and concern. "How'd they find out?"

"My mom found the screen on the ground outside my window."

"Your screen was off? That doesn't make any sense, Destiny. I specifically remember putting it back on. I know I did because it was a pain to put back in from so low on the ground."

"Well, there was that storm the next day. Maybe you didn't get it back in properly, and the wind knocked it down."

I nodded thoughtfully. It made sense. I crossed my arms over my chest. "I'm sorry. I feel terrible that you got in trouble because of something I did."

She reached up and uncrossed my arms, taking my hands and stepping closer so that our noses were almost touching. "Don't feel bad. Please."

Well, when she asked that way… I inched closer so that our lips met and kissed her deeper this time. All too soon, she pulled away again.

"Isaac…um. I've been thinking." She scrunched her forehead up, creating a neat wrinkle of her perfect brow, like whatever she was about to say would be hard for her. "We should go back to keeping our relationship a secret." I started to protest, but she put a finger to my lips. "It would be for the best. Just think about it. You could have your phone and your truck back, and everyone would chill out. I know it would feel like we were letting everyone else win, but we would know the truth."

I reached out and tucked a chestnut strand of hair behind her ear, taking a minute to absorb her words. "As much as I don't like hiding, I have to admit you've got a point." I grinned. "It really would be nice to have my phone back."

"Exactly! Then we can text at night. It won't even be hard. We can just disguise each other's contact info in our phones with code names. And we can have more of these meetings under the stairs, but we'll have to change up the times so that people don't catch on."

I laughed. "You've really put some thought into this, haven't you?"

She shrugged. "Just a little. I'm sure we'll figure out better ways to hide as time goes on."

"So, are we going to have an 'official breakup'?"

"No, I think as long as we aren't glued to each other's side people will get the message."

"What are we going to tell people when they ask if we've broken up? Because, believe me, they're going to ask."

She smiled ruefully. "Yeah, I remember at Homecoming how many girls flocked to you when they found out that you and Aspen had broken up."

I dodged her last remark carefully. "Well, if anyone approaches me about it, I'll just tell them I'm not looking for a relationship at the moment."

Chapter 4

Under the Bleachers

Destiny

"See you later, Destiny," Hannah called with a wave as she climbed into Evan's yellow Jeep. Through the driver's side window, I could see them leaning in for a kiss. Other than our conversation before school when I asked her to deliver the note to Isaac, it was the only time she'd spoken to me all day. All day she and Evan had been inseparable. Normally, I wouldn't have noticed, but it was hard to sit next to them being all lovey-dovey when Isaac was across the room sitting at a table full of football players. It just didn't seem fair that we had to hide and they could be as open with their affections as they wanted. I missed him.

I retreated to the sidewalk that wrapped around the corner of the high school building and scanned the line of cars to see if Mom had arrived yet. I couldn't see her anywhere. Michael had football practice today, so I couldn't ride home with him unless I stayed late. As soon as Mom and Dad realized I only stayed for football practice to watch Isaac, they banned me from it.

My phone rang in my pocket.

"Hey, Mom."

"Hey, I'm stuck over at the dentist's office with Elijah and Brianna. I need you and Olivia to stay after with Michael today."

I couldn't help but smile. And watch my sexy boyfriend play football? What an inconvenience. "Sure thing, Mom. I'll let Livie know." I ended the call and looked up to see Olivia approaching me with a group of her eighth-grade friends from the direction of the middle-school building on campus. The middle school was further back from the loading zone, so those students usually congregated with the high school kids when it was time to wait for their rides. Despite being the only Mormon in eighth grade, Olivia hung out with the popular crowd. I would have liked to assume that my lack of popularity was due to the fact that I was one of the freaky Mormons, but Olivia and Michael blew that theory out of the water. You'd think that dating the student body president would get me some popularity points, but it seemed to do just the opposite. Sure, I got noticed—just not in a positive way.

The strange thing was I honestly didn't care as much about popularity anymore. Sure it was nice to be well liked, but as long as I had a few key friends who stood by me fiercely, it really didn't matter what the majority of the student body of Bethel thought about me.

"Livie, Mom's stuck at the dentist with Elijah and Brianna. We have to ride home with Michael today."

She made a face. "Are you serious? It's freezing out here."

"Then don't watch them practice," I said, rolling my eyes. "Go in the building and do your homework."

Usually, I hated the cold, too, but I would gladly endure the weather if it meant I could watch Isaac play. My chances to spend time with him suddenly seemed to be slipping away from me. Every moment I could have with him was precious, even if it was just watching from afar.

I walked past the school buildings to get to the football field. As I rounded the corner of the middle school and the back of the bleachers came into view, something caught my eye. Aspen and Will were under the bleachers about thirty feet from me, only this time they weren't making out like Hudson had reported the day I'd discovered that Aspen and Isaac had broken up. From the looks of it, they were having a massive fight. Aspen had her arms crossed and her hip jutted to the side. Her blonde hair was pulled up into a high ponytail, and she was wearing her cheerleading uniform. Even from where I stood, I could tell she'd been crying.

"How could you do this to me?!" she flung the words out of her mouth like daggers, enunciating each syllable with deadly precision. "You saw how horrible it was for me when my dad cheated on my mom."

I froze in place. Aspen hadn't noticed me yet, and I wasn't sure what to do. Unless I walked all the way around the middle school building to reach the other side, I'd have to pass them to get to the front of the bleachers.

"You're no better than him," she said, the venom in her voice turning to pain and disbelief. "I *trusted* you, Will. You were supposed to be there for me. I gave up Isaac for you! You're not even half the boyfriend he was. Sure, he ignored me sometimes, but at least he was loyal."

Through all of this, Will stood there, impervious to the emotional pain in front of him. Her dagger-words glanced off him harmlessly. Not even the comment about Isaac seemed to faze him.

That was when she saw me. Her expression shifted rapidly from shock to mortification to hatred. I waited for her to walk away. When she didn't, I moved past them quickly and awkwardly, relieved that I could finally escape their private moment of upheaval.

By the time football practice was over, my bottom was numb from sitting on the cold metal bleachers for so long. I'd seen Isaac look over at me several times though, so it made it somewhat worth it. Michael crossed the field, and I climbed down the bleachers.

Honestly, I was so upset by what I'd heard transpire between Aspen and Will that I couldn't focus on the practice. Their timing really stunk. Between today's decision to keep my relationship quiet and what I assumed was Aspen and Will's fresh breakup, she'd be swooping in on Isaac like a hawk intent on its prey. It made me want to punch something. I had to admit, I'd felt sorry for her at first, but the moment she mentioned Isaac, my sympathy had vanished. Who was she to whine about being cheated on when she was a cheater herself? She'd had it coming to her.

Big time.

Still, I dreaded the moment Isaac found out. He'd be sure to sympathize with her. I highly suspected that, even now, despite every rotten thing she'd done to him, he still had strong feelings for her. It really wasn't fair, but what could I do about it?

As I reached the bottom of the bleachers and stepped out onto the field, Isaac approached me. For a moment, I was worried he'd say something to blow our cover in front of Michael, but he looked away, letting his hand brush mine as he walked past.

When Michael and I passed the spot where Aspen and Will had been fighting, they were gone.

"Where's Olivia?" Michael asked as we approached the high school building.

"She's in the high school building somewhere. She didn't want to sit in the cold." Michael gave me an appraising look, and I immediately wished I hadn't added that last part about the cold. Michael knew how much I hated to be cold and how much I liked Isaac. I really wasn't doing a very good job convincing people that we weren't together. Oh well. It didn't really matter, did it? As long as they didn't see us constantly together, they couldn't say anything. I was allowed to want whomever I wanted in my heart.

Michael pulled out his phone and began composing what I assumed was a text for Olivia, telling her to meet us at the car. Hudson Brown walked past us as we reached Michael's green Honda Civic, and Michael lifted his hand in greeting.

"Hey, Hudson," I said. He came over, smiling his usual devil-may-care grin. "What are you still doing here?"

His smiled twisted into an annoyed expression. "I was over in the chem lab. Dr. Spencer's having me do some extra credit to pull my grades up."

"Do you have a car now?"

"Yep. I just turned sixteen last week. My mom hooked me up with that sweet little Mercedes C250." He pointed three empty spots over to a gleaming, cherry red sports car.

"For real?" Michael dropped his hand from his door handle and turned toward the Mercedes, his eyes caressing it like it was a beautiful woman. "I saw that car this morning, and I was wondering whose it was."

"Can I say that your mom is officially awesome in my book?" I said after we'd walked over to inspect it more closely. I smiled to myself. Somehow, since he'd gotten it, the interior was already cluttered with a random assortment of both opened and unopened cans of Monster, a scattered stack of car magazines, and a rolled-up bag of Doritos.

He shrugged. "I think she's trying to make up for everything she's put me through with the divorce this year. I kept trying to convince her to buy me a Bullet bike, but she insisted on this car instead since it was much 'safer.'" He said this with a roll of his eyes, like she was totally ridiculous.

"She's worried about a Bullet bike, but she lets you longboard down 'wicked steep hills'?" I asked, mimicking his description of his favorite longboarding spots.

He flashed a grin that reminded me of a kid getting away with something naughty and swept his long, blond bangs out of his eyes. "Who said she lets me? When your mom works 70 hours a week, you tend to have a lot of time to yourself."

Olivia emerged from the building and came across the parking lot. She glanced at Hudson leaning casually against his new car, looked away, and bit her lip as a blush crept across her face.

"Hey, Olivia," he said, one side of his mouth pulling up in a cocky, self-satisfied smile.

She looked up at him for a fleeting moment, her blush deepening. "Hey."

Wow. She had it bad. Usually when guys from school tried to give her any kind of attention, she gave them a rejection that was quick and to the point. But she seemed truly flustered by Hudson. Didn't see that one coming.

Chapter 5

My Precious

Isaac

I was starving after football that night. Mom still wasn't home and Dad was on the phone in his office, so I scrounged in the fridge. I pulled out a dish of leftover mashed potatoes and ham and dumped it into a frying pan with some butter. I probably should have melted the butter first, but I didn't think about it until it was too late, and I wasn't in the mood to pull everything out and start over. Once the smell of browning potatoes and ham filled the air, Dad appeared, looking over my shoulder.

"Hey, Dad," I said. "I need to talk to you."

"Yeah?" he said, reaching past me to turn down the heat under the skillet.

"I know what you did," I said seriously

He avoided my eyes. "What I did?"

"The car wreck? I got my memory back. I remember everything now."

His face paled for a moment, but then his jaw clenched and he looked out the window overlooking our backyard.

"Not that it matters anyway," I continued coolly. "As soon as Destiny's parents found out she was dating a Baptist, they totally freaked on her, and now they're doing everything they can to keep us apart. Destiny's not the type to go against her parents' wishes." *In most circumstances, anyway*. "I hope you're happy. You almost killed yourself and your own son, and it was all for nothing." I threw him an accusing glare for good measure.

My carefully crafted little speech must have worked because later that night, when I was finishing up my calculus, Dad appeared in my doorway, reaching out and knocking on the open door.

"Isaac?"

"Yeah?" I looked up from the book, calculator, and paper spread on the bed in front of me.

He was cradling something in his hands. Was that, by chance, my keys and phone? Oh *heck* yes!

"I owe you an apology for my behavior that night. I took things too far. I put your life in danger, and I'm sorry for that." For a moment I thought he actually meant it, but then he crossed his arms, something flashed in his eyes, and he lifted his chin defensively. "But I still don't approve of you having any kind of relationship with her, and I stick by my same stance in the matter."

What kind of piece-of-crap, flimsy apology was that? He almost killed me, and he's defending himself as part of his apology?! He thought he was excused from responsibility—that he was justified since it was "for a good cause"?

I was about to give him a piece of my mind, but instead, I held my breath as he walked to my dresser. He set my keys and phone on the silver tray where I kept random stuff like paper clips, receipts, and a wound-up headphone cord. He turned around and droned on about the dangers of Mormons for another twenty minutes. I sat perfectly still, my eyes occasionally drifting to the silver tray as he preached his perfectly rehearsed sermon. It was a serious challenge to keep from rolling my eyes, but somehow I made it through the entire thing without a single sarcastic remark. When he finally left, I leapt from my bed, promptly locked the door, and grabbed my phone, pushing the button on the side to activate it.

I frowned. Of course the battery was dead. It had sat somewhere in Dad's room, collecting dust for days. I fished the charger out of my sock drawer and plugged it into the outlet behind my nightstand. When the phone had powered up again, it took forever for the OS to load. I soon found out why. I couldn't wait to text Destiny, but the texts just kept coming, interrupting me and making my phone freeze up. By the time everything had come in, I had 287 text messages and a bazillion notifications from Facebook, Kik, Instagram, and Twitter.

Good grief.

I didn't look at them, but I imagined that they all said something like "we're praying for you," or "get well soon." I guess that's what happens when you're the student body president, and the entire school is worried you might either die from a car wreck or lose your salvation because you're dating the Mormon girl.

Fifteen minutes later, I was finally able to send the text to Destiny.

Guess what?? I got my phone back. It's a freaking miracle!! Your evasion plan worked like a charm.

When she didn't reply immediately, I began going through my phone, switching around the privacy settings. I made a new password and changed Destiny's name into Hannah with a lower case 'h' to differentiate from the real Hannah, who was still entered in with the capital 'h' intact. Then, for good measure, I deleted the message I'd only sent moments ago, just in case Dad decided to come back to check my phone before he went to bed.

As I waited for Destiny's reply, I began sifting through the text messages. Ninety percent of them were genuinely kind, but a few, like Aspen's, for instance, made me cringe at the blatant hypocrisy. Most of them were from numbers I didn't even have saved to my phone. How'd all these people get my phone number? It made me wonder if Aspen or Will had given it out. Apparently she hadn't realized I'd had my phone taken away at the time.

By the time I'd read all the text messages and notifications, an hour had passed and Destiny still hadn't replied. I sent her two more texts, and I turned back to my calculus with an impatient sigh.

Chapter 6

Code Name

Destiny

Later that night, after the kitchen was clean and my homework was finished, I found Olivia sitting in bed with her phone, fingers flying across the touch screen, probably gushing to Brinlee about the amazing Hudson Brown.

I walked over to the denim jacket hanging on the back of my desk chair and pulled my phone from the pocket. I stared at the display, and my pulse quickened. I had three unopened messages from Isaac. He'd gotten his phone back!

Olivia giggled to herself from under her piled-up blankets as she tapped in a quick reply. I was lucky I'd had my phone on silent or Olivia probably would have heard the incoming messages and snooped to see who they were from. And I hadn't even thought to change his name to some code name yet. I'd change it, but first I had to open his messages. I couldn't wait a second longer.

I smiled to myself as I read his first message. What a sneaky guy. I was curious to know what he'd said to his dad. I hoped he wasn't too convincing. I didn't like the idea that he might have been bashing me to his dad. His next two messages were only two minutes old.

Where are you, gorgeous?

And then one minute later:

I'm dying here waiting for your reply.

I made him impatient? It was still so hard for me to imagine that he was that crazy for me. What we had between us seemed so surreal, like somehow it wasn't quite solid and might vanish at any time.

I pushed the negative thoughts away and decided to put Isaac out of his misery. I tapped in a reply, carefully guarding my face in case Olivia happened to glance over to see me grinning from ear to ear.

Hey! I'm so, so glad you got your phone back! Now we can talk at night again! Sorry I made you wait so long. I was busy with dishes and homework, and my phone was on silent way back in my room.

As soon as the message was sent, I opened the edit contact screen for Isaac's number. I thought for a moment. What would be the best code name? I could put something random in there like "spaghetti," but that would just end up being a red flag to anyone who picked up my phone. I considered putting in another guy's name in there like DeShawn or Hudson, but if I did that and was discovered saying lovey-dovey stuff to them, I'd still be in big trouble for dating a nonmember. Just then, the most brilliant idea came to me, and I punched in:

Preston ;)

Not to be confused with the real Preston who was entered into my phone as *Preston Nelson.* In all honesty, wasn't Preston the perfect Mormon boy? He was the kind of guy my parents would handpick for me to marry and have seven kids with. It was devious and foolproof, yet dangerous. If anyone found my phone and saw that I was texting Preston the kinds of messages I was planning to send to Isaac, they'd think Preston and I were in a relationship. Then they'd really get off my back about dating a nonmember.

It would just be a little awkward if it ever got back to Preston. He'd be sure to deny it, but of course they wouldn't believe him since they'd seen the texts with their own eyes.

Just then, a text from *Preston ;)* popped up on my phone. I replied to Isaac, and we texted back and forth for a few minutes. I glanced over at Olivia to see if she noticed what I was doing, but she was too absorbed in her own phone to pay any attention to me. Isaac and I continued texting off and on for the next hour.

It wasn't until we'd said goodnight, long after the lights were out and Olivia was snuggled deep under her covers sound asleep, that I realized I'd completely forgotten to tell Isaac what I'd witnessed under the bleachers between Aspen and Will earlier that day.

Chapter 7

Chapel

Isaac

I sent Destiny her good-night text and rolled over in my bed to review the notes scribbled in a spiral-bound notebook on my bedside table. They were for the speech I had to give the following day. As the student body president, I was required to speak to the students in Chapel twice a semester.

Twice a week, after lunch, we had Chapel in the Bethel Baptist Church sanctuary. The church building was the original structure that had housed Bethel Baptist Academy back when it was first formed many years ago. Since we were nearing Thanksgiving, it would be my second time speaking.

Normally, the past student body presidents spoke to the students about their big plans for the upcoming few months or got them excited about the next fundraising project, but as I stared at my notes outlining the plans for the Winter Wonderland banquet and the Christmas food drive kickoff, I couldn't shake the feeling that something important was missing.

I glanced at my car keys lying on the silver tray on my dresser. For the past month, I'd had a lot of reasons to be angry with a lot of people. First, it was Aspen and Will. Seeing my girlfriend and my best friend making out was something that tortured me, even now. Saying that it had been a hard blow to take was a massive understatement. That was bad enough, but then, she just couldn't leave me alone. Why couldn't she let me find happiness somewhere else? It was impossible to understand why she persisted in torturing me even after she'd decided to shift her affection from me to Will. It was one thing for her to torture me, but when she'd started up on Destiny, it was too much to handle.

Then there was Dad. It was so frustrating that he couldn't accept my relationship with Destiny. Why did he have to insist on being so obstinate about it? When he stopped the car in the middle of the road that stormy day, demanding that I break up with her, he'd taken it too far. And then he had the nerve to offer up that flimsy apology.

And what about all the kids who were so against my relationship with Destiny? They'd started a prayer group to keep me from becoming a Mormon. At the time, I'd been so angry with them that I'd wanted to punch my fist into a locker.

Feeling uneasy, I hopped from my bed and went downstairs to pop myself a bag of popcorn. The kitchen was dark, except for the light from the microwave, as I watched the bag expand with popped kernels. I returned to my room with the popcorn and ended up staying up until midnight. I spent the time poring over the Bible, praying, and brainstorming. Despite all my efforts, I still couldn't completely release the anger gripping my heart.

The next day, when the entire high school had assembled in the sanctuary, I climbed the carpeted steps to the pulpit and gazed out into the sea of faces before me. I stacked my note cards neatly in front of me and began with my prepared speech, outlining the plans for the next few upcoming events. Just before I finished my address, once more, the thought popped into my mind that something was missing from my speech.

My eyes roamed over the packed room in front of me. So many faces in the congregation had been in the "Save Isaac" prayer group just last week. They had worn those ridiculous "Save Isaac" badges and passed out the yellow papers announcing the meeting times to pray for my soul. My face burned with humiliation. What was I even doing up here? I felt like such a fool. I was beyond ready to give some hasty closing statement and escape their scrutiny. Even returning to my seat next to Aspen and Will on the front row with the other student body officers was better than this extension of the public humiliation.

But as I gripped the edges of the podium and stared out into the crowd, I began seeing individual faces rather than the angry mob I'd envisioned only seconds ago. There was Seth Carter from the junior class who'd sent me a text message, saying he hoped everything was okay with me. He was staring up at me, and for the first time since I'd gone public about my feelings for the forbidden Mormon girl, I realized the expression on his face, so similar to other students who'd worn the "Save Isaac" badges, wasn't one of malice or disapproval. He was looking at me with genuine concern.

It was at that precise moment that a powerful realization struck me. Aspen and Will may have had malicious intentions toward me, but the rest of these kids didn't have anything against me personally. They'd been taught, just as I had been, that Mormons weren't Christians. Could they help what they'd been raised to believe? They hadn't had the opportunity to learn any better. What if our roles were reversed? What if Seth Carter was the one dating the Mormon girl, and I hadn't taken the chance to get to know Destiny? I probably would have been one of the first ones to join the prayer group to save him.

My eyes scanned the crowd again, and I saw more like him. There was Jackson Palmer, Susanne Weeks, Amy Walker, and Carlos Rodriguez. Their texts were all genuinely supportive, as well.

I was suddenly tired of all the anger controlling my life. As I came to this realization, I finally knew what was missing from my chapel talk.

Forgiveness.

I swallowed dryly, and for some reason, before I began speaking again, my eyes drifted to where Aspen and Will sat. Instead of giving the standard closing of, *Let's pull together for a great year*, I said, "As we approach the holidays this year, I'd like to encourage all of you to reach out to those who have wronged you and find it within yourself to forgive them. As you do, you'll discover God's love shining brighter in your life."

As I spoke, the anger and resentment lifted from my shoulders tangibly. I continued, and the words poured from my mouth. Although I hadn't spoken specifically of what had been done to hurt me, I sensed a distinct shift in the room. The crowd had split into two. Half the room was nodding receptively, watching me intently with misty eyes, or smiling encouragingly. The other half of the room was staring back with hardened expressions, passing notes to their neighbors, or sleeping, completely oblivious to my words.

Neither Aspen nor Will seemed to show any reaction whatsoever to my words. She was sitting with her crossed legs twisted away from him, her eyes glazed over and staring at nothing in particular. He was sitting with his elbows propped on his knees and his forehead resting on his clasped hands, bent down toward the carpet, like he'd rather be anywhere but listening to me talking.

It didn't matter though. I'd said what had needed to be said, and I'd meant it. It was going to be hard to fully forgive them, but I was definitely on the right track.

After I'd closed my speech, I grabbed my note cards and stepped down from the podium. I took my seat next to Will. Throughout the rest of the meeting, he refused to meet my eye, but I caught Aspen glancing over at me more than once with an unreadable expression.

When the meeting was over, I stood, and my eyes automatically traveled to the left side of the room where Destiny had been sitting with the other sophomores. She wasn't looking at me. Instead she was smiling and talking to that little blond kid who had played paintball at her house and sometimes ate at her lunch table. What was his name again? Oh yeah. Hudson. He was a nice enough guy, even if he did look at Destiny like he wanted more than friendship with her.

A small hand touched my bare elbow, and I turned to see Aspen looking at me with a solemn expression. Immediately, my defenses shot up. My first instinct was to jerk away from her, but I took a deep breath and faced her instead. She dropped her hand from my arm once she saw she had my attention, and I breathed a sigh of relief. I really couldn't handle her cheating hands touching me.

I silenced the acidic thoughts flowing through my head. *Forgiveness.* I had to try harder.

"Can I talk to you for a minute?" she asked quietly, her voice steady and serious.

Everything in me was screaming at me to get away from her, but I swallowed my resentment and nodded. This forgiveness thing was much harder than I'd imagined. It was one thing to forgive the various kids in the congregation. Forgiving Aspen was an entirely different matter altogether. It seemed so achievable looking down from the pulpit, but now that she was right in front of me, smelling like coconuts with her long, blonde hair practically brushing my arm, the agony of her betrayal came back to attack me full force.

I followed her down the aisle to the back of the sanctuary, hyper aware of the eyes focused on us as we pushed through the crowd passing row after row of students filing out to leave. It infuriated me that being seen leaving with her had such an effect on me. Why should I care if people see me with her? I should be able to talk to my ex-girlfriend without people stirring up rumors.

Aspen opened the door to the stairwell that led to the balcony seating. She wanted me to go in there with her? No way. I stood my ground, crossed my arms over my chest, and said, "What do you need, Aspen?"

She dropped her hand from the door handle, and it began to close slowly. She turned to look at me, her bright blue eyes pleading. Around us the foyer was packed with people and she glanced around at them uncomfortably.

I took a deep breath. *Forgive her. Just let the pain go.*

As though she'd plucked the thought from my mind, she said, "Isaac, can you ever forgive me for what I did?"

I drew in a sharp breath and looked away from her pleading eyes. Why did she have to look at me like that?

"I'm so sorry. I treated you so horribly. I wouldn't blame you if you hated me until the day you die, but if you could somehow find a way to forgive me…" Her voice trailed off. After all the fake, twisted crap she'd done to me, how dare she have the nerve to look sincere?

I bit back the retort on the tip of my tongue and said, "Aspen, I want to forgive you. I know it's the right thing to do, but what you did was…beyond horrible." I hated how thick my voice was becoming. "I'm going to need some time." And a ton of help from God. Because at this point, He was the only One who could make this better.

"I understand," she said seriously, her eyes full of repentance. She dropped her eyes and began twisting a strand of her golden hair around her pinky finger. "I'm guessing by now you heard what happened."

My brow furrowed in confusion. "No. What are you talking about?"

With the noise of the chatting girls passing by us, her voice was too soft to catch her next words.

"What?" I asked, leaning closer.

"Will has been cheating on me with Jessie Larsen."

I rocked back on my heels, stunned. No freaking way. He sure knew how to pick them. Jessie was even more despicable than Aspen—and that was saying something. "I—I'm sorry," I stammered. I didn't know what else to say.

"He knows my dad cheated on my mom. I just don't understand how he could do this to me, Isaac…" Two fat tears rolled down her cheeks.

Great. Now what was I supposed to do?

"I was such an idiot for ever leaving you," she said, sniffling. "It was the worst mistake of my life. You were…" She took a deep breath and started again. "You were so amazing to me. You helped me through my parents' divorce when I was at my lowest. I'll never forget that for as long as I live. I never deserved you in the first place, and then I was so awful to you."

I still didn't trust her, but I couldn't deny that despite all she'd done to me, there was a small part of me that felt compassion for her.

"I'm sorry," I said quietly.

She must have taken my apology as permission, because without warning, she threw her arms around me, hugging me tightly.

How awkward.

I moved to push her away, but before I could, my eyes fell on Destiny's ashen face across the crowded foyer, just before she turned to disappear into the milling crowd.

Chapter 8

Forgiving Forgiveness

Destiny

Hudson had been telling me about the new longboard he was getting that weekend when I saw them together. I think he saw it, too, because when I turned away from Isaac and Aspen's intimate scene with fury boiling inside me, he stopped talking abruptly.

After we'd walked away a few paces, he said, "Dude! When Isaac was talking forgiveness, he sounded totally sincere, but did he have to take it to this level? She was kinda rotten to him."

I fought with everything inside myself to resist the urge to march over to her and rip handfuls of blonde hair from her head. How could Isaac do this to me? I fought back the tears threatening to spill down my cheeks.

I wouldn't cry here. I simply wouldn't.

Hudson glanced at me uneasily, "I'll see you around, okay?"

I nodded miserably and wrapped my arms around my torso as he disappeared into the crowd. He must have sensed that I needed some space.

Aspen wasn't wasting any time trying to get Isaac back. Even from where I stood, I could tell that she'd turned on the waterworks for him. It was probably natural for her to cry, too. Her boyfriend had just cheated on her. It was a good reason to cry. I just wished she'd go pick some other guy's shoulder to cry on. I walked down the hallway, passed the kindergarten classrooms, and followed the crowd through the cafeteria. I pushed open the double doors that led to the path to the high school building, and a hand clamped on my wrist, pulling me to the side. I twisted to see Isaac.

"You're not supposed to talk to me anymore," I said dully, loud enough that the group of freshman boys who were passing could hear. They were friends with Isaac's little brother, Josh, and the last thing Isaac needed was a report reaching his dad that we were still together.

Isaac frowned and dropped his hand from my wrist. "I don't care. You have to know that I didn't want Aspen to hug me."

I rolled my eyes. "Sure you didn't."

"No, actually, I didn't. Why are you being like this?"

"We can't talk here," I said, eyeing the people watching us. "Meet me under the stairs ten minutes after the next period starts."

Isaac nodded, shoved his hands into his jacket pockets, and walked away with a worried look on his face.

Shanice walked up to me with concern in her dark eyes. "Hey. Are you okay? What's going on with you and Isaac lately?"

Ever since Jessie Larsen had ditched me for the popular crowd at the end of seventh grade, Shanice had been my one friend until Hannah had showed up at the beginning of the school year. Hannah and I had become closer than I'd ever been with Shanice. I'd told Hannah everything, but for the past few days she'd seemed too absorbed in Evan to spend time with me like she used to. I hadn't really noticed it when I spent every spare moment with Isaac, but now that we were forced into yet another layer of secrecy, it was glaringly obvious that she was more interested in talking to Evan than she was to me.

I sighed and turned back to Shanice, surprising myself by telling her everything from our parents' disapproval to our decision to keep our relationship quiet, to the breakup under the bleachers, and finally, to Aspen hugging him outside the chapel.

"Oooh! I don't know how you haven't killed that blonde witch already."

"I do have to admit, I've had to restrain myself around her a few times," I said with a smile. "So, how are you and DeShawn?"

She shook her head. "You just had to bring him up, didn't you?"

"What's going on?"

"Absolutely nothing." When she took in my disbelieving eyebrow, she said, "No. I mean it. Nothing's going on between us because all he cares about is basketball. When he's not at practice, he's at home shooting hoops, and when the weather's bad, he's sitting in front of his Xbox playing some basketball game with the guys who live on his street."

"Guys can be so dumb," I said.

"Isaac didn't do anything wrong though," Shanice said. "That is, if he's actually telling the truth about not wanting her to hug him."

Part of me desperately wanted to believe that he truly didn't want her to hug him, but I'd seen how hard he'd taken it when she'd dumped him. I couldn't push away the doubt lingering in the back corner of my mind.

Normally, Mr. Campbell made American History come alive for me. But today there was something about the cadence of his voice as he described the Louisiana Purchase that made me want to fall asleep. By the time Isaac met me under the staircase, I'd calmed down considerably.

"Hey," I said. I didn't step closer to him.

"Destiny, please understand that I didn't want Aspen to hug me." He must have noticed my reluctance to close the gap between us, because he didn't come toward me. "She told me Will had been cheating on her, and she started giving me this big sob story. I feel like I'm supposed to forgive her, you know, to move on and stuff, but she's so manipulative. I don't trust her..." His voice trailed off.

I studied him for a moment. His eyebrows were drawn together in frustration. His beautiful mouth was twisted into a slight frown. His fists were clenched at his sides.

I wanted to believe him. I really did. But there was this small feather of doubt that had slipped into my heart. I couldn't shake it off. The negative voice in my head kept telling me he still wanted her. Why wouldn't he? They had been happy before, why couldn't they put their differences aside and start over again? She was just the type of girl to date him: gorgeous, blonde, petite, and talented. She was easily the most popular girl in school. He was the most popular guy—or at least he had been, before he'd started dating me.

I was a huge threat to his popularity. Didn't that bug him? He'd said it didn't, but maybe he was just saying that so I wouldn't feel bad.

"You have to believe me," he said when I still didn't step closer, panic rising in his voice. "I had so many harsh feelings toward Aspen that it was starting to eat away at me. I can't live that way. So, when she came up to me, I knew I had to forgive her, but she was just so emotional. It sucks for her. I mean, Will cheated on her with Jessie. That's gotta hurt."

I sucked in a large breath of air. "He cheated on her with Jessie?" I couldn't help the small flicker of satisfaction. I couldn't feel sorry for

Aspen. Isaac may have been embracing the spirit of forgiveness, but I wasn't feeling it.

He nodded. "According to Aspen, anyway."

So Jessie finally got a jab at Aspen. She'd been competing with her for years. It was surprising that she'd succeeded. Especially since Aspen was two years older and already dating Will. How did Jessie manage to pull it off? She was dirtier and craftier than I gave her credit for.

"Jessie used to be close friends with you, didn't she?"

I nodded. "Yeah. I'm surprised you noticed."

"Well, you guys did call me all the time back when you were in middle school."

"You knew that was us?" I gasped, horrified, and all thoughts of Aspen flew from my mind. Jessie and I used to prank call Isaac back when we were younger and we'd recorded the conversations with this little digital recorder. We'd been so careful to hide our identity.

"Oh yeah, I knew the entire time," Isaac said with a shrug.

"You must have thought we were so dumb." How mortifying.

"Only slightly dumb." He flashed a teasing smile.

I punched his muscled bicep. "Ow!" I said, holding my hand. "Seriously? Why is your arm so hard?"

He chuckled, a low throaty sound, and took my hand in both of his. "You know, you really shouldn't go around punching people." He brought my hand to his lips and kissed it tenderly, his dark, smoldering eyes fixed on me.

"Yes, sir," I said softly, my eyes locked on his. I stared at his intense brown eyes and melted. He was so beautiful, inside and out. I hated it that we had to have these issues. I reached out and took his hand. "I believe you, Isaac."

"You believe me?"

"Yeah. I believe that you weren't trying to rekindle things with Aspen." I wasn't sure if I believed him completely, but enough of me trusted him to say that I did.

He squeezed my hand and relief flooded into his eyes. "I can't lose you again," he said, his voice suddenly thick with emotion.

"I'm not going anywhere," I said, pulling him closer to me.

He wrapped his arms around me and held me to his chest. Through his uniform shirt, I could feel his heart beating steadily. When he held me like that, nothing else mattered. Together we were strong, a force to be reckoned with.

How could I have questioned him only moments before when I felt this way now?

Chapter 9

A Heart Full of Love

Isaac

I checked my watch and said goodbye to Destiny reluctantly. If we stayed under the stairs too much longer, our teachers might get suspicious.

That night, as I was driving home from work, my phone rang. I worked part-time for Hannah's parents—they were also my aunt and uncle—at their Christian music company. I picked it up and answered it, just as my eye caught the caller ID.

I held back a groan as I held the phone to my ear. "Hello?"

"Hey, Isaac!" Aspen's voice sounded a bit too shrill, and her cheerful tone was obviously forced. Why the *crap* was she calling me?

"Hey." It was so tempting to hang up the phone and block her number, but I could at least *try* to be polite, right? I cleared my throat. "What's up?"

"We have to rehearse 'A Heart Full of Love' tomorrow for Primus so I was thinking I'd swing by your place tonight so we could get one more last-minute practice in."

Seriously? Just invite yourself over already. "You want to come over?" Saying I didn't want to spend time with her would be a massive understatement. How could I put this politely? I racked my mind, trying to come up with an excuse of why I was busy.

Technically, Destiny was supposed to sing with us as well since it was a trio, but Aspen didn't even consider inviting her over. I just imagined her offering to swing by and pick up Destiny and held back a bitter laugh. Like that would ever happen. Inviting Destiny into my home would be complicated on so many levels. I could always come up with the excuse that we weren't dating and just had to sing together, but that seemed too much like playing with fire so soon after our supposed breakup.

That was when it hit me. If I had Aspen over, it would only reinforce my separation with Destiny in my family's eyes. They'd really get off my back then. "What time were you thinking?" I turned into my subdivision and drove up one of the many steep, wooded hills in my neighborhood.

"Can I come over in about thirty minutes?"

I bit back another groan. "Sure. That should give me enough time to grab some dinner."

"Want me to stop by Smokey Bones on my way over?" I clenched my jaw. Now she was totally pushing her luck. Pain twisted within me as I thought about the happy evenings we'd spent eating Smokey Bones barbecue sandwiches last summer. She really was trying to get back together. And she thought she had a decent shot. Well, she was seriously mistaken.

"No, that's okay," I said brusquely.

"It's really not a problem," she insisted.

"Aspen, let me make something clear to you. I don't want to eat barbecue with you. You can come over to practice, but don't think you have a chance at getting back together with me. That opportunity came and went last October, and it's gone for good now."

"That was a terrible mistake," she said in a small voice.

Her sad, forsaken tone tore at the armor I was trying so hard to keep up. "Yes, it was," I said gently. "And I'm trying to forgive you for that. But that doesn't mean I want to open a door that should stay closed."

"I understand," she said in a syrupy sweet voice, which only led me to believe that she really didn't understand at all.

We hung up just as I pulled into my driveway. Once I was inside the house, I made a beeline for the kitchen. Josh was sitting at the table eating a big plate of leftover lasagna.

"Is there any more of that?" I asked.

"Nope. This is the last of it."

I opened the fridge and scanned the contents. Near the back was a Ziploc bag with a couple of slices of the frozen pizza we'd baked two days ago. "Thanks a lot. Did you really have to eat the rest of the lasagna? There's enough of it on your plate for five people. Now I'm stuck with nasty old freezer pizza."

"Ya snooze, ya lose, bro," Josh said, shoveling another bite of lasagna into his mouth.

Stupid punk.

I threw the pizza onto a plate and warmed it up in the microwave. "Where's Dad?" I asked. If he wasn't home, I was calling Aspen and canceling right away. The whole point of suffering through a practice with her was so he could see it.

"He's back in his office."

I wasn't sure whether I was relieved or disappointed. Part of me was looking forward to canceling with Aspen. The microwave dinged a few times, and I took out the pizza. "Guess who's coming over."

"Destiny?"

Crap. Did he think we were still together? "No," I said slowly fighting the blush that was threatening to creep into my face. He'd totally caught me off guard with that one. "Aspen."

"Aspen? I thought you were done with her."

"We have to practice," I said cryptically.

"So, you invited your ex over?"

"Not exactly. She kind of invited herself over."

"Dang. She must really want you." A wistful look crossed his features for a fleeting moment. "You should capitalize on that. I heard she broke up with Green. Some people were talking about it at lunch today." He knew before I did? What the heck?!

Josh certainly had changed his tune since the day I'd discovered Aspen was cheating on me with Will. "I don't get it, Josh. You seemed so happy to see me break up with Aspen before, and now you think I should get back together with her?"

He shrugged. "Well, face it. She's a whole lot better than that stupid Mormon girl. No comparison."

Anger welled up inside me, hot and furious, and I balled my hand up into a tight fist, ready to throw a punch to hit Josh squarely on the nose. But then Dad walked into the kitchen, and I uncurled my fist reluctantly.

After I finished my pizza, I retreated to my room and began texting Destiny. Maybe I should have told her about Aspen coming over, but I didn't think it would be the best idea at this point. She'd been pretty upset earlier.

All too soon, the doorbell rang. I kicked back on my bed and smiled to myself at Dad's pleasantly surprised reaction as he opened the door. This was working out a bit too well.

"Isaac," his voice boomed up the stairwell. I opened my bedroom door and descended the stairs, my feet tapping against the polished wooden steps. There she was. She looked positively, mouthwateringly gorgeous. Her hair was down and curled into these perfect, shiny ringlet curls. Her creamy skin was flawless, and her navy sweater and skinny jeans tucked into brown boots showed off her every curve. I released a puff of air and averted my eyes. This was going to be much harder than I'd expected. I was an idiot for thinking that this was a good idea.

She stepped closer to me and flashed me a secretive smile. "Hey," she said. "You look nice."

Oh, this was bad. She even smelled heavenly. "Thanks." My eyes roamed all over the room, desperately looking for something else to look at beside her.

Dad was grinning so broadly, you'd think we were happily married and presenting him with our firstborn son. "Well, I'll leave you two alone so you can get busy practicing." How'd he know why she'd come? Josh must have been talking to him about it while I was up in my room texting Destiny. Oh man. Destiny could *not* find out about this. She would flip out.

"Thanks, Dr. Robinson!" she said cheerily. She walked over to the grand piano in the living room and sat down at the bench. If she thought I was sitting all cozy next to her, she was out of her mind. I shouldn't be getting within a mile of her, let alone in the same room.

"Were you planning on playing?" I asked. She could play a little, but I was by far the more experienced pianist.

"No, I was hoping you could," she said.

When she didn't move, I gave her a hard look. "I don't mind playing, but I'm going to need a little more space than that." She scooted over an inch. "No. I meant you're going to have to get up."

"What's the matter with you? I don't bite."

Yeah, actually, you do. I gave her another hard look, and she stood up sheepishly.

"Gosh, Isaac, you don't have to be like that," she said, a pout forming.

Oh yes, I do.

I slid onto the bench and opened the three-ring binder of *Les Mis* music that had made its home on the piano since the beginning of the school year. Aspen and I had already sung out of it so many times at this very piano. I was beginning to realize that it probably wasn't even necessary for us to have this last-minute practice. Boy, was I an idiot.

I began playing and did my best to ignore her, but it was impossible. I could feel her watching me out of the corner of her eye, and my face started getting hot. I could just imagine the worshipful expression on her face. I'd seen it dozens of times before as we'd practiced. Now I was beginning to wonder how genuine it had been. I had to keep reminding myself that she'd been cheating on me with Green all that time. I could never forget what a cheating liar she was. Every word that tumbled from her mouth was for her own benefit. But why did she have to be so hot?

We went over two or three of our songs together. Her voice was incandescently light, her notes pure and clear. It was much harder to sing with her than I'd anticipated. I stood to get up, but Aspen put her hand on my shoulder.

In that instant, I had a flash of memory. Aspen was before me, caressing my face just before kissing me like she had so many times before. I craved her powerfully. I wanted to kiss her, to touch her, to feel her small body enveloped in my arms again. She was right here, and she wanted me.

It would be effortless to be with her. We wouldn't have to hide. I would have my reputation more or less restored at school and at church. But it would be hollow. My heart and soul craved Destiny. She was selfless, loyal, courageous, and bold. She chose to stand by me even when it meant her life would become hard. Aspen wouldn't even stay with me when it was as easy as breathing.

But it was so hard to focus on Destiny when Aspen was standing before me like an evil temptress. I hated the effect she had on me. Thinking about how pure and beautiful Destiny was compared to her made me feel like the scum of the earth.

I didn't deserve her.

Chapter 10

Yucky Chemistry

Destiny

The next morning in chemistry, we were assigned lab partners. I was assigned to Hudson. Hannah was assigned to Jessie. I shot her a sympathetic look.

I still couldn't believe Jessie had bested Aspen. I honestly wasn't sure how I felt about that. On the one hand, she'd given Aspen a taste of her own medicine. On the other, she'd made Aspen available to chase Isaac. Not so cool.

There were moments when I believed Isaac would never be tempted to be unfaithful to me. All I had to do was think about the magical moments we'd had together at the hammock spot, visiting the horses, sitting in his truck after Homecoming, and best of all, stargazing on his land at Walnut Ridge. But then that old self-doubt would creep back in, and I'd remember how lovey-dovey they'd been at the retreat and at lunch. I'd have these images flash across my mind of them kissing behind her locker door or holding hands in the hall.

"Are you okay?" Hudson asked from the stool beside me.

"What?" We were supposed to be starting up the Bunsen burner.

"You're way zoned out."

"I have a lot on my mind."

"Care to share?" he asked, his blue eyes fixed on me.

I glanced over my shoulder to where Hannah and Jessie were scowling at each other two rows back. "Isaac and I are having some issues," I explained in a hushed tone.

"I'm sorry."

"I think Aspen's trying to get him back," I whispered.

"Whoa. She's hot enough, but I'd stay far away from her. I'm not into lying hypocrites." He poured a foul-smelling yellow liquid from a vial into the beaker on the burner and the mixture turned jet black.

"It wasn't supposed to do that, was it?" he asked.

"I have no idea."

"And this is why I hate chemistry," he said, pushing back from the table in frustration.

"This is the fun part. It reminds me of cooking. I hate all the equations and formulas."

"You like cooking?" he asked.

"I don't mind cooking, but put me in front of a sink full of dirty dishes and I'll find any excuse I can to leave," I said. "What about you?"

He shrugged. "I don't cook much beyond Hot Pockets and pizza rolls. I have to fend for myself most of the time since my mom's always working."

"What does your mom do?"

"She's a stock broker."

That explained the massive house on top of Walnut Ridge. I was about to ask him what his dad did, but Dr. Spencer walked by to inspect our work.

"You know, if you cut out the chitchat, you might actually get to step four like the rest of the class." Dr. Spencer was a tall, gray-haired man who took chemistry a bit too seriously, if you asked me. He seemed to think the entire world revolved around his class, like we didn't have any other teachers who piled on the homework. His long-winded explanations of how we could apply the concepts behind the formulas were vague at best, and I always ended up feeling a bit disconnected during his lectures.

Hudson rolled his eyes, but turned to focus on the beaker filled with murky black liquid. "Everyone else's is white, what did we do wrong?"

"Maybe we had the heat turned up too high. Or you added the vials in the wrong order," I suggested. Thinking about chemistry experiments hurt my head, and I was beginning to think it was much worse than cooking. At least after cooking a meal, I could have a nice dinner. What was the point of this? Sure, I knew chemistry had its place in the world, but sometimes it was hard to see the big picture.

I checked my phone between classes to see if Isaac had texted me recently. No messages. I walked with Hannah and Evan to the cafeteria and sat beside her while Hudson and Evan had a long discussion about the best spots on Walnut Ridge for rock climbing. Usually I would have joined in the conversation. I loved rock climbing and had been to almost every spot they'd mentioned. Michael and Preston had taken me dozens of times. But my eyes were glued to Isaac's table across the room.

I missed him.

He was sitting between two of his football buddies, but Aspen was only two seats down from him. She was sitting with Sydney Carter and the rest of the cheerleaders. At least, for the moment, she wasn't talking to Isaac. She was too busy staring at Will and Jessie with a look that could kill on the spot.

Isaac looked so happy with his old friends. They were talking and laughing, and Isaac wore his trademark grin, the one that always made my knees feel like jelly.

Only he wasn't smiling at me. He'd forgotten me already. It was like I was a freshman again, sitting alone. Sure, Shanice had sat with me, but she'd mostly talked to the other kids around us. So, I would eat my ham and cheese sandwich from my little brown bag and watch Isaac from afar. But why should it surprise me that today felt so much like old times? If it weren't for Hannah bringing me into Isaac's life, our social circles would be worlds apart.

Hannah was the bridge between our two worlds, the catalyst that brought us together, and now she was drifting further and further from me. She was so obsessed with Evan that she barely even spoke to me anymore. Even if she didn't have a boyfriend, she wouldn't be allowed to hang out with me. Her mom was strongly opposed to Mormons and had totally freaked out when she found Hannah holding a Book of Mormon one afternoon when the missionaries coincidentally showed up on her doorstep.

Later, on my way to Primus, I followed Evan and Hannah into the chapel where we were meeting to rehearse *Les Misérables* again. I filed into the choir loft, which was considered the backstage area.

Mr. Byrd called for our attention. "We're going to start out with 'In My Life' and 'A Heart Full of Love,' so I'm going to need Michael, Aspen, Isaac, and Destiny center stage."

Oh man. I'd completely forgotten today was our first rehearsal in front of the entire choir.

Don't hyperventilate. Don't you dare.

I'd been so stressed about chemistry and all my drama with Isaac that I hadn't practiced *Les Mis* for the past two weeks. Great. Just watch me forget my words and make a complete fool of myself. How could I have forgotten? I'd been dreading this song since I'd been cast as Éponine, and I was terrified of acting out my true feelings onstage. But then when Isaac didn't seem to care so much about his Cosette anymore it didn't seem to matter. At that point it was just acting, but now that I'd seen that hug I wasn't so sure.

As I walked to the middle of the stage with one of the most awkward groupings of people I could imagine singing with, I told myself I was jumping to conclusions. It was just a hug. Isaac had promised that it didn't mean anything. She'd forced it on him. He couldn't help that, could he? Why did I have to be paranoid?

The song began with Aspen singing alone. She sang about how confusing her life was and then how Isaac's character, Marius, had walked into her life and they'd fallen in love quickly and unexpectedly.

Gag.

Then Michael, who was playing her dad, Jean Valjean, walked up to her and sang with her about their daddy-daughter issues. She wanted info from him about his mysterious past. He wasn't willing to share, and it was supposed to frustrate her. I had to say, she was doing an amazing job looking irritated with him.

Suddenly, Isaac walked to the center of the stage singing with such passion it took my breath away. But he was singing about her. Going on and on, spouting all this poetic garbage about how wonderful she was. And then he turns to me and thanks me for bringing him to her.

Yeah. Like I'd ever do that.

Not on your life, buddy.

If I were really Éponine, I'd keep him as far from her as possible. I never understood that part of the musical. Why does Éponine help Marius find where Cosette lives? Does she truly have such unwavering, unselfish love for him that she would go out of her way to help him get together with another woman just because she knows it would make him happy? Would I do that for Isaac if I thought it would make his life better?

I couldn't think about it. And I had a good reason, too. It was my turn to sing. I sang of his words being daggers in me, and a lump formed in my throat. Never had those words been truer than they were at that moment. The next words were nearly impossible to sing, but somehow I did it. I sang of how amazing he was, and how if he'd ask me to be his, I would. And I meant every single word. For a few short moments Isaac's voice joined with mine, but he was singing about how he wanted her. His voice sounded earnest, genuine. It wasn't like the practice at Aspen's house when we'd all sung it together for the first time. He'd been so guarded that day. No. Today his voice throbbed with emotion, and it sickened me. His performance was so stellar that I felt my face growing hot with embarrassment.

It doesn't matter how in love Isaac and Aspen look as they sing to each other, it's just an act.

Aspen began singing to Isaac, and she sounded incredibly passionate. And I swore I saw her eyes and cheeks brighten with the glow of a first love. Was she remembering their first kiss? Or was it some other private moment they'd shared?

I clenched my shaking fists, and suddenly it seemed that all eyes in the room were on me. I felt the blood drain from my face. It was my turn to sing again, and the next words were ten times harder to sing than the first. I did my best, but my throat was tight from the lump that wouldn't go away. The sound that came from my mouth was much worse than any of my past rehearsals. I barely recognized it as my own voice.

Oh my gosh. This was it. The moment I'd gone to great lengths to avoid. I'd created a fake boyfriend to keep this from happening, for goodness' sake.

But it was all for nothing. My humiliation was complete. They all thought I was the spurned lover, and now there would probably be rumors flying around the school that Aspen and Isaac were getting back together.

I was so busy basking in my embarrassment as the three of us blended our last harmony that I almost missed the kiss.

Somehow, in some way, Aspen's lips ended up on my boyfriend's. *My* boyfriend's! His lips belonged to me! My jaw should be dropping. I should be screaming, rushing across the stage to pull out her disgustingly perfect blonde hair, but I was too shocked to move. My face was frozen and completely expressionless.

But wait. Was he actually kissing her back?

She had to be the one who surprised him with the kiss. My beautiful, perfectly loyal boyfriend would never ever do such a thing to me. I mean, come on, he stood up to his dad for me. He gave up his truck and his phone and almost died in a car wreck in order to stay by my side. No matter how realistic he'd sounded in his passionate addresses to her, it was all an act. Inside, he was devoted to me.

Right?

He stepped away from her, a wild, dazed look in his eyes. Several shocked gasps sounded from the choir loft.

Mr. Byrd cleared his throat disapprovingly, and Isaac wiped his mouth with the back of his sleeve.

That befuddled look in his eyes was just a look of surprise and...and...intrusion. Yes. It had to be. He wouldn't be breathless from that kiss because he actually enjoyed it, would he?

Oh my gosh. The room began to spin. I was going to faint. I stumbled back to my seat and put my head in my hands. For a long moment, the entire room was silent. I looked up and was startled to see Mr. Byrd crouching before me. He put a kind hand on my shoulder and met my eyes with a fatherly expression. "Are you all right?"

I shook my head slightly.

"If you need to go out and sit in the hall for a minute, you're perfectly welcome to. We can move on to other parts of the musical."

Oh yeah. I was still supposed to be onstage. Great. Now no one would miss the spectacle I'd made of myself. How lovely. I pushed the image of their kiss out of my mind and looked around the room. Everyone was watching us. This was going to be talked about for weeks. No, more like years. Well, let them talk. I threw my shoulders back and managed a brave smile.

"No, thank you, I'm fine," I said in a steady voice, loud enough for everyone to hear. "I just didn't realize we were continuing on with the scene."

I strode back onto the stage with my head held high to perform the next scene. It was the one where I sacrifice my home and standing with my family to protect Cosette by screaming to alert Jean Valjean that my dad and his band of ruffians were outside ready to attack them.

I stared back at my seat. It was calling to me desperately. But it was my turn to sing "On My Own," my weepiest, most pitiful song.

Perfect.

Just perfect.

I looked across the room at Isaac. He met my eyes and looked away guiltily. Whatever. I would deal with him later. Right now, I had to sing. I pushed away all thoughts of a possibly cheating boyfriend and focused on the pure technicalities of the music. I ignored the words describing my unrequited love and instead focused on controlling my tone and supporting my notes with a firm diaphragm. Altogether, it wasn't too bad of a performance, but it was nowhere near as emotional as I usually sung it.

As I walked off the stage and returned to my seat, I realized Isaac had moved over to where I'd been sitting. At first, I considered moving to a new seat, but then decided against it. Who cared whether or not people saw us together? At this point, I was desperate to know he still wanted to be near me. I needed to know that the kiss with Aspen had been revolting for him. That he'd wanted to shove her away, but was too much of a gentleman to do it publicly.

Just then, I had an interesting thought. What if the kiss was in the script? I'd never seen Aspen and Isaac perform their song onstage. Although I'd seen various performances of this song hundreds of times online, I'd never noticed whether or not there had been a kiss. Whenever I'd watched the videos online, I'd always been so busy focusing on my own part and doing my best to ignore the chemistry between Marius and Cosette that I honestly couldn't remember if there had been a kiss involved. Maybe I was blowing it all out of proportion and it was something Isaac knew all along that he'd have to do, but didn't want me to worry about. I wasn't sure whether I'd have wanted to know in advance or not.

I sat on the pew next to Isaac. He took my hands in his and brought his forehead close to mine. "Destiny," he said in a low whisper. "I had no idea that was going to happen. Please forgive me."

I pulled away, my eyebrows drawing together in confusion. Was he saying it was his idea? That he'd gotten carried away and moved in for the kiss? She was his ex, after all. He'd taken the breakup so hard. Maybe all of this was just too much temptation for him.

He shook his head. He must have recognized my expression and followed my reasoning because he raised his eyebrows and said in a quiet voice, "You do know that was one-hundred-percent Aspen, right?"

I felt my anger melting away a bit. "I wasn't sure," I whispered a bit sheepishly. It really had seemed like he was kissing her back for a moment. Maybe he was just taken off guard.

Relief coursed through my veins. Why had I ever doubted him? Isaac had stood by my side through much worse than this. He'd deserved my trust.

Chapter 11

Can't We All Just Get Along?

Isaac

"Isaac," Mr. Byrd called out to me as the class period ended. "Can I have a word with you?"

I turned around. I'd been halfway down the aisle leading to the exit of the sanctuary. "Sure thing." I strode back to where he stood by the score stacked neatly on the front pew where I usually sat with Aspen and Green during chapel.

I glanced toward the exit to see if Destiny was going to wait for me, but she was already gone. Hannah had swooped in on her pretty quickly when the class period had ended. Knowing Hannah, there was no way she'd want to miss the conversation waiting for her after that horrible kiss. Aspen might have ruined everything for me this time. I was beginning to think it wasn't worth it to stay in the musical. She was messing with my head. She knew it, and she loved it. Maybe it was time for me to drop out.

But it was my only valid excuse to see Destiny publicly these days, and I didn't want to give it up. Why did Dad have to be such a stubborn jerk about who I dated? Why couldn't I just date who I wanted without having to worry about being grounded and having my stuff taken away?

Mr. Byrd looked around the chapel. When the last student had exited, he turned back to me. "Isaac." He crossed his arms, stood a little taller, and exhaled. "I'm going to be blunt with you."

"Okay?"

"We have to get the drama straightened out in this choir. If we're going to pull this musical off, we have a tremendous amount of work to do. All this tension is sapping the energy out of our production. I'd hate to lose some of the best talent in this choir, but what happened just now was completely unacceptable. I don't know what's going on between you and Destiny and Aspen and Will, but this was the final straw for me. The four of you had better get it straightened out, or you're going to face not only losing your spots in the musical, but possibly also your spots in Primus."

Whoa. I'd never heard such a stern speech come from his mouth. He was dead serious. "Yes, sir."

"You have an amazing talent for influencing others. Use it to help everyone get along. You all have until the end of January to work it out or the musical won't be happening."

"Maybe I should explain a little bit about what's been going on."

He gave me a tired look, but nodded seriously. "I suppose that could be helpful."

I told him everything. I started with Will's plan to dig up dirt on the Mormons when we were at the retreat, and how he'd discovered that Hannah had made friends with the Mormon girl. Then I explained how I'd tried to execute that plan by purposely seeking Destiny out to learn more about Mormons. Only, it hadn't worked. I'd only been attracted to her and intrigued by her beliefs. Then I filled him in about Will and Aspen making out in the car. I purposely left out the part about them doing drugs. I figured if I confided something like that to him that he would be required to report it, and that would only stir up more trouble. As I progressed through the story, his face was sober and his arms remained folded.

When I told him about how Destiny and I had found ourselves in a serious relationship, his face softened a bit and he nodded at the familiar parts.

I explained that Aspen had begun attacking us. She started with the "Save Isaac" prayer group. Then, when our parents found out we were dating, they began harassing us, too. He knew of that firsthand. Finally, I explained about Will cheating on Aspen with Jessie and my quest for peace and forgiveness. This was where the story got sticky for me. "Ever since I spoke in chapel, Aspen's been throwing herself at me. She thinks Destiny and I aren't together anymore."

"Why would she think that?" Mr. Byrd asked, clearly confused.

"Destiny and I decided it would be better for us to keep our relationship quiet."

"I don't think you should be dishonest, but it wouldn't hurt to be a bit more private about your affection. I gave Destiny similar advice when you were in the hospital."

"You did?"

He nodded and then paused as though he were processing everything I'd just told him. "So, now that Aspen thinks you're available, she's doing her best to patch things up?"

"Pretty much."

"I don't want to sway you in either direction, but have you ever considered that your life would be much simpler if you just decided to rekindle things with her?"

Sure, I'd thought it to myself, but there was no way I was admitting it to Mr. Byrd. Anyway, it was a terrible idea. "I don't trust Aspen. Also, I think I've changed too much. I could never be happy with her now."

Mr. Byrd nodded. "I thought you might say that. I think you're making the right choice."

"You do?"

"Yes. Definitely. But it's the harder road, not just for you two, but for all of us."

"I was thinking about dropping out. If I left, you could just put someone else in as Marius."

"After hearing what you've had to say about this situation I'm beginning to think that wouldn't be the best solution, after all. Why should you be punished when you haven't done anything wrong? I'd say we should just pull Aspen out, but I don't have enough proof that she's actually done anything wrong. She'd be incredibly difficult to replace, anyway. Her voice is absolutely perfect for the role."

"I agree. Her voice really is."

"No, the best solution is to convince your friends to work it out. I meant what I said about you earlier. You have a gift for influencing others. Do your best to inspire them to lay aside their grudges to bring our choir back into harmony again."

Chapter 12

Funny Business

Destiny

Just after the last bell of the day, Isaac approached me in the hall. "Hey, Destiny."

I looked at him guardedly. Why was he talking to me so openly? "Hey."

He gripped the straps of his backpack and casually leaned his shoulder against the lockers. He looked so amazing that it hurt. I couldn't even remember the last time we'd kissed. I had to fight the urge to grab his backpack straps myself and pull him toward me.

"So," he said in an easy tone. "A bunch of us are meeting this Friday night at my house to practice *Les Mis*. Do you think you and Michael can make it?"

He was kidding, right? He wanted me to go to his house? It was like he was asking me to take a stroll through a pit of vipers for him.

Just then, Will Green walked by, and Isaac called out, "Hey, Green, you gonna be there Friday?"

"Yeah, I'll be there," he replied.

"What's going on?" I asked quietly.

Isaac's brow arched as he threw a quick look over his shoulder like he was checking to see if Will was still back there. He turned back to me. "Mr. Byrd had a little talk with me today. He's not happy about all the unrehearsed drama happening lately."

"How is inviting us all to your house supposed to help? It sounds like you're trying to stir up drama, not fix it."

An irritated expression flashed across his face momentarily before being replaced by that same composed look he'd had before. "I think it'll be good for us, actually. Trust me. They just need to get to know you better."

"So, does this mean we're not hiding our relationship anymore?" I asked warily.

"Not necessarily. I think we should still keep it under wraps for now. We need to get our parents on board before we try anything that drastic."

"Good," I exhaled. I couldn't deal with Isaac not having his phone anymore. Plus, his dad had put him in harm's way once before. Who knew what he'd do next?

Mom and Dad left to go to California on a business trip for the weekend, leaving Michael in charge. Friday night, around five, Michael parked his Honda Civic on the street in front of the Robinson's two-story house. The Colonial home had tan siding and dark green shutters. Two massive oak trees shaded the carefully landscaped front yard. Clutching my choir folder, I opened my car door and stepped out onto the pavement. The driveway was full of cars, including Isaac's black truck, Evan's yellow Jeep, Aspen's red Mustang, and a black sedan that must have belonged to Will.

We stepped onto the front porch and rang the bell. It was so weird to stand on Isaac's front step. On Dr. Robinson's front step. I shuddered in the cool November air. The door swung open, and Isaac greeted us with a smile that caused a different kind of shiver to run down my spine. "Come on in!" He had on a green plaid shirt with straight-legged jeans, rolled up at the ankles. I walked past him and breathed in his intoxicatingly familiar sandalwood scent.

We were standing in a foyer with wood floors. Directly in front of me, a flight of stairs led straight up. To my left was an elegant dining room with a chandelier hanging over a dark cherry table. A few of Michael's football buddies congregated near a large dark cherry china hutch full of expensive-looking figurines. The upper walls were painted a silvery blue with glossy white wainscoting below the chair rail. Ivory drapes hung from the ceiling to the floor.

Michael strode over to his cohorts and performed a manly exchange of mock punches and handshakes.

I glanced into the living room to the right. Several Primus members crowded around a dark walnut grand piano. At the far end of the room was a white fireplace. Above it was a painting of Dr. Robinson and his wife. Hannah and Evan were snuggled on a sofa beneath a huge framed picture of Isaac posing with a brilliantly white smile. It was one of his senior portraits. I had a wallet-sized variation of it buried in the bottom of my sock drawer.

Will was sitting at the piano, playing "One Day More." Aspen and Sydney were standing around the piano chatting idly. Isaac walked into the center of the room, singing softly in a velvety voice that took my breath away. As it came closer to her part of the song, Aspen stepped closer to him, harmonizing with him in her incandescent soprano voice like it was specially crafted to blend with his.

Although it was freezing outside, she wore a tiny white skirt with a gray tee and a military green canvas jacket that was almost as long as her skirt. Long silvery, chandelier earrings flashed from within her perfectly-crafted blonde waves. I looked down at my own outfit. I had on jeans, boots, and a red V-neck sweater over a black long-sleeved shirt—attire that was more appropriate for the forty-degree weather outside, but completely forgettable compared to her trendy get-up.

Isaac stopped singing and turned around. He watched me like he wanted to say something, but couldn't in front of the others in the room.

"I like your house," I said.

"Thanks." He'd said it simply, but his eyes spoke much more. In them I could see his desire for me to be accepted and comfortable here. He wanted me to be able to come in and out of his home freely.

It broke my heart that the only way I could be welcomed into to my own boyfriend's home was with a group of other people.

"Oh," Aspen said in a triumphant tone. "Is this your first time here?"

Yes, Aspen. Unlike you, I'm not welcome in his home. What was I even doing? I didn't know what Isaac was trying to accomplish, but so far, it wasn't working at all.

"Get a life, Aspen," Hannah said from the couch. Her long brown hair was curled into waves similar to Aspen's hairstyle. "What's your problem? Why do you always have to butt into Destiny's life and say something snotty?"

"Hannah," Isaac said. "There's no need to be rude."

He was defending Aspen? Seriously? She was the one stirring up the trouble.

"No," Hannah said. "She's the one being rude."

But Isaac didn't seem to hear her. His back was turned to her, and he called out to the people in the dining room, "Hey, guys, listen up. Can everyone come in here for a minute? I think we're ready to get started." The chatter died down as Michael and a few others came in from the dining room. Hannah and Evan joined the group gathered around the piano. Isaac clasped his hands together just like he always did when he went into presidential mode. "I want to thank y'all for coming tonight. I know we've had some issues, but honestly, we just don't have time for drama."

Sydney and Aspen exchanged a look, and Sydney rolled her eyes and snickered.

Isaac looked over at them, and when their expressions sobered, he continued, "Mr. Byrd informed me this week that if we can't pull this musical off by the end of January, he's going to cancel it."

One of the football players swore softly behind me. Aspen kept her face neutral, but I could see fear in her eyes. Will had his eyes trained on the music in front of him as though it was suddenly important for him to study it carefully. Hannah looked so furious, I wouldn't have been surprised if she'd ripped up her sheet music in frustration.

"But that's not going to happen. I know you all want this musical to work just as much as I do. So, let's put our differences aside and pull together to make the most of the time we have tonight."

"Seriously," Evan said to Michael behind me, and I heard Michael grunt in agreement.

"Let's get started with 'One Day More,' since pretty much everyone's in that song and then we'll go from there."

And yet again, I had to listen to Isaac and Aspen proclaim their love for each other while I sang on the sidelines about my rejection. Hannah gave me a sympathetic look. She'd been so nice the other day after I'd seen Isaac kissing Aspen. He'd sworn up and down that it wasn't his idea. I should trust him more. No one was forcing me to sing as Éponine. Mr. Byrd had even given me the opportunity to back out, but I had committed to stay, no matter how hard it might be at times.

By the time we'd sung for an hour, the crowd had thinned. A bunch of the people who didn't have major roles had taken off since there was nothing for them to do.

"Hey guys," Isaac said after we'd finished another grueling run-through of "A Heart Full of Love." "Anyone want to put money together and order pizza?"

We discussed what kinds pizza places we liked and what toppings to include, and Aspen said, with her phone in front of her, "I have the number right here. If y'all give me the money, I'll take care of the order since Isaac was nice enough to open his home to us tonight."

There she was again, stepping up beside him, acting like they were in some kind of partnership together and it was, therefore, her duty to take some of the workload off of him. But if anyone else noticed or cared, they didn't say anything. They were too busy reaching into their pockets and bags to pull out their money.

I'd left my wallet out in my purse in the car and Michael had the keys. I walked over to where he was sitting at the dining room table. He was sitting across from Will and had a defensive look on his face.

"Can I get your keys, Michael? I need to get my money from the car."

He reached into his jacket pocket and deposited the keys into my open palm, as he said, "I really don't want to discuss it any more, Will."

"The Bible is perfectly clear on the subject. Even an idiot could understand that."

My heart slammed in my chest. I didn't know what particular point of doctrine they were disputing, and I didn't want to. I stepped away from them quickly and spun around toward the front door, knocking into Isaac on my way out.

"Whoa. Are you okay?" I pushed past him, out the front door, and into the chilly, moist night. I ran across the front lawn and past the massive oak trees, tears pricking my eyes. It was one thing when Aspen attacked Isaac and me because she was jealous. Or when Dr. Robinson was concerned that I was going to convert his niece or his son. I didn't like it, but I understood.

What Will was doing was entirely different. He was attacking Michael just for the sake of argument. What had Michael ever done to him? He was kind, friendly, and the best brother I could ever ask for. I could handle their attacks, but going after my brother was the final straw.

"Destiny," Isaac called after me. By the time I had the key in the car door, he'd caught up to me. I reached into the front passenger seat, pulled my money from my purse, and put it into my jacket pocket. I tried to wipe the tears away with the sleeve of my sweater, but he grasped my shoulders, turned me around, and saw the tears before I could fully wipe them away.

"Hey," he said softly, wiping them for me with the sleeve of his Abercrombie shirt. He smelled so good. "What's going on?"

"Did you hear Will in there? What did Michael ever do to him? I can't take it anymore." I slammed the door and leaned against the side of the car, pulling my jacket tighter to block the wind.

He leaned on the car next to me and wrapped an arm around my shoulder, reeling me close to his warm body. I breathed in his sandalwood cologne and let out a breath, releasing the tension coiled within me. I wrapped my arms around him. Beneath his green plaid shirt, I could feel the hard muscles of his torso. How did I ever end up with him anyway? I thought back to Homecoming when Jessie had told me that eventually Isaac was going to get tired of me and dump me like a bag of garbage. Was that what he'd been doing, bit by bit? Was he getting tired of me?

As though he sensed my thoughts, he moved in until our noses were practically touching. It was incredible how sensitive he was to my moods, like our brains were connected.

Isaac's expression suddenly became solemn, and fear crept into my heart. "I need to tell you something important," he said with a sadness I couldn't understand. "I've put it off long enough." His eyes lit up like something had just occurred to him. "But first, I have to do this…"

He leaned forward and kissed me slowly, gently. I memorized the feel of his lips on mine, the way his arms wrapped around me protectively. I wanted to freeze this moment in time forever. Then the kiss changed. His tenderness became something reckless and yearning. He kissed me desperately, like it was our last, and he had to squeeze every emotion he'd ever wanted to show me into that one kiss. Whatever he was about to say was going to end our relationship. I felt it deep down, and the agony was almost debilitating.

We pulled apart, and I said, "Can we put this conversation on hold? Please? I just want to be with you right now without worrying about our problems." He must have seen the hurt in my eyes because I was beginning to see it reflected in his as well.

He shook his head sadly. "No, I need to tell you. There's something I've been keeping from you for a long time. I wanted to tell you, but it just never seemed like the right time."

As his words sunk into me, a dizzying fear clutched my heart. Had he kissed Aspen again? Like, outside the musical? I'd seen so many signs over the past week. The hug. The tiny moment when it had seemed like he'd been kissing her back onstage. His campaign for everyone to get along. He should be pushing her away, not trying to forgive her!

He was going to break up with me. I could just feel it. But a small voice in the back of my head asked, *If he wanted Aspen, why would he kiss me like that?* It didn't add up.

Just then a set of headlights turned the corner, and the car began slowing. It pulled up behind Michael's car and Isaac's back went rigid beneath my embrace and his next words scared me more than whatever he'd been about to say. "That's my dad."

The headlights turned off, and we were left in darkness. Then Isaac was tugging my hand, pulling me rapidly back into the house.

Chapter 13

Truth Revealed

Isaac

I swung the front door open, cringing at the scene before me. Everyone was seated around the dining room table either participating in or listening to a heated discussion. Even Hannah and Evan seemed completely engrossed in what was being said.

Michael put his hands up in surrender. "I'm honestly trying to be as nice about this as possible. I don't want to fight with you. If you want to learn about my church, then great! I'll set you up to meet with the missionaries, and they can talk to you all day long about it, but please, stop harassing me about it."

"You see that? He can't answer the question because he knows he's wrong, and he doesn't want to admit it!"

"Green!" I growled. "That's enough."

"Where have you two been?" Aspen asked in a slightly strangled voice.

Destiny reached into her pocket and pulled out the money. "Here's what I owe you," she said, extending her hand with the folded bills.

"Whatever," Aspen muttered in irritation. She took the money from Destiny's open palm with her finger and thumb like Destiny had dirtied it somehow.

Destiny walked back to Michael and handed him his keys. "Are you okay?" she asked him quietly.

Before he could answer, the front door swung open, and Dad stepped in, his face completely devoid of emotion.

Aspen hopped up and chirped, "Hey, Dr. Robinson!"

He looked at her and nodded slightly. "Hey there, Aspen." He scanned the room, and when his gaze fell on Destiny standing between Michael and me, his eyes narrowed.

"Isaac, what's going on here?"

"It's just another *Les Mis* practice, Dad."

"I'm not so sure I like what goes on at your *Les Mis* practices." He said it like he'd found us all drunk and passed out on the floor.

"What's that supposed to mean?" Hannah said.

"I'm talking about the filth I just witnessed in the front yard."

"What filth?" I asked incredulously. Dad hadn't even seen us kissing. We were just talking.

"Oh that," Green waved Destiny and me away like we were insignificant. "I thought you were referring to the way Michael's been sitting around trying to cram his religion down our throats."

Whatever! From what I'd seen, Green was the one cramming religion down Michael's throat, not the other way around.

"I just saw my son with his hands all over the Mormon girl, practically undressing her on the street in front of my house, and now you're telling me her brother's been poisoning innocent minds under my roof?"

How dare he accuse me of treating Destiny with anything more than the utmost respect!

Before I could open my mouth to form a coherent reply, Green said, "You know, Dr. Robinson, you really shouldn't worry about Destiny and Isaac. He's perfectly aware of what he's doing."

Oh no. He was *not* going to go there. I shot him a lethal glare. He'd better keep his mouth shut, or so help me, I'd beat him until his scrawny body was nothing more than a lifeless heap on the ground.

Just then the doorbell rang and Aspen darted over to answer it with a fistful of cash.

Whew. Saved by the pizza delivery guy. Aspen paid him and took the stack of boxes from him, almost dropping them.

"Here, let me help you with that," I said. I really wasn't in the mood to scrape pizza sauce off the floor.

"Oh thanks, Isaac!" She gave me a flirty smile and made a point of brushing her hand against mine as she passed the boxes to me. I ignored her and carried the pizza to the table.

"Hey, Isaac, do you by chance have any paper plates?" Evan asked.

"I dunno. They're around here somewhere." I walked toward the kitchen.

"They're in the cabinet over the stove," Aspen said, following a bit too closely behind me.

I refrained from rolling my eyes. Apparently, she knew my kitchen better than I did, and she wasn't about to let it be forgotten. She brushed past me and stood before the stove. She reached up on tiptoe, stretching her petite body until a three-inch strip of perfectly-formed midriff was exposed above her miniskirt.

Wow, all that cheerleading sure kept her toned up. She must have been hitting the tanning bed, too, because her skin was still just as dark as it had been all summer when she'd sunbathed religiously—something I had very fond memories of.

Evan reached up to help her and grabbed the plates. I felt a pair of eyes on me in the doorway. I turned to see Destiny frowning, her face angled downward.

I averted my eyes, and my face flushed. I'd just done it again. I'd been careless with my thoughts, but this time, it was right in front of Destiny and I'd hurt her. The pain in her eyes would haunt me for a long time.

I was the biggest, most worthless, piece-of-crap boyfriend ever.

Aspen waltzed past us and helped Evan and Hannah pass out the plates. I looked around the room for Dad, but he must've gone upstairs to talk to Mom where she was working on some real estate stuff. Great. I could just imagine the conversation they were having up there. He'd probably already confiscated my keys from my dresser. At least I still had my cell phone in my back pocket.

I sat next to Destiny at the table. There was no point in hiding things now. As we ate, she barely spoke. It wasn't unusual for her to be quiet, but this was different. She was withdrawn, distant. She wouldn't meet my eye or anyone else's, for that matter. Ugh. What on earth was going through her head?

I had to tell her the truth before Will blabbed everything. What was he thinking? Now, after she'd caught me checking out Aspen, she was going to be even more upset. I wouldn't blame her if she kicked my sorry butt to the curb.

"Hey, Destiny," Hannah asked after we'd eaten. "Can you critique my solo?"

"Okay. Sure," she said.

"Would you mind playing, Isaac?"

"No prob, cuz. I'll give you some good feedback, too, if you want."

"All right, but don't be too harsh. I know you're awfully picky when it comes to music."

We listened to Hannah's song twice, and Destiny offered some polite suggestions, not that there was much to say. Hannah's voice was fantastic and she had been practicing her song faithfully for the past couple of months.

"Y'all keep at it," Destiny said. "I'm going to go grab another drink from the kitchen."

"What's going on between y'all?" Hannah asked sternly. "You need to fess up. Are you going after Aspen?"

"No way. Do you think I enjoy pain?"

"I don't know. I'm beginning to wonder if you do. If you don't stay away from Aspen, Destiny's going to show you the true meaning of pain."

I exhaled loudly.

"You'd better go talk to her. You have some major sucking up to do after that onstage kiss. She was seriously ticked about that."

I went into the kitchen and found Destiny sitting sullenly at the kitchen table with her back to me.

I froze in the doorway. Green and Dad were in the middle of a heated discussion back in Dad's office, a small room off of the family room. They were two rooms away, so they didn't see me, but they were talking loudly enough for me to hear them clearly.

"He was worried about Destiny converting Hannah," Will was saying. "He told me he didn't want the Mormons poisoning her mind. He didn't want you to know because he was afraid you would overreact and drive Hannah to do the exact opposite of whatever you said. So, he decided that the best way to protect his cousin was to have the Mormons leave the school once and for all. He talked to me about it at the retreat and together we came up with a plan. We decided that if he got close enough to Destiny she would open up to him and expose what really went on in her family. Then, he'd have enough dirt on the Mormons to get them kicked out of the school."

Destiny turned around, her face ashen, and saw me standing in the doorway.

Chapter 14

Shattered

Destiny

I couldn't move. My legs wouldn't operate. I was glued to the wooden chair. Everything Will had just said was true. I could see it on Isaac's face as plain as day.

No.

I didn't need to see it on his face to know.

The story made logical sense. I thought back to the day of the retreat when Will had discovered my infatuation with Isaac. That must have been when the plan started. Then, as I was getting into my car to leave with Mom the next morning, Isaac had sought me out to wish me luck with my Primus audition. That had never made sense to me before. It did now. Now I knew. He was only saying it to soften me up so he could expose my family somehow. We didn't have anything to hide! How could he not see that? He'd been to church with me!

"Destiny!" Isaac's voice was frantic.

Dr. Robinson's voice boomed from the other room. "I agree now more than ever that the Mormons need to leave the school." Isaac's eyes flicked to the office and a tortured look came over his face. "But I don't think this is the way to go about it." Dr. Robinson paused as if deep in thought. "I'll come up with something. In the meantime, he needs to stay away from that girl. She's nothing but trouble."

A wave of nausea hit me like a semi-truck. I leapt from my chair and launched myself toward the open door of the powder room on the opposite side of the kitchen. I slammed the door and twisted the lock just in time. Within seconds, I was heaving the contents of my dinner into the toilet bowl. Shaking, I flushed the toilet and rinsed and wiped my mouth with a hastily grabbed wad of toilet paper. I slid my back down the hunter green striped wallpaper until I landed on the linoleum floor. This room hadn't been remodeled in years. Apparently, the Robinsons hadn't gotten to it yet. I found it strange that I noticed such a meaningless detail at a time like this. It was like my brain was trying to disconnect from the situation, the reality around me.

A soft knock sounded on the door. "Go away," I said in a strained voice.

"I need to talk to you," Isaac said.

"You've talked enough," I moaned.

"Please, just let me explain."

Explain? What could he possibly explain? That he was a deceitful jerk? That everything he'd done to make me feel valued was an act? There'd been moments when I'd seen how easily he could lie. How smooth his voice could become when he wanted to mislead someone. What about after our kiss in the woods when Preston had shown up? Don't think about the kiss. Don't! I'd given him my entire heart, beating and achingly vulnerable, and he'd been slowly smashing it all along. A wrenching sob shook my body before I could stop or control it, and I fought to keep it silent. I couldn't let Isaac know how badly he'd hurt me.

Ever.

I would just tell him I'd had food poisoning...from the pizza... And then, I'd tell him to stay away from me…

Forever.

I stood up and checked my appearance in the mirror. My hair was braided in a side braid that was looking a bit thrashed and not in a casual, trendy kind of way. I wiped the mascara that had been smudged and re-braided my hair. I took a deep breath and opened the door to find Hannah sitting at the kitchen table. She rushed to me and threw her arms around me. "Destiny, are you okay?"

"Yeah," I said, smiling weakly. "Just a little food poisoning."

Hannah raised her eyebrows disbelievingly. After all, no one else was puking her guts up, and they'd all eaten the same pizza I had.

Upon hearing my voice, Isaac shot into the room, panic written all over his face. "Destiny, we need to talk."

"Nah, I'm good." My voice was cold and detached. "I don't have anything to say to you." I pushed past him and slammed my shoulder into his muscled arm. I twisted away. Just touching him was so painful I felt like someone was ripping into my gut with a barbeque fork.

He grabbed my arm and turned me to face him. "Wait!"

"Take your hand off me. You don't get to ever touch me again." My words hit his face like acid.

"You'd better do what she says," Michael said. He'd just come in from the living room where he'd been sitting on the couch talking to Evan.

Isaac looked from Michael to me. Finally, he dropped his hand and stepped away from me in defeat. The look on his face was one of unfathomable guilt.

"Michael, can you please take me home now?" I hardly recognized my own voice.

He wrapped his arm around me defensively. He looked over his shoulder toward Isaac. I couldn't see the expression on his face, but I could easily imagine the accusation Isaac saw there.

He helped me down the steps and out to the car. "I just want to go home," I said as I stared out the window of the car. I felt Michael's gaze when we came to a stoplight. I glanced over, and worry was etched deeply into his face.

"What did he do to you?" Michael finally asked as he put the car into park in our driveway. "Can you tell me? Because, honestly, you're kind of freaking me out."

I stared out the window.

"Did he rape you?"

"No! Gosh," I said, snapping out of it a little.

Michael let out a heavy sigh. "Well, the way you're acting…"

"He was only dating me to dig up dirt on our family because we're Mormons." I spoke mechanically, like a robot processing information with detached logic.

"What? That's crazy. Are you sure?"

"Ask him yourself. He certainly didn't deny it."

Michael sat in stunned silence.

"I need to get out of here." I opened the door. "I need to go somewhere to be alone for a while." I started walking toward the woods.

"Are you sure you should be alone at a time like this? It's dark and cold out there."

"I don't care about the cold."

"At least tell me where you're going." Michael said. Worry crept back into his eyes.

"I'll be at my hammock spot," I said automatically, and then my face crumpled as I remembered our first kiss there. "No...actually. I won't."

"What's wrong with your hammock spot?" Michael paused, and in the dim light inside his car, I could see the wheels turning in his head. "You know what? Don't answer that question. I really don't want to know. Why don't you just go hang out at the tree house? You never go there anymore. It's private, and you can cry your eyes out all you want."

I nodded and stumbled through the darkness, tears flowing like they'd been given permission to come. My feet slogged through leaves, wet from yesterday's rain. At least it wasn't raining now. But it was cold. I pulled my jacket tighter around myself.

When I finally made it to the tree house, I climbed the steps Dad had built when I was younger and pushed open the plywood door with a creak. I threw myself onto the army cot we kept up there for campouts and finally allowed my body to convulse with the sobs I'd been holding back for the past half hour.

Chapter 15

What Goes Around, Comes Around

Isaac

I deserved it. I deserved all of it.

I couldn't blame her. Her reaction was mild compared to what mine would have been if I'd been in her place. I'd broken her trust, and if she never forgave me…well, it would feel like a freight train slamming into me, but I'd understand.

Well, shoot, it already felt like a freight train slamming into me. I stood at the dining room window and watched her get in the car with Michael. He opened the door for her and helped her in like she was as fragile as a cracked china doll and would shatter at any moment.

I did that to her. I caused her the deepest pain imaginable. She was trying to hide it, but I didn't miss the way her lip had quivered, how pale her face had been.

"What are you still doing here, you idiot?" Hannah scolded. "Go after her!"

I considered the idea. Michael had looked like he wanted to kill me. I wasn't sure whether or not he could take me in a fight. I'd seen him knock down plenty of guys on the football field. But then again, so had I.

Not that it mattered. I wouldn't even fight back. I didn't care if Michael beat me senseless. Right now, I was so emotionally numb that it would feel nice to have someone punch me in the jaw. At least I would be feeling something.

"Listen to me, Isaac." Hannah insisted. "You can't let her think you really did that crap."

"That's the thing, Hannah," I said as I stared aimlessly into the dark. "I did do it."

She recoiled from me. "What?" she murmured. "You don't actually mean that, do you?"

"I hate to say it, but yeah."

"You slimy piece of shiz!"

Shiz? She sounded like Destiny now.

"I did it to protect you."

"I didn't need protecting. I'm a big girl. I can take care of myself."

"I didn't know better back then."

"So that first day you showed up at my house to help her practice to get into Primus, that was all staged?"

"Do you really want to know the answer to that?"

Her hand flew out of nowhere and hit me across the cheek with a loud smack. "You dog!" she spat. "How could you? She trusted you!"

Aspen looked up from where she was talking with Sydney and Evan with a smirk.

I rubbed my cheek where Hannah had hit me. Man, Hannah sure could pack some power into her smackdown. That shiz *stung*. Great. Now *I* was using the stupid word.

"Do you have any clue how much she cared about you, even then? You toyed with her heart! On purpose! I'm so mad I could kill you right now."

"Hannah, why do you like the Mormons so much anyway?" Green asked, stepping into the room. "They're nothing but a bunch of liars."

"No, Will. You're the liar. You think you're so holy. But you're not. Last time I checked, God doesn't approve of hypocrites, and you happen to be the biggest one I know."

"Since when did God put you in the judgment seat? God knows my heart."

"Yes. He does," Hannah agreed. "And when you die, you're going to have a rude awakening. You know what they say. 'What goes around, comes around.' You may be getting away with everything now, but eventually you *will* get what's coming to you."

"That's enough, Hannah." Dad said, coming into the room from the kitchen. "Isaac, I think the party's over."

"Really?" Aspen said. "I thought it was just getting started."

I ignored her and nodded at Dad. "You're right. If this gets back to Mr. Byrd, it won't be pretty. I'm sorry guys. I tried so hard to get everyone to get along, but now I've just ruined everything."

Hannah grabbed her coat and purse from next to Evan on the couch. He was staring at his phone, and when he didn't look up, she tugged on his arm. "Come on. Let's go. If I don't get out of here, my big mouth is going to get me into more trouble than I'm already in." He stood, and they headed toward the door.

"Before you go, you need to understand something, Hannah." I glanced around the room. Everyone was looking at us. I cleared my throat. At this point, they all needed to hear what I had to say. "I admit I may have done everything you accused me of in the beginning, but after a while, I didn't feel that way anymore. Somewhere along the way, her religion stopped mattering so much. They're not bad people. I've been to church with Destiny and Michael. It's a nice place. Heck, I may just go again."

"Robinson, you're crazy," Will said. "See, Aspen? I told you they'd gotten to him." He looked back to me. "She wouldn't believe me. And she wonders why I picked Jessie over her. The entire time we were together all Aspen would talk about was you. She kept thinking she could save you, but obviously, she was wasting her time. You're just as far gone as Michael. Why even bother?"

"Because he's my son. And last time I checked, he was your best friend, Will."

I snorted. "Dad, Will's not my best friend. He's not even my friend at all."

"That's a little harsh, Robinson," Green said.

"Don't act like you don't know what I'm talking about. What kind of friend rips his best friend's girlfriend away from him? You knew how much I loved Aspen!"

Hannah glared at me. From the corner of my eye, I saw a flutter of movement and I glanced over. Aspen had thrown a hand to her chest, and the mask she usually wore had fallen away for a brief moment. Beneath it was raw, fragile emotion.

My face burned. Oh crap. Why was I saying this in front of her? I had zero intention of rekindling things with her, no matter what happened with Destiny. I'd given her a false hope that I'd only have to crush later. Regardless of what a stuck-up brat she could be, I didn't want to cause her unnecessary pain. But my mouth was running away from me, and I felt powerless to stop it. "And just now you exposed me in front of Destiny. I probably lost her, too." As I said those final words, my throat thickened and tears threatened to spill down my cheeks. I couldn't lose her. I'd do everything in my power to make it up to her, to prove I was worthy of her. It didn't matter how long it took or how many people it alienated. I would fix this. Because being with her turned a bad day into a bright one. I craved her like I craved sunshine on a stormy day. Whenever things got tough for me, she was there by my side, even when it meant she was giving up her reputation and her parents' blessing. I could search for decades and never find another girl as amazing as her.

"Good," Dad said. "Will may have just done you the biggest favor of your life."

I ignored him. I could still make this better. All I had to do was explain everything to her. If I could just tell her how much I loved her…

Whoa. I *loved* her. Of course I did. How long had I loved her? I thought back over the past few months. It had begun so slowly. Ever since I first saw her at Hannah's house that day. I'd been so drawn to her. We were magnets with opposite poles attracting.

She'd felt it, too. I'd seen it reflected in her eyes countless times before. I had to tell her I was in love with her. I peered out the window. The streetlight in front of my house spotlighted the glossy red finish of Aspen's Mustang. Perhaps not coincidentally, her car was blocking my truck.

But Dad's car was parked next to the curb all by itself, and I knew he kept a set of spare keys behind the spice rack in the kitchen. I glanced over at Dad. At the moment, talking to Green was keeping him distracted. They were ranting about the Mormons and how to stop them from corrupting more of the school.

Whatever. That topic ought to keep them busy for a while.

I strolled into the kitchen and nonchalantly grabbed for the keys from behind the spice rack. Good. They were still there. I closed my palm around them and slipped out the back door. I walked down the steps of the deck and around the house to the gate of the wooden fence that surrounded our backyard. I lifted the latch and made my way to Dad's car unnoticed. Just as I started the engine, the front door opened, and Aspen came out with Sydney. They froze on the front porch when they saw me and turned back to the house, probably to tattle on me like a couple of first graders.

As I drove out of my neighborhood and turned onto Acorn Creek Road toward Destiny's house, I pulled out my cell phone and called her.

Chapter 16

Memories

Destiny

Sometime during my bawling, my phone buzzed in my jacket pocket. Sniffling, I pulled it out and stared at the display.

Preston ;)

My heart leapt as it always did when Isaac's code name popped up on my phone, but now, I couldn't bear to answer it. He left a voice message and then called again and again. I thought about turning it off, but part of me wanted to hang on to the idea that he still wanted me and this was all a big misunderstanding.

Maybe this was just a bad dream, and I'd wake up and he would still be mine. But this was no dream. He'd betrayed me. He was a liar, a hypocrite, and a skilled actor. It was all true. All of it. The tears poured down my cheeks and left wet spots on my jeans.

As time passed, I quieted, my sobs giving way to shuddered breaths, and I finally took notice of my surroundings in the glow of my cell phone. Surprisingly, the floor had been swept clean. The corners were devoid of cobwebs and there was a broom behind the door. Against the wall was a line-up of my old, ratty Barbies that Olivia and I had passed down to my youngest sister, Brianna. Pinned to the door was a list of clubhouse rules written in neat, little-kid handwriting. The members listed were Brianna and her friends, including one of Preston's younger sisters.

Elijah was specifically mentioned as someone not allowed to join. Brianna and Elijah tended to butt heads a lot. He always accused her of being a spoiled brat. But the more he said stuff like that, the harder she tried to find new ways to rile him.

I smiled for the first time in hours as I remembered a time when Olivia and I had ruled this tree house. It was our castle, and we took turns being the princesses. Or we were supposed to, anyway. Olivia always threw fits when it was my turn. Those were the days. Back when my biggest fears were the spiders and falling off the tree house stairs. Back when Preston would push me into the creek, and I'd get out and ask him to do it again. I remembered the day when we'd finally convinced him to come play Rapunzel with us. It had made me so happy when he'd call to me, and I'd throw that rope. Then he'd climb it, and I'd see his face appear in the window. He had always looked so proud of himself. Then he'd just stopped coming.

What had happened to us? He was so intent on his lawn-mowing business. I was so wrapped up in school, popularity, Primus, and Isaac.

Isaac.

I shuddered at the thought of him and fresh tears streamed down my cheeks as the sobs overtook me again.

Chapter 17

Tree house

Preston

I swept the floor in the kitchen where one of the twins had spilled pretzel sticks and had walked over them until they were pulverized. Mom and Dad were out on a much-needed date, and Megan and I were in charge for the night. I was finally tucking the rambunctious little fellas into bed when my phone rang.

"Go to sleep, guys. I gotta take this call," I said, stepping from their darkened room to the hallway. I shut their door until it was open just a crack and answered my phone. "Hey, Michael, what's up?"

"Hey. Is there any way you can get over here, like, right now?"

"I'm babysitting at the moment, but if it's important Megan could probably take over," I said glancing into Anna's bedroom. She was fast asleep with about thirty stuffed animals scattered around her.

"It's Destiny. She needs you."

My hand dropped from the doorknob. "Is she okay?"

"Not really."

"What happened?" I asked, jogging down the stairs to the basement where my room was. My heart pounded in my chest. If anything had happened to her…

"Let's just put it this way: I don't think she's going to be talking to Isaac anytime soon."

I stopped in my tracks at the bottom of the stairs and released a massive sigh of relief. "Did they break up?" I asked. Megan and Brinlee were on the couch watching some girly movie in the family room as I turned the corner. I scooped my keys from my dresser and shoved them into my back pocket. Megan and Brinlee stared at me, wide-eyed at the mention of a breakup, and began whispering furiously.

"Oh yeah," Michael said seriously. "You have no idea how bad it was."

"What did he do to her?" I asked, imagining the worst.

"He was only dating her to dig up this supposed dirt on the Church so we'd get kicked out of the school," Michael said.

Okay. I didn't want to kill him anymore. Thank goodness my fears were wrong. Instead of being a low-life dirtbag, Isaac was a conniving bigot who had played with Destiny's feelings just to make Mormons look bad. I couldn't imagine doing that to someone, even a person I didn't like. To have fooled us all so well, to have made Destiny believe that he loved her and then for her to find out it was all a lie from the start…

Okay, I was furious again.

I walked back into the family room where Megan and Brinlee were still watching their movie. "I have to head over to the Clarks'. Are you guys good to stay here and hold down the fort for a while?"

"Sure you do," Megan said with a broad smile. "Yeah, we'll be okay."

"Oh my gosh!" Brinlee squealed. "This is so freaking epic! He's going to go rescue her like a knight in shining armor!"

I pretended I hadn't heard Brinlee's outburst as I headed for the garage with Michael still on my ear. "You may want to grab a flashlight,"

Michael said, stifling a chuckle. Apparently he'd heard Brinlee, too. How could he not? She was practically screaming her head off. "She's out in the tree house. Just try to cheer her up. She's totally freaking out right now. She was really scaring me on the drive home from his house tonight."

I grabbed my electronic lantern from one of the shelves where we kept our camping gear, clipped a carabineer to my belt, and left through the garage door to where my old white truck was parked in the driveway. I shut the garage door after me with a keypad mounted on the outside of the house to make sure the kids would be safe while I was gone.

I'd never driven so fast to the Clark's house. All I could think of was how she was hurting, and how I had to cheer her up. I had no way of knowing if it would work, but I had an idea.

When I got to her house, I parked the truck at the edge of the woods and sprinted to the tree house. This was it. Maybe, just maybe, if I didn't screw it up, I could have a chance with her.

Hope swelled in my heart, and an involuntary smile spread across my face as I approached the tree house. But then, when I got as far as the bonfire spot, the sound of soft, pitiful sobs reached my ears. My smile disappeared, and for a moment I wasn't sure what to do.

Her crying stopped for a moment, and I mustered the courage to call out to her. Maybe there was something to this knight-in-shining-armor thing.

Chapter 18

Rapunzel

Destiny

I bit back the sobs and took a deep, shuddering breath. That was when I heard it. A voice straight from my past. But this voice was different.

Older. Deeper.

"Rapunzel, Rapunzel, let down your hair."

I blinked back my tears, thinking I'd just imagined it, like a specter from my past, a dusty memory re-emerging. I was legitimately going nuts.

This time, the voice came again, sounding slightly impatient. "Rapunzel, Rapunzel, let down your hair." I stood up from the army cot, stretching muscles that were stiff from sitting for so long. I looked out the window, and there was Preston, standing in the glow of the little electronic lantern he was holding, in his faded jeans and nicely-fitting black T-shirt.

"Oh you *are* up there!" He grinned. "So, are you going to throw me the rope, or am I going to have to take the stairs? You do still have the rope, right?"

"I'm not sure. Let me see." I searched around the room with the dim light of my phone to guide me and found it coiled neatly at my feet. Maybe Brianna liked to keep the tradition alive with the Nelson twins. I giggled at the idea of them fighting over her.

I tossed the rope down to him and gawked as he hooked the lantern to a carabineer attached to one of the belt loops of his jeans. Then he climbed up with ease, hand over hand, his muscles rippling beneath his black T-shirt. He grasped the bottom of the window, and I took a couple of steps back. I stood awestruck as he pushed himself up and over the wall without difficulty. The light from the lantern filled the room with a soft glow.

"Hey," he said, smiling broadly, dusting his hands off on his jeans. He unhooked the lantern and set it onto the cot where I'd just been sitting a moment before.

"Hey," I said. "I remember that being a lot harder for you when you were a little kid."

"So do I," he said with a chuckle. "Man, I was pretty scrawny back then."

"You were the best Prince Charming though." I smiled wistfully, remembering.

Preston grinned broadly, like I'd said just the right thing.

"How'd you know I was up here? It's not exactly my favorite hangout anymore."

His expression sobered. "Michael told me you were upset and could use a friend."

The fact that Michael just told his best friend to go find his sister alone and emotionally vulnerable in a dark tree house spoke volumes of the respect and trust he had for Preston.

But that trust was something I understood completely.

He sunk down onto the cot and leaned back against the plywood wall behind him. He slapped a hand onto the seat beside him. "Sit. Tell me what's going on."

I eyed the empty spot next to him warily. I wasn't ready to get into another relationship. He was nuts.

"I'm just asking as a friend," he said gently.

I exhaled and sank down onto the cot. I started with the beginning and told him everything, sparing hardly any details, but I didn't miss the way he cringed when I told him about the times Isaac and I had kissed.

Just as a friend. Yeah, right.

I didn't mind though. It was nice to have someone to talk to about all of this. Somehow, I just felt like opening up to him. But when I got to the hard parts, my voice became thick and strangled, and the sobs took over again for a while.

"It's okay. You don't have to talk about it if you're not ready to."

"No. I want to tell you. I think it'll help." So I did. Somehow, miraculously, the words poured from me. Preston put an arm around my shoulders, and I huddled close to his chest, my body convulsing with grief. As I continued talking, he stroked my hair soothingly, not saying anything. Just being there, stalwart and strong.

"It would've been one thing if he'd just wanted to go back to his girlfriend. I could understand that. I thought it was coming anyway." Could Isaac have really been faking all of his sadness over Aspen? Was her relationship with Will all just a ploy, a part of their master plan?

I gripped handfuls of Preston's black T-shirt and buried my face into his chest. "Why? Why was I so dumb?" We'd had so many amazing moments together. I ached for him. To feel his arms around me. To tell me that he loved me. We'd never progressed that far in our relationship. Was it because lying to me about being in love was where he'd decided to finally draw the line?

I realized it with a jolt, even as Preston wrapped his arms around me, that I'd been very much in love with Isaac. And although the thought wasn't recognized in my mind at the time, I'd given him my heart, all the same. Had he been able to sense that? Regardless of what he'd understood about my feelings for him, he never should have toyed with my heart the way he did. It was unforgiveable.

Every stolen moment we'd had was an excuse to get me to open up more about my church so he could exploit it. But each second with him had been precious to me. I missed him fiercely. More than anything, I needed to feel his arms around me again, telling me that it was all a misunderstanding, that Will was a big liar. But I knew better.

If a genie appeared before me right now, I would wish for his betrayal to be erased from my mind so I could still be with him in ignorant bliss. Everything would go back to normal and this pain in my chest would be gone.

My scattered emotions continuously wove themselves around each other chaotically, growing from a few errant threads of thought into a tangled mess, snagging tighter and tighter until I was ready to explode.

I began wailing, and Preston grabbed me by the shoulders, pulled me back, and said, "Destiny, stop." But I couldn't. The tears kept coming. Living without Isaac was like being held underwater and being told to breathe. I would take water into my lungs, and it would burn. And eventually, everything would grow dimmer until it became black.

Preston shook my shoulders, jarring me from my despair. "Look at me, Destiny." I cracked open my eyes and peered into his trustworthy green ones. They were so full of concern. "He's not worth your tears. Do you hear me?"

I stared back at him. Not worth my tears? Did he have any clue what Isaac meant to me?

"Don't let him hurt you worse than he already has. It's going to be hard for a long time, but you're going to survive this."

"How can you possibly know that?" What did he know about getting his heart ripped out? He'd never even had a girlfriend.

A corner of Preston's mouth quirked up. "Because the Destiny Clark I know is a fighter."

I sniffled. "I'm not feeling it at the moment."

"Just wait and see. You'll get through it. You're an amazing, strong girl."

I almost laughed off his praise. But the fierce look he held in his green eyes stopped the strange combination of half-sob, half-giggle in my throat. What exactly did he see in me that I couldn't see for myself?

Chapter 19

Turned Away

Isaac

Destiny's phone went to voice mail for the fourth time. I bit back a curse. I didn't usually swear, but her not answering her phone almost warranted it. Apprehension dropped into the bottom of my gut as I turned into her driveway. The headlights of Dad's car created strange shadows in the trees.

Dad was going to be so furious when I got home. He was more protective of his car than I was of my truck. The guy was totally OCD about it. He always kept it spotless. He wouldn't even let anyone unwrap a burger in his car. The thought that I'd stolen it to go see Destiny would torture him. I hoped Sydney and Aspen actually had told him. The thought that I was on Mormon soil, romancing a Mormon girl with his car would drive him nuts. He was probably picturing me making out in the backseat with Destiny right now. After the way he'd taken my truck, I didn't feel even an ounce of guilt. Who knew how long it would be before I saw my truck again? I wouldn't even put it past him to sell it at this point.

Did it really matter? I was going to be eighteen in two weeks, and then he couldn't tell me what to do. Even if Aunt Bethany fired me, I could find another job somewhere else. I thought about living in a small apartment somewhere with a crappy job at a fast food joint and cringed. Okay, maybe I needed to graduate so I could get into a good school, but after that, I'd be out of there so fast he wouldn't know what hit him. If it weren't for Destiny, I'd pick a school on the other side of the country. No one in California would care who I dated.

I pulled up to Destiny's house and turned off the engine. The lights were on in the formal living room, and I could hear music playing. The house sat up on a hill and there was a long sidewalk that curved up and around the hill from the garage to the second floor where the front door was located.

This was a lot more intimidating than I'd imagined. What was I thinking coming here? Did I think I could walk right up to the front door and expect to be welcomed inside? I'd probably find myself face-to-face with her dad, and I already knew firsthand how much he liked me. He used to like me, though. When I was little, he taught my Sunday School class at Bethel Baptist Church. Couldn't he learn to like me again in time? After he forgave me for breaking his daughter's heart, of course.

I took a deep breath that was shakier than I would have liked as I faced the heavy, solid-wood door. I could still hear the music coming from the living room, but now I recognized it as piano playing. Whoever was playing was really good. I knocked on the door, but the piano continued to play. I knocked again, and nothing happened. I walked to the French doors that lined the porch. They led to the large family room, and the light poured out onto the cement of the front porch floor. I peered inside. Michael was sitting on the couch with an old Nintendo controller playing a Zelda game from fifteen years ago. Destiny wasn't kidding about them being behind on technology. How weird. They had this gigantic house, but they lived modestly inside. It was so different from Hannah's house where they had everything name brand and top-of-the-line. Even at my house, we at least had the newest Xbox. But there was something so wholesome about her family's lifestyle. Although I wouldn't want to live without my iPhone or plasma screen TV, I could honestly respect the way they lived.

The piano playing stopped, and Olivia came into the room. I was hoping to catch Destiny alone. Where was she anyway?

I might as well find out.

I tapped on the glass of the French door I'd been peering through, and Michael's head turned in my direction curiously. Olivia came over to open it, but he waved her back cautiously. He squinted in my direction as though he couldn't see my face in the shadows. He reached out and flipped a switch, flooding the porch with light. His face darkened as he twisted the deadlock and opened the door.

"Who's out there?" Olivia asked from over his shoulder. Was it just me, or did she seem kinda apprehensive? Maybe it was freaky for her to live way out here in the woods like this, but I didn't really see why. Their house was surrounded by mansions, each with their own long driveways and acreage.

Michael cracked the door open wider, and she stepped closer and said, "Oh. It's only him."

Michael stared at me, long and hard, his face stony. Talk about intimidating. At 6'4" he stood a good two inches taller than me—not to mention the fact that I stood a step down from him on the porch.

"What are you doing here?" he asked. Was it just my imagination, or did his voice seem deeper than the last time I'd talked to him? The way he was looking at me, I half-expected him to pull a shotgun out. At the very least a handgun from some holster hidden behind his back.

"I really need to talk to Destiny. Is she here?"

He stared at me for another long moment. "Yeah. I'm gonna tell you right now, that's just not happening."

"You don't understand…"

"Oh I understand, all right. You want to sweet-talk my sister into believing whatever jacked-up story you have prepared for her so you can crush her heart all over again."

"I care a lot about her. I would never do that."

He began shutting the door in my face, but I pushed out a hand to stop him. "Wait. You have to let me talk to her. She isn't answering her phone!"

"If she's not taking your calls, then she doesn't want to see you."

"Don't I deserve the chance to defend myself?"

"Are you telling me you're innocent? That you didn't do any of that stuff Will was talking about?"

"No, I—"

"Then I can't think of any possible explanation you could give her to make this better."

"Michael, please." Now I was begging like a desperate loser.

"Stay away from my sister. I mean it. If I see you hanging around here again, I'm going to beat the crap out of you."

I eyed him warily. The whole idea of letting Michael beat me up was starting to sound quite a bit less appealing now that he was actually towering over me.

"I get the message," I said brusquely. "See you in school." I turned on my heel and descended the stone steps of the porch and the sidewalk that wound around the house. Now that the outdoor lights were on I could see another vehicle parked beneath some overhanging branches bordering the driveway. As I came closer I could see it was a white truck. I had a fleeting memory of Destiny walking out of Hannah's house toward a white truck just like that one.

Holy crap! He was here with her. Otherwise he'd have been playing video games with Michael. Where were they? Somewhere in the woods? I spun around and peered into the trees surrounding me.

Chapter 20

Coping

Destiny

"It's getting late, we should probably get you back into the house before you freeze," Preston said, pushing up off of the creaky cot.

I really didn't want to face Olivia. Didn't want her sympathy, or worse yet, her "I told you so."

"Come on." Preston grabbed my hand and pulled me up to stand.

"Do I have to?"

"Eventually, yes. Aren't you half frozen by now?"

When we got to the house, Olivia was lounging on the couch in the family room watching Korean dramas. She glanced at me and Preston and said, "Yay, Preston! You brought her back from the dead!" She turned to me. "You shouldn't cry over Isaac. There are way better guys out there." Easy for her to say. Her heart wasn't the one aching for the guy who'd just betrayed her. "Want to have a movie party with me tonight? I'm going to have a Korean drama marathon! I have snacks!" She held up a basket with a gigantic hot pink bow fastened to the handle, stocked with glass bottles of root beer, Sour Patch Kids, gummy bears, and several kinds of chocolate.

My scowl melted away as I eyed the basket of my favorite snacks. I was a huge sucker for Korean dramas. Olivia's best friend from Bethel was from Korea, and she'd gotten us hooked on them. "Michael put you up to this, didn't he?"

"It was actually my idea, but he took me to the store while you were hiding in the tree house."

"Well, I'm going to head home. I can see that you'll be well taken care of," Preston said.

I smiled at him gratefully. "Thanks for tonight. It really meant a lot."

"Anytime," he said as he opened one of the French doors that led to the front porch. "It's what I'm here for."

Chapter 21

A Friend in Need

Preston

My mind reeled as I walked down the Clarks' porch steps. Hate, envy, ecstasy, despair, hopelessness, and joy swirled within me. I could still feel her body against mine, the way her body had fit so perfectly in my embrace. Surely she had felt it, too. But just because she trusted me with her secrets didn't mean she wanted me like she wanted him.

But she *had* trusted me. It was a start. She'd opened up to me on a level I'd never seen from her before, and now I felt bonded to her in a way I hadn't thought possible.

I climbed into my truck and drove home. As glad as I was that Destiny was single, that Isaac wouldn't be allowed to put his hands on her again, I hated to see her in pain. I'd felt so completely helpless. How could I make it better for her? I couldn't take away his actions. No matter what I did or said, those bad memories would still be in the back of her mind, torturing her.

The best thing she could do at this point would be to search within herself to find the strength to pull through it. But she could do it. And I would be there by her side for as long as she would allow.

When I came in the house, through the garage, Megan and Brinlee pelted me with questions.

"Preston! You're back!" Brinlee squealed, jumping from the couch.

"Was Destiny okay?" Megan asked.

"She was having a hard time," I answered.

"How'd it go? Did you kiss her?" Brinlee asked.

I pointed a finger at her. "I refuse to answer that," I said, my cheeks reddening.

"What happened with her and Isaac?" Megan asked.

"If you guys want to know, you'll just have to ask Destiny yourself."

"Ugh," Brinlee said. "You suck."

"But don't call her right now. Olivia's cheering her up with Korean dramas."

"I'll text her later, then," Megan said. "She needs to know we're here for her."

That Sunday, forgiveness seemed to be a recurring theme at church. I glanced over at Destiny from where I sat in the chapel, but she wore a hardened expression. Guess she wasn't feeling it.

After the meeting, I followed her out of the chapel. The missionaries approached her with friendly smiles on their faces. "Where's your friend, Isaac? He told us he was going to start coming to church with you from now on."

He'd come with her for the second time a couple of weeks ago, and he'd acted pretty interested. Who knew if it wasn't all just an act, though?

Destiny peered down her nose at Elder Benson, the missionary with blond hair. "Yeah?" she said. "Well, I guess you can't believe anything he says because he's not here," she said bitterly and turned and walked away.

The elders watched her retreat and gave me a quizzical look. I only shrugged. It wasn't my place to tell her story.

I watched as Olivia caught up to her in the hall on her way to Sunday School. "I know Isaac dumped you," Olivia scolded with her hands on her hips. "But you don't need to be rude to the missionaries because of it. They didn't do anything wrong."

"Don't say his name around me," Destiny said with a warning in her voice. "Anyway, he didn't dump me. I dumped him. Get it straight."

I came up behind Destiny. She sounded so broken. Oh, how I hated seeing her like that. "Maybe you should just head to class, Olivia."

Olivia nodded slightly at me and said, "I'll see you later."

"Chin up." I tapped Destiny lightly under the chin with my forefinger. "You'll get through it."

"I really don't want to go to school tomorrow," she said. "Can I just start going to school with you and Megan?"

A smile twitched on the corners of my mouth.

"It wouldn't bother me!" Megan said, coming up beside me. "You should!"

"I'm considering it," she said.

She was willing to give up her choir, even her part in the musical to escape having to see him every day? "What about *Les Mis*?" I said. "You're one of the leads. You can't give all that up just because of some jerk."

She sighed. "Of course, you're right. Why are you always right about everything, Preston?"

I shrugged, and the right side of my mouth tugged upward.

Chapter 22

Hope is Lost

Isaac

I called in sick to Aunt Bethany Saturday morning. I was too much of an emotional wreck to deal with people professionally. I ended up spending most of the day on my land, sitting in my truck, staring at the spot where Destiny and I had been stargazing. When Sunday morning came around, I thought about going to church to see her, but I didn't have the guts. Going to church with Aspen was out of the question, so I ended up attending church at Bethel with my family. Dad could tell I was upset, and he kept trying to cheer me up. It was so freaking annoying. Halfway through the service I got up and walked out. I couldn't take another one of Dad's triumphant smiles. So, he'd won. Did he have to keep smashing it in my face?

Just before first period, I found Destiny switching out books at her locker. She looked up and saw me walking toward her. My mouth set into a determined line. Finally, after spending the entire weekend in agony, I could set things straight. "Destiny! I need to talk to you!"

She glanced at me for a moment, and then, as though she were casually ripping my heart from my chest, she stared at the crowd behind me like I was invisible. She turned and wove through the students, putting people between us. Before I knew it, she had vanished completely from sight.

Did it even matter how hard I was trying to get through to her? She hadn't replied to any of my texts, even when I'd told her that I loved her.

"Did you just see that?" some girl said over to my left.

"She has a lot of nerve rejecting a guy like him," a different girl said.

"Did they break up again?" a third voice said. "I heard they were back together."

My cheeks burned with humiliation as the rest of their conversation was drowned out in the chatter of the crowd.

After Bible, I stepped out into the hallway and saw Destiny, Hannah, and Shanice walking with their backs to me. I pushed through the crowd to get closer, so I could talk to Destiny.

"I'm so mad at him right now," Hannah vented. Hannah was still mad at me? What had Destiny said to her?

"Me, too. You know what? We should do something to get even," Shanice plotted.

"No," Destiny said in a tired voice. "Fighting back will only make it worse."

"The person we should be taking down is Will," Hannah said icily. "According to Isaac, it was all his idea."

"We're not taking anyone down," Destiny said in irritation. "I just want to stay away from them."

No! She couldn't push me away. I had to tell her how I felt, or I was going to explode. But then the editor of the school newspaper came around the corner and started asking me a bunch of questions about when we could get together for my upcoming interview in next month's issue.

I glanced over his shoulder hopelessly as Destiny and her friends walked away.

I made one last attempt to talk to her at lunch. I walked into the room with my lunch tray and started toward the table where Hannah and Destiny were sitting with Evan, Shanice, and Hudson.

Destiny glanced over her shoulder at me, darted her eyes away, and said, "Hannah, tell him to go away. I can't even look at him."

Okay, now I was mad. I'd done everything I could to make amends to her. She couldn't even respond to my texts when I was so obviously pouring out my heart and soul? She was such an ice queen.

Then Hannah turned around and gave me this nasty glare that clearly said, "Don't even think about coming over here." *Et tu Brute?* Destiny must have really poisoned her against me.

All of a sudden, it felt like everyone in the lunchroom was staring at me standing in the middle of the room looking completely lost and rejected. I swallowed thickly.

But then, a group of girls surrounded me like a swarm of butterflies. "Isaac! You should come sit with us!" one of them said. I gave one last glance at Destiny, and she stared back coldly. Evelyn, the cute blonde junior class president, smiled at me like I was the sexiest man alive. I shrugged bitterly. If that's what Destiny really wanted… A guy could only try so many times to make things right, couldn't he?

As we walked from the lunchroom, Evelyn said goodbye, and I ended up behind Destiny and her friends again.

"Destiny, if it's too hard for you to sing with Isaac today, I can talk to Mr. Byrd to see if he can postpone it," Hannah said.

Destiny considered this for a moment, but before she could answer Hudson interjected, "What's going on with y'all and Isaac? Why didn't you want him to sit with us?"

"Destiny dumped him," Hannah said. Hannah and I really needed to have a little chat to set some things straight. Whose side was she on, anyway?

"So, Destiny's available now?" Hudson asked.

Oh, if he even tried… I would… I would what? There was nothing I could do. Destiny could make her own choices. Even though it hurt like hades, I wasn't going to be the jealous ex, sabotaging every relationship she ever wanted to get into.

"No! Definitely not!" Destiny said. "I am *so* not available."

I released a tense breath. Well, *that* was good to know.

"Sorry I asked," Hudson muttered.

"She means no offense, Hudson. She's just really beat up over the breakup. It was pretty ugly," Hannah said.

"I know how that can be. My girlfriend dumped me last year, and it sucked. Majorly," Hudson said. "I wanted to slash her tires, but I didn't."

"That's good to know," Destiny said, cringing.

"We're going to do something to get revenge on Isaac for what he did to her. You in?" Shanice said.

Whoa. Revenge?

"What'd he do?"

Hannah and Shanice relayed a shortened version of the story.

"What a jerk!" Hudson said. "Yeah, let's get him for what he did!"

"Please, don't go slashing anyone's tires," Destiny pled.

"Shanice and I," he said, waving a finger between them. "We'll think of something else."

I was about to pull the little punk aside and tell him to leave me alone, when Destiny said, "Seriously? I don't care about revenge! I just want him to leave me alone. I don't want anyone to try to kick me out."

"They'd better not," Shanice said. "Cuz that would be messed up."

"You didn't hear Dr. Robinson when he was talking to Will. He said something about finding a way to get the Mormons to leave the school."

"What!?" Hannah exclaimed.

"Are you serious?" Evan said.

"I don't know what I'd do if you left!" Hannah exclaimed. "And it would all be because of my stupid uncle."

I clenched my jaw. I couldn't help but agree.

"Man, sometimes I really hate this place," Hudson said. "These people need to realize that we live in the twenty-first century. The stuff they come up with is ridiculous."

"I'm with you, man," Evan said. "All the way."

I didn't see Destiny again until Primus when Hannah was hugging her in the hallway. "I'm sorry all this is happening to you," she said. "Even though I get busy with Evan and school and *Les Mis*, I'm always here for you if you need me."

"Thanks, Hannah."

I walked past and moved into the chapel. I found a seat in the choir loft and sat morosely by myself. Jessie Larsen edged her way onto the pew about fifteen feet from me. I glanced over at her. She was staring at me with her mouth twisted into a self-satisfied smile.

Destiny and Hannah filed into the pew in front of us about ten feet from Jessie. Jessie stood with her hands on her hips and said, "See? It's just like I told you at Homecoming. Just a bag of garbage thrown to the curb."

What? She'd said that to Destiny at Homecoming? No wonder Destiny had been so upset. I'd thought it was just about the punch being dumped down the front of her dress, but now I was realizing there was much more to that conversation than I'd realized.

Destiny's eyes grew distant, and she angled her face away from Jessie like she hadn't heard her, but as I studied the rigid way she held her shoulders, I realized that definitely wasn't the case.

"What the crap does that mean?" Hannah said, going into attack mode. She had her hands on her hips, mirroring Jessie's posture, and her eyes were on fire.

"Isn't it obvious? It means that Isaac finally came to his senses," Jessie replied with a snort.

"*She* dumped *him*, you malicious witch," Hannah said.

Ouch. Just shove it in my face already. Thanks a lot, Hannah.

"You weren't even there, Jessie," Aspen said, rolling her eyes. "You didn't see how she treated him. He was trying to apologize, and she wouldn't even listen." Aspen turned her frozen blue eyes on me. "From what I hear, she still won't accept his apology. You know, Destiny, in the Bible, it says that we should forgive."

"The Bible also says you shouldn't judge. So, maybe you should take your judging butt someplace else," Hannah retorted.

Aspen looked down her nose at Hannah, but turned and moved across the room to talk to Sydney.

Mr. Byrd came into the room shortly after the hour and said, "Sorry I'm late, after some of the events of the past weekend I feel that it would be the most beneficial if we go back to the beginning of the musical and start over." Destiny relaxed visibly, and I suddenly understood why. Today, Destiny and I were scheduled to sing "A Little Fall of Rain," the scene where Éponine and Marius sing as she lays in his arms dying. Hannah must have told him about our breakup.

Great. Singing that song with Destiny might have been my best chance of rekindling things with her. If we were starting again from the beginning, we probably wouldn't get around to singing it again for months, especially with Christmas coming up. Who knows what our relationship will be like by then?

Chapter 23

Holidays

Destiny

It was starting to get too cold to enjoy the tree house, but I was determined to still make it out there. At first, I'd just brought out a heavy coat, but as the temperatures dropped, I eventually brought out a sleeping bag as well. After my homework was finished, a lot of times I'd read my scriptures or sit and think. Olivia called it moping. I claimed I was pondering life.

One day, a few days before Thanksgiving, I was up in the tree house, and Preston called up to me. "Rapunzel, Rapunzel, let down your hair."

"You insist on still using that rope like when you were a kid?"

"Of course."

I laughed, threw it down to him, and watched as he climbed up hand over hand.

"I brought you something," he said, sliding his backpack off once he'd climbed up. I couldn't believe he'd climbed the rope while wearing that thing.

"What'd you bring me?"

He set his backpack on the floor between his feet, unzipped it, and pulled out two thermoses, his hair falling into his eyes as he leaned forward.

“Hot chocolate?” I asked hopefully.

“Yep! It’s the mint kind,” he said, sweeping his hair back from his eyes.

I grinned. He’d remembered it was my favorite.

“You know, you’re totally nuts to be out here in this weather,” he said with a teasing smile.

“I thought you were the one who said the cold was invigorating,” I teased.

His smiled vanished. “It is. For me.” He regarded me seriously. “But I don’t think you come out here because you feel that way.”

“What do you mean?” I asked.

“I think you come out here to punish yourself.”

“Punish myself?” It kind of made sense. I carried a heavy load of guilt concerning my relationship with Isaac. I’d broken a lot of rules and had really pulled away from my friends and family.

“Maybe you should take up a more productive pastime. Try something like poetry.”

I rolled my eyes.

“That wasn’t supposed to be a joke. I think it could help you.”

Not likely. There wasn’t much that could help me. “I’ll think about it,” I said, mostly to keep from hurting his feelings. I sipped the hot, creamy liquid and sighed as it warmed me.

Preston's family came over for Thanksgiving dinner. Grandma and Grandpa were spending it with Dad's sister in Ohio, and Mom wanted to take some of the pressure off of Preston's mom, since her depression had been pretty rough lately. After our big dinner, Olivia and I were poring over the Black Friday ads with Brinlee and Megan, and the guys were watching football. The younger kids were all crowded in Brianna's room playing board games. The house smelled like warm pumpkin pie, and there was Christmas music on in the room where Mom and Sister Nelson were making wreaths.

"Are you guys doing anything fun for Christmas?" Megan asked.

"Not really," I said.

Dad muted the TV for the commercial and glanced over at us. "Actually, I was just talking to your mom about an idea," he said to me. He glanced back at Preston's dad. "I was thinking your family might want to come along as well."

"Oh yeah?" Preston's dad glanced over with interest.

"My parents called to wish me a happy Thanksgiving earlier today, and they let me know that there's been a last-minute cancellation at their cabin for the weekend of Christmas. They decided to gift the weekend to us as part of our Christmas present rather than trying to fill it at the last minute."

"Oh my gosh! That's awesome!" Olivia jumped out of her seat. She turned to Brinlee. "My grandparents own this huge cabin up in the Smokey Mountains, and they rent it out for extra money and stuff. Y'all should come. That would be the best Christmas ever!"

"Please, Dad! Can we do it?" Brinlee asked.

"I'll have to talk to your mother, but I don't see why not," Brother Nelson said.

So I might spend Christmas with Preston in a cabin? I didn't see that one coming.

The next few weeks flew by. Isaac and I continued to avoid each other. I spent more time in the tree house with Preston. Sometimes he'd find me up there, and he'd bring his homework with him. After about a week of that, it became a regular thing. I would have thought someone would say something, especially my parents, but either they didn't notice Preston's truck or they thought he was hanging out with Michael. If they suspected something was going on between us, they didn't say a word to me about it. Honestly, I wasn't so sure what was going on between us. Preston came to do homework with me, but he wasn't super talkative. He just kind of showed up, telling me he didn't think I should have to be all alone. Part of me wanted him to leave, but this other part kept me from showing it. It was the part that needed him near me, like a pillar of strength. It needed him to stay, so I wouldn't break apart again.

The days Preston didn't come I couldn't focus on homework. Instead, I stared out the tree house window listlessly. Sometimes my mind would drift to *him*, like an unsuspecting fly to a light bulb. I'd hover close to the thought of him, only to get too close and get burned again as I remembered. And the pain was terrible. Agonizingly so. I'd been shoved under deep black water and told that I'd never be able to resurface. Where were my gills? Maybe in the future, I'd learn to grow some; but before that time came, each breath would be either raw or numb, depending on the moment. Every day, walking past him in the hall was torture. Whenever he returned one of Evelyn's persistent smiles, the pain ached inside me. Oh, how I wished she would leave him alone. But even if she were to go away, another girl would come. And then another.

Every night, sometimes for hours, I begged God to erase the desire, the anger, and the pain from my heart. Occasionally, a tiny moment of clarity and relief came. But the next morning, the instant I saw him, I was plunged back into the water and the debilitating chasm of nothingness threatened to drown me again.

And then there were the dreams. Some were snapshots taken from our past. We played paintball, sang our duet at Hannah's house, or stargazed on his land while I ran my hands through his hair. Each dream was so real, so vivid. When I woke from them, they left me gasping with the knowledge that I would never have those moments again.

But those were the good dreams.

The nightmares brought a pain so unspeakable that I withdrew into a sullen state of silence for the rest of the day. Those days scared Michael. He was so amazing and supportive. He tried to get me to talk to him about what I was feeling, but I usually ended up telling him I was fine or I made up excuses. I didn't want him to worry about me. Hannah made several efforts to cheer me up. But it was obvious that she wanted to focus on Evan. No matter how hard they tried, no one could pull me from the dark, frozen depths that had captured me.

Except for Preston. Somehow, while he sat with me in the tree house as our pens scratched across our papers, the iceberg around my heart began to thaw. It never vanished completely, but melted enough to allow small, sporadic moments of laughter. Even if those fleeting moments of happiness didn't warm my heart completely, they pulled me into the sunshine just enough to carry on, one foot in front of the other.

Midterms were over and Christmas break was upon us, and the Nelsons and our family caravanned up to the Smoky Mountains. I sat in the backseat of our Suburban, staring out the window at the cars we were passing on the interstate. For the next two weeks, I was free from enduring Isaac's presence. I should be relieved, right? Wrong. Being away from him made everything worse. When I was at school, I could at least see him. There was this little back corner of my mind that still fantasized that he'd come back to me. And somehow, he would realize that what he'd done was wrong, and on bended knee he'd beg me to forgive him. And I would graciously agree.

But he'd stopped caring. He hadn't even attempted to talk to me in weeks, which only reinforced my belief that he'd never truly wanted me in the first place. Jealous rage sliced through me. He'd replaced me with Evelyn just as quickly as he'd replaced Aspen with me. Except, I'd had such a short time with him, he probably didn't even remember that we'd even been together. I'd never hated and loved someone so much in my entire life. But it had to stop. This trip was my chance for a fresh start on life.

We arrived at the cabin with the Nelsons pulling up just behind us. The mountains loomed over us, and there was snow on the ground scattered with melted patches so that the field before us looked like a Dalmatian with spots across its back. I had to wait for everyone else to leave before I could get out, and by the time I was out, Preston was already stepping out of his family's van, stretching his arms behind him. I couldn't help but stare. He was awfully beautiful sometimes, and it came through at the strangest moments. One minute he was being a bit annoying and sarcastic, the next he was doing something like stretching outside his family's minivan, looking like a Greek god. Truthfully, I hadn't seen his annoying side in a long time. Not since my breakup.

So far, he'd just been…well, awesome.

He turned and saw me staring at him, and a corner of his mouth pulled upward in a friendly way. "So, we heard on the weather report on the drive up that they're expecting more snow here." It was cute how excited he always got whenever there was even the slightest chance of snow. I think it had something to do with his early years spent in Utah playing in the snow every winter.

"Really?" Brianna squeaked. "We haven't had any real snow in forever."

"Well, they get a lot more snow up here than we do," Preston said, lifting the hatch on the back of his mom's minivan. He slung a couple of pink backpacks, a Barbie pillow, and two sleeping bags onto one arm, and with the other he grabbed two more backpacks and began heading toward the cabin.

Inside it was huge and clean, but desperately in need of a renovation. We helped our parents unload the rest of our luggage and discussed where everyone was going to sleep. Mom and Sister Nelson decided that the guys should take one half of the cabin, and the girls should take the other half, with the parents sharing the two largest bedrooms.

I piled my stuff next to the bed I was sharing with Megan and went outside to see what everyone else was doing.

Preston was standing on the porch looking out at the expanse before us. Far off in the distance there were fields with horses and sheep, and beyond that, there was an old, white brick house that looked as though it dated back to the Civil War.

"Wanna go check out the horses?" Preston asked, a hand tucked into a pocket of his dark wash jeans.

"I'd love to," I said.

As we passed the cars, Michael poked his head out of the Suburban with his backpack slung over his shoulder. "Where are y'all going?"

Preston told him, and for a moment, I thought Michael would say he wanted to come with us, but something strange flashed across his face, and in the end, all he said was, "Awesome. Have fun."

We trudged through the snow, and I listened to the muffled way it crunched under my feet, breaking the perfect silence.

"How was your drive up?" he asked.

I shrugged. "It was fine, I guess," I said, trying not to dwell on the fact that I'd thought way too much about Isaac.

"Well, ours was horrible. One of the twins got carsick and threw up, and Anna whined about the smell for the rest of the trip."

I couldn't help but giggle. "Sorry, I know I shouldn't be laughing."

He glanced sideways at me and grinned. "Oh I see how it is. You think my misery's funny?"

"It's just nice to know I'm not the only one getting tortured in the car by annoying little brothers and sisters."

He laughed. "That's what iPods are for."

"True story," I said, nodding. We followed the gravel driveway that led to the old Civil War farmhouse.

Preston walked up to the barbed wire fence and whistled to the horses. One of them perked up his ears and trotted over to us. Preston put his hand out, and the horse nuzzled it like he expected a carrot. When the horse didn't find anything, he turned away disinterestedly.

"We should have brought him a snack," I said.

"We'll just have to come back tomorrow," Preston said.

"Definitely," I said.

"You seem much happier today," Preston observed.

"You tend to have that effect on me," I replied.

"I'm glad. Sometimes it seems like I'm not getting through to you." His green eyes focused intently on me.

"Are you kidding? Everything that happened with Isaac would have been so much harder if it hadn't been for you."

"You've been really distant, so it's hard for me to tell what you're thinking," he explained.

"Preston, there were so many days that I'd be in the tree house, not knowing how I could face another minute of life, and the next thing I knew, you're down there calling out to me. And even when I wouldn't say much, you never gave up. You just kept coming." I looked out across the snowy field. "It's still so hard. Every day."

He studied my face and his mouth formed a serious thin line, but his eyes were compassionate.

"Sometimes it just aches." There were moments when I could joke around with Preston. During those short times, I'd forget for a while. But then, as soon as there was a lull in the conversation or he left my side, the iceberg would harden up again.

He put an arm around my shoulder and pulled me close to him until my cheek rested against his shoulder. I breathed in the smell of his leather jacket, and some of the ice slowly melted away. "But the good news is, I won't have to see him for another two weeks," I said. "We're going to have fun this week, and I'm not going to wallow in my misery."

Preston held me for a moment, and we gazed out across the field, watching the horses pawing at the ground as they looked for grass to eat in the bare patches of ground. As I felt his arm encircling me, I thought back to the time we were walking to the paintball field, and he'd put his arm around me. I'd been so focused on not giving Isaac the wrong impression about my fake relationship with Preston that I hadn't thought about how Preston must have felt. My cheeks burned. I'd been so awful to him. Then I thought about how I'd put his name in my phone to hide the fact that I was still dating Isaac. I'd used him to get to Isaac repeatedly, and all he'd ever done to deserve it was give me his undivided attention. If he ever knew how I'd used him, he'd be so hurt. All I ever did was mope about my sad life and whine about how my ex-boyfriend had betrayed me. And yet Preston kept coming back. What had I ever done to deserve him?

After dinner, back at the cabin, Michael and Preston were building a fire together in the huge stone fireplace. Preston bent over the hearth, reaching back and forth as he added sticks to the cold fireplace. I couldn't help noticing the way his shirt clung to his shoulders as he worked. A stray lock of his wavy blond hair fell forward and he shoved it back distractedly, his eyes focused on the small flames he'd just kindled.

He really was beautiful.

Within minutes, a cozy fire blazed, warming the room.

Chapter 24

Snowball Fight

Preston

I looked up from the hearth and felt Destiny's eyes on me. Our eyes met, and she blushed and looked away. Was I imagining it, or was she checking me out just now?

Well, that was new. Maybe there was hope, yet. And she hadn't pushed me away when I'd put my arm around her today. I'd been a little hesitant to do it at first, but it felt right at the time.

For the past few weeks, I'd kept expecting her to push me away or to somehow forgive him and go back to him, but she hadn't so far. Every time I'd come to her tree house, I'd wondered if it would be the day she'd turn me away. She still thought about him constantly. She'd get this faraway look in her eyes, and then the sadness would overtake her all over again.

I felt myself being pulled toward her, but at the same time she was so broken and fragile. It was clear that she still wanted him. At any time she could wave me away and decide she was willing to take him back. It was what kept me from kissing her when I'd had so many opportunities. That and sheer terror.

But that didn't mean I didn't think about kissing her.

I did. A lot.

Destiny was addicted to ChapStick. She was always putting it on, and every time she did, it was like she was begging me to kiss her by drawing attention to her lips. And she wore these flavors that smelled like dessert. Talk about torture.

Speaking of ChapStick, she was pulling a tube of it out of her jacket pocket right now and running it all over her lips. Oh dude, don't look. I turned back to the fire and busied myself with rearranging one of the logs, even though it was roaring cheerfully and wouldn't need attention for a while. Just then, the twins ran through the room chasing Drianna, who was squealing gleefully. Both of them had it bad for her. They were always getting into these lengthy arguments over who would end up marrying her one day. I couldn't blame them. She was a carbon copy of what Destiny had been like when I first met her.

Destiny twisted around, smiling at them as they ran past. It was good to see her smiling again. There was something magical about this cabin. I wasn't sure if it was the Christmas tree set up in the corner, or the fact that it was filled with our closest friends, but it definitely felt special. Destiny could probably sense it, too. It would explain her lighter mood since we'd arrived.

The next morning, Michael and I woke up to Elijah and the twins screeching something about snow. I rolled over and groaned, but sat up to see how much snow we'd gotten. I peered out the window, and sure enough, there was at least six inches and it was still coming down.

I grinned. "You know what this means, right?" I asked Michael.

"Snowball fight," he said, returning my grin.

"Heck yes," I said, climbing out of bed. I hadn't seen this much snow since my last visit to Utah two winters ago. I rifled through my bag, grabbing my toothbrush and the clothes I planned to wear for the day. I was lucky enough to actually find the bathroom open. Not sure how I achieved that since I'd waited a full hour to get five minutes in the bathroom last night. After getting dressed and brushing my teeth, I slung my leather jacket over my arm and headed to the kitchen to scrounge up some food.

"Good morning," Destiny said from beside the kitchen table. "Hungry?" She was chopping green onions and bell peppers.

"When am I not hungry?" I asked with a grin. "Whatcha making?"

"Omelets," Megan answered from beside Sister Clark who was standing at the stove.

"The first one's about to come off the skillet right now. Want it?" Sister Clark asked.

I glanced over and noticed Mom lying on the couch by the fire. "Mom, have you eaten yet?"

She nodded.

"How are you feeling this morning?" I asked. She'd gotten so much weaker lately.

"I woke up with a massive headache," she said, pressing a hand to her forehead.

"I'm worried about you," Megan said. "You look really pale."

"I'm fine," Mom insisted.

"Why don't you go back to bed," I suggested.

"I need to be out here to help supervise the kids," she said.

"I'll help get them breakfast and take them outside to play," I promised. "Just go get some rest."

She nodded and returned to her room. I turned to see Destiny watching me with a pensive look.

Megan and I helped the rest of the younger kids get ready to eat breakfast. By the time they'd all finished up and I'd helped clear the dishes, the kids were all bouncing up and down, bursting at the seams, wanting to go play in the snow.

"Who wants to have a massive snowball war?" I bellowed, throwing my arms into the air.

The twins went berserk, and even Brinlee and Olivia looked interested. I glanced over at Destiny and said, "You coming?"

"Of course," she said. "Like I'd pass up another chance to take you down."

My mouth quirked up into a smile again. Now that was the Destiny I knew so well. "You wish."

"I don't wish. I know," she said.

"Psh. Whatever." I seriously couldn't wait to see her covered from head to foot in snow.

Fifteen minutes later, we all congregated on the porch. We split up into two teams and left to scout out the best places to set up our headquarters. Olivia, Brinlee, and I were on a team together with the twins and Anna, while Michael, Megan, Destiny, Elijah, and Brianna were on the other team. We picked a spot behind a rusty shed next to a small stand of trees. Michael's team chose a spot behind a gigantic fallen log.

"Okay, guys, start making snowballs and stockpile them over behind the shed," I said. I gazed across the field to where Destiny and Megan were scooping up snow and rolling it into balls. As I looked, I noticed the snow had stopped falling. I bent down and began forming my own pile of snowballs in a series of rapid movements. Before long, we'd cleared out all the snow in the general area, and we had to move out to farther ground to find more snow. When we had a good-sized pile, I said, "Okay, guys, that's good enough. Let's go hit them with a surprise attack."

"Yaar!" the twins roared. So much for the surprise. Michael looked up and pointed Elijah in our direction.

"Charge!" I commanded, and we flew forward with armfuls of snowballs. Our two forces collided, and snow exploded around us like a full-blown blizzard. I lunged for Destiny and threw a snowball that splattered across her arm. Her eyes grew wide as she looked down at her arm, her brow set in determination as she pelted me with five snowballs in a row. They slammed against my chest, my shoulders, my back, and right smack on my cheek. "Dang," I said, rubbing the snow off my face. "Don't mess with Destiny."

"That's right," she said, with her arms crossed and her chin thrust out. But her eyes were twinkling.

We were out of snowballs, so we had to go back to our piles to restock. Then we were all back on the field, colliding in a flurry of white. I hit Destiny right above her ear with a huge snowball. She shrieked a feminine war cry and clobbered me with two snowballs, one on either side of my face. My cheeks stung with the cold, and I ran back to the fort to get more snowballs.

As I was reaching down behind the shed to restock my supply of ammo, Destiny barreled into me, knocking me off balance. Her arms wrapped around me, and we fell into the snow on my side. I struggled to break free, but she had me pinned at a strange angle. Technically, I could have thrown her off at any time, but that would have ruined the fun.

I howled as she shoved snow down the back of my shirt, and we rolled several times down the slope as I struggled to get free. But her arms were locked around my neck. And then, somehow, she was pinned under me. Every vein in my body was on fire as I gazed into her crystal clear blue eyes. She released her arms from her vicelike hold on my neck. Her eyes grew wide and her lips parted slightly as though she'd just realized how close our faces were.

I had no idea what possessed me to do it, or when all reason had suddenly flown from my mind. But as I leaned forward and kissed her tenderly, all I could think about was how beautiful and pure she'd looked lying there in the snow with her hair splayed all around her in wild waves of perfection.

Honestly, if I'd stopped to think about what I was about to do, I never would have been able to go through with it. I mean, come on, how many years had I imagined what it would be like to kiss Destiny Clark? But that had always been pure fantasy. Especially after her nasty breakup. If I'd taken the time to consider kissing her, I would've convinced myself that the last thing she'd wanted was a kiss.

As my lips met hers, Destiny froze under me, shocked. At first, I thought she was going to push me off or slap me in the face, but after a moment, her body relaxed beneath me and, miracle of miracles, she wrapped her arms around my torso and pulled me in even closer. Her cold nose brushed mine, and her breath was warm on my mouth as she exhaled. Her lips were amazingly soft as she moved them over mine, and she tasted like…vanilla frosted cupcakes.

I'd never experienced anything so heavenly. It didn't matter that there was melted snow dripping down my back or that I couldn't feel my toes anymore. I finally had her arms around me, and she had just kissed me back. My legs could be broken at this point, and it wouldn't matter.

She pulled away and looked up at me, her liquid blue eyes vulnerable. I vowed in that moment to do everything I could to cherish and protect her.

Her bottom lip trembled, and she bit it hesitantly as a shudder ran through her. She was thinking of him. Somehow, I could just tell.

I sat up and looked away.

How could I have been such an idiot? She obviously wasn't ready for another relationship. I'd acted out of selfishness and desire for one thoughtless moment, and it would probably cost her countless days of pain and confusion. I'd just been thinking about how I wanted to protect her, but instead, I was the person inflicting the pain. I should have known her feelings were still too raw to handle something this serious.

Chapter 25

Snow Kissed

Destiny

I gazed up into Preston's green eyes, and a shudder ran through me. I totally hadn't seen that kiss coming. But wow. Seriously. Just wow. Who knew Preston Nelson was such an amazing kisser?

My head was spinning as he pulled apart from me and sat up. His eyes shifted away from me, and I suspected the redness in his cheeks wasn't just from the cold. This wasn't going to make everything awkward between us, was it? Because, honestly, I couldn't afford to lose him.

But before I could tell him that, the twins came around the corner of the shed and screeched. "Get her! She took Preston down!" They pelted me with snowballs, aieee-ing like a couple of Native American braves. I scrambled onto my side to grab some snow into balls, but it was too late, I was toast. The rest of Preston's team came around the corner and bombarded me as well.

"Guys, back off!" Preston said. "Give her some room to breathe." He stood and grasped my hand, helping me up off the ground. I stood and gazed into his eyes. They were full of concern and something else I couldn't quite put my finger on. Regret? Guilt? Fear? Was he having second thoughts about kissing me?

Well, I certainly wasn't having any regrets. In fact, I was kind of wishing he'd do it again.

"Oh my gosh," I said. "I'm freezing." And I was. I couldn't feel my feet anymore.

"Hot tub!" Brinlee chimed.

"Yes!" Olivia said.

"That actually sounds really amazing right now," I said. "You guys coming?" I turned to Michael and Preston. I think Preston's jaw dropped a little.

"Sure, I'm in," Michael said.

Preston didn't say anything, but followed us back to the cabin. Once I was back in the room I shared with Megan, I put on my little, yellow, polka-dotted tankini. I twisted my hair up into a ballerina bun and wrapped my pink and black zebra-striped beach towel around myself.

Preston used to swim with us all the time when he was younger, but last summer he'd been so busy mowing lawns he hadn't swam with us even once. That was why when I'd seen him shirtless that night we stole his underwear it was such a shock to me. His body had changed so much since two summers ago when I'd last seen him shirtless. He used to be such a scrawny kid. But now? He was absolutely drool-worthy. And that was last fall. Since then, he'd only bulked up more.

Olivia and Brinlee came into our room with their towels wrapped around them. "You guys ready to go?" Brinlee asked.

"Yep," Megan said.

Preston and Michael met us in the kitchen where the sliding glass door led to the back porch. Preston had on a navy blue BYU T-shirt and the silver athletic shorts he was wearing the day we'd stolen his underwear.

The twins ran out in their swimsuits, but Mom stopped them. "Where do y'all think you're going? You're still too young for the hot tub."

"No fair!" the twins said in unison.

"Rules are rules. You know we don't let you in the hot tub at our place either. Not until you're twelve."

Personally I thought the rule was kind of dumb, but Mom was a big stickler for the rules. But who was I to complain? That was two less kids to splash me in the face.

Michael slid open the glass door, and we stepped out. As soon as the frigid air hit us Brinlee and Olivia shrieked, and we scrambled across the deck to the hot tub. They jumped in together before anyone else. I kicked off my flip flops, draped my towel over the deck railing, and dipped my foot into the scalding hot water. I looked up just in time to see Preston peel off his shirt.

Holy freaking cow! A flush crept up into my face. His arms were massive, his chest was chiseled, and his abs could keep my clothes clean. *Can I just say yum?* My heartbeat flew into overdrive. I was staring at him openly. I knew I was, but I couldn't take my eyes off of him. And he noticed, too. How did I know this? Well, it was pretty easy to tell because he was staring right back at me like a starving man looking at a feast placed before him.

Chapter 26

Hot Tub

Preston

Destiny and I locked eyes, and I felt my entire body heat up despite the freezing air biting at my bare skin. She was beautiful standing there in her yellow swimsuit with one foot in the hot tub, her skin flawless and creamy. She lowered into the water, breaking the spell, and Megan climbed into the hot tub after her.

What was I thinking coming out here? How could I stay just friends with her when she looked at me like that? She may think that this was going somewhere, but there was no way she was ready for another relationship. What if I did something stupid to her and ruined everything and broke her heart all over again? I almost did earlier in the snow, and I wasn't going to be stupid enough to do it again.

There were two open spots in the hot tub. One was next to Destiny, and the other was on the opposite corner from her, about as far as I could get from her. I let Michael climb in before me, thinking he'd take the spot closer to Destiny. But of course he didn't. He took the spot next to Megan and Brinlee.

I climbed in after him, grateful for the excuse of the steamy water to explain my red face, in case anyone noticed. No one seemed to. They were too busy joking around and playfully splashing each other.

"Hey, are you okay?" Destiny asked me.

"Huh?"

"You seem kind of quiet."

"Me?"

"Yeah, you," she nudged my knee with hers underneath the water.

I ran my fingers through my hair, wetting the unruly waves down. I was far from okay. I was trying to forget about that kiss, but it was all I could think about, and now she was sitting inches away from me in a swimsuit.

"Hey," she said, reaching for my arm. "Talk to me." Her fingers trailed down my arm beneath the surface, sending electrical jolts through me. This was incredibly hard. More than anything, I wanted to take her in my arms and kiss her again, but I couldn't risk hurting her.

"We can talk about it later if you want," she whispered, her face dangerously close to mine. And just like that, she turned back to Olivia and splashed her in the face. Megan and Olivia started whispering and then teamed up to dunk Michael under. When he came back up, a full blown water fight broke out, and we all joined in.

Sister Clark slid open the door. "Y'all need to calm down out here. Either get out or stop with the water fight. You're going to splash water all over the deck, and it's going to freeze over and break someone's neck."

"Yes, ma'am," Michael said. "Sorry about that, Mom."

She slid the door closed again, and Megan and Brinlee started whispering again, this time with Olivia and Michael as well. I figured they were all just going to start something else, to somehow circumvent the no-water-fight rule, and I prepared myself to be ambushed.

But instead, Brinlee said, "Hey, let's go get some hot chocolate." And they all agreed and left one by one until Destiny and I were alone. I was too stunned to leave. They were trying to set us up? Didn't they realize she didn't want to get back in a relationship so soon? She had told me so herself. She'd been very clear about it. Hadn't she told them? They were her closest friends.

Destiny didn't seem to mind at all. She turned toward me and smiled. "So? Can we talk now?"

I was in so much trouble. "Sure." I swallowed.

"Tell me what's going on. You kiss me, and now you're acting all weird. I don't want this for us, Preston."

Neither did I, but I couldn't see a way around it. "I'm sorry about earlier. I acted on impulse, and I was totally out of line."

"Oh my gosh! Don't apologize for that."

"You were okay with it?"

"Did I ever give any kind of sign that I wasn't?"

"No..." I said, my voice trailing off. "But you said yourself you didn't want to get into another relationship, and I didn't honor your wishes."

Her face grew thoughtful. "I can understand that, I guess, but right now what I need more than anything is to move on. And I can't do that until I forget him," she said, getting on her knees on the ledge in front of me and inching closer. "Who better to help me forget than you?" She rested her hands against my bare chest, electrifying my skin with her touch. "I need you to help me forget. Right now." She trailed her hands up my arms and over my shoulders like she was on a mission to explore the contours of my body. She wrapped her hands around my neck. Now her face was inches from me, and her eyes were locked on mine.

She wanted to forget him? Oh, she was going to. She was going to forget the guy even had a name. "Okay. I'll help you," I murmured. "Just remember, you're the one who asked for this."

I finally allowed myself to touch her. I wrapped my arms around her waist and pulled her in closer. And then my lips were on hers. I kissed her the way I really wanted to. All the desire I'd been holding back for the past hour—for the past several years, actually—flowed into the kiss.

Her lips moved in perfect synchrony with mine, soft, yet firm, at the right moments. She pulled away, resting her forehead against mine, sighing in satisfaction. I drew her torso closer. Her body fit perfectly against mine, like she was specifically crafted for me.

We pulled apart, and I gazed into her eyes, my head spinning.

Just then the sliding glass door opened, and Sister Clark called out to us, "Hey, you two, how about you come inside for some hot chocolate, too." She'd tried to keep her voice light, but I didn't miss the slight undertone of disapproval she must have felt at seeing us out here alone together.

Little did she know…

Chapter 27

Poetry

Destiny

A few days after Christmas, Preston and I were hanging out in the tree house again. A tinkling melody filled the chilly air in the tree house. Preston reached into his back pocket and yanked out his phone.

"Hey, Dad… I'm over at the Clarks' right now." Preston's face paled, and he sat forward a bit. "Oh no."

I studied Preston's face with the hope that it might reveal some bit of information.

"Yeah, I'm heading home right now," he said, scrambling to his feet. "Yeah, I'll see you in just a few. Bye." He crammed the phone back into his pocket and twisted to look at me.

"What's wrong?"

His eyes had a haunted look in them. "My mom got her results back from the doctor today. Dad's calling the family together so she can tell us all in person."

"That doesn't sound good." Dread settled into the pit of my stomach.

He put a hand to his brow and inhaled jaggedly. "What'll we do if we lose her?"

"I'm so sorry," I said. "I'll pray for your family."

"Thanks," he said from over his shoulder as he jogged down the stairs to the dried leaves below.

That night, while we were doing the dinner dishes, the house phone rang. "Hello?" Mom answered. Suddenly, the only sound in the room was the water running. Mom covered her mouth with a hand and squeezed her eyes shut. Fat tears rolled down her cheeks.

I stopped rinsing the food from the pot I was scrubbing and turned the water off.

"Yeah, I'm still here," she said, blinking back tears. She glanced over her shoulder at our curious faces. She turned away from us and scurried into the formal dining room and shut the door.

Olivia and I exchanged a somber look and went back to doing the dishes. Five minutes later, Mom came out of the dining room with a tearstained face.

"What's wrong, Mom?" Brianna asked.

Mom looked at Brianna like she was considering sending her away on an errand or changing the subject, but in the end, she simply said, "Sister Nelson is very sick."

"What do you mean?" Olivia asked, her voice tight.

"Her cancer's back."

I turned around, fear slamming into my chest. I'd suspected as much, but I'd hoped it wasn't true.

"That's horrible," Olivia said.

"What are they going to do?"

"They're going to put her on chemo, but the doctor said it didn't look good. Out of four stages she's at stage three." Mom slumped into a chair at the kitchen table. This wasn't just some lady from church. Preston's mom was her best friend.

"Are they still coming over for New Year's Eve?" Olivia asked.

"I don't know." She rubbed her temples. "They probably won't be feeling up to it."

"I hate cancer," Brianna declared, storming from the room.

"I think we can all agree to that," Michael called from the family room. "I'm going over to Preston's." He jumped out of his chair.

"I'm going with you," I said.

"Me, too." Olivia threw the dishrag into the sink.

"No." Mom raised her head, her eyes firm. "You three stay here. Give their family some time to sort through this together. If you want to contact them, send a text so they can reply on their own terms." She pointed a finger to the sink. "Anyway, there are dishes to be done." She put her head back in her hands morosely.

"Mom," I asked. "Are you okay?"

Without a word, she got up, went into her bedroom, and shut the door, her shoulders slumped.

After finishing the dishes, Michael, Olivia, and I sent texts, and the younger kids made cards for their friends.

Later that night, I felt tense. If I wasn't able to see the Nelsons soon, I'd explode. I trudged back to my bedroom and flopped onto my bed. Olivia was digging through her closet.

"What are you doing?"

"I just have to clean something right now." Over her shoulder, a red ballet flat flew out of her closet. She hadn't worn those shoes for about three years. It landed on a heap of shoes she'd found from the depths of her closet.

"You're cleaning out your closet?"

"Yep," she said, tossing out a teddy bear I hadn't seen since seventh grade.

I'd sent individual texts to Megan, Preston, and Sister Nelson, but it didn't feel like enough. More than anything, I wished I could be there for Preston like he'd been there for me when my heart was broken. I couldn't imagine the pain he was in. Feeling helpless, I pulled out a pen and notebook and began writing poetry like Preston had suggested.

It was surprising how easily the words flowed from me. Powerful similes and metaphors wove themselves into the rhyming lines. That night, I wrote a poem about mothers and how they sacrifice for their families.

The next day was December thirtieth. Mom was out grocery shopping, and I'd finished all my chores. I put on my heavy coat, grabbed my pen and notebook, and slipped on a pair of mud boots in the garage. I trudged through onion grass and brown crispy leaves until I reached the tree house. I climbed the stairs and breathed a sigh of relief. I kicked off my boots and snuggled into the sleeping bag, arranging the pillow behind my back. I clicked open my pen, and this time, the words and emotions I'd been trying to suppress flowed from me explosively.

First, I wrote about Preston's mom and how he must feel about her illness. Then the following poems were a bit more general. They were about grief over losing a loved one. Before I knew it, the floodgates had opened, and I was finally able to write about Isaac and the pain he'd caused, how it burned inside me like fire. I wrote about feeling alone and unwanted, lost and broken. After some time, it began raining outside, and I wrote a poem, likening the rain to my tears. Time passed, and my hand began cramping up from writing so much.

I dropped my pen onto the sleeping bag and surveyed my work. I'd written eleven poems. I felt lighter than I had in weeks. All the anger, frustration, and anguish I'd felt had been taken from me and had come alive on the paper instead.

Feeling rejuvenated, I returned to the house.

The next day was New Year's Eve. I had three more days until school started again, and I'd be expected to sing during rehearsals. I hadn't practiced my music in weeks. I couldn't bear to. I pulled out the music to "On My Own" and began playing it at the piano. I stumbled over the notes, rusty because I hadn't played for a long time, other than the occasional Sunday when they needed me to play at church. I hadn't had the heart to be around music more than necessary. I hadn't wanted to do much of anything other than sit in the tree house and "ponder life."

After pounding out the song a couple of times, I started getting the hang of it enough to sing along without constantly pausing for my fingers to find the next notes.

As I sang it over and over, some of the words struck me. It was about living in my own fantasy world and pining over a guy who would never love me back. It was pretty relevant, right? All this time, I'd been idolizing Éponine. I'd loved how sneaky and brave she was, how determined she was to get Marius. I'd taken everything she was and had assumed I was exactly like her.

When Éponine sings "On My Own," she's just been cast off from her father and feels that she's friendless and no place to go. When I discovered the truth about Isaac, I felt the same way, so alone.

Suddenly, a revelation hit me. I wasn't alone. God had been there by my side the entire time, and He hadn't left me friendless. I had a family who loved and supported me. I would never forget how Olivia went out of her way to cheer me up the day my heart shattered, or how Michael put his arm around me and took me home. Hudson and Shanice had banded together to fight for me. Hannah was on my side against her own family members. Finally, I thought about Preston, how he climbed the rope, held me, stroked my hair when I cried, and brought hot chocolate when I was cold.

Most of all, God had given me myself. I didn't need a guy to give me self-worth. I played and sang with power and determination, and as I did, a tiny portion of my heart stitched itself back up.

"You're really good, you know," Preston said from the doorway.

"Preston!" Without thinking, I jumped up from the piano bench and threw my arms around him. I felt his shoulders stiffen under me, and I stepped back, suddenly bashful. "I'm sorry about your Mom," I said softly.

He shoved his hands in his pockets and stared away morosely. He looked like a train-wreck survivor.

"Hey, Destiny," Megan said. She stood in the foyer next to Brinlee.

"Y'all decided to still come over to celebrate?"

"Yeah, Mom wants to live life as normally as she can."

"Megan, I'm so sorry."

"I'm still pretty much in shock, you know?" Megan said.

"I can't even imagine."

Sister Nelson walked into the room, a cheery smile on her face. "Hey, everyone! We brought seven-layer dip!"

"You brought us food? We should be the ones taking it to you!" I said.

"I'm not feeling that bad, yet." She grinned sardonically. "Just wait until my treatments start on Monday. Then you can bring me all the food you want."

"Mom was on the phone with someone from church this morning, signing up to bring you a few meals. Don't worry. You'll be taken care of."

"Brinlee's already been online picking out wigs for me. We found a cute red one. What do you think, Preston? Would I look good as a redhead?"

"I think you'd look awesome, Mom." He'd said it with a smile, but there was sadness in his eyes.

We gorged on party food, played Apples to Apples, and just before midnight, we turned on the TV to watch the ball drop. As the clock struck midnight, the married couples kissed, and I sat awkwardly on the couch trying not to think too hard about Isaac and whether we'd be kissing at that very moment if we hadn't broken up. Instead, I was sitting all alone, and it stunk. Royally.

As I sat there bemoaning my own little problems, I looked and saw the pain in Brother Nelson's eyes. This might be his last opportunity to kiss his wife on New Year's. After that realization, I just felt like a whiny brat. I needed to snap out of it.

After toasting with Martinelli's Sparkling Cider, we went out to the driveway to light up the fireworks. Preston was sitting on the sidewalk with his knees brought up and his arms crossed loosely over them, his expression sullen in the glow of the outdoor lighting on our house. Not even little exploding rockets could cheer him up tonight.

Throughout the night, Preston had sat apart from the group and had only spoken when someone had asked him a question directly. I'd missed him teasing me with that lopsided smile of his. I wanted to do something to cheer him up, but I couldn't figure out what. I remembered watching the fireworks when we were little kids. He was always right on his dad's heels, trying to be in the middle of the action. But for the last couple of years, the two fathers had taken a bit of a step back, letting Michael and Preston take over the majority of the production. Tonight was different, though.

How much was he suffering? I ached inside as I thought about it. He was there for me when I was broken. It was time to return the favor.

I wrapped my favorite silver velour blanket around my shoulders and lowered myself onto the sloping sidewalk next to him.

"Hey," I said, nudging his elbow with my blanketed one. He lifted his head from between his knees, gazed at me, and grunted in acknowledgement.

"Not feeling up to fireworks tonight?" I asked.

"Not really. I know I should be acting happy in front of my mom, I see Megan doing it, but, I dunno, I just…can't." He looked up to where Orion stood sentinel in the clear night sky.

"It's okay to feel sad about your mom."

"Sitting here, wallowing in my sadness, feels selfish. It's making me feel guilty."

"You don't have anything to feel guilty about. Everyone deals with it differently."

He stared ahead vacantly.

"I don't know much about all of this, but to me, you seem like you're still in shock."

"Well, that's an understatement."

I racked my memory trying to think of some way to distract him, to cheer him up. Then it came to me. "I took your advice," I said.

He glanced at me with mild curiosity.

"You have no idea how right you were about the poetry thing."

He raised his head, his eyes brightening. "You wrote some poetry?"

"Yep, pretty much all day yesterday. If you want, you can come over tomorrow and I can show them to you. We can even have a Mario Kart tournament."

"I'd like that a lot." A hint of a smile appeared on his lips, and butterflies fluttered in my chest as I remembered our kiss in the snow. I ducked my head, a blush creeping onto my cheeks.

We sat watching the fireworks for a few more minutes, neither of us saying much, but something had changed within him. Then, his smile broadened and he stood up, calling out to Michael, "Hey, do you guys still have some more that I can shoot off?"

"Yeah, c'mere. We still have an entire pack of bottle rockets and about three of the Roman candles left." As he walked down the hill to join the others, a weight lifted from my shoulders.

"How've you been, Destiny?" Dad asked the next morning as I stirred a gigantic bowl of pancake batter.

"It's been pretty rough the past couple of months, but you know what? It's a new year, and I'm determined to make it a better one." I passed the bowl over to Dad, and he began pouring circles of batter onto the electric griddle.

As Dad flipped the pancakes, one by one, he leaned casually against the countertop, asking me about my friends at church and what subjects I liked in school. After a few minutes, it became obvious that he was tiptoeing around the topic of Isaac. He still hadn't spoken to me about him since our breakup.

Olivia walked into the kitchen and snatched a steaming pancake from the top of the growing stack. She tore off a piece and shoved it into her mouth.

"What do you have planned for the rest of the day?" Dad asked.

"Not too much. I know Preston's coming over a little bit later."

"I heard about that," Dad said. "It sounds like he's been coming over more to see you than Michael here lately."

I blushed. You think?

"I think Preston has a thing for you, Destiny," Olivia said.

"Nah, we're just friends," I said, throwing a nervous glance in Dad's direction.

"Isn't that what you said about Isaac?" Olivia pointed out.

I winced, but for some reason, it didn't hurt quite as badly to hear him mentioned. The iceberg was still there, but it had shrunken considerably.

"I would rather she stay my little girl forever," Dad said. "I don't like all this talk about you pairing off with boys."

I glared at Olivia. I didn't appreciate her bringing up my boy drama. Ignoring my angry eyes, she said, "But Dad, if Destiny had to be paired up with someone, wouldn't Preston be a good choice?"

"Olivia, why don't you set the table? We're about ready to eat." Dad said, indicating that the conversation was over.

She didn't get the memo, apparently, because she went on to say, "We should have a surprise party for Michael's birthday. We can invite all his attractive friends."

"Oh yeah. He's almost eighteen now." With everything going on, I'd totally forgotten his birthday was coming up.

"You never know, you might end up with a bunch of dates out of the deal."

Like something as simple as a birthday party would score me a load of dates. Probably not going to happen. "I'm not so sure about the party idea." What was the point anyway? "I'll probably be too busy with *Les Mis* rehearsals."

Dad's face twisted as though the mere mention of *Les Mis* caused him pain. "I think you should plan the party," he said. *Les Mis* rehearsals involved Isaac, and if I was passing up an opportunity to date Mormon boys because of an obsession with my Baptist ex-boyfriend, Dad didn't see that as healthy.

Guilt seeped into me. I'd let Dad down enough. "Okay," I said. "I'll talk to Mom about it."

"Hey, Preston!" I said a couple of hours later when I opened the door. "Ready for some Mario Kart?"

"Definitely," he said. It was amazing to see his smile back again.

After we'd played several rounds, he flopped onto the couch and said, "You kicked my rear, woman." I wasn't very good at most video games, but I did have a knack for Mario Kart. "This may sound funny, but I like this old-school version of Mario Kart the best," he said, motioning a hand toward the GameCube console.

"Remember when we used to play it at your house? That was forever ago. I think I was about ten. We found your family's stash of ice cream sandwiches and sundae cones and went through the entire twenty-five pack in one Saturday."

"I remember. It was the best day ever," he said.

"I could never eat that much now without getting sick."

"Wasn't that the same day I found the snake in the woods behind my house and hid it in my room?"

"Oh yeah! How could I have forgotten? We were all so freaked out when you told us about it the next morning."

"I remember naming it Yoshi."

"You named it? That's so cute and gross all at the same time."

"I put it in my old, empty fish tank, and I tried convincing my mom to let me keep it."

"And as I remember, that didn't go over so well."

"Yeah. Not so much." He smiled lopsidedly. I looked up and met his eye, and as we basked in the funny memories, an unexpected electric current ran down my spine. What exactly was this between us? We'd shared a couple of knock-your-socks-off-amazing kisses, but now it was like we were still just friends, pretending it had never happened.

He tore his eyes away from mine, and an uncomfortable space grew between us. He cleared his throat. "Do you want to show me your poetry now?"

"Yeah," I said, recovering. I looked outside at the unseasonably warm day. "It's nice out for once. Want to go hang out and read it by the creek?"

We took the same trail that led to the paintball field, but as we neared the bridge that led over the creek, we turned onto a small path into the woods. Pretty soon, the creek appeared, babbling with its freezing water. All around it, tulip poplars grew with gigantic exposed roots, big enough for me to wrap my arms around. The roots looped through the sides of the stream bank, like the scaly arms of a sea monster imprisoned by the dirt.

My favorite tree was particularly strange with several knots the size of pumpkins arranged in a triangular pattern like a face watching me. Beneath the face, two roots shot out from the tree like tentacles that formed a place to sit. I sat on the roots, dangling my feet down above the water. Preston sat on a boulder with his knees about six inches from my shoulder. I angled myself so my back was against the trunk of the tree, and I faced Preston.

I flipped through the book and read my first poem to him. It was the one about the sacrifices mothers make. Although it was painful for him, Preston gave some surprising insights, leaving me with a lot to ponder and several ideas for future poems.

"You're good at this," I said. "You should write some, too."

Preston shifted on the rock, positioning himself into a sunbeam that peeked through the bare branches overhead. The light hit his hair, and it shone like gold. "I have an entire notebook full, actually."

"Oh, you should have brought it!" I exclaimed. "I bet your stuff is fantastic."

A muscle twitched in his jaw. Was he blushing? "Maybe I will one day," he said in a soft, hopeful voice.

Something about the way he said it made him seem so vulnerable. It made me think of a day months ago when Hannah had found a journal on the shelf in his closet. Realization hit as I thought about the longing I'd heard in his words as he spoke of a girl.

A blush crept onto my cheeks, and I found that I could barely meet his gaze. All words fled from me. For a time, I allowed my ears to fill with the sound of the water moving playfully over the stones in the creek. The smell of the moist, loamy earth filled my nostrils. A centipede scuttled out from under a brittle leaf about three feet from me. I watched as it crept up and over a fallen seedpod.

I felt Preston's gaze on me. I lifted my eyes to his hesitantly. In the sunshine, the green in his eyes was a brighter shade. Somehow, he just looked like he belonged, like he was a part of the woods.

He was beautiful and strong, sitting there gazing at the water as it flowed downstream. This was the boy who had helped heal my hurt, had sat with me the day my heart had broken, had held me in his solid arms. He was loyal down to the marrow in his bones, and I knew, like I should have always known, he would never break my heart if I gave it to him.

He must have felt my scrutiny because he turned and regarded me, the same longing reflected in his eyes. My pulse quickened. He wanted me. Not just as a kissing partner, but as something more. I had suspected it before, but now, I was almost sure of it.

"Is that it, or are there any more poems?" he asked.

"Actually, there's one more." I flipped the page of the notebook and paused. The next page was all about Isaac. I stared at it without reading the words. I didn't need to. Suddenly, I wasn't sure I wanted to talk about him anymore. The words had been transferred from me to the page. Why not tear it out and float it downstream?

"Why the hesitation?" Preston asked softly.

"I dunno..." I stammered. "It's about Isaac. I'm sure you're tired of hearing about him."

A faint smile played upon his lips. "Nah, let's hear it."

I smoothed the page and read the first three lines before I faltered.

"What's wrong?" he asked, his voice low.

I squeezed my eyes shut to ward off the tears. It wasn't working. "I just...can't. It hurts too much."

Preston lowered himself from the rock to the spot on the tree root beside me, lighting my skin on fire and heightening my senses.

"It'll get better. It's already better for you. Am I right?" He was so close.

I nodded. "I'm scared to see him again. I've gotten much stronger, but when I see him, I feel so weak."

"I wish there were some way I could help you," he said.

I smiled as I remembered the last time he'd helped me forget Isaac. It had definitely worked at the time, but after a while, the memories kept coming back.

It was time for me to help myself.

I ripped the sheet off, balled it up, and threw it into the creek. As I watched it bobbing in the water, traveling further away, my heart thawed even more.

It was gone.

"Feel better?"

"I do, actually," I said with a smile. "Well, that's all the poetry I have. Does this mean you're going to let me read your poetry now?"

"I don't know..."

I twisted to look at him. He was sitting so close his arm brushed mine. My breath quickened. He smelled woodsy and clean. "Is there some way I can convince you otherwise?" I asked.

His eyes widened, and his breath caught. "What do you mean?"

I hesitated. I was so afraid of getting hurt again. He wanted this with me, I could see it in his eyes, but something was holding him back. Maybe he wasn't ready to get into a relationship. Or maybe he felt vulnerable because of his mom. We were the same. We were two broken souls, floating along, desperately looking for someone to cling to.

He needed me. If he felt the way I imagined he did, I could help him more than anyone. I remembered him touching me, running his hands down my arms. "What would I do without you?" I whispered. "I'll never forget how you were there for me that day in the tree house. I've thought about it a lot since then."

"Me, too," he said.

"I want you to kiss me."

Our eyes locked, and my heart sped. He leaned his face close to mine hesitantly. I could feel his breath on my face as his forehead touched mine. I closed my eyes and exhaled. It felt so amazing and terrifying all at once to be this close to him again.

He wrapped a hand around the back of my neck, barely touching my skin and traced a thumb down my cheek. I opened my eyes and saw his green eyes regarding me searchingly. "I'm so afraid of hurting you. You've been through so much already."

"You would never hurt me." I trusted him completely. He was the kind of guy who would devote his life to the woman he loved. I took his other hand and held it in my own. It was strong and callused. I traced my thumb around one of his calluses. It was like a trophy commemorating all the hard work he'd done for his family. I gazed into his eyes. I thought about how they crinkled at the corners when he laughed. Now they were serious and tender.

"Are you sure this is what you want?" Behind the fear in his eyes lived a glimmering hope.

"I'm sure."

He leaned forward, and I clutched the edge of his leather jacket, pulling him closer to me. He brought his lips to mine, kissing me slowly and tenderly. Just as I was starting to really get into it, he pulled away.

"What's wrong?" I whispered.

"I'm not so sure this is the right time."

I studied his face and understood. "You're worried that I'm still not over him."

"I think we're both too emotionally messed up to start a relationship right now."

But what if starting a relationship was exactly what was best for us? We needed each other. But before I could say that, a voice rang out far above us in the treetops. "Bang, bang! Y'all are so totally dead!"

I lifted my eyes to the high branches of a nearby sweet gum tree and spotted Elijah standing on a sturdy limb, his right arm clinging to the branch above him and his other hand outstretched, holding a gun-shaped stick. His dark, wavy locks were tousled, and he had a wicked grin on his face.

I scrambled up and began gathering armfuls of pinecones, fallen from a nearby loblolly pine. I chucked them in his direction, missing him by about two miles.

"Aughhh!" Elijah screamed, as I continued pelting. I sharpened my aim and one hit the trunk a few feet from his mud boots. He chortled with delight. "You almost got me that time."

"You deserved it, you little spy."

"Spy?" he called down. "What were you and Preston doing down here all alone, anyway?"

"We were waiting here, hoping you'd come attack us, of course," I said, trying to keep my voice sounding lighthearted.

"Shouldn't you be getting back, Preston?" Elijah asked. "I heard you promised your mom you'd still spend part of the day with her."

I hadn't thought about it, but he had given up a large portion of what could quite possibly be the last New Year's he may ever have with his mom. Just to spend time with me.

Preston tore his eyes from me and grunted in irritation as he pushed himself up from the oversized tree root.

We swished through layers of sycamore and tulip poplar leaves as we made our way back to the main trail.

"I was talking to Olivia today, and she had this cool idea. I was wondering if you'd be willing to help out," I said.

"Probably. What'd you have in mind?" he said.

I told him about the surprise party, and he agreed to come over early to help decorate and to invite people from church.

"I'll work on his school friends, then."

His face darkened for a moment, and I knew he was thinking about Isaac again. "Don't worry. Isaac's one person who won't be on the list."

"Am I that easy to read?" he asked.

"Only when Isaac's involved. Believe me, half the time I have no clue what you're really thinking."

He chuckled softly. "I had no idea you wanted to figure me out so badly."

"You're kind of a mysterious guy."

"Me? I've always thought of myself as pretty straightforward."

"You're honest, but that doesn't make you easy to read. There are still all these thoughts swarming through your head that I don't know about."

He smiled, and his eyes grew distant for a moment.

"See?" I said.

"What?" he asked.

"Exactly."

Preston smiled and stared at the driveway as we approached his truck. He looked over at me after he'd opened the driver's side door.

"Thanks for inviting me over today." He stared off into the tops of the trees. "For a little while I was able to forget. I needed that."

As he climbed into the truck, I realized I could say the same thing.

Chapter 28

Back to School

Isaac

The morning Christmas break was officially over, I gripped my coffee and headed into the building. Across the parking lot, Destiny climbed out of Michael's car. She'd used gel to enhance her natural curls, a hairstyle I'd never seen her wear before. It looked so different, leaving me wondering what it would be like to pull a curl down and watch it spring back up. Better yet, what would it be like to tangle my fingers in those curls? I'd never made out with a curly-haired girl before.

But I'd lost that chance with Destiny. She didn't even glance in my direction as she walked into the building with Michael, talking and laughing easily with him.

Even when I came up right behind them and said hi to Michael as they were opening the doors to the building, she didn't acknowledge me.

Michael waved stiffly and turned away from me.

"Destiny!" Hannah called to her in the hallway.

"Hey," she said.

"I heard about Megan and Preston's mom. How're they dealing with it?"

"They're coping, I guess. Preston and I read poetry by the creek and…" she looked around nervously, but still didn't seem to notice me. The hallway was pretty crowded, so it made sense.

"Are you dating him now?"

I walked past. I really didn't want to hear the answer, but this other part of me had to know.

"We're still trying to figure it out." I felt her eyes on me as I walked to the water fountain and stooped to take a drink.

I turned around to see Hannah staring at me with raised eyebrows. "I can see that."

At lunch, I ended up sitting with Evelyn again. This time, she picked the table directly next to Destiny and Hannah's table, facing them. I cringed but sat down anyway. Hannah was picking at her sub sandwich, eventually shoving it away with a groan of disgust.

"What? You don't like the delicious cafeteria food they have here?" Hudson teased.

"I'm not feeling it today."

"Did y'all hear the news?" Destiny asked. "Michael's turning eighteen, and we're throwing him a surprise birthday party."

"Am I invited?" Hannah asked.

"You're all invited," Destiny said.

"Epic party at Destiny's place? I'm in." Hudson said.

"I'll be there," Shanice said.

"I haven't even told y'all when it is yet." As she filled them in on the details, her eyes fell on me and widened slightly as though she'd just noticed my presence. Her eyes slid over to Evelyn, and they narrowed.

Somehow, I got the impression I wouldn't be invited.

Chapter 29

History

Destiny

I shoved the last bite of my chocolate Pop-Tart into my mouth. Hannah was totally obsessed with them, and since I'd hung out with her so much last fall, it had rubbed off on me, too. It had taken a while, but I'd finally convinced Mom to start buying them for our after-school snack. I went back to my room, scooted my chair up to my desk, and flipped open my American History book to catch up on my reading assignment. We were studying the migration of the pioneers into the West, a subject that I was quite familiar with. As I scanned the reading material, my eyes snapped to the word "Mormons."

There was an entire box featuring the Mormons and their struggles to find a safe place to settle. I was surprised to see that Joseph Smith's martyrdom was mentioned. It also described Brigham Young's role in leading the exodus that led the early Latter-day Saints to their final destination in Utah. My heart swelled with pride for those who had gone before and had sacrificed so much just so that they could live their religion in peace. My mind drifted to Preston, and I remembered several stories he had shared over the years about some of his pioneer ancestors. He came from some amazingly strong people.

I collapsed into the desk next to Hannah the next day. Mr. Campbell was the coolest history teacher I'd ever had. He always encouraged the students to be open minded and to study our findings from multiple angles to form our own opinions about what we were learning.

Mr. Campbell captured my attention as he began explaining the migration of the early settlers into the American West. I'd felt so proud to read about the pioneers last night when I was alone in my room, but now a heavy apprehension fluttered in my chest.

Mr. Campbell seemed like he might just gloss over the Mormon section completely, but then, five minutes before class ended, he said, "In 1830 the Mormon Church was founded by a man named Joseph Smith. He and his followers received harsh treatment by those around them. After the assassination of Joseph Smith in 1844, it became clear to the Church that they could no longer stay in their home of Nauvoo, Illinois. In the year 1846, they were led by their new leader, Brigham Young, on a massive exodus to what is now the state of Utah."

The entire time he spoke I kept my eyes forward. I felt the eyes of some of my peers watching me, but I didn't meet their gaze. Just as he was finishing up, Mr. Campbell raised his eyes past me and called out, "Yes, Jessie?"

"Don't Mormons believe that Joseph Smith and Brigham Young were actually prophets?" she asked.

My face grew hot. Jessie knew very well that I believed in modern-day revelation and a living prophet. Back when we used to be best friends, we'd had plenty of discussions about my faith. She even knew that we had a church-wide conference twice a year to listen to our prophet and other church leaders give messages to the world. The only reason she would have to bring it up now would be to make me feel like even more of a freak and an outcast than I already did.

Mr. Campbell nodded. "That's right."

"Do you think it's possible that there might still be prophets out there today?"

"Absolutely not," Mr. Campbell said, getting all fired up.

Why couldn't the ground open up and swallow me whole? I stared at my backpack near my feet. I could understand Jessie bringing this up in Bible class, but did she have to start up a religious discussion in history, too? History and all my other secular classes were supposed to be a break from all the religion being crammed down my throat. But no. Every class was about religion at Bethel. They all started with a prayer and Mrs. Smith even read from a devotional book at the start of every geometry class. It wasn't like I had a problem with religion—I loved the gospel—but when it was someone else's spin on the Bible and it was inserted into almost every discussion in almost every class, it tended to get a little exhausting.

"The Bible explains that very clearly. God gives a very serious warning to anyone who tries to add or take away from the Bible. You can find many examples with supporting evidence in both the Old and the New Testament."

He expounded forcefully on the subject, but I tuned him out. I expected more from Mr. Campbell. He'd always seemed so open minded, but everything he was saying was the same stuff the other teachers had pounded into my head a million times before. I couldn't be sure, since I was so young when we joined the Church, but Michael seemed to think that since we'd converted, Bethel had gone on a special campaign to disprove every doctrine my family believed in. They must have tried so hard to convert us back, but it never worked. Every time they tore down my religion or preached doctrines we disagreed with, we clung to our faith even tighter. That had to be why Dr. Robinson was so determined to get rid of us.

When the bell rang, Mr. Campbell called out, "Don't forget to get together with your partner and pick a topic for the presentation due next week."

Hannah looked over at me. "Want to get together after school to knock this out?"

"Okay," I said tightly. "Want to come to my place? Or will your parents get mad?"

She cocked her head to the side and asked, "Are you okay? You seem a little tense."

I stood and scooped up my books. "I just—I don't know—I felt like everyone was staring at me during the section on Mormons."

"Jessie's such a brat. I know she totally did that on purpose."

"There's no doubt about that."

"Don't worry about her. She's just still bitter that you got to date Isaac and she didn't." She cringed at the sharp look I gave her. "Sorry, I shouldn't have brought that up. Anything good happen with Preston this morning in seminary?"

Other than him looking super attractive and answering all the tough questions correctly? Not that that was anything out of the ordinary for him. If she was trying to calm me down by changing the subject, then she was on the right track. Thinking about him melted the hurt away.

"You mean Mr. Mormon Pioneer Stock?"

"Huh?"

"Preston descended from the pioneers we were talking about today. It just made me think of him, that's all." I could definitely see in him the values of hard work and honesty that had been passed down through the generations in his family. I felt an immense respect for him because of it.

"Hmm. You sound like you really like him."

I grinned. "What makes you say that?"

"You got all starry-eyed when you talked about him."

I blushed furiously. "I did?"

"Mm-hmm."

"It would be so simple to be with him. He can date me with my parents' permission. There would be no need for lying or sneaking around."

"Yeah, but that's half the fun." Hannah said with a naughty smile.

She was right. Sneaking around with Isaac really had been fun, but I wasn't going to admit it to her.

We turned the corner, and I almost slammed into Isaac. His eyes widened in surprise, but changed quickly to a mask that reminded me of his dad.

"Watch where you're going, Isaac," Hannah teased good-naturedly. My heart slammed against my chest. *Bam, bam, bam.*

He flashed her a smile, but stepped around me like I was a tree trunk in his way, not even bothering to look in my direction again. Why should I care? He was the one who'd tried to hurt my family. Hurting me was one thing, but when you go after my family as well? You'd better watch out. I was still riled up from that history lesson.

At lunch, Hannah and Evan were bickering worse than Elijah and Brianna. I wasn't even sure what they were mad about, but Hannah was fuming. Finally, Evan just got up, threw his trash away, and walked out the double doors.

"He makes me crazy," she said. "It's like he's been disagreeing with everything I've said this week."

"Maybe it's time to find a new guy," I suggested.

"You shouldn't put up with that," Shanice agreed.

After school, Hannah came over in her new red Toyota Corolla. She'd turned sixteen right before Christmas, and for her birthday she got a car straight from the factory.

I didn't know whether or not her parents knew or cared that she was coming to the Mormons' house. She didn't say, and I wasn't going to ask.

We kicked Olivia out of the room and settled onto the plush white carpet next to my bed. "I was thinking we could do our project on the pioneers crossing the plains." I scooted a stack of books I'd borrowed from Preston earlier that day. His dad was a huge family history buff and collected books on his ancestors trials as pioneers.

Hannah made a face. "Oh really?" she challenged. "I had my heart set on doing it on the history of plantation houses in Tennessee. I've always been fascinated by them. I've practically worshipped Scarlett O'Hara since I was five."

"Oh," I said. "But I've spent half the afternoon studying all these books." I pulled out three pages of notes I'd painstakingly written out.

"Why'd you even want me to be your partner if you were planning on taking over the entire project before I even showed up?" she snapped.

I sat back, blinking. "I didn't think you'd care." I'd never seen Hannah so angry before. It was like she'd switched bodies with Jessie Larsen. My brow furrowed in irritation, but then I took a deep breath. She'd been fighting with Evan. Maybe he'd been really hard on her. "Okay," I said. I pushed the books to the side. "What ideas do you have so far?"

She stared at me blankly. "Well, I haven't actually given it too much thought yet."

I wasn't sure I could take anymore of her crazy mood swings. My *Les Mis* rehearsal was looming ahead of me, and I felt completely unprepared. I could have been practicing my solo instead of doing all that pioneer research. It seemed like such a waste, and it was all because Hannah was being moody. I didn't have the time, energy, or patience for it.

Hannah pulled out her laptop and began typing. I eyed it enviously. My connection to the outside world consisted of a cell phone that didn't connect to the Internet and one desktop computer at the other end of the house, closely monitored by my mom who sent me to do chores whenever she noticed me online. She considered it a big waste of time. She didn't understand that half of the average teenage kid's life was online now. Either that or she didn't want me to fall into that category.

Hannah pulled up several articles from historical blogs and put together a PowerPoint presentation on the decline of plantations in

Tennessee after the Civil War. It was fascinating stuff, but since I was still irritated that she'd completely disregarded my research, I sat back and let her do most of the work.

"Enough of this. I'm dying for some Taco Bell. You wanna come with?"

Girls' night with Hannah in her new car? Yes, please! Even if she was in a bad mood. "I could use some Taco Bell right about now."

Hannah packed her laptop, and as we were heading out the front door, Mom called to me, "Where are you going?"

Whoops, I'd forgotten to ask permission to leave the house. "Oh, is it okay if Hannah and I make a quick Taco Bell run?"

"I suppose so. Just don't stay out too late. It's a school night, and you have seminary in the morning. You know I like you to be in bed by nine-thirty."

"Don't worry, Mrs. Clark. I'll have her home safe and sound by nine," Hannah said in a deep voice like she was pretending to be my date.

"Cut it out, you dork."

We considered going through the drive-thru, but decided to eat inside in the end. "You know, they add all this fancy stuff to the menu, but when it comes right down to it, I always get the same old bean burritos. And then I'm never disappointed."

"You're making me want one, too."

She giggled. We took our orders of bean burritos and grabbed a table. I crinkled the paper away from the burrito and sunk my teeth into the warm beans and gooey cheese. Hannah peeled back the wrapper on hers and took a bite as well.

"When I was twelve, I saw *Gone with the Wind.* I loved it so much that I got the book and read the entire thing."

"You read *Gone with the Wind* when you were only twelve? Isn't that book like a thousand pages long?"

"Nine hundred and sixty." She said it automatically, like she'd bragged about it many times before.

I'd seen Mom's copy, and it was thicker than a brick.

"Did you know that before the war the O'Haras' plantation was successful because Scarlett's mother was so involved with the management of it? I mean, talk about a successful businesswoman back in the day."

I'd eaten through my entire burrito and Hannah had yet to take a second bite. She bit into the burrito again, and her face turned slightly green. She put the burrito down. "Ugh. This just doesn't taste good." She stared at it for a minute and then screwed up her face. "I'm going to be sick." She leapt from the booth and darted into the restroom. Should I go in after her? No. She probably wanted privacy.

Five minutes later, the door squeaked, and Hannah came out. She slid into the booth across from me, her face pale, but there was something else there as well. Worry? Fear? Suspicion?

"Are you okay?" I asked.

She shook her head half a shake. "I think…" She looked around and leaned forward. "Before I tell you this, you have to swear you won't tell anyone."

"What?"

"Promise!" she hissed fervently.

"Okay, I promise."

"I'm late."

"What are you talking about?"

"I mean *I'm late*. You know? Aunt Flo? She hasn't come to visit this month."

"Ew, gross. Why are you telling me this in the middle of Taco Bell?"

"Because I'm freaking out here! Can't you tell?"

"Hannah, it's normal to be irregular sometimes. It happens." Maybe that was why she'd been so moody lately. Her hormones were probably all messed up from being irregular.

She let out the puff of air she'd been holding. "I hope you're right."

"I know some girls just get on birth control, and it helps them get things straightened out."

"I've never been late before though…" The haunted look crept back onto her face. "And I'm sick. I've felt like taking a nap all day. Bean burritos taste disgusting when normally they're my favorite. Something is wrong with me."

"It sounds like you have a stomach virus."

Hannah shook her head. "I'd like to believe you, but I'm getting this feeling that you're wrong."

I cocked an eyebrow at her. "What are you trying to say? Quit beating around the bush."

Her eyes were wild with fright. "I think I'm pregnant."

"You're what!?"

"Shh. I'm serious."

"How could that even be a possibility?"

She looked at me pointedly.

"What the heck, Hannah!" I stood up from the booth, trashed my wrapper, and bolted toward the parking lot with Hannah following closely.

We settled into her Corolla and an awkward silence grew between us. Finally I said, "So you and Evan…?"

Hannah rolled her eyes. "Obviously."

"You know there are ways to prevent pregnancy, right?"

"We weren't planning to take it that far," Hannah insisted. "At least, I wasn't." She stared at the steering wheel. "I don't know what to do." She sounded like a lost little girl. "Tell me what to do."

"Go take a test."

She nodded. "Okay, but you can't tell anyone."

"I won't. I already promised."

"They sell those at Walmart, right?" She reversed out of her parking spot.

"Yeah, my mom picked one up a couple of years ago when she had a false alarm."

"Maybe that's all this is." She sounded like she was trying to convince herself, but it wasn't working very well. I'd never seen her so scared.

She drove to the store, her shoulders hunched as though sitting in that position would somehow lessen the blow of her situation. She pulled into a parking spot and said, "I can't be pregnant. I'm only a sophomore. I still have to finish high school. What am I going to do with a baby? I don't babysit. I don't even know how to change a diaper. If my parents find out, they're going to freak. How am I going to hide this?"

"Calm down. You might be freaking out over nothing."

"I can't. I can't." She held her arms around herself and rocked back and forth. "I can't go in there. I don't want to know."

"Hannah! Just go pee on the stick and get it over with. Don't think about what you're doing."

"I can't do it." She reached into the backseat and brought out a Coach purse. She unzipped it and pulled out a twenty.

"What are you doing?"

She shoved the money into my hands. "Can you buy it for me?"

Seriously? Buying a pregnancy test in public would be horrifying! But her hands were trembling. Whatever embarrassment I might feel buying this test for her would be a zillion times worse if she did it herself—because for Hannah, the humiliation was real.

I creased the bill in half and pocketed it. "All right, I'll do it." I opened the door and crossed the darkened parking lot. I walked inside the sliding glass doors and passed the shopping carts, not bothering to grab one. On my way to the pharmacy, I passed a young mother with a cartload of tiny kids. Two of the kids were having a poking match. One of the toddlers jabbed his sister in the eye, and she let loose an ear-piercing scream.

It was a good thing Hannah hadn't come with me. The last thing she needed was to hear some kid crying. I checked two or three aisles finding only shampoo and hairbrushes. Then, finally, I located the pregnancy tests next to an array of other items I didn't even want to think about. If Hannah hadn't been so supportive about my heartbreak over Isaac, I'd say she seriously owed me. I stood in front of the tests, trying to figure which one to buy. I eventually settled on the generic brand. I reached for it apprehensively like it was covered in prickly thorns.

A woman with gray, curly hair turned around, saw me holding the test, and shook her head disapprovingly. "What is the world coming to? These trashy girls just keep getting younger and younger."

I bit back the snippy reply sitting on the tip of my tongue. Conjuring an extreme amount of self-control, I turned and walked toward the registers. The lines were always bad at this particular Walmart, but they seemed especially bad at the moment. I got into line behind the young mother I'd seen previously and picked up a copy of *In Style* to distract myself from the task at hand.

"Destiny?"

I didn't need to turn to see who was addressing me. I'd know his voice anywhere.

Chapter 30

Walmart

Isaac

"I don't know why you're bothering to hide that since I saw it from like twenty feet away," I said bitterly.

Destiny stared back at me with wide eyes.

"Who did this to you?"

"This has nothing to do with you, Isaac."

Seeing her beautiful eyes flash at me, hearing her say my name like it was a curse, it was ripping my heart to shreds. "Well, that's one thing I'm definitely sure of."

Shock registered in her eyes as she caught my meaning, and she flicked her eyes away from me, blushing deeply. We stayed like that for a moment. She stared at her feet morosely, and I stood like an idiot in the middle of the store, gaping at her. "I'm starting to wonder if I had something to do with this indirectly, that I drove you to this."

"Don't flatter yourself." She rolled her eyes bitterly.

"Who did this to you? Preston?" Had she thrown herself at him? Slept with him so she could forget me?

"What? No!" She blushed furiously and glanced at the lady in front of her. She looked so furious, I half-expected her to throw the pregnancy test across the store. Maybe she really was pregnant. She certainly had been acting a bit hormonal. Who was it then? Did she get raped? Maybe she had an entirely new guy from church.

"I know I've hurt you. I can't tell you how sorry I am for that, but if you're in trouble, you shouldn't have to go through this alone."

"Well, you'll be glad to know you don't have to bother yourself over me. It's not mine. I'm here for a friend."

"So, you're not pregnant?"

"No, I'm not."

My defensive mood evaporated immediately, replaced by relief that flooded me to the core.

Then who was? I narrowed my eyes as I studied her, and suddenly, it dawned on me. I knew what this was all about. Hannah had been acting even crazier than Destiny lately. "Is it Hannah's?"

She tore her eyes away from my scrutiny. "You don't know this person."

She was obviously lying. "Oh, man," I spoke softly with an undercurrent of knife-twisting. It really was Hannah's. "You're lying, aren't you? You're a terrible liar."

She stared at the box in her hands silently. It was all the confirmation I needed. What had Hannah gotten herself into this time?

The lady in front of Destiny took her receipt and pushed away her cart.

Destiny placed the box on the conveyer belt and kept her eyes away from me. "I wish you would just go away."

"Who, me?" The large African-American cashier asked in an insulted voice.

"No, him."

"Is he the one who did this to you?" She swiped the box over her bar code scanner.

I laughed easily. Destiny gave me a weird look.

"Oh yes," I said. "We just got married, and we're expecting our first already!" I put my arm around her.

Destiny's jaw dropped.

The cashier eyed me suspiciously. "You look awfully young to be married."

I shrugged and bit back a laugh. "I just couldn't stay away from her." Destiny turned bright red and hid her face in her hands.

"That'll be ten sixty-eight."

She stepped away from my arm and pulled out a twenty. I put my hand over hers. "No sweetheart, I'll pay for it. You save that money to get something pretty for the nursery." She lowered her hand and looked at me like I'd lost it. Then her face softened, and I got the impression she'd finally understood what I was trying to do.

I had no idea what Hannah's future held. What if she decided to keep the baby? Would her parents throw her out? I could picture Dad doing something like that. Was Aunt Bethany much better? I hoped so. I pictured her and Evan living together in some dump trying to raise a screaming baby, and I shuddered.

I yanked my wallet from the back pocket of my jeans and pulled out my credit card. I slid it through the slot in the electronic keypad and signed the screen.

"Have a nice day! Y'all take care," the cashier called out cheerfully.

Destiny grabbed the plastic bag, and I fell into step with her as she headed to the front door. "What were you doing back there?" she snapped.

"Protecting your honor."

She clenched her jaw like she was trying to keep it from dropping again. "Why are you being so nice to me?"

I stood still. "I never stopped being nice. That was all you." When she didn't reply, I continued. "I've tried to apologize so many times."

"This really isn't a good time for this conversation. I have someone waiting for me," she said coldly.

My brow creased with worry. I'd almost forgotten about Hannah. "You're right. I'm sorry."

For some reason, my apology seemed to exasperate and annoy her even more.

When we reached the doors, she said, "You can't follow me out here."

I continued on as though I hadn't heard her.

She grabbed my arm from behind just as I stepped through the automatic doors. As though my arm had burned her hand, she let go just as suddenly as she'd grabbed it. I spun around to face her. Her blue eyes smoldered with repressed emotion. Was she looking at me like that because she was worried about Hannah or was it because she'd just touched me?

"She's my cousin. She needs help." I strode forward purposefully.

"I swore to keep her secret!" she called out to me. "She's freaking out enough as it is."

"That's all the more reason to comfort her." I stood on my tiptoes and scanned the parking lot for Hannah's car.

"Come on. She's this way," she said in a deflated voice.

We walked in silence to Hannah's car, and when we arrived, Destiny knocked on the driver's side window. The engine was running, and *Les Misérables* blasted through her speakers. I found it particularly ironic that "I Dreamed a Dream" was playing since it was about a woman who'd had her life ruined by an unplanned pregnancy. Hannah looked up at Destiny and wiped her eyes with a napkin from a fast food place. She rolled down her window, and her eyes widened with fear when she saw me standing with Destiny.

"What's he doing here?"

"It's nice to see you, too, Hannah," I joked.

She didn't smile.

"Interesting choice of music," I said dryly.

"You told him?!" The glare she gave Destiny was lethal.

Great. Now, I'd gotten Destiny in trouble. Destiny was mad enough at me as it was.

"She didn't tell me anything," I assured her. "I ran into her at the store and figured it out." When she opened her mouth to protest, I said, "I won't tell anyone. You have my word. If there's anything I can do to help you, let me know."

"She might not need any help at all. She has to take the test first," Destiny pointed out.

"Come out of the car and go take it in the bathrooms here," I said.

"I can't."

"Why not?" I asked.

"I just…can't. I'm just so scared to know."

Evan Bellingham was going to pay. Hannah was such a vibrant part of my life, and seeing her debilitated terrified me.

"Sitting in here, listening to that depressing song, isn't going to help you." When Hannah didn't move, I reached inside her open window and popped open the lock on her car door. "Come on. You don't have to do this alone."

"He's right. I'll go in there with you if you want," Destiny offered. She reached down and tugged on Hannah's hand.

Hannah turned off the motor, gathered her purse, and climbed out of the car. Together, the three of us crossed the busy parking lot back into the store. We walked through the automatic doors and past the shopping carts. Hannah's teeth chattered next to me.

"Why are your teeth chattering?" Destiny asked.

"I'm just really freaked out right now. Sometimes they do that, okay?" she barked.

I threw Destiny a cautioning glance, and she smiled back tightly. She was actually going to smile at me now? Well, that was something, at least.

Chapter 31

Bathroom Test

Destiny

Isaac waited on a bench outside the restroom. Once we were inside the ladies' room, I breathed a little easier. If I had to hang around him one second longer…

I handed Hannah the Walmart bag with the test inside, and she motioned me to come inside the handicapped stall with her.

"I have no idea how to even use this thing," she said.

"Here, let me read the instructions." I unfolded the inserted paper and scanned the illustrations. "It says you're supposed to take it first thing in the morning, but I think it will still work now." I explained the basics of peeing on the stick, capping it, and laying it flat while the test developed. "All right, you ready?" I handed her the uncapped stick with the absorbent strip exposed.

She gave me a queasy look, but took it from me.

"Do you want me to leave?"

"No. Just turn around."

"Okay." I turned toward the corner and stared at the dirty grout of the bathroom floor. In an attempt to lighten the situation I said, "I think this was the strangest trip to Walmart I've ever taken." I relayed my experience with the old lady and then my exchange with Isaac. It must have helped, because by the time I told her about the cashier's reaction, Hannah was giggling.

"That's totally awesome!" I heard her snap the cap onto the test just before she flushed the toilet. "I told you Isaac still has it bad for you."

I turned around and looked at her soberly. "You think he really does?" A small flame of hope flickered in my heart, and the ice started melting again.

She pursed her lips like she wanted to say something, but didn't dare.

"What?"

"He doesn't feel that way about Mormons anymore."

The cold blew into my heart like a blizzard—swift and furious—and extinguished the flame. "How do you know? He could just be saying that to placate you. The bottom line is, I can't trust anything he says." The numbing cold spread in my chest again. What about the time he'd taken me to his land and told me he believed I was a Christian? Was it all an act? How many of his kisses were even real? I recalled the way his lips had moved over mine and shuddered. There was no doubt about it. Those kisses were real. That would mean that he was attracted to me, but kept his ulterior motives in the back of his mind the entire time. That explanation made sense. So, he just wanted me for my body? *Lovely*. Anger burned inside me again.

Hannah choked back a sob. "The line. It's there."

I snapped my head up, jerking myself out of my pity party and back to Hannah's desperate situation. "Both lines? There have to be two lines to get a positive."

"Yes!" she cried.

I stepped over to where the test was resting on the toilet paper dispenser and glimpsed the solid double lines.

I held back a gasp. So, it was true. Hannah looked at me in fright. "This can't be real. The test has to be wrong."

"I read on the paper that false positives are extremely rare. Even if there's a faint or broken line, it still counts as positive."

"What am I going to do?" she wailed. "I keep thinking I'm going to wake up and find out this is a sick, twisted dream."

"I'm so sorry."

"I hate Evan. I hate him and his stupid pressuring."

"What do you mean?"

"He'd been pushing me to take our relationship to the next level for months, but I didn't want to."

"Do you think he did this on purpose?"

"Not exactly. I think he wanted it so badly he couldn't think straight."

"How did y'all even have the opportunity?"

"Whenever his parents weren't home, he'd text me, and I'd sneak out the back door to go see him. My mom always thought I was watching TV in my room. I'd sneak up to his room, and we'd cuddle up and watch movies, eat, and usually end up making out. Some days we'd just jump right to the kissing. It was like he couldn't think about anything else."

"How did your mom never find out?"

"She was swamped with work. Then it was Christmas time, and she was out doing last minute shopping. You know how it can be."

We heard several pairs of feet shuffling as a young mother with a toddler came into the bathroom. The little girl was cranky and the mom was trying to soothe her, but it was late and obviously past the kid's bedtime.

Hannah wrapped the test in layers of toilet paper, shoved it into her purse, crammed the empty box into the tampon disposal, and unbolted the bathroom stall. She washed her hands methodically, and we listened as the mom talked sweetly to her little girl, despite the child's nonstop whining. Hannah looked at me with panicked eyes that said, "I'm not ready for this."

When we walked out, Isaac stood, his eyes so full of concern, one might think he was the father instead of Hannah's cousin. The tenderness displayed so openly on his face tugged at my heart, and I had to look away.

"So?" he asked finally.

"Positive." Hannah said the dreaded word softly.

"This is happening, isn't it?"

I nodded morosely.

We stood silently as people crisscrossed past us through the store.

Isaac cleared his throat and indicated that we head back to the car. "What does Evan know about this?"

"He knows it's a possibility, but I don't think he wants to admit how real it might be," Hannah said.

"Did he force you into this?" Isaac asked like he'd been holding the question inside himself for a long time and had finally decided to let it loose.

Hannah glanced away from him uncomfortably. I got the impression she didn't want to have this conversation with Isaac. "He didn't force me, but he was very persistent."

"I'm so mad at him right now I could…" He glanced in my direction. "Well…never mind."

"You make it sound like you're contemplating taking away his manhood," I joked.

"Something like that," he muttered.

"I don't know what to do," Hannah whispered. She sounded like a song stuck on repeat.

"Why don't you go home and get some rest," Isaac suggested. "You don't need to make any decisions yet."

"I have to drop Destiny off first."

"I don't mind taking her."

"Yeah, that's not happening," I said. There were way too many painful memories associated with his truck, and if I went in there I'd have an emotional breakdown.

I didn't miss the pain in his eyes at my rejection. Just because we'd touched and had a few conversations didn't mean I was going to rush back into his arms. I had something good going with Preston, and I didn't want to mess it up. There was another reason anyway. "My parents are just starting to trust me again. If I show up with you, everything I've done to build that trust will be thrown away." If Michael or Preston saw me…

"Did I really cause that much trouble for you?" he asked softly.

Was he that clueless? "Why are we talking about this?" I snapped. "Hannah, can you please take me home now?"

"Sure." She looked over her shoulder at Isaac. "And, to answer your question… Are you stupid?! You freaking ruined her life."

It was sweet of her to say it, considering her situation. She had way more cause to be angry at Evan than I had to be at Isaac. Isaac had only broken my heart. My heart was mending, and I would be whole again one day. Hannah? She would be stuck with a kid for the rest of her life. She would have a much longer, more painful road to travel before she found peace. Her youth was snatched away from her, and she would never get it back.

Chapter 32

Where Have You Been?

Isaac

I stood in the middle of the Walmart parking lot and stared after Hannah and Destiny as they climbed into the car and drove off. I couldn't get Hannah's words out of my head. Had I really ruined Destiny's life? It was so hard to know if she still had feelings for me. She always kept her emotions so guarded when I was around.

The following evening, I was working in Aunt Bethany's office when Hannah came in the front door. Aunt Bethany was in another part of the house doing laundry.

"Hey, Isaac." She came and sat down in her mom's swivel chair.

"Where've you been?"

"Over at Evan's."

Again? Hadn't she learned her lesson about that guy? "Have you told him yet?"

Her face paled. "No."

"When are you going to?"

"I have no idea. I need some time to figure stuff out, you know?"

"I guess that makes sense." I leaned back in my chair thoughtfully. "I was so scared when I saw Destiny standing in line with that test. You really do owe her for that."

"I know. She's been super supportive. I was afraid to tell her, because I thought she would get all judgy on me, but she totally didn't."

She leaned forward with an earnest question on her face. "Something's been bugging me, and Destiny wouldn't talk about it on the drive home."

"What?" I asked.

"How'd you figure out Destiny was buying the test for me?"

"Well, at first, I thought it was hers."

"Seriously? Come on, Isaac! The girl doesn't even wear sleeveless stuff, for Pete's sake. She's the last person out of everyone I know who'd get herself knocked up."

"She doesn't wear sleeveless stuff?" How had I never realized that? How much else was there about her that I didn't know?

"No. Where have you been? You were her boyfriend. Maybe you should have asked her a few more questions about what she believed. Oh wait. I forgot. You did. That's what you were trying to do all along."

"Hannah, you have no idea how much I wish I could erase some of that stuff from my past."

Her face softened. "I'm sorry. That was uncalled for. I've just been so snippy lately."

"I understand. You have a long road ahead of you."

"I'm trying not to think too much about it."

"Mormons don't wear sleeveless stuff?" I asked.

"That's what Destiny said."

"Huh," I said.

"So, when you saw Destiny and jumped to conclusions, whose baby did you think it was?"

"Well, since she's back together with Preston again..." my voice trailed off.

"Again?" Hannah's eyes brightened with amusement. "You still think… Oh my gosh. Y'all weren't very good at communication, were you? I can't believe she never told you!"

"Told me what?"

"Let me clear some things up for you. You're all sorts of confused."

I raised my eyebrows, leaned back in my chair, and crossed my arms. This ought to be interesting.

"Okay, first of all, she's not with him. Second of all, Preston's an even bigger goody-two-shoes than she is. I wouldn't be surprised if he's never kissed a girl. Third of all, I can't believe Destiny never told you the truth about the fake-boyfriend thing!"

"Fake-boyfriend thing?" What the heck was she talking about?

"Well, Destiny and I might have fed you a few teensy lies about Preston."

Lies? "What are you trying to say?"

"Destiny and Preston have never dated. And, last time I checked, they've never kissed either. Unless she's been keeping things from me… Come to think of it, she has been starry-eyed lately. We're going to have to have a little talk about that sometime soon."

Why was she rubbing it in my face? It must be a hormonal thing. "Getting back to the fake-boyfriend thing... Y'all guys made that up so Destiny wouldn't feel embarrassed about singing as Éponine?"

"Yeah. I bet she wouldn't have done it if she'd known how much trouble it would have caused her later."

I'd felt so threatened by him back then, and all along she'd just wanted me. "What does Preston think about all of this?"

"As far as I know, he's totally clueless."

Interesting.

"Sometimes I wonder if it would've given him the courage to go for her," Hannah said. "But honestly, it would probably just make him mad. She kind of used him to get to you."

"What do you mean?"

"Oh, well, part of that was me, actually. I kept trying to get you to be jealous of him."

I clenched my jaw. Why did that not surprise me?

Chapter 33

A Little Fall of Rain

Destiny

The Wednesday before the birthday party was the day Isaac and I were supposed to rehearse "A Little Fall of Rain." I'd been dreading it for weeks. Whenever we'd rehearsed it before, we'd been next to a piano, but this time we were going to have to appear onstage to act out the hands-on version.

Some of the choir members were hanging out in the pews of the choir loft, goofing around. I was on the stage, leaning against the choir loft and tapping my fingers on the ledge apprehensively as I waited for Mr. Byrd to arrive. Evan bounded up the maroon-carpeted steps and greeted Isaac, who was standing about fifteen feet away from me onstage. I watched as Evan slid into the pew beside Hannah and held his face close to hers as he murmured to her.

I fidgeted with the buttons on my navy cardigan and pulled a long, curly, brown hair from the sleeve of my sweater. I'd decided to allow the natural curl in my hair to take over today since it was cold and rainy, fitting weather for the song we'd be singing today.

Mr. Byrd walked down the aisle of the chapel, and a hush came over the room. Isaac glanced at me and smiled lightly, but I looked away, pretending I hadn't seen it.

After a quick prayer, Mr. Byrd said, "Okay, let's dive in with 'A Little Fall of Rain.' Marius, Éponine, thanks for being in place and ready."

I glanced in Isaac's direction. I was nowhere near ready.

The music started, and we stepped toward the center of the stage, carefully keeping a safe distance from each other. We hadn't practiced our song in months, and we'd gotten a little rusty. Especially me. I was holding back so much that it sounded a bit dull, even to my ears. When he reached the last note, Isaac sang it with aching tenderness.

Mr. Byrd pressed his lips together and studied his stack of papers pensively. Finally, he looked up and spoke slowly, like he was choosing each word carefully, "I'm sure you know this is meant to be a very intense scene. I need to see more action." He paused thoughtfully. "Let me go into a little bit more of the background of the story to emphasize what I'm trying to say here. Éponine is shot during the battle at the barricade and spends her last moments in Marius's arms. Destiny, let's have you enter from the right side of the stage," he said, indicating the spot.

"Once we're in costume, you'll be disguised as a boy," he explained. "When the intro begins, you'll rush past Isaac at the center of the stage. Isaac, you'll recognize her, grab her arm in surprise as she passes, and berate her for putting herself in harm's way. Then you'll ask her whether or not she's made contact with Cosette. Destiny, as you're explaining things to him, you collapse from the pain. Isaac, that's when you'll catch her and lower her to a sitting position on the ground," Mr. Byrd said, gesturing to show what he meant.

My face reddened at his mention of Isaac's arms around me, and I took a deep breath to calm my racing heart. It didn't work. I was starting to have second thoughts about doing this.

"That's when Marius discovers the blood she's been hiding on the inside of her coat. At this point, things rapidly become very tender between them. Éponine was his friend, and she was the person who brought him to his precious Cosette, so he's very upset about her impending death. Éponine, on the other hand, is savoring her last moments with the man of her dreams. This is the moment she's been waiting for. This is her one and only chance to have any kind of intimacy with Marius. It's the only chance she ever gets. Destiny, you need to show that here."

I swallowed and nodded bravely. I'd told him there wouldn't be a problem with me playing Éponine, and I intended to stand by that. I couldn't let him know how hard this was for me, or he'd be sure to pull me from the musical.

Mr. Byrd waved his hand, indicating that he wanted us to move into our places. I walked to the side of the stage, hands trembling. When the pianist played the first notes, I walked toward Isaac hesitantly and, as planned, collapsed into his arms.

I looked up into his brown eyes. I couldn't be this close to him. Real pain exploded in my chest. I wanted to pull away, but his strong hand wrapped around my head, his fingers entangled into my curly locks.

The melody came to an awkward stop, and Isaac cleared his throat, looking slightly amused. His face was only two inches from mine.

He gave a small chuckle. "You're supposed to be singing right now," he whispered.

"Hello? Éponine? You haven't died yet," Sydney said sarcastically from the soprano section.

"Pull yourself together, girl," snickered someone I couldn't see.

"All right, that's enough," Mr. Byrd scolded the girls giggling in the choir loft. "Let's take it from measure twenty-two."

Isaac repeated his last few lines, and this time, my brain decided to function properly, enabling me to sing my next few lines without forgetting anything. Isaac shifted me so that my back was leaning against his chest. As his face pressed against mine, the slight stubble on his chin brushed my forehead. I repressed a shudder. While he sang, I could feel the vibrations his chest made against my back and I impulsively wrapped my hands around his muscled arm. Heat came to my face as I realized how it must look to the other students.

I sat up quickly to put a few inches of distance between us, but he pulled me back close to him so that I was cradled in his arms with my face only inches from his. Suddenly, it was like we'd never been apart. There were no lies, no difference of religion. It was just Isaac and me, and for that precious, intense moment, that was all that mattered. I stared at his lips as he sang and craved to feel them on mine once again. I ceased to even hear what he was singing about anymore. I lay there, savoring the feeling, not wanting it to ever end.

As I sang my last notes, I began feeling lightheaded, whether from being so close to Isaac, or from breathing his expelled air, I wasn't sure. I turned my face away and inhaled deeply to clear my head.

Right on cue, Isaac repeated my last dying words, and I collapsed back into his arms pretending to be dead. After a pause, he finished the song with a single, melancholy note. He then crushed me to his chest, rocking me as he cried out: "Éponine!" in a tortured voice.

In that moment, reality crashed upon me, slamming my vulnerable heart. This wasn't about Isaac and me. He was only playing his role as

Marius. He was such a good actor that I actually believed he'd fallen for me.

The choir behind us burst into applause. "Well done! Well done!" Mr. Byrd said emphatically. He stood, looking very impressed. "As far as initial run-throughs go, your performance today was the most realistic rendition I've ever seen of that number."

I wasn't sure whether to be embarrassed or proud.

"That was…beyond words," I heard Hannah from behind me. Was she *crying*?

"I thought they broke up," someone hissed from the choir loft.

"Take a break, get a drink, and in two minutes we'll move on to the next scene," Mr. Byrd announced.

Isaac pulled his hands from my hair, his class ring catching on a snarl. "Oh sorry, did I hurt you?"

I looked at him sharply for a moment as though there might be a double meaning in his words. *Did I hurt you?* What kind of question was that?

Isaac stood, reaching down to offer me his hand. I took it, and it was warm and strong. My heart pounded wildly, but immediately my wall of protection went up.

As I walked to the hall outside the chapel, Michael studied me with concern. "I can tell this is hard on you. You know, if you don't want to be Éponine, you don't have to do it. I'm sure there are plenty of other girls who would love to take over."

I considered his words. "No, I want to be Éponine," I insisted. "I'm fine, really. Please don't worry about me."

"Okay, but if Isaac ever hurts you again, let me know, and I'll make sure it doesn't happen another time."

I arched an eyebrow. "What's that supposed to mean?"

"I'd try not to do anything violent, but I can't make any promises," Michael said firmly as he stepped through the doors and into the parking lot.

Chapter 34

Birthday Party

Destiny

Olivia, can you hand me that roll of tape?" I asked from the top of a kitchen chair. She handed me the masking tape. I ripped off a piece and taped the end of the neon green streamer to one of the corners above the kitchen table. "Okay, I'm ready for the balloons."

She passed me the cluster of hot pink and neon green balloons. Stretching awkwardly, I attempted to tape them into the corner.

"Hey!" Preston came into the room with a gigantic smile. He wore a well-fitting red plaid shirt and jeans. He looked amazing, better than I'd seen him look in weeks. Megan followed beside him wearing a bright blue, belted mini dress paired with leggings and black knee high boots. She set a present wrapped in glossy red paper on the table.

I smoothed the tape over the rubber stems of the balloons and leaned back to inspect my work. The balloons promptly fell on my face. "Oof," I said. "That didn't work so well."

Preston grabbed my hand and pulled me down from the chair. "Want me to give it a try?"

"Feel free. I was about to pop them and say forget it."

He climbed up on the chair, and I tore off a few long strips of tape for him. He took them from me, and our hands touched momentarily, causing a shiver to go down my spine.

He must have felt something, too, because he pulled his hand away with a hint of inhibition. With a determined look on his face, he crisscrossed the tape over the taped up knots of the balloons.

"I think I need more."

I tore off two more strips, and as he took them from me, the tape wrapped around one of my fingers binding our hands together.

"The tape is trying to send you a message," Olivia said.

Preston grinned as he peeled the tape off of our fingers with his other hand. I hadn't seen him so happy in such a long time. It was like I had the real Preston back again.

He stuck the tape to the balloons and ran his hand along the messy crisscrossing layers of tape. "It doesn't look that great now, but if you let go, the balloons hide the mess."

"That actually looks great," I said. "Thanks for the help."

"Anytime."

"Just in time, too." I glanced at my watch. "I think people should start coming any minute now."

The doorbell rang.

"Right on cue," Preston said.

I opened the front door, and found Hannah and Evan standing there together. "Hey!" Hannah said.

"You came! I wasn't sure your mom would let you," I said.

"She doesn't know," Evan said. "She thinks I'm taking Hannah out to dinner and a movie right now. And I will after this, but we still wanted to swing by."

"So, she has no clue we still hang out all the time?"

"She knows we're in the musical together, but she doesn't know about the times I've gone to your house. She doesn't ask, and I don't tell. When's Michael getting here?" Hannah asked as they came into the room.

"In about five minutes."

We walked across the room and settled ourselves on the couch we'd pushed up against the back wall to clear a spot for mingling, games, and dancing. There were more streamers and balloons strung above our heads and a "Happy Birthday" pennant banner hung over the fireplace.

There were kids clustered around the room in groups. The girls to the left were planning which guys to snag for the night.

"Hey, Hannah," Olivia said, taking a seat beside me on the couch.

Hannah gave her a small wave and then turned to me. "Who else did you invite?" Hannah asked from beside Evan on the couch.

"Pretty much everyone we know from church between the ages of fourteen and eighteen," Olivia said.

"I kind of went overboard inviting friends from church," Preston said.

"It's okay. You did great," I said.

"It won't just be our ward either," Olivia said. "We have people coming from all over the stake."

"Ward? Stake?" Evan asked. "Is that some kind of Mormon talk?"

"Yeah," Preston said. "Our church groups its members into congregations according to where they live. It's all very organized. A ward is a congregation of about five hundred people, and a stake is a bunch of wards across the city."

"I don't know exactly how big it is," I said. "But I know one of the buildings is about an hour away."

"Back when I lived in Utah our stake covered two neighborhoods because the Mormons were so densely populated." Preston lowered himself into a cross-legged position on the floor in front of the couch.

"Some of the kids here live an hour away?" Hannah asked.

"I don't see any of those people, but a few live at least forty-five minutes away," I explained.

More friends from the stake arrived at the same time Hudson, DeShawn, and Shanice did.

Preston stepped up onto the hearth of our giant stone fireplace and whistled loudly. "Hey! Everyone, listen up!"

The room grew quiet, and a few people from the kitchen came into the doorway. "I just got a text from Michael's dad. They're on their way home from dinner and should be here in about two minutes. We're going to bring him in through the basement door by the kitchen, and we're all going to crowd into this room and shut the door." Everyone, including Elijah and Brianna, who didn't want to miss out on the fun, moved into the room. There were probably fifty people in there.

Preston, Olivia, and I stepped into the kitchen. The plan was that we were supposed to look like we were hanging out with Mom while she put the finishing touches on Michael's birthday cake. As far as Michael knew, he was having a steak dinner with his dad and then cake with his family and his best friend. Preston checked the dining-room window, which overlooked the driveway.

"They're coming up the driveway," he said, moving back into the kitchen.

"Shh!" Olivia popped her head into the family room. "Everyone be quiet. They're here."

By the time Michael came up the stairs with Dad, the entire house was silent. "Hey, Michael," I said, doing my best to not crack a smile.

"How was your dinner?" Mom asked.

"It was great," Michael said.

Preston repressed the sneaky grin playing at the corners of his mouth. "You should take a look at what Destiny and I fixed up for you in the family room."

"Okay," Michael said as Preston opened the door to the family room.

All fifty people chorused, "Surprise!" and Michael just about jumped out of his skin.

"Whoa!" Michael said.

"Happy Birthday!" I said with a laugh as Michael went around greeting all his friends. He knew each of them by name like they were best buds.

Preston and I opened the doors to the formal dining room where we'd stashed veggie trays, bowls of chips and dip, and platters piled with brownies and cookies. Earlier that day, we'd spent hours over at his house preparing everything so Michael wouldn't know. Then Mom had helped us transfer it all over in her Suburban.

Olivia cranked up an old Justin Bieber song, and a few people started dancing. I wandered into the kitchen where throngs of people crowded around Mom as she filled cups with punch.

"So, this is how Mormons throw a party, huh?" Hudson said, coming up beside me. I nodded and took a sip of punch. He continued, "This is squeaky clean compared to the parties I used to go to back in

Atlanta." I looked back into the family room and nodded. The couples that were slow dancing had about a foot of open air between their bodies.

"No wild partying for me. My parents stick around the entire time." I dipped a carrot stick in ranch dressing and took a bite.

"I'm actually a Mormon, too," Hudson said.

I almost choked on my carrot. "What? No way!"

"Well, I think I am. My mom took me when I was a little kid, but we never go to church anymore."

From the corner of the room Olivia stood backed against the cabinets, her mouth agape. "You should come with us," I said. "The church is just down the street from here." I'd never seen Olivia so reticent before. She really did have it bad for Hudson.

A set of pretty, blonde twin girls walked into the kitchen talking animatedly, "Have you met that new guy that's been coming to our ward lately?"

"Not officially. But I walked next to him in the hall last week, and I almost passed out."

The other girl dissolved into hysterical giggles.

Hudson looked over his shoulder at the two girls and grinned wolfishly. "Maybe I will go to church with you sometime."

I was pretty sure he didn't notice the dark look he won from Olivia for making that comment. I didn't bother telling him those two girls didn't even go to church in our building.

I wandered into the family room, and leaned against the wall. Near the fireplace, Preston was smiling and talking to a girl with long, honey-colored hair. Preston said something to her that made her laugh, and she laid a hand on his arm to emphasize her enthusiasm.

Hannah got up from where she was sitting across the room on the couch next to Evan and walked up to me.

"Who's that girl talking to Preston?" Hannah murmured.

"That's Lindsay Keeton."

"She seems pushy. I don't like her."

"You're not the only one," I said under my breath.

She used to be in my ward when our family first converted. But then, her family moved to a more affluent area in town, and she switched into another ward. We still saw her a few times a year at our stake conferences, dances, and stake youth activities. She was my age, but she never smiled or said hi. She acted like the year and a half when we were in the same Sunday School class had never happened, like we'd never played as kids. It wasn't like I hadn't tried being her friend either. I'd said hi to her on a few occasions, and she'd say hi and then promptly walk away to talk to her snotty little group of friends, leaving me to feel like a complete loser. That was when our parents weren't around. Whenever our families saw each other in the halls after Sunday morning stake conferences, she always smiled sweetly at my parents and acted like we were old friends.

She always dressed in the most expensive name-brand clothing, and the tuition at her private school was quadruple what Bethel's was. I'd been to her family's mansion for a church activity once about a year ago, and it made my house look like an outdated shack.

"She has a lot of nerve, moving in on your man underneath your own roof."

"He's not exactly my man," I pointed out.

"Close enough. I say you go over there and show her what's what."

"Or not." Lindsay Keeton terrified me. There was no way I was going anywhere near her if I could help it.

A soft, romantic ballad came on, and a few couples began pairing up to dance. Hudson drew Olivia to the center of the room to dance. Through the crowd, I spotted Michael dancing with Megan on the far side of the spacious family room. With the feeling of a knife twisting in my gut, I watched as Lindsay linked arms with Preston and led him to the dance floor.

Hannah's eyes darkened, but before she could say anything, Evan came up to us and extended his elbow to her. She took his arm, and they joined the couples. I stood against the wall watching Lindsay flash Preston a flirty grin.

"I heard that Lindsay's parents are commissioning a fashion designer to make her prom dress this year." Annabelle stood in the kitchen doorway to my right. She was one of the girls from Lindsay's ward. Her jet black hair was gathered into a high pony tail, and she had a Prada bag slung over her arm.

"Already? It's only January," said Emory, another girl from their clique. She sported tight, blonde, corkscrew curls that bounced when she moved.

"Those kinds of things can take months," Annabelle said like she was a superior source of knowledge on custom-made prom dresses.

Emory sighed. "It's like they're designing her wedding dress."

"I heard her mother say she wanted Lindsay to have something with sleeves, but I think she actually just likes the idea of having something custom made."

"Have you heard if Lindsay is running for the pageant again this year?" Emory asked.

"Oh yeah, she's already signed up."

A kid named Paul from my ward who hung out with Michael and Preston came up to Annabelle and said, "Would you like to dance?" He had glasses and an acne problem, but he was a pretty funny guy. Sometimes he came over to play paintball with us, and he'd been to several Boy Scout campouts on our land.

Annabelle regarded him with an apologetic look that I suspected was less than sincere. "Oh, I'm sorry. I was just about to go to the bathroom. It's kind of an emergency."

"That's no problem. Sorry to bother you," he mumbled. I caught his eye and gave him a sympathetic smile. He ambled my way.

"Hey, Paul."

"Hey! Do you want to dance?" he asked.

"Sure."

He smiled shyly, and I took his extended arm. He was about six months younger than me and two inches shorter, but I didn't mind. At least someone wanted to dance with me. He led me to an empty spot in the room that just happened to be within earshot of Preston and Lindsay.

"I love your shirt, Preston," Lindsay gushed. "Red is a good color on you."

"You're so lucky you're sixteen already," Paul said. I tore my gaze away from Preston's plaid-covered back and returned my focus to my dancing partner. "Have you gotten your license yet?" Paul asked.

"Not yet. I think my dad's taking me this week. He's the one who usually lets me practice driving. My mom gets too nervous to let me drive.

I think she's still trying to heal from the scars she got from dealing with Michael's insane driving."

Paul laughed heartily. "That sounds just like my mom!"

"I heard you're having your Eagle Court of Honor next week," I said.

"Yeah, it's about time."

"You're only fifteen. That's not bad. Most guys get it when they're about to graduate from high school, and you're still a freshman."

"It's still not as impressive as Preston or Michael. Weren't they like thirteen?"

"Yep. My mom says that's because they were so focused on competing with each other. Whenever one of them would pass off a merit badge, the other would pass off two more just to show him up."

"That's awesome."

The song ended, and the couples scattered as a fast-paced song came on next. Hannah and Evan came up to me. "We're gonna head out," Evan said.

"I need to go to the bathroom first," Hannah told him. "I had a little too much punch."

"Okay, just find me when you're done. I'll be over by the food." Evan flashed her a dimpled grin before sauntering toward the kitchen. Hannah walked toward the guest bathroom, but turned around when she realized it was occupied.

"You can use the girls' bathroom in the hallway back by the bedrooms," I offered. I opened the door that led to the long hall leading to four bedrooms and two bathrooms. The lights were out since this part of the house wasn't open for the party. I shut the hall door behind me.

"Have you told him yet?" I asked.

She shook her head. "He still doesn't know."

I opened the door to the bathroom and said, "When are you going to tell him?"

"I was actually planning on telling him tonight at dinner, but tonight's been so much fun. Part of me doesn't want to ruin it."

"You might as well just get it over with."

She looked down at her belly and placed a hand there. "I still can't believe there's a little person inside me. It doesn't seem real," she whispered.

"Have you been to the doctor yet?" I asked.

"No. If I go to the doctor, she'll just tell my parents."

"Go to the health department. They won't tell anyone, but I'll warn you, they might make you wait all day to be seen." Mom had taken us there when we'd gotten sick, and our insurance was messed up because Dad was in between jobs. "But you need to make sure everything's okay with you and the baby."

"How am I going to go there without my parents finding out?"

"Just tell the school office you're not feeling well, and you need to go to the doctor. It wouldn't even be a lie."

Hannah nodded and went into the bathroom. I turned back to the family room. Through the closed hallway door I could hear a song blasting from an upbeat boy band. I opened the door, and the noise level increased dramatically. Hudson and Michael were sprawled on the floor in an arm-wrestling match with kids circled around them as spectators. Olivia stood with a couple of girls her age who swooned openly at the muscular display before them. A few of the boys chanted Michael's name loudly as the two guys battled.

"Go Hudson!" Olivia screeched. Hudson looked up in her direction, and it was just the distraction that Michael needed to smash his hand down. I was impressed. Not only was he a small guy, but Michael was two years older and a football player. Despite all of that, Hudson had still held his own fairly well.

"I think you've got some competition coming your way with the ladies, Michael," I said as he climbed from the floor.

"Nah, I was going easy on him," Michael said.

"You don't have to worry too much about him," Paul said, slapping Michael on the back. "The main girl he seems to have eyes for is Olivia."

"What?" A shadow clouded Michael's face.

"He danced with her once. I don't think that counts," I said.

"I heard he's a Mormon. Is that true?" Paul asked.

"Yeah, he told me so himself," I said.

"I hadn't heard that," Michael said. He whipped his head around and scrutinized Hudson with a new light in his eyes.

I glanced into the kitchen and chuckled to see Hannah smack Evan playfully on the arm with the back of her hand. "Hey, we're supposed to be going to dinner in a few minutes, and you're not even going to be hungry by then."

"Don't worry, I ran five miles today. I could eat three more dinners." It was probably a good thing he was eating before he got to the restaurant because once Hannah delivered her news his appetite would be gone altogether.

"That's so not fair." Hannah rolled her eyes. "Guys get to eat like pigs without gaining a pound."

"Well, especially not when we're running five miles a day."

Preston stepped out from behind two girls refilling their cups with punch.

"Hey, Destiny, I was looking for you."

"You were?"

"Yeah, do you want to dance?"

He came all the way into the kitchen to find me so he could ask me to dance? A smile tugged at the corners of my lips. "I'd love to."

Hannah and Evan walked past as Preston and I moved into the family room. "See you later, Destiny. Happy birthday, Michael!" Hannah called and waved.

Preston slid his arm around my waist comfortably, and I reached up and curled my hand around his shoulder. It felt so right being with him, like coming home. I could practically feel the goodness radiating from him. There was something about him that set me at ease and made me feel like I belonged. I looked up into his green eyes and smiled. Suddenly, I was ultra-aware of the way his thumb moved over my hand absently, how his fingers felt interlaced with mine, and the warmth of his arm around my waist. How muscular his shoulder felt under his red shirt. I had a flash of memory back to the day we'd stolen his underwear, and he'd walked back to his bedroom bare-chested. He was so beautiful, inside and out. Whether I was willing to admit it to myself or not, I'd known it all along. Other girls were beginning to notice it, too. If I wasn't careful, I'd lose him. I'd seen that tonight with Lindsay.

I felt an intense desire to show him how I felt, but I didn't know how. How could I ever allow my heart to heal enough to let someone back in, to trust again? My wounds were healing, but I was still so raw inside.

Chapter 35

Gift

Preston

The song ended, and Destiny and I had hardly even spoken to each other. But somehow, it was okay. It was like we didn't need to, we were just happy to be together. I crooked my arm, and she nestled her hand around it. I led her to the side of the room, and when she began to withdraw her hand, I held my hand over hers and leaned my head toward hers until our foreheads touched. "I have something for you, but I don't want to give it to you with everyone else around."

Her eyes widened. "For me? But it's not my birthday."

"You'll see."

"Okay." She shrugged. "We can go to the screened porch if you want."

I inclined my head. "Grab your jacket and meet me out there."

I ran out to my truck and grabbed the gift for Destiny from under the driver's seat. When I got back in the house, I went through the kitchen to open the door to the deck.

"Where are you going?" Olivia asked.

I just looked at her for a moment. "Out."

"Oh my gosh. You're having a secret rendezvous with Destiny, aren't you? I totally just saw her go out there."

"Well, I guess it's not a secret now," I said, glancing over my shoulder. One of Lindsay's friends slinked away into the family room. Before anyone else could comment, I slipped through the door and clicked it shut behind me. The deck connected to the pool area and the spacious screened porch where they did all of their grilling. On the screened porch, the Clarks had a long cushioned swing and a patio set. Against the back wall of the house was a set of decorative shelves where they kept their pool supplies and beach towels during the summer when it was warm enough to swim. Usually, her mom stored the cushion from the swing over the winter, but she hadn't gotten around to it this year.

Destiny stood in the middle of the porch, and I strode toward her with the present. "This is for you."

"Thanks." She took the small, rectangular gift and slid a finger underneath the tape securing the black and white polka-dotted paper. The paper fell away, revealing a red leather-bound journal with gold-tipped pages.

"It's for your poetry. I wanted you to have something nicer than that spiral-bound notebook you've been using."

"Preston, I love it!" She stepped forward and threw her arms around my neck.

"There's something else, too," I said apprehensively, taking a step back. "Open to the first page."

Destiny found the gold satin ribbon marking the beginning of the book. When she saw my poem, a small gasp escaped from her lips. "You wrote this? For me?"

I nodded. "Sit down. I want you to read it." I put my arm around her shoulders and led her to the swing. I sat close, pulled out my cell phone, and turned on the display so she could have a little reading light. I could have just turned on the light over our heads, but wanted to avoid the attention it would bring.

We bent our heads over the book and read.

When days are dark
And nights are long
And music dies
Without a song
And wrongs are right
And right is wrong

When lovers lie
And liars love
And crows outfly
The hopeful dove
And voices cry
To God above

When saints lament
And sinners pray
And sturdy trees
Begin to sway
She's there ahead
She lights my way

Her smile so bright
And eyes so blue

Her angel ways
Her heart so true
I pray someday
To walk with you

As she read, I felt my face grow hot. I'd never put myself out there like this, and quite frankly, it terrified me. "It's a little rough, but there it is," I said, shrugging off the embarrassment.

"No, no. It's amazing. I love it!" She took my hand, lacing my fingers with hers. My fingers curled around her hand like they had always belonged there. I looked down into her blue eyes that sparkled like sapphires even in the dim light of my cell phone.

"Does this poem mean you like me better than Lindsay?"

"Lindsay Keeton?" A slow smile spread across my face, and I tilted my head to the side. "Do I sense a touch of jealousy here?"

She stopped smiling.

Great. Now I'd made her mad.

She tried to jerk her hand away from mine, but I held it firmly. "Destiny, you have nothing to worry about," I said reassuringly. "She doesn't even hold a candle compared to your flame. Not even close. She's a nice enough girl, I guess, but she kind of threw herself at me tonight. The entire time I was dancing with her, I just wanted to be with you."

She searched my face in the dim glow of my cell phone, and her features softened. She relaxed the pull on my hand, and I drew her closer.

"You have no idea how much that means to me," she whispered.

I released her hand and gently cupped her face. I leaned in so close I could smell the sweet vanilla scent of her ChapStick, and it took me back to the day of the snowball fight. It was one of the happiest moments of my life. As I brought my face to hers haltingly, her sweet breath hit my face and my pulse quickened. When my lips brushed hers, she responded by kissing me back tenderly. I pulled back for a moment to take a breath, and she released a small sigh. I gave a low laugh and leaned in to kiss her again, this time for real.

Chapter 36

Knight in Shining Armor

Destiny

Preston leaned back, and my head was spinning with him, all of him. His smell, his muscular body, and his rock-solid stability. He was trustworthy and loyal to the core. We'd been through so much together, and he'd been the answer to so many of my problems. Being with him was so simple, even our silences were effortless.

He pressed his forehead to mine, his hand still around the back of my neck. "Destiny, you're so beautiful."

I couldn't help the smile that pulled my lips upward. "I could get used to hearing you say that more often."

"I'll make sure you hear it every day then. I could stay out here all night kissing you like this." He reluctantly slipped his hand from the back of my neck, the sensitive skin back there still tingling from his touch. "But as much as I would love to do that, we should probably get back in the house."

He brushed my hair back from my face. "You're the most beautiful, talented, adventurous girl I know, and I've been crazy about you for a very long time."

"You have? Like how long?"

"You didn't have a clue, did you?"

"What do you mean?"

"Destiny," he said, his voice low. "I've been crazy about you since the first day I saw you."

"What?" My eyes widened. "All that time…"

He nodded eagerly. "I'll never forget it. It was Easter Sunday, and your family had just gotten baptized. You walked in wearing this bright green dress. You were with your entire family, but all I could see was you." I shuddered, and he looked down at me with such tenderness in his eyes I thought my heart would burst with joy.

I wrapped my arms around him, and he held me tightly. His body was warm and protected me from the cold.

Preston kissed the top of my head and said, "I have to say, I've been to some good parties, but this one tops them all."

I laughed. "Understatement of the year."

"I say we go get some food." He took my hand in his.

"Good idea. I'm freezing," I said with a shudder.

"Nah, it's invigorating," he said with a boyish grin. "I really am hungry though."

"You're seventeen, and you're a guy. When are you ever not hungry?"

"Good point." He opened the door to the kitchen.

Hudson sat at the bar surrounded by five girls, Olivia and Megan included, and they were all laughing. He spun around toward us on his stool and said, "What are you two smiling about?"

I blushed, but my smile only got bigger.

"Someone needs to spill," Olivia said.

"They look like they found a little pot of gold on the back porch," Megan said.

Preston grinned.

The pretty blonde twins from earlier rushed into the kitchen. "Oh my gosh. Oh my *gosh*. I'm trying so hard not to freak out right now."

I eyed them curiously.

"I can't believe he's here."

"He's so amazingly gorgeous."

"Do you think he saw me?"

"We should go talk to him."

"Do you think he has a thing for twins?"

"Do you think he has a brother?"

"I wish *he* were a twin."

The words were spouting from their mouths so rapidly I could hardly understand them. A few months ago when I was doing a research paper for English, I stumbled across this article online that said it was common for twins to have their own language as babies. Maybe this insane babble was some offshoot left over from their twin language in their toddler days.

Megan met my eye with a curiosity that equaled my own. "Excuse me," I said as I maneuvered around the twins, who were still speaking their strange hyper-nonsense, and made my way through the kitchen. I walked into the living room and didn't see any sign of who they might be talking about. There was a small commotion outside. I stepped onto the porch to investigate. I walked down and around the sidewalk as it curved around the corner of the house and stopped in my tracks.

Michael was at the bottom of the sidewalk where it joined with the driveway. He was talking to Isaac. This was the guy the twins were babbling about? Isaac? How did they know who he was? How did Isaac know we were having a party tonight? I certainly didn't invite him, and I doubted Hannah would have done so, unless she was secretly plotting to get us back together. There might have been a chance for us at one time. Maybe if I had listened to what he'd had to say and worked on forgiving him…but it was too late for that now. I'd made my decision. My heart belonged to Preston.

Come to think of it, I remembered telling my friends about Michael's party in the lunchroom. Isaac had been there. He'd been sitting at that table with Evelyn. He must have been eavesdropping. How sneaky of him!

"You shouldn't be here," Michael said.

"You're not turning me away again. I'm not leaving until I see her!"

Again? How many times had Isaac tried to see me only to have Michael turn him away?

"Isaac?" I called down to him.

"Destiny!" He pushed past Michael and rushed toward me, his face eager.

"Stay away from her," Michael said, balling up his fist and drawing his arm back.

"Michael, it's okay. He came all the way over here. Let him speak."

Michael looked at me in surprise, but unclenched his fist and took a step back.

"What's going on?" I asked Isaac.

Preston came down the steps of the front porch and stood beside me with an alarmed look on his face. "Isaac…"

“Preston.” Isaac nodded in acknowledgement and then turned back to me. “Can we talk for a minute?

I nodded at Preston and Michael. “Just give us a second.”

Preston leaned close to me and murmured in my ear, “I’ll be up on the porch. Let me know if you need me.” He squeezed my arm and then left with Michael.

Isaac’s eyes trailed after Preston, and he frowned.

“You’ve been to my house to see me?” I asked.

His eyes flicked back to my face. He nodded slightly.

“When?”

“I came to see you right after you left my house.”

My jaw dropped. “You did? Michael never told me. What happened?”

“Michael wouldn’t tell me where you were and threatened to hurt me if I came back again.”

“Yeah…Michael kind of has a temper.”

“I’ve noticed,” he said dryly.

“So, what were you going to tell me?” I knew I shouldn’t ask the question, but curiosity had gotten the best of me.

“Destiny, I’ve been trying to tell you all along that I only went along with Will’s idea for few days. When I saw you at Hannah’s house for the first time and heard you sing, I knew I could never do anything to hurt you. I saw how much Hannah liked you, and I knew what Will wanted me to do was totally and completely wrong. My mistake was that I didn’t confront Will about it, and I will never stop paying for that mistake because it hurt you. I can’t even stand to think about what I did to you. I don’t blame you for hating me.”

"I don't hate you." As I said it, I realized that the words were true. I didn't hate him anymore. I could feel the heavy burden of anger and hatred being lifted from my shoulders and my mind.

"You don't?"

"Nope, I forgive you." Saying the words felt like unlocking the door to a musty old room and letting in fresh, spring sunshine.

Isaac stared at me and blinked twice. "Thank you."

"I'm sorry, too." I stared into the glow of the outdoor lights shining on our heads. "For not letting you tell me any of this before. And for being so quick to throw you aside and to assume the worst. I should have known you better than that, but I let my anger and hurt control me."

"How about we put it in the past and start fresh?" Isaac asked. "Friends?" He stuck out his hand.

"Okay, I can live with that, I guess." I took his hand and gave it a firm shake.

"Now that that's settled…" He extended his other hand offering me a gift bag. I took the bag by the bottom, to avoid touching his hand. I'd forgiven him, but I wasn't stupid enough to think I was completely immune to him, either. I pulled out a large, hardcover book. It was a book about *Les Misérables* and the journey it took from being a novel, to the stage, and finally the screen. It was full of glossy photos and little tidbits of information.

"Wow, this is awesome!" I'd never seen a book like it before.

"It's a pretty fun little book, but there's a surprise in the front."

With a feeling of *déjà vu*, I turned to the first page, half-expecting a love poem to be written there. Instead, there was a note written in a feminine hand.

Destiny,

Congrats on landing the part of Éponine!

Never stop singing!

Love,

The name was written in a flowing scrawl across the page. I squinted at the looping letters and was only able to decipher the first name: *Samantha*.

No freaking way… "Who signed this? This can't be…"

"It's the real deal."

"Samantha Barks!?" I squealed. "How on *earth* did you get this?" Samantha Barks played Éponine in the Twenty-Fifth Anniversary Edition of *Les Misérables* on the stage and was later cast in the movie for the same role, alongside an all-star cast. I'd been idolizing her since September.

"My uncle got a couple of them at some party or convention and gave them to me and Hannah because he knew we're in the musical. But when I got it, I immediately thought of you. I know how much you like her. Oh, and she signed page ninety-three as well."

I turned to page ninety-three and found a full-page photo of Samantha on the red carpet with her signature scribbled in black Sharpie.

"This is just so amazing, Isaac! I don't even know how to thank you!"

"I have a pretty good idea of how you can," he said quietly, his eyes intense, yet vulnerable.

A shiver ran down my spine. He stepped closer, and I froze, lost in the smell of him. I shook my head to clear the haze that was threatening to overcome me. "No, Isaac," I whispered.

"Don't say that. I know you still care about me. I can see it in your eyes. I saw it when we sang together this week." He leaned in close.

I tore my gaze from his dark, fathomless eyes. Looking at them would make this completely impossible. I focused on my hands instead. "Isaac…I can't." Betraying me, my eyes flicked up to his ardent gaze. So eager. I took a deep breath. I had to keep talking. "I—I just don't think we can be together." That wasn't exactly the speech I was supposed to make.

He stepped forward, and my heart raced more furiously. "I think you're wrong," he said. I shook my head, unable to speak. He was now only inches from my face. "I'm in love with you."

"No." I said, my voice barely a whisper.

"I tried to tell you before, but you never gave me the chance."

He was so close. My head was screaming that I needed to back away, but I was frozen in place. He stared at my lips like he wanted to kiss them, and my eyes widened.

I couldn't lead him on anymore. It was unfair that I'd let things go this far.

"Isaac. I can't be with you."

"What do you mean?" An edge of panic crept into his voice.

"We're too different. We tried it, and it didn't work."

"We'll make it work. We'll learn to compromise. I'm willing to change for you. If you had listened to me before, you'd know that."

"What do you mean by change?"

"I'm reading the Book of Mormon."

"You are?"

"I wanted to see for myself what you believe. I've gone to your church five times now."

"What are you talking about? I'm at church every Sunday, and I'm pretty sure I would have noticed if you'd shown up."

"I never said I was going to your ward."

"You—" *What?* The twins…so that was how they knew Isaac. They went to a ward building about fifteen minutes away in a different neighborhood closer to where Isaac lived in comparison to my house. Come to think of it, his house was in the boundaries for that ward anyway. "You've been going to church? To a Mormon church?"

He nodded. "The Sunday night after our breakup the missionaries stopped by my house. My dad was livid. I've never seen him so mad. I was out of my mind with grief," I winced, "and said some things I'm not very proud of. After the missionaries left, I called and told them I'd meet them at their place in the future. They explained that technically I wasn't in the right area for them, and they referred me to the right missionaries for my area. I started taking the lessons with the new missionaries the very next week, and they had me go to the other church building. I was glad for the change, because I figured your family wouldn't want me around anyway."

By the time he'd finished his explanation, I was mortified. "Isaac, I'm sorry. We've been horrible to you."

He looked away, the pain evident on his face.

"Why are you doing all this?" I asked.

"You know, at first, it was just to win you back. But now…" He ran a hand through his hair. "I don't even know anymore."

"What do you mean?" I shifted my weight from one leg to the other.

"I'm still trying to figure it all out."

"That's great. I hope you do." I meant it, too. Regardless of our relationship status, I still wanted the best for him. "So, how much have you read in the Book of Mormon?"

"Last night I finished up Alma."

"Whoa, you're more than halfway through!" *He'd been reading it on his own?* "What do you think about it?"

"It's a good story. If you're asking if I think it's scripture, I can't tell you that. But I will tell you this: it's definitely not evil like my dad would have me think."

That was reassuring. At least he didn't think I was a freak. "So, why do you keep going back to a Mormon church? I don't get it."

"At first, it was just to spite my dad and to win you back, but now, I don't know, I just like it. The people seem genuine."

"That's good. I hope you keep going."

"Destiny."

I looked up.

"I want things back the way they were with us."

I clenched my fists at my sides. "That can't happen."

"Why not? I'm doing everything I can here. Don't you see that?"

"Isaac." I sighed. "I'm already dating someone else." There. I'd finally said it.

"What? You're pulling the 'I'm dating Preston' card again? Hannah told me you were faking that. Do you know what I think? I think you're scared to commit. You're afraid of getting hurt again. We belong together. Can't you feel that? Look me in the eyes and tell me that you don't still feel something for me."

I studied the bushes.

Isaac took my chin and turned it toward him. "Look me in the eyes."

I bit my lower lip to keep it from trembling. It was impossible to look in his beautiful eyes. I couldn't say it because my heart was overflowing with my feelings for him.

"You can't say it, can you?" He placed his hands on either side of my face, and I finally looked him in the eyes. I had to do what was best for him. He deserved better. I only had one heart to give, and I'd just pledged the entire thing to Preston.

It was time to finally push the muddled cloud away from my brain and treat Isaac fairly, once and for all.

He leaned in closer to kiss me, and I placed both hands on his chest to push him away. But I was too late. He pressed his lips fervently to mine. I angrily forced my hands against his chest. "Stop it, Isaac!" I pushed forcefully, and he stumbled down the hill, caught off guard.

Preston must have heard my cry, because he immediately came jogging down the hillside from the front porch, which was out of sight from where we were standing.

"Destiny, are you okay?"

"He just kissed me!"

"Dude! When are you going to get the message? Stay away from my girlfriend!" I'd never heard Preston raise his voice before, but he was absolutely out of his mind with rage.

Isaac's lips formed a small 'o.' "So y'all are really dating this time?"

Preston gave me a funny look. "This time? What's he talking about?"

Oh shiz! "I'll explain it later," I promised. "Seriously though, Isaac. Preston and I really are dating now." I slipped my arm around his waist to emphasize my point. Preston wrapped his arms around my shoulders. "That's what I've been trying to tell you."

Isaac looked from Preston to me, and his expression hardened. He looked away, running his hand across his forehead and down the side of his face. "I think I'd better just go." He turned around, shoulders hunched, and walked down the long, car-lined driveway to where he'd parked his truck. I couldn't help it. As I watched his defeated gait, my heart shattered all over again.

"Are you okay?" Preston asked gently.

I turned toward Preston and looked up into his beautiful, caring, supportive face. He was there for me. No matter what.

He wrapped his arms around me, and I buried my head in his chest, my cheek pressed to the soft cotton of his plaid shirt. He smelled like the woods after a rainstorm and like the comforting, clean smell of his family's home. It took me back to my childhood and the many happy hours I'd spent playing there. I lifted my chin, and his lips found mine like they'd come home. While our lips were still locked, a bright light flooded us like a spotlight on a stage. We pulled away, blinking, and heard the revving sound of an engine starting. We twisted to see Isaac's truck turning around in the driveway, and then, his tires squealed as he peeled out.

"Do you think he saw us?" Preston asked.

"Yeah. Wasn't it obvious?"

"Good. It's about time he feels a little bit of what he's put the rest of us through."

"Preston! I'm shocked."

"Why should that shock you? Do you have any clue how horrible it was for me to see you with him? Every time I saw him touch you, I wanted to beat him senseless." The agony in his voice was unmistakable. I had no idea he'd felt that strongly at the time. It was amazing to know he'd cared. "But I never did anything to him. I just stood aside and allowed it. And then, after all that, I had to watch you suffer from what *he* did." He spat the word *he* like it was rotten in his mouth. "He treated you like crap! Then he thought he could waltz back in here and take you away from me again? Did he think that a present and a flashy smile would make you forget everything he did to you? No, I don't feel sorry for him. Not one bit. It's his turn now," he said with a voice full of triumphant justice.

It wasn't exactly fair to say that Isaac had treated me like crap, but I wasn't about to correct him. Not now anyway. Preston deserved this moment of triumph. He'd worked hard to earn it.

"I'm glad you came for me. There you were, once again, my knight in shining armor." His eyes softened as they looked down at me.

"Yo! Preston!" Michael called from the porch. "Y'all had better come back in. People are starting to look for Destiny."

I looked up to the window of the formal living room and saw Megan and Olivia's faces gawking openly at us through the curtains. "Well, this was a lot less private than I'd thought."

Preston laughed when he saw their faces in the window and said, "I don't care. Let 'em see." He turned me toward him and kissed me right in front of them. I could hear their squeals. Thank goodness it was muffled by the glass of the windowpane.

We walked up the porch steps past Michael. "I'm going to give you a little heads up about something, bro."

"What's that?" Preston asked, glancing up at him.

"You might want to steer clear of Lindsay Keeton for the rest of the night. She's not that happy with you."

He strode past Michael easily without even a wince. "Sure thing."

Chapter 37

Walnut Ridge

Destiny

Later that night—after Preston and I had gotten plenty of teasing—the candles had been blown out, the presents opened, and the guests bid farewell, Hannah called me. "Did you tell Evan?" I asked from my bed. I had on bright blue satin pajamas, and I'd just finished washing my face in the bathroom. Olivia had already gone to bed, and Michael was in his room, quietly listening to music.

"Yes."

"And?" I shut and locked the door to the bathroom in case Michael decided to take off his headphones.

"He wants me to get an abortion."

My heart sunk. I shut the lid of the toilet and lowered myself onto it. "Are you considering it?"

"Never in a million years. Of course, to Evan, it makes perfect sense. Just wash the entire situation away like it never happened. Well, guess what? Because of him and his out-of-control hormones, this *did* happen. Selfish jerk! I think he needs to man up, face the facts, and take care of this kid he helped make. But he doesn't see it that way. To him, it's just a mass of cells that's threatening to ruin his life."

That surprised me. I couldn't imagine Evan acting that way. Maybe I didn't know him as well as I thought I did. Or maybe, because he was under extreme stress, his uglier side took over.

"What did you tell him you wanted to do?"

"I'm giving it up for adoption. I like the idea of adoption because I could go back to high school and get back to just being me. I don't know if I ever even want kids. I definitely don't want one now!"

"I'm surprised you seem to know what you want to do. It seems like in most stories, the girl feels all torn about what to do."

"It's pretty simple. I don't want to be a mom, and I don't want to kill an innocent baby. That's all there is to it."

"Good for you, Hannah. I think it's a great idea. You can find some amazing family for your baby, and give him or her a beautiful life."

"My best friend in elementary school was adopted, and I've always thought it was awesome. She told me her birth mom lived in a crappy trailer with about ten cats, but her adopted parents lived in a nice, clean house with a big backyard and a swing set."

"If you decided to keep the baby, your parents would help you take care of it, right?"

"Oh, I'm sure they would, but I'm not keeping it, so what's the point of even asking them?"

"You may end up changing your mind. I mean, what if you get attached and decide you can't go through with it?"

"No, I don't even want to think about it. All the crying, the dirty diapers, spit up? No way. You may be good with kids, but it's just not my thing. I'm so not the domestic type. I mean, you've seen my cooking skills! I'm proud to have mastered the Pop-Tart!"

I laughed. She had a point.

Sunday morning, I walked into the church building early with a bounce in my step. We had choir practice before church since we were performing that day, which meant that most of our family would be on the stand throughout the meeting. Dad was up there because he was the bishop. Michael, Olivia, and I were in the choir, and Mom was the pianist. Elijah and Brianna sat in the Nelsons' pew waiting for them to arrive.

As I sang from the front of the chapel, Preston came into the room. His eyes went directly to where I was standing near the piano. He gave me a lopsided smile, and my heart melted a little bit in my chest. My eyes trailed after him. He looked amazing in his light blue tie and navy suit. His thick, wavy, dirty-blond hair was combed neatly. He walked up the aisle, took the steps jauntily, and greeted Dad.

"Good morning, Bishop Clark." Dad shook his hand vigorously. Dad was so pleased my attention had turned toward Preston. Six months ago, he probably would have given me a talk about not pairing off with boys too early, but after my drama with Isaac, he was grateful I was focusing on a Mormon boy. Still, there were probably a few parental discussions coming our way. It went with the territory.

Preston walked past Dad and made his way over to Sister Poff, the ward choir director. "Am I still allowed to join? I'm not too late, am I?"

"No, of course not! We can always use more men." She handed him a copy of the music. "What part do you sing?"

"I'm a tenor."

My jaw dropped of its own accord. Since when did Preston sing? I'd never heard a note of music come out of his mouth the entire time I'd known him.

"We're performing today, so you'll have to pay close attention to the music."

Preston scooted into the aisle behind me, next to Michael, who was also singing tenor. "We don't have much time left today, so we're going to get through this as quickly as we can." Mom played the intro, and we dove right into the music. I had a solid grip on my notes since the alto part was fairly simple on this particular arrangement. Without being too obvious, I strained to hear Preston's voice, but all I could hear was Michael overpowering the entire section. I refrained from rolling my eyes. Didn't he know this was no time to show off? My new boyfriend was singing with me for the first time, and all I could hear was Michael belting his notes. Like I hadn't heard that before.

Yes, Michael, you're an awesome singer. We all know that. Now please let us hear the hot guy next to you sing. Mmmkay?

I wished there was some way I could telepathically communicate the message to him, but finally, when we came to a break in the music, I gave up and turned around, tapping him lightly on the knee.

"Psst. Michael."

"What?"

"Can you keep it down a bit? You're overpowering the entire tenor section."

"Sorry?" He cocked an eyebrow at me.

Olivia twisted around. "Destiny wants to hear Preston sing." I elbowed her, but then nodded emphatically.

Preston shifted awkwardly in his seat. "Hey, give me a bit of a break here, guys. It's my first day. Do I have to go all solo on you already? I don't even know the music yet."

I liked the way he said "first day." Did that mean there would be others? The music began again, and I turned back to Sister Poff. As we sang, I still couldn't hear anything but Michael's voice coming from the tenor section. Maybe it was just as well. For all I knew, Preston couldn't even carry a tune. Although, logically, it would seem that he'd at least have some talent since Megan sang and played the flute and Sister Nelson had joined the choir from time to time over the years.

When the meeting had concluded, I slung my purse over my shoulder and returned my music to Sister Poff. I'd failed to hear anything from Preston as we sang, but I was determined to get some music out of him before too long. I sensed Preston at my elbow, and I turned to see him grinning down at me. I knew then that he'd joined the choir just for me. It didn't matter whether he was a good singer or not. He'd gone out of his comfort zone to do something to make me happy, and that was incredibly awesome.

Preston and I walked to Sunday School side-by-side, picked out chairs together, and when class was over we, reluctantly said goodbye for the third hour when the guys and the girls went to separate classes. I walked into room for the Young Women. Olivia was already playing the piano. A couple of girls looked at me and then pressed their heads together to whisper. Megan slid into the chair next to me. "What's with them?"

"I think they heard about Preston and me."

"It was bound to get out eventually," Megan said.

"Did you know he liked me?"

"Oh yeah, I figured that out back in fifth grade," she said dismissively.

"You knew he liked me all that time, and you never told me?"

Megan shrugged. "I was sworn to secrecy. Preston had gotten ahold of my diary and knew enough of my secrets to keep me quiet."

"So, what? You and Preston would have special meetings about me?"

Megan laughed. "Something like that."

Brinlee leaned forward from her chair behind us. "She's not kidding. Preston would come and sit in our doorway every Sunday night after everyone else had gone to bed, and he'd ask us for girl advice."

"What?" Man, what I would have given to be an invisible observer at one of those sessions. "What kind of advice did you give him?"

"Mmm." Megan pressed her lips together thoughtfully. "Mostly to make sure he was well groomed and to open doors for girls. It was pretty basic stuff."

"She means the rest is top secret," Brinlee piped up from behind us.

I didn't have a chance to reply because our Young Women leader came to the front of the room to start the meeting. All this time, Megan and Brinlee had been conspiring to get me together with Preston? Those little sneaks!

When class let out, Preston found me in the hall. "Hey there," he said.

"Hey. What are you up to this afternoon?" I asked.

"Michael asked me to hike Walnut Ridge. You want to come with us?"

"Sure! I haven't climbed Walnut Ridge in a while." Usually Michael and Preston hiked the ridge behind our house with for scout campouts. Now that there were houses up there, they had to walk quite a ways to the north of Hudson's neighborhood to find a camping spot. They knew the man who owned the land, and he had given the scouts permission to camp. Now, Elijah was the one going on those campouts, but Preston and Michael still went fairly often to help out.

An hour after church, Preston arrived with Megan and Brinlee.

"Y'all are coming with us to the top of the ridge, too?" I asked.

"Yep."

"It's a pretty easy hike, right?" Megan asked.

"Oh yeah. The ridge isn't very high. It takes about thirty minutes to get to the top," Preston explained.

Olivia came into the foyer from the family room. "Brinlee, I have to talk to you!" They dashed off to the back of the house, whispering fervently to each other.

"How's your mom, Preston?" I asked. I'd noticed she hadn't shown up to church.

"She's been fighting some severe nausea today, but she's still keeping her spirits high." Preston frowned a little. "I don't know how she stays so upbeat. If it were me, I'd be whining like a two-year old."

"I don't believe that," I said, "You're a tough guy."

"You haven't seen it," Megan said, rolling her eyes. "He's the biggest baby."

"Do you even get sick?" I couldn't remember a single time he'd missed anything because he'd been sick.

"Once in a while. It isn't pretty," Preston said. "Where's Michael?"

"Probably in his room." We walked down the hall together to find him. Preston knocked on Michael's door.

"Hang on a sec," Michael called.

As Preston and I stood there, my eyes slid to my open bedroom door. I hadn't left a stray bra out in the open in my rush to get ready for church that morning, had I? Thankfully, all I saw was Brinlee and Olivia sitting on Olivia's bed and giggling softly, probably about Hudson. They hadn't seemed to notice we were standing so close.

"Should we see if he's home?" Olivia giggled.

So, that was the sudden interest in this hike. Hudson. I should've known. He'd probably be glad to see us. I pulled out my phone to send him a warning text.

Michael opened his door. "Hey. Y'all look like you're ready to go."

"We're ready when you are," Preston replied.

I tapped the message into my phone. *I'm hiking Walnut Ridge with some friends today. Can we swing by and say hi?* I grinned secretively to myself. It would be hilarious to see the look on Olivia's face if he showed up in the woods.

"Who are you texting?" Michael asked.

"You'll see," I said with a suppressed grin. Preston gave me a funny look. Uh-oh. He didn't think I was sneaking around with Hudson, did he? "I just arranged a little surprise for Olivia and Brinlee," I clarified hastily.

"What kind of surprise?" Preston asked warily.

I showed him the sent text. He didn't smile. He just turned his broad shoulders away from me.

"Let's do this, Michael," he said, his voice tight.

Shiz! What had I done now? Did he think I had a thing for Hudson? Hudson was too immature for me. Simply put, I just wasn't into him, but maybe Preston didn't understand that.

We gathered in the grass just behind the pool area and then started on the trail that led to the hammock spot. I'd forgotten about that part. To get to the trail that led up the mountain we had to cross through that area. I hadn't been back since the day Isaac kissed me. I couldn't bring myself to do it. Preston was the only person I'd ever told.

As we walked toward the clearing, our feet crunched across the dry, fallen leaves. All around us, the woods were filled with signs that the once-thriving life had died. As we neared it, the hammock appeared, now abandoned by me. If the other kids in the family used it, I didn't know. It was a cursed place in my mind.

Sensing my discomfort, Preston wrapped an arm around my shoulder protectively. I looked up to see his green eyes regarding me seriously. "I'm here for you," he whispered.

I inhaled deeply, released the breath, and we stepped into the winter sunlight together.

Once we passed through the hammock spot, the ground sloped upward dramatically and the trees thinned. The gray trunks were tall and skinny without lower branches to obscure our view. The woods were beautiful, even in the winter.

Preston and I hung back, allowing the rest of the group to distance themselves about twenty paces ahead of us.

"When are you going to read me some more of your poetry?" I asked. "And why's it so top secret?"

"Believe me, there's a good reason," he assured me. "If you saw what was in there, you'd think I was so lame."

"I'm pretty sure I already know." I slid my hand around the inside of his bicep where his skin was soft. "But I'm still with you, so it's all good."

"Speaking of you being with me, what was Isaac talking about at the party?"

"What do you mean?" *Oh shiz*. He just *had* to bring this up, didn't he?

"He said something about us dating before."

"I think he was confused."

Preston gave me a pointed look. "Destiny."

A sharp mixture of embarrassment and guilt sliced through me. "Okay, okay," I said, cringing. "I just really don't want to tell you."

"What did you do?"

I told him how Hannah had humiliated me by telling Mr. Byrd about my crush, how it had gotten back to Isaac, and how I'd felt it necessary to use him as a cover to convince Isaac that I wasn't some desperate reject.

"How'd he find out it was fake?"

"I think he started suspecting the day he met you, but then Hannah confirmed it after we'd broken up."

"You mean the day he asked my permission to go play paintball with you? I was wondering what was up with that."

"I tried to cover that up by telling Isaac the next day that we'd broken up, but Hannah eventually told him the truth."

I traced my fingers down his arm and nestled my hand into the protection of his strong palm. "Right after Hannah and I came up with the whole fake-boyfriend thing, I started wondering what it would be like to actually be your girlfriend."

"Really?" Preston looked down at me in interest. "When was this, again?"

"This was back in September, I think."

"Around the time you stole my underwear?" Preston asked, his green eyes teasing.

I blushed. "It was right before that."

"And you decided it would be weird and gross to be my girlfriend, so you went for Isaac instead?"

"No," I said slowly. I was on treacherous ground. I could feel it. "I liked the idea," I explained. "I guess it just wasn't the right time. If you think about it, a lot of why I'm with you is because of Isaac. If it weren't for my experiences with him, I would've been too scared to let you know my true feelings. I'm sure we wouldn't be together right now."

"I'm not following," Preston said, lifting our clasped hands over the jagged splinters of a fallen tree stump.

"Let me put it this way. Isaac was the catalyst. Because he broke my heart, you were able to bond with me and help me through that rough time." I watched my feet as I climbed the steep incline. "It started that day in the tree house. I didn't realize it yet, because I was too emotional, but I can see it now, looking back. I mean, come on? What girl wouldn't have swooned over this totally hot guy climbing a rope and then holding her while she cried?"

My phone chirped. Ever so slightly, Preston tensed up. I pulled out my phone and read Hudson's excited message. *Awesome! Feel free! I'll be here all day just chillin.*

Cool. Which house are you?

I'm at the end of the street. 3204 Emerald View.

"Who was that?" Preston asked, attempting to keep his voice light, but failing miserably.

"It was Hudson," I replied. "He said we could come over."

His lips formed a hard line, and he stared at the top of the mountain. We climbed over another fallen tree, and a gravel path came into view. One of our neighbors owned the land we were on, and he'd faithfully maintained the trail. It wound up the mountain in switchbacks, and every now and then there were small benches made with flat rocks found on the mountainside.

Hudson wasn't mentioned again until soon after we'd reached the top and caught up to Michael, Megan, Olivia, and Brinlee.

Olivia and Brinlee kept exchanging glances and smiling, and Megan pointed toward the south. "Is that a house through those trees?"

"Yeah," Michael said. "They put in a new neighborhood up here recently."

"Oh," she said. "I've seen those houses from the road. There's a pretty clear view of them from Acorn Creek High."

We hopped along the tops of the smooth, flat boulders that ran along the top of the ridgeline. In-between bare trunks, I caught glimpses of the valley below, but it was nearly impossible to see much since the trees grew so closely together.

Suddenly, the woods parted to reveal a mansion built from the same mountain stone the homemade benches had been made from.

My breath caught, and I stopped walking altogether. Beyond the stone wall surrounding the back of the house, the world opened expansively. I stepped forward eagerly.

"Where are you going?" Michael said. "You can't just walk on someone's property like that."

"I don't care," I said. "I have to get a better look at this view." I rushed to the edge of the wall where it curved behind the end of the driveway and took in the world before me. Rolling green fields of what used to be farmland were now dotted with mansions and horse pastures. To the southwest was Acorn Creek High. I couldn't see our house because we lived right at the base of the mountain, but directly west was the road I lived on. When I gazed down it far enough, the outer edges of Preston's neighborhood were visible.

I turned back to the group. They were all standing on the edge of the woods staring at me like I was nuts. Just behind them, leading up to the mansion, was a winding driveway that led down a slight, wooded hill to a street Hudson probably longboarded on.

I turned to Olivia and Brinlee, who were whispering again, and I pulled out my phone to see which house number Hudson had said his was.

It was at 3204, and it was at the end of the street. Hmm. Where was the number on this house? I glanced around for a mailbox and saw 3204 in expensive-looking gold numbers. Suddenly, even though I'd been invited, I felt like the creepiest stalker. Should I text him again, or should I knock on the door? Or just tell Olivia and run away like a bunch of cowards?

I was being ridiculous. I strode toward the front door. "What are you doing, Destiny?" Preston asked.

"This is Hudson's house," I said.

Somehow, Olivia didn't seem that surprised. She'd probably been tracking his house on her google maps app this entire time.

I rang the doorbell and glanced to my left. The trees had been cleared from the side of the mountain and there was a clear view of the other side of the gap. Less than a mile away, a tree-covered mountain rose before me, shaped like a giant Hershey's kiss that had melted down slightly. It was majestic and beautiful and reminded me of the wooded hills that surrounded the lake at the retreat.

Suddenly, I realized what I was looking at. That very peak was Isaac's land. It had to be. I could even see the road winding through the trees. Immediately, the memories of that night came crashing down on me so heavily that a knot twisted in my stomach.

The door opened and Hudson stood in the doorway casually. "Hey, hey. What's up?"

I managed a smile and resisted the urge to turn around and look back at Isaac's land. It was symbolic of everything I thought I might have one day.

The white house with the wrap-around porch.

How many times had I dreamed of standing on that imaginary porch, gazing out into the valley with Isaac's arms wrapped around my waist? Mom and Dad couldn't see it, but what if he converted one day?

What was the point of pushing him away when he was actually interested in learning more?

He was, wasn't he? Or was he still on a secret mission to "expose the Mormons"? If he was still bent on his original plan, he was being awfully persuasive. But then, he usually was. He was like Hannah in that way. His words were so powerful. It was nearly impossible to tell him no, or at least it had been on the sidewalk. But that was more than just his words. It was his…everything. His eyes, his smell, the sound of his voice as he said my name. A chill ran down my arms, and I shivered.

Preston's voice jarred me from my thoughts. "Hey, Hudson."

Hudson's eyes moved past Preston and fell on Olivia and Brinlee, who were hanging back shyly on the driveway. Michael came up the steps with Megan. "S'up, Hudson. Nice place you have here," he said, looking around appreciatively.

Hudson shrugged. "It's my home sweet home. You guys want to come inside?"

"Sure," I said. I was seriously dying to see what the view was like from inside the house. We moved into the rustically trendy foyer. Almost every surface of the room was covered in mountain stone, slate, polished wood, or rusty metal. To my right was a staircase made with wrought iron and golden pine. The entire room had the feel of an upscale Rocky Mountain ski lodge.

"You guys like hockey?" he asked, walking down a short hall that led into the great room. The ceiling in this room was two stories high and the back wall was mostly glass. The gigantic TV that took up a generous portion of the wall to the left was showing a hockey game.

"Whoa," Michael said. "Is that a seventy-inch TV?"

"It's a seventy-two-inch, actually," Hudson said. "My dad was pretty unhappy when my mom got it in the divorce."

"I can imagine," Preston said. "I bet you didn't mind so much."

Hudson shrugged. "My mom probably would have just bought another one."

"Is your mom from out West?" Preston asked, looking around at all the western décor.

"Not originally. She grew up here, but she went to college in Colorado and fell in love with the whole snow-skiing thing," he said. "We still go back a few times during the winter when she has a moment to get away."

Who *does* that?

Someone with a lot of money—that's who.

Someone extremely talented, who could land a big-time recording contract, could do that. Someone like Isaac. I pushed the thought from my mind.

I walked over to the windows and gazed down. Somehow I'd missed that Hudson had a pool back here. The water came all the way to the edge of the wall like it was being held up by the air itself. I'd only seen pools like that on celebrity home TV shows.

There was even a round hot tub built into the cement. Did Hudson ever bring girls back there with him? I wouldn't have been surprised.

"This view is gorgeous," Preston murmured in my ear.

"Yes, it is," I said, smiling up at him.

"Ugh. Really?" Olivia groaned. "Do y'all have to do that?"

"Sorry, but yes," Preston said as an unapologetic grin stretched across his face.

She rolled her eyes.

"What's wrong with a little bit of cuddling, Olivia?" Hudson asked from several feet behind her.

She spun around, her head whipping toward him when he spoke, and her cheeks turned crimson. "Nothing." She gave a small, strangled cough and cleared her throat. "I just don't like to watch my sister cuddle with Preston. It's weird."

"I bet you've done more than cuddling," Hudson said to her.

Olivia turned away from him, focusing on the hockey game instead.

"Hardly," Michael said. "Olivia's determined to not date until she's sixteen," Michael said.

"Oh really, now," Hudson said, regarding her with new interest. "That's fascinating," he said, one side of his mouth drawing up.

There was something strange about the way he was looking at her with an amused twinkle in his eye.

"Yeah, it's kind of a Mormon thing," Megan said. "You're a Mormon, right?"

"Well, kind of," Hudson said. "I was baptized as a kid, but I haven't been back since."

"You should come to church with us sometime," Michael said.

"Yeah, I was thinking about it," Hudson said, glancing at Olivia.

Even then, she stood rigidly with her back to him and her eyes on the hockey game.

On the way back down the mountain, Preston seemed oddly detached.

"Are you okay?" I asked.

"Something's bugging me," he said.

"What?" I asked.

"How did our walk up the mountain turn into a walk to Hudson's house?"

"It's not like that."

"Oh really? What's it like, then?"

"I'm not into him that way. We're just friends." I didn't want to tell him about Olivia's crush. I was on her bad list enough these days. What was with Olivia anyway?

"This was supposed to be a way for us to spend more time together. Why does it feel like every time I get a moment alone with you, some other guy is always popping up?"

"Just because they do, it doesn't mean I don't care about being with you," I said.

"I guess I'm just tired of being the second-rate guy."

"How could you think that?" I asked. "You're anything but a second-rate guy. You're hardworking, honest, loyal, funny, gorgeous, and spiritual."

He looked over at me and his eyes softened. "Thanks." His green eyes regarded me soberly.

"I'm serious," I said. "You know those lists of qualities we'd like to see in our future husband the girls make at church?"

"Yeah, I've seen Megan's. Her list would be impossible for any guy to ever achieve."

"You think so? I've seen her list. It's not that different from mine," I admitted. "And it's not that impossible. Preston, you fill every category for me."

His eyebrows rose.

"I have so much respect for you. When I found out what you've been doing for your mom…"

His brow lifted higher. "You know about that?"

"Megan told me the last time I slept over."

"She told you?"

"Yeah, it bugged me that you were always gone working, and she told me you were helping to pay for her antidepressant medication."

"What else was I supposed to do? Stand by while my mom committed suicide because she didn't have her medicine?"

His mom was suicidal?

The shock that radiated through me must have been written all over my face. "Please keep that part about my mom being suicidal between the two of us," he said.

"Of course, I will." How much had he been through? I'd known she was depressed, but I hadn't known it was that bad. My heart went out to his family and to him. How could he have been strong for so many years, knowing that any day he could walk into his house and find her dead?

Preston was more amazing than I'd given him credit for. How was he not this totally messed-up kid? He was strong, driven, and hardworking. He deserved someone better than me, someone who didn't have feelings for her ex. Maybe I should have taken the advice he gave me by the creek on New Year's when he suggested we give ourselves more space.

Chapter 38

Ex-Girlfriends

Isaac

It had been an especially dark weekend. I'd put myself out there, taken a risk, and I'd come so close to getting her back—or so I'd thought. I'd made such a fool of myself. When I saw her kissing Preston the night of the party, it was like my worst nightmare had come to life.

My insides were still raw when I saw her Monday morning, and the burning ache to be near her became unbearable. Knowing that she belonged to another guy, who could put his arms around her whenever he wanted, drove me insane.

"Hey, Destiny." I wasn't planning to say anything to her, but the words leapt from my throat as I approached her taking books from her locker. She spun around, and I silently cursed myself for my stupidity. What was I supposed to say to her? Was I supposed to congratulate her on her obvious happiness in her new relationship? They'd fit into each other's arms like they were made for each other. I should be happy for Destiny. He was good for her. Shouldn't I congratulate her and walk away? But I couldn't, not when it felt like a sledgehammer was hitting my chest every time I pictured them together.

She met my eyes, and I fully expected to see the animosity that had taken up permanent residency on her face every time she'd looked at me since our breakup. But surprisingly, her expression was softer this time. Although not welcoming me with open arms, she no longer cringed just at the sight of me.

"Yes?" she asked in a steady voice.

"I need to talk to you." I had no idea what to say, but I had to talk to her.

"About what?" She clutched a stack of books to her chest as though she were trying to use them as a protective barrier between us.

"Um..." I looked over her shoulder, and my eyes fell on Hannah's locker. *Bingo!* "I'm worried about Hannah. She pretends she's fine, but I think, deep down, she's broken. I was wondering if maybe you knew anything."

Her face grew serious, and for a precious moment, her reserve fell away completely. "She talked to me after the party. He wants her to..."

Her eyes darted around the hall nervously, and she leaned close enough for the smell of wildflowers and sunshine to flood my senses. The urge to pull her toward me and to kiss her soft, shimmery lips was overwhelming.

I suddenly knew the true definition of aching for someone. She was right in front of me, and I couldn't have her. I clenched my fists at my sides to keep my hands from reaching out to run my fingers through her hair.

"He wants her to have an abortion," she said in a low voice. She pulled away from me, and I felt the disconnection between us like a slap in the face.

Once she was a safe distance from me, my mind cleared enough to focus on what she'd said. Panic ripped through my heart. Hannah couldn't do that! It would wreak havoc on her conscience, and she would regret it for the rest of her life. I'd sat through enough of the pro-life chapel meetings Bethel frequently held to know what having an abortion could do to a woman's emotional state. "Is that what she wants?" I asked. Because, if it was what she wanted, I would do everything I could to talk her out of it.

"No, of course not," she said.

I breathed an audible sigh of relief. My little cousin in her tummy was safe. And as an added bonus, I got to avoid an awkward conversation. If she wanted to raise the baby herself, I'd do everything I could to help her. Either that, or I'd beat some sense into Evan to get him to man up and take care of his own kid.

Destiny slammed her locker door shut and leaned her shoulder against the row of lockers. "But now she's fighting with Evan."

"Do you think they're going to break up?" I asked. That would be rich. It would be so easy for him to walk out on her when she needed him the most. Guys like that infuriated me to no end. She was so young—too young to deal with this burden alone. Aunt Bethany was constantly on her phone, messaging agents, scouting for talent, or setting up appointments with clients. She hadn't even noticed how Hannah picked at her food or escaped to the bathroom to throw up whenever she cooked Hannah eggs in the morning.

"I don't know." She twisted a strand of hair around her finger. "Evan has been under a lot of stress lately. Maybe he'll come around."

It's not like Evan's stress was going away anytime soon. It was only a matter of time until Hannah's belly got big enough for people to notice. In the meantime, his stress would grow steadily, and I'd be danged if he took it out on my cousin. The dude wasn't handling things so well. If

I was ever stupid enough to get a girl pregnant, I'd do everything I could to take care of her. I was already willing to do it for Destiny when I saw her in line to buy that test in Walmart, and it wasn't even my kid. I shuddered. "It was so horrible when I saw you with that pregnancy test." Did I just say that out loud? Ugh. Watching her play with her hair was so distracting.

"You should've let me pay for it," she said with a determined set to her jaw.

"No way." I stood straighter, puffing my chest a bit. "Paying for it was the least I could do to help."

Aspen walked around the corner with wide, shocked eyes. "Isaac…"

Oh *crap!* She hadn't overheard us, had she?

"You have a lot of nerve. Acting like you're so holy," she sneered, jabbing a finger at my sternum.

"Don't touch me," I said, stepping away from her. "What the heck are you talking about?"

"I'm talking about how you always say you're waiting until marriage."

Where did she get off talking to me like that? I gritted my teeth and took a deep breath to hold off the string of insults straining to fly from my mouth. The last thing I needed right now was to make her more angry and jealous than she already was. "What I choose to do or not do with my body is none of your business," I said stiffly. It didn't matter that I hadn't done anything. It bugged me that she thought she had a say over anything in my life.

Something tightened around her eyes, and she said, "You're nothing but a fake and a liar."

With great effort, I held back the fury threatening to erupt. I could spend a good two hours straight putting Aspen in her place—bare minimum—but at this point, what did it matter? Letting my anger overtake me would only complicate my life even more. Some people weren't worth the trouble.

"If it makes you feel better, you can tell yourself that." I turned to walk away, but just before I did, I caught a glimpse of Destiny's face. Her hardened exterior had chipped away and she was looking at me with a tenderness that gave me the tiniest bit of hope that maybe, just maybe, one day, I could get her back again.

Aspen and Sydney spent all of Primus whispering, provoking Mr. Byrd's wrath more than once. They kept throwing scornful glances at Destiny and me. Destiny refused to meet my eye. Once again, just before class ended, Mr. Byrd gave his little speech about class members getting along. He was absolutely right.

As we were leaving the chapel to cross the campus to the high school, I fell into step beside Destiny.

"Hey," I said, flashing her a smile. I tried to ignore the way my heart was pounding, but it wasn't working.

She stared at me and blinked twice. "What are you doing?"

"Is it okay if I walk you to class?"

"Why?"

"What? I can't even walk with you as a friend?"

"We're not friends, Isaac."

Ouch. What happened to the sweet girl who'd returned for a few minutes by her locker this morning? It was like talking about Hannah and her problems made her forget for just a moment that she was still mad at me. Well, she'd forgotten now. Was she upset because I hadn't completely refuted Aspen's accusation? I ignored the excruciating pain her words caused and said, "That's something that needs to change."

"And why is that?" she asked, crossing her arms.

I stared into her bright blue eyes and said, "Look, I'm sorry about what happened in the hallway with Aspen earlier. But we're going to be spending a lot of time together during the next six weeks until this musical is over, and I'd prefer to not be fighting with you the entire time."

She looked away but continued walking next to me.

"Is that a yes?" I asked hopefully.

"A yes to what?"

"A yes to us being friends?"

She sighed. "Okay. We can be friends."

"Awesome," I said, strolling a bit more lightheartedly. On the outside, I was smiling, but inside, I still longed for what we used to have.

The short time I'd had with Destiny had been a precious gift. Even if I'd lost it, I still had the memories stored away. Each recollection was like a candle on a shelf. Whenever life got hard, I could take a candle down and light it, and for that moment, I could bask in the steady, warm flame. The best thing about my memories was that they were safe. No one could take them from me.

But I took Destiny's from her. Every kiss was tarnished. She'd thought I was a fake and a liar. Looking at her face just now, I hoped she no longer felt that way, but there had to be some lingering doubt.

Otherwise, she would be with me, regardless of whether or not Preston had captured her attention.

Being just friends with her would never be enough.

Chapter 39

Rumors

Destiny

"What's with you? I've asked you three times to hand me that beaker." Hudson's voice broke through my thoughts later that day in chemistry.

"Sorry, I have a lot on my mind. You know, the musical and all," I said.

"I saw Isaac talking to you in the hall earlier." I winced. Unfortunately, Hudson had seen straight to the root of the problem. I couldn't stop thinking about Isaac and how Aspen had overheard our conversation. I had to protect Hannah's secret, even if it meant Aspen would be spreading rumors about me.

"Does he still think he has a chance with you after what he did?"

"Isaac says he wants to be friends now."

Hudson let loose a bark of laughter. "Sure he does."

"Why's that funny?" I asked.

"Destiny, come on. Everyone knows there's no such thing as a single guy who wants to be 'just friends' with a girl."

"That's not true," I insisted.

"Oh, he may say it, but he doesn't mean it."

I didn't have long to contemplate what he actually meant by that because there was a commotion across the room. A few students scrambled around, opening a window to allow in a frigid burst of air.

"Oh my gosh. That's freezing." I reached for my jacket on the back of my chair, but it wasn't there. Then I remembered stuffing it in the bottom of my locker earlier, because the hall had felt stuffy after I'd talked to Isaac.

"You want to borrow this?" Hudson offered me his black skater jacket.

"Thanks," I said, taking it from him and slipping it on. It was still warm from his body and smelled like surfer-boy cologne. Wouldn't Olivia be jealous if she saw me now?

When the bell rang a few minutes later, Shanice came up to me, to set up a study date at her house. We got into a long conversation about how DeShawn had been treating her. By the time we were finished talking, Hudson was long gone and I was still wearing his jacket. Oh, well, I'd just get it to him later. But I had a *Les Mis* practice during lunch, and I didn't see him again for the rest of the day.

After school, in the parking lot, I had my regular jacket on and Hudson's slung over my arm as I looked around for him. A strange ringtone sounded, and I fumbled with Hudson's coat to see where it was coming from. I reached my hand into a pocket and pulled out his phone.

As I pulled it out, my finger slipped, effectively answering the call. Whoops.

"Hello?" I said, quickly pressing the phone to my ear.

"Destiny?"

"Olivia?" She'd worked up the courage to call him?

"Oh. I must have misdialed your number. I meant to call someone else. Sorry about that."

"No problem," I chirped. Seconds after the line went dead, the phone rang again, but this time, I knew better than to answer it. She left a voice mail and then a text as well.

Part of me was dying to see what she had to say to Hudson, but at the same time I remembered how she'd snooped on my texts with Isaac. I would be the better person and give her the space and respect I'd wished she'd given me.

Across the parking lot, Olivia was walking toward me like nothing had just happened. Behind her, a crowd of junior girls passed, staring at me and whispering furiously. I didn't have much time to contemplate the meaning of it because, seconds later, Isaac and Evelyn stepped down from the sidewalk together. She ran her fingers through her luscious blonde hair and let it fall around her face like gold shimmering in the winter sunlight. He gave her a prize-winning smile and laughed at something she said.

I hated to admit how good they looked together. And she was genuinely a nice girl. As far as I knew, she was a good Christian girl, not at all snotty like Aspen. I should be glad for him, right? He deserved to find happiness again.

I turned away, and continued scanning the parking lot for Hudson. If he didn't show up soon, I'd be forced to take his stuff home with me. Michael came out of the building to drive us home, and by then, I realized Hudson's car wasn't even in the parking lot anymore. I shrugged and stuffed his jacket into my backpack.

That night his phone went off so many times I decided to silence it before Olivia discovered I had his phone. As I unlocked it, my eyes caught on the images displaying three missed calls and ten unopened text messages. It was tempting to check them, but I restrained myself.

As I fiddled with the phone to figure out how to put it on silent another text from Olivia flashed onto the screen. *So you're going to kiss me again and then not talk to me all day?*

Kiss!? I stood frozen, staring at the screen in disbelief. The door opened and Olivia came into our room with her phone in hand. I slipped his phone into the back pocket of my jeans casually. *Shiz.* I still hadn't silenced it.

"What's up, Livie?" I said, forcing nonchalance into my voice.

"Not much," she muttered, her thumbs flying over her phone. She sunk onto her bed, eyes still focused on her phone, and kicked off her pink, fuzzy slippers.

A light knock sounded on my door. "Come in," I called.

The door cracked open hesitantly.

"Oh hey, Preston," I said, hopping up from the bed. It felt like ages since I'd last seen him, even though I'd just hugged him goodbye in the church parking lot this morning after seminary. "I didn't know you were coming over!"

"I wanted to surprise you," he said.

"What's the occasion?" I asked stepping out into the hallway, shutting the door behind me.

"Do I need an occasion to see the most beautiful girl I know?" he asked with an irresistible grin.

"Of course not," I said.

"Good. But actually there is a reason I came over. Know what today is?" he asked, leaning closer to me and lowering his voice.

"Nope," I stepped into the hallway and shut the door behind me.

"It's the one-month anniversary of our first kiss," he murmured.

"Oh wow. It totally is." How romantic was it that he remembered that? "We should do something to celebrate," I said, stepping closer with a coy smile.

"I'm way ahead of you," he said with a grin, taking my hand in his.

As we walked through the family room, Mom came to the kitchen doorway. "Have fun, you two."

"She knows about this?" I squeaked, once we were on the front porch. So not cool.

"She just knows I'm taking you on a date tonight," he explained in a deep, quiet voice. "She doesn't know we're celebrating anything."

"Good." As far as I knew, my parents were almost completely in the dark about how serious my relationship with Preston was, and I hoped to keep it that way. They didn't like the idea of high-school romance much. They were always saying kids should wait until they're out of their teens to get serious. How serious was too serious? How could we know when we'd crossed that line?

As we approached his truck, he surprised me by guiding me toward the woods instead. As we neared the tree house, the forest parted to reveal golden light peeking through the windows.

Preston led me up the steps and pushed open the door. The army cot was missing, and so were all the ratty Barbie dolls and Brianna's poster on the wall. Instead, there was a table set up with a candlelight dinner, complete with steak, shrimp, baked potatoes, and cheesecake. The windows were covered with heavy curtains to keep out the cold, and in the corner there was a little kerosene space heater running. Preston pulled out my chair, and I sat down.

"This is incredible," I breathed. "Did you set this up all by yourself?"

"Not completely," he admitted. "Megan and Brinlee helped some."

I looked over at Preston. How did he do it all? More than once I'd seen his brow crease with worry when he thought I wasn't looking. He'd been through so much lately. "Preston, sometimes I think you try so hard to be the strong one that you don't stop to think about yourself."

"I get that from my mom, you know," he said, smiling thoughtfully. "She's always doing that. She puts on this big smile even when she's going through chemo and throwing up."

"Sometimes it's okay to let go and show your true feelings. You know that, right?" I asked.

"I know," he said softly.

"How is your mom really doing?"

"She's suffering horribly, but like I said, she puts on a happy face. I know she does it for us. She watches the way her failing health is affecting our family, and she worries about being a burden."

"But that's totally valid. It's hard on your family. I've seen what it's done to you."

"And she sees it, too. No matter how we try to sugar coat it, she knows how hard it is for us."

"Well, yeah. She has six kids. You and Megan help out a ton, but you can only do so much."

"Even though we'd give everything to keep her alive, all she sees is how much trouble she causes for us. She knows there's no way we can afford all the treatments she's getting. I think she feels a lot of guilt about it, especially because of the way my dad plans to pay for the treatments."

"What do you mean?" I asked.

"Well, Dad's draining all the kids' college funds. And that won't even pay a quarter of what they're going to owe."

"Wow." I hadn't even though about the financial aspect of it.

About halfway through dinner, the phone in my pocket buzzed, and I glanced at it under the table. *You aren't mad at me, are you? When you get this please just message me back.*

I looked back up to see Preston studying me.

Chapter 40

Secret Messages

Preston

Destiny looked down at her lap, her brow furrowing for a moment, before looking up at me hesitantly, indecision written all over her face.

"Is everything okay?" I asked.

Fear clenched my stomach. She wasn't texting *him*, was she?

"I'm worried about Olivia."

My brows shot up. "Olivia?" She was the last person I expected Destiny to be worried about.

She launched into this story of how she'd been borrowing Hudson's coat, and had found his phone in the pocket when Olivia had called it.

"Is that it?" I asked, pointing toward the phone she'd been trying to conceal in her lap.

"Yes," she said, pulling it out reluctantly.

"Can I see it?" I asked, reaching for it.

She handed it to me reluctantly with a guilty expression on her face. I scanned through the messages on his phone, checking several messaging apps as well. "Destiny, this is serious."

"What is it?"

"If this were my little sister, I'd be furious with the guy."

"Why. What did he do?" she asked.

"It looks like they've been meeting at night in the woods for months."

"What?" she yelped. "That can't be true."

"No, it definitely is," I confirmed, studying the texts a second time.

"How? If she'd been sneaking out, I would have heard her leaving."

"Well, not that I would know from personal experience," I said slowly, my face heating up at the thought of spending my nights with Destiny by my side. "But according to Olivia, you're an extremely sound sleeper."

She gaped at me. "The missing screen…" she said under her breath, and then her face twisted in furious disbelief.

I had no idea what she was talking about, but this missing screen was clearly a sore spot with her.

"And it hasn't been back on in months because the frame was bent. We kept meaning to replace it," she said more to herself than to me.

"What do we do now?" I asked. "Tell your parents? Have Michael threaten the guy?"

"No," Destiny said firmly. "She told on me behind my back like that, and it was awful. Let me handle it. I'll talk to her and see what's really going on."

My jaw tightened, but I nodded. "Okay. If you think that's best, I'll trust your judgment." I didn't know how Olivia had gone behind her back, but I was pretty sure it had to do with Isaac. The less I heard about his time with Destiny, the better. I still felt a sickening rage whenever I thought about him touching her. If he ever tried it again…

She brightened and reached a hand out to take the phone from me. Without even glancing at the display or scrolling through any of the messages, she slipped it into the back pocket of her jeans.

Chapter 41

Return the Phone

Destiny

"You and Olivia, huh?" I said coming up behind Hudson as he stood at his locker.

"I don't have any idea what you're talking about." He turned around to face me, one side of his mouth hitched up.

"Sure, you don't," I said slapping the phone into one of his hands.

"So, that's where it's been!" he said without a shred of guilt on his face.

"I tried to give your coat back to you after our chem lab yesterday, but you took off."

He shrugged. "Doctor's appointment. I have ADHD, and I was due for a checkup."

"Whatever. I just want you to know I wasn't snooping. I was trying to give you back your jacket, and she wouldn't stop calling and texting you."

He smiled brilliantly. "I can't even tell you how amazing your sister is."

I punched him in the arm. Hard.

"Ow! What'd you do that for?"

"That's my baby sister! If this gets back to Michael, it won't be pretty."

Fear flashed across his face momentarily. But then it was gone, replaced by his usual cocky nonchalance. He shrugged. "Whatever happens, happens."

"Olivia's not allowed to date until she's sixteen," I said.

"Who said we were dating?" he said.

"I…uh…" He had a point. Technically, they weren't going out on official dates to dinner or the movies, but still. "Well. Er. Don't you think meeting in the woods counts as dating?"

"Who said we were meeting in the woods?" he asked smoothly.

"Your phone did," I said. I didn't see it with my own eyes, but Preston would never lie to me.

He shoved it deep into his back pocket deliberately. "And you can prove that, how?"

"Look," I said. "I'm not trying to be a tattletale. I'm the last person to ever do something like that. I know how horrible it can be, but that doesn't change the fact that if Michael or my parents find out, it's not going to go so well for y'all."

"Thanks for the tip, but I'm pretty sure we can handle it."

"I won't tell your secret, but you'd better not break my sister's heart or I'll break your face," I said.

"I'd like to see you try." He chuckled.

"Oh no, you wouldn't," I said, beating my fist into an open hand with a wicked grin. "And when I'm done, I'll send Michael after you next."

"Whoa, down girl." His face softened. "I have no intention of breaking your sister's heart. I wouldn't do that."

"Sure you wouldn't," I said, rolling my eyes. I could spot a player from a mile away, and Hudson fit the profile to a tee.

A group of girls passed and stared at Hudson talking to me like we were the scum of the earth. They whispered something, and all I could catch was "trashy." Another girl shook her head and said, "Guys, sometimes people make mistakes. We shouldn't judge her."

What was *that* supposed to mean?

After school, when I was in the bathroom, a few girls came in talking. It sounded like Jessie Larsen and Sydney Carter, which was weird because they didn't usually get along. "I heard she seduced him into going to church with her," Sydney said.

"Yeah, well, look where that got her," Jessie said. "Although I have no idea how she could possibly seduce him."

"I know. Aspen said he kept pretty strict standards."

"That's not what I meant. I don't see how he would be attracted enough to her to take it that far."

"Jessie, that's horrible!" Sydney cackled gleefully.

Tears burned my eyes, and I waited for them to leave before I came out of my stall. I hated the stupid rumors going around about me. I growled in frustration. I clenched my fists to keep from beating the wall shattering a mirror. How could I refute them without exposing the truth about Hannah?

My fists unclenched at my sides as a realization came to me. As long as they were fixated on me being the one pregnant one, Hannah was off their radar. Did it matter what they thought about me? They already thought I was a freak. Why not add a teen pregnancy to the list? It was something I could actually do to help her. I wasn't sure how long Hannah would be able to keep her pregnancy a secret, but hopefully she'd be able to last until we performed *Les Mis*.

I came out of the bathroom and headed to the parking lot to find Michael's car. Instead, I found Isaac. He was getting into his truck, but the moment he saw me pass by, he called out to me.

I turned to him and made a face. What now?

Chapter 42

Reputations

Isaac

"Destiny!" I called to her from across the Bethel parking lot. Her head whipped around, and I waved her closer. She glanced at the group of senior girls gossiping around Aspen's Mustang, and even from fifty feet away, I could see her chin lift in resolution. She approached me, keeping her eyes away from the group of girls to her left.

"I owe you an apology," I said seriously, standing by my open truck door.

For what?" she asked as she approached.

"For talking about the pregnancy test so openly," I said once she was close enough to talk quietly. "Because of me, Aspen's been spreading rumors that you're pregnant."

"Yeah. I've noticed," she said, crossing her arms.

"Well, we need to tell them it's not true."

"Why? So you can protect your precious reputation?"

"No. So we can protect yours," I said.

Her mouth fell open, and she stepped so close that my breath caught in my throat. "Listen, Isaac. There's no 'we.' I told you before. I'm with Preston now."

Ouch.

"And I don't care about my reputation," she said offhandedly. "I care about protecting Hannah. She's my best friend. She'd do it for me in a heartbeat. My heart aches every time I see her escape with a hall pass and a green face to go throw up. It's been tough."

"I know you say you don't care and you want to protect Hannah, but she's the one who made the mistake. You shouldn't be punished for her sins."

"She's your cousin. Listen to yourself, Isaac. You're starting to sound like one of them."

"I *am* one of them."

My words hit her in the face like a wave of icy water. "You're right," she said softer, taking a step away from me. "Somehow, along the way, I forgot."

Ugh. When was religion ever going to stop coming between us? "I'm sorry, Destiny. I didn't mean it that way."

"Look, Isaac. Hannah can't change what she did in the past. Life's going to punish her enough as it is. Do you know how helpless I've felt around her lately?"

"Yeah, I do. Because that's exactly how I feel," I said.

Her eyes softened. She bit her lip and averted her eyes. "Well, I've finally found a way to help her. Let me do this," she said with a stubborn tilt to her chin.

"No way. It's going to spiral out of control until you find yourself in the headmaster's office again."

"I'm not scared of your dad," she insisted, staring back at the school.

Yeah, right. I didn't believe *that* for a second.

Chapter 43

Seminary

Destiny

It was one of those glorious spring mornings where the sunbeams filter through the trees like beacons of sparkling gold and the birds serenade you with their achingly sweet songs. The freezing days of winter were long behind us. All around, the redbuds and dogwoods bloomed. Their blossoms were scattered clusters of pink and white, peeking through bare branches that had sprouted tiny green leaves. Isaac and I were curled up in the hammock together, and he sang a magical tune softly in my ear. When the song ended, he whispered in my ear, "Man, I've missed you. You have no idea how much I care about you, Destiny."

Like I had so many times before, I traced the white calluses on his fingertips he'd gotten from playing his guitar. It made me think of the times he'd serenaded me at Hannah's house. "Yes, I do. I'm pretty sure I feel the same way about you, too."

"Please…don't ever leave me again," he said huskily. His voice sounded so heartbreakingly vulnerable. I couldn't let it go on. Suddenly, I was filled with an intense desire to help him mend his broken heart.

I twisted toward him and placed my hand against his clean-shaven jaw. "I'm not going anywhere. I promise."

His eyes crinkled softly around the corners. He brushed the hair back from my eyes like he had so many times before. The transcendent smile that appeared on Isaac's face was the last thing I saw before I woke up to the darkness of my room. My heart pounded heavily against my ribcage. Was my heart speaking what my mind refused to admit? Did I really miss Isaac, or was this all just a silly dream?

It wasn't the first night I'd had a dream about Isaac. For a while I hadn't had any, but the more he kept popping up in my life, the more frequently the dreams came. The other dreams had been snapshots from the past, almost like reliving my memories. This one was from the future.

I reached for my phone on my bedside table and lit the display. I had three minutes before my alarm was supposed to go off. I rolled onto my back and stared into the darkness as my mind reeled. I was supposed to be over Isaac now. We were going to be just friends and everything was supposed to be okay. But it wasn't. I wanted him more than ever now.

My alarm went off, and I rolled out of bed. As I went through the motions of getting ready for the day, confusion swirled through my mind, alternating between the two guys.

Preston. Isaac. Preston. Isaac.

Michael and I walked into the building at six twenty. Brother Bernard brought donuts and orange juice to seminary every Friday. I grabbed a plastic cup, filled it, and gingerly picked up a glazed donut with a red-checkered napkin.

"Sleep well?" Preston asked as he came up beside me.

"Not really."

"I shouldn't have kept you up so late last night." Preston had helped me with my geometry homework over the phone until Mom made me hang up to go to bed. But that wasn't why I hadn't slept well. Dogwood blossoms and a warm breeze flitted through my mind again.

Focus, Destiny. Focus. Preston is talking to you. Remember him? Your boyfriend? I plastered a grin over my face. "I don't mind you keeping me up."

"Y'all are kind of nauseating. You know that, right?" Michael said as he passed us with a mouthful of donut.

"We're nauseating? You're the one talking with your mouth full," I teased.

Michael made a face and took a seat around one of the folding tables arranged in a u-shape in the center of the room. Preston and I sat around the corner from him, holding hands under the table.

Michael noticed, but looked away with a slight smile on his face.

"What the heck is he doing here?" Preston growled under his breath.

Good question. I twisted around in my chair and locked eyes with Isaac. My breath hitched in my throat as I relived the feeling of my hand on his clean-shaven jaw. My cheeks burned furiously hot as the vivid dream came rushing back to me. I angled my face away from Preston so he wouldn't see my face turning beet red.

Isaac walked up to Brother Bernard and shook hands with him like a Mormon who'd been born and raised in the Church. "You must be Isaac. The elders called me last night to tell me you'd be joining us." He turned to the class. "Everyone, this is Isaac Robinson. He's been taking the discussions with the missionaries for a few months now and has decided to join our seminary class."

Michael and Preston gaped at him for a moment, but Michael composed himself and stood to greet Isaac with a polite handshake.

Megan, who had taken the seat next to me, shot me an inquiring look, but I gave what hopefully looked like a casual shrug.

"Did you know he was coming?" Preston leaned over and whispered to me.

"I had no idea."

I sat up straighter as Isaac lowered himself into the empty chair next to Michael, around the corner of the tables, so he was seated directly diagonal to me. I'd thought for sure he'd given up on anything having to do with the Church when I'd rejected him so openly on the sidewalk outside my home, but apparently I was wrong. I carefully avoided his gaze but felt his eyes on me, burning holes into my skin. The heat in my face traveled down my neck as I remembered how vivid the dream about Isaac had been. Preston shifted closer to me, cutting off the fantasy threatening to replay through my mind.

A few minutes later, we delved deeply into the lesson. We were studying the book of Romans, something Isaac knew better than the lyrics to *Les Mis*.

I watched Isaac out of the corner of my eye. He kept strangely quiet, taking notes in a spiral-bound notebook. I would've expected him to have more to say. Preston was quiet as well and sat rigidly in his chair.

Seminary ended, and Preston and I left without a word to Isaac. I climbed into Michael's car before Isaac could have the chance to talk to me. I wasn't going to fall for him again. We were over. I told myself that repeatedly, but why did my heart still ache when I looked at him? Michael came out of the building with Isaac. They talked like old friends. Had Michael assumed that since I was with Preston it was okay to be friends with Isaac? It was nice to see Michael finally being nice to Isaac. He must have forgiven him.

I felt a tug in the pit of my stomach as I watched him give Michael a friendly, grateful smile. Guilt seared through me. I should have been the one to welcome him, set aside my feelings, and reached to him as a friend. Maybe if it weren't for the dreams I'd been having about him I would have. But there was no way I could face him when every time I looked at him all I wanted was to reenact everything I'd just dreamt about.

Isaac climbed into his truck and shut the door, pulling on a hat before backing his truck out. As he passed, I got a clear view of his profile. I caught my bottom lip between my teeth and my stomach twisted into a strange knot. It was his favorite hat, the same one I'd thrown at Michael when I'd found it in my room the day after the breakup. I couldn't bear to give it back myself. Michael never told me he'd actually given it back, and I hadn't seen Isaac wear it in months. A shudder ran through me as I remembered the night he gave it to me. Everything had felt so perfect at that moment. Seeing him wear it again made me want to snatch it off so I could run my fingers through his lush, dark hair.

I jumped as the door to the Civic opened. Michael climbed into the driver's seat. "You okay?"

I shrugged my coat off, suddenly feeling hot even though the air was chilly. "Yeah. I'm fine."

Michael studied my face for a moment before cranking up the engine. "You just seem a little on edge this morning."

"Nah, not really. It's cool that Isaac came today, huh?" I forced my words to sound casual.

"I have to admit, I was kind of surprised by it."

"I feel kind of bad that I wasn't friendlier to him."

"That's what I'm here for, sis."

Suddenly Michael's welcoming attitude toward Isaac made perfect sense. Dad had probably put him up to it to keep me from feeling obligated to spend time with Isaac if he ever came back to church.

I narrowed my eyes. Why couldn't they just mind their own business and let me talk to Isaac whenever I wanted? I didn't need Michael's protection. I was perfectly capable of befriending Isaac all on my own.

As Michael drove out of the parking lot I pulled out my phone, and stared at the screen. It was time to do something I'd been avoiding for what seemed like a very long time. I opened my text messages folder and scrolled down until I reached November.

There they were. The last texts Isaac had sent me. I'd never allowed myself to read them before.

I'm sorry for what I did.

Please forgive me.

I'd give up everything for you. Do you actually think I still feel that way?

I had no idea who you really were then. Now that I know better, I would never do anything to hurt you or your family.

Can't you see how much I've changed? It was you. You made me a better person.

Please answer me. I have to tell you something important.

By the time I read his final message, tears had formed in the corners of my eyes.

Destiny?

There was so much hopelessness in that last plea. After that, nothing. He'd given up. And then Evelyn had stepped into his life.

What had I done? Because of my own stubbornness, I lost this amazing guy. He'd put his heart on a silver platter for me, and I'd trampled it carelessly.

"Whatcha looking at?" Michael asked.

"Just trying to figure some things out."

His brow lifted inquisitively, but he kept his eyes on the road.

Could I ever consider going back to Isaac? If I did, would it be for the best, or would I be walking into one of the biggest mistakes of my life?

Chapter 44

Eternity

Preston

When I spotted Isaac walking into the chapel on Sunday, I shifted in my seat on the stand uncomfortably. Really? Was he going to start following us everywhere? Destiny's mom chatted easily with him and Dad and Michael crossed the room to welcome him. Bishop Clark even went up to him and shook his hand. It seemed like everyone had completely forgiven him for what he'd done. During sacrament meeting he sat between Michael and the missionaries on the opposite end of the pew from where Destiny was sitting. It seemed that Bishop Clark and Michael were doing everything they could to keep him away from Destiny, while still giving him the opportunity to feel like they wanted him there. I thought Destiny would have been upset, but she didn't seem to mind that he'd come. She gave him a polite smile and a wave, but thankfully, kept it to that.

The next Monday Isaac showed up at seminary again and began participating more in the lesson. Everything seemed to be going fine, until the subject of eternal marriage came up.

He looked from me to Destiny and then away, his expression unreadable. Brother Bernard got into some deep doctrinal stuff about marriage in the covenant, and as Isaac grilled him with questions, Destiny squirmed in her seat.

"The missionaries were teaching me a little bit about this. You go to the temple to be sealed, right? Then, when you die, you're never parted? I have to say it definitely holds some appeal."

Destiny's knuckles were white as she gripped the table in front of her. What was with her? I thought she was over him finally. Maybe I'd thought wrong. I stared at her white knuckles and my heart raced. Was she imagining marriage with him? When she was in the tree house the day she'd broken up with him, she'd admitted to me that she'd dreamed he'd convert and build her a white house on some piece of land he had somewhere. At the time, she'd sounded a bit crazy, but now I was wondering if maybe there actually was a piece of land like that. Was that what she was thinking about now? I gripped the table as well. Now *my* knuckles were white.

Throughout the next several days, Destiny gradually began warming up to Isaac. She laughed at his jokes and helped answer some of his questions. Despite her insistence that she was just friends with him, I caught her staring at Isaac more than once when she thought I wasn't watching. Every time I caught him smiling at her or sharing an inside joke with her, I wanted to pound his face. By the time Friday rolled around, I'd seen Isaac every day, except Saturday, for the past seven days, and I was at the edge of my breaking point.

Most of the class had left, but Isaac was at the front of the classroom, asking Brother Bernard some deep doctrinal questions. Finally, Brother Bernard excused himself with the promise that he'd be sure to answer more questions when he wasn't running late for work. Destiny and I were sitting in the back of the room talking with Michael and Megan, and we got up to go at the same moment Isaac turned to leave. As we walked toward the cabinet to put our scriptures away, Isaac walked past and bumped into my shoulder with his. "What was that for?" I growled.

He turned to face me. "Are you accusing me of doing that on purpose?"

"Yeah, I am. What are you gonna do about it?" I said, stretching to my full height.

Isaac stepped closer, his eyes level with mine as he said, "Just because I had her first doesn't give you an excuse to treat me like I'm a jerk."

"What are you even doing here?" I spat. "Why don't you just go back to being a Baptist and leave us in peace?"

"Whoa, take it easy, bro," Michael said from behind me.

"Preston," Destiny scolded. "Don't talk to him like that! That was totally out of line!"

Isaac's eyes flicked to Destiny and one side of his mouth pulled up. "You can't handle the fact that she might still want me," Isaac taunted.

I slammed him against the wall with one hand and landed a punch into that pretty-boy face of his with the other. And man, it felt good to finally do it. Adrenaline coursed through me as I pounded my fist into his gut. He responded by shoving me back into the table and chairs behind me. I flew my hands backward and used the table as a springboard to bounce back into the fight. I thrust another punch at him, but he grabbed my arm and twisted it behind my back. He held me there pinned, my heart pounding as Destiny stepped forward, her eyes flashing.

"Let him go, Isaac."

He immediately released my arm, and I stepped away.

"I'm ashamed of both of you! Especially you, Preston. I thought you were better than this." The disappointment in her eyes was the punch to the gut I never received. "I guess I was wrong."

She ran from the room, and I rushed out into the hall to find her. She had her back to me with her arms crossed and her head leaning against the wall.

"I'm sorry, Destiny."

"What is wrong with you?" she asked in a disgusted voice, without turning around.

"I'm sorry." Was I really? I hated that Destiny was there to see it, but I didn't regret punching Isaac, even for a moment. He'd had it coming to him for a long time.

"Is that all you can say? He's making an effort to learn more about our church. Whether he wants me or not, you have no reason to say that stuff to him."

"I know. I've been an insensitive jerk."

"Yes. You have," she interjected. "You might as well face it, Preston. Isaac is a part of my life. He's going to be coming to church, and he just might be here to stay. My family has put their hard feelings aside to help Isaac feel welcome at church. You should learn to do the same."

She walked toward the exit and out into the cold morning air. What she was asking felt completely impossible at the moment. How could I continue going to church and be expected to be nice to this guy when he was constantly shoving it in my face that my girlfriend still has a thing for him? I had to figure it out somehow or I could very well lose Destiny over it.

"Let me make it up to you," I said when we neared my truck.

"I don't know. I'm starting to think that maybe we should cool things off between the two of us."

My heart plummeted to my feet. She wasn't serious, was she? "Please, Destiny. I said I was sorry. Just give me another chance."

She stared at my pleading face, and slowly her hardened expression softened. "What did you have in mind?"

"Dinner tonight. I'll take you anywhere you want to go."

"How about the Japanese place over by Gold's Gym?"

Relief washed over me. "That sounds perfect."

Just then Michael, Megan, and Isaac came out of the building. Isaac glanced at Destiny leaning against my truck, huddled up close to me, and his eyes jerked away.

As they approached, Destiny gave my hand a squeeze and took a step away. Isaac watched her steadily as she climbed into Michael's car.

Why, oh why, couldn't he go away and leave us alone?

Chapter 45

The Fountain

Destiny

Isaac pulled into the Bethel parking lot immediately after Michael and I arrived. He'd been following us the entire way from the church. The more I thought about it, the more I realized that other than taunting Preston about me still wanting him, Isaac really hadn't done anything that wrong to Preston. In fact, Preston had been getting on my nerves lately, and now that I didn't have a good reason to reject Isaac, the list of reasons to stay away from him was getting shorter and shorter.

Isaac crossed the pavement to me from his assigned parking spot. "Hey, Isaac," Michael said.

"Hey, man." His eyes slid to me, and the apology I read there was unmistakable. "Can I talk to you for a second, Destiny?"

"Um. Sure." I glanced in Michael's direction, but he didn't budge from his spot. "Give us a minute, will you, Michael?"

A muscle twitched in his jaw and I thought he wasn't going to, but after a moment he mumbled, "I'll see you guys around."

Isaac and I watched Michael walk toward the building, and when he was out of earshot, Isaac turned to me. "I'm sorry about what happened earlier."

My mouth twisted downward. "Yeah. That was intense." I raised my eyes to meet his. "But thank you for your apology. I appreciate that. Can I ask you a question?"

"Yeah."

"Why didn't you punch him back after he hit you twice?"

Isaac threw his hands to the sides. "I'm just trying to be the bigger man."

"Preston and I aren't doing so well." The words popped out of my mouth unexpectedly. Why did I suddenly feel the need to announce that to Isaac?

"Well, if you ever decide to walk away from him, I'll always be here waiting for you."

"I appreciate that, I really do, but we're trying to work things out."

Isaac shrugged uncomfortably. "Okay. But my offer still stands."

That day in study hall, Hannah told me that she was still craving Mexican, despite her fiasco at Taco Bell. She was raving on and on about this new restaurant with an amazing romantic atmosphere that Evan had taken her to. By the time school was over, my mouth was watering for the Mexican place. Hopefully, Preston wouldn't mind me switching restaurants at the last minute. I pulled out my phone and sped down my contacts list to send him a quick text.

I changed my mind. Can we have dinner tonight at the new Mexican place over by Acorn Creek High?

Immediately, a reply came.

Absolutely!! What time?

Is seven too late?

Of course not. I'll see you tonight.

When Preston came to pick me up, it was dark, cold, and rainy.

"Have you talked to Olivia about Hudson yet?" he asked.

"No, not yet."

"You said you were going to handle it. Destiny, she could end up getting raped by this guy. How well do you actually know him?"

"Hudson would never do that. I talked to him. It's obvious that he cares about her."

"Oh sure. He cares enough to sleep with her and get her pregnant."

I cringed at his words. They were hitting way too close to what I'd been helping Hannah through for the past few weeks.

"Destiny, you need to put a stop to this by telling your parents." I hated his bossy tone. It just irked me.

"No, I refuse to be that girl. I hated how everyone was trying to tell me who to date. If I went to Olivia and tried to tell her what to do with her love life, I would be just as bad as she was."

"So you're just going to be stubborn and watch her flush her life down the toilet? Nothing good can come from this. And it's even worse for her because she's only fourteen. Did you know that the younger girls are when they get their first boyfriend, the more likely they are to end up pregnant out of wedlock?"

"Preston! Back off. You've made your point. Now just drop it."

"Didn't you learn anything from your time with Isaac? Look what happened to you when you dated a nonmember."

Oh no. He did *not* just go there. Had Michael been poisoning his brain about Isaac all this time? "I was wrong about Isaac," I said.

"You were wrong about him?" his voice escalated. "So you're considering going back?"

"I didn't mean it like that," I protested a little too defensively. There was an awful lot of truth to what he was implying. Wasn't that exactly what I'd been debating in my head for the past week? That my dream was a prediction of the future, that Isaac and I were meant to be together, and that the white house would actually become a reality for us? I had to patch this mess up, and quickly. "What I meant was, he might have started out hating Mormons, but he doesn't hate them anymore."

Preston relaxed a notch. "How can you be sure, Destiny? I don't trust the guy. He's such a smooth talker you never know what he's really thinking."

I used to think that, but not so much anymore. What if I had been wrong about him? I couldn't imagine everything he would be suffering if that were true.

He flipped on his blinker and took a right turn.

"What are you doing? You were supposed to turn left there."

"No, I have to turn right. You're not making any sense."

"But we switched it to the Mexican place," I reminded him.

"Since when?"

"Since this afternoon, remember?" I said. "I texted you."

"No, you didn't."

"Yes, I did! Don't tell me I didn't text you when I know I did."

"Well, I didn't get it. I checked my phone right before I came over to pick you up, and I specifically remember that I didn't have any texts."

Why would he lie to me about something like that? He was being so weird. "You don't have to be so rude about it," I said.

"I'm not being rude!" he said defensively.

"Can we please just go to the Mexican restaurant?" I asked.

"Whatever," he muttered. He turned into a neighborhood and headed back in the direction of the Mexican restaurant.

A few minutes later, Preston turned into the parking lot of the restaurant. "Wow. This place is packed."

My phone buzzed in my hand, and even though I knew it bugged him when I paid more attention to my phone than to him, I looked down at it.

I'm here now. I just got us a table next to the fountain.

It was from *Preston ;)*

I swallowed back a gasp. Suddenly, I knew where the missing text messages had gone.

Preston circled the parking lot slowly, looking for an open spot as the rain beat down on the windshield.

Isaac thought I was ready to forgive him, and instead of being bitter and resentful and angry like he had every right to be, he was in there waiting for me. And he was willing to give me a second chance.

But what about Preston? He couldn't know Isaac was here waiting for me. He'd find out that I had used his name as a code word to hide my relationship with Isaac last fall, and it would crush him. He was suffering enough with his family's issues as it was.

"Would you mind dropping me at the door?" I asked. "I need to go to the bathroom."

"Sure," he said. "Just try to get our names on the list. It's probably going to be a long wait."

"Okay," I said, opening the door and stepping out into the downpour. When I got inside, I walked up to a plump Hispanic hostess with tight black curls, whose name tag read *Isabel*. "I'm dining here with my boyfriend, but I have another friend who is here as well. Is it all right if I go say hi to him super fast?"

"Sure," Isabel said. "Let me get you on the list, and I'll give you your buzzer so that when your table is ready you can know to come back to the front."

"Okay, thanks," I said, giving her my name and taking the buzzer from her. "Oh," I said, remembering. "He said he was sitting over by the fountain. Which way is that?"

"Well, the fountain is in the very center of the restaurant. What does your friend look like?"

"Um." I blushed. "He has dark hair. He's eighteen."

"Hmmm."

I sighed. I couldn't believe I was admitting this to her when I'd just told her I was here with my boyfriend. "He's, uh." I cleared my throat. "Really attractive."

She got all starry-eyed for a minute. "Oh, I know *exactly* who you mean. You're looking for that hottie over there in that sexy V-neck sweater. I could never forget a face like that," she said passionately.

I rolled my eyes. I knew the feeling well.

She gave me directions, and I thanked her again, tucking the buzzer into my coat pocket.

"Have fun talking to your *friend*. Hopefully your boyfriend won't mind too much," she said with a dimpled grin.

I turned from her as she gave me a wink. Hannah was right about this place. It was absolutely beautiful. It was like I'd stepped into a charming little Mexican town. The restaurant was designed to feel like a courtyard with the fountain situated in the center of the room. The glass ceiling was surrounded by fake, clay-tiled rooftops, supported by decorative archways made from adobe. High above my head hung star-shaped lanterns and lacey, colorful banners stretched across the expanse of the room. The floor was paved with flat stones, and there were potted palms, ferns, and brightly colored flowers everywhere.

The fountain itself was stunning. Its three rounded tiers were covered with intricate detail, and beneath all the pennies, the bottom was covered with bright blue tiles with the occasional yellow or orange accent tile. Flowering lilies floated on the surface of the water.

My eyes drifted past the fountain, and I spotted him sitting on the other side of the courtyard. I stood motionless, watching as he accepted a drink from his waitress. He thanked her and sipped it thoughtfully. He looked nervous, like he didn't expect me to show. At that moment, his eyes lifted and focused on me. Immediately, he pushed up from his chair and crossed the courtyard.

Chapter 46

Angel

Isaac

As I walked toward her, every step seemed to be in slow motion. She was so beautiful, standing there like a mirage. Her hair was pulled back from her face with tiny braids woven through her curls, and she was wearing a white dress that reached all the way to the floor. She looked like a blue-eyed Latina angel standing in the middle of a Mexican courtyard. I had the sudden urge to pluck one of the red flowers from the vines creeping up the side of the archway next to me and tuck it into her hair.

But I didn't.

I still wasn't sure what this meeting was all about. What exactly did she change her mind about? Did she want me back, or was she just accepting me as her friend? I would take anything I could get at this point.

"Isaac," she said, her voice barely above a whisper when I came close to her. I almost didn't hear it with the babbling of the fountain beside us.

"Hey," I murmured.

"I finally read your text messages," she said. "You know, the ones you sent…before."

"You mean from back in November?"

She nodded.

"You hadn't read those before?" Well, that explained a lot. She wasn't nearly as heartless as I'd thought she had been. So, what did it mean now?

"You said you had to tell me something important. What were you going to tell me?"

How could I ever forget? "I was going to tell you that I was in love with you."

She bit her lip and tore her gaze from mine. "I realized that day that I loved you, too."

"Loved? Like, as in past tense?"

"Isaac, my heart still needs to mend. It's going to take me some time to sort everything out."

"I can respect that, I guess."

"I still really care about you. I want you to know that. The way I treated you…you didn't deserve it. I feel terrible about the way things turned out." Did she mean between the two of us, or ultimately with her and Preston? Did she break up with him? I had so many questions, but if I asked them all at once it might scare her off.

In the end I simply said, "I care about you, too."

Her brows knit together, and my heart twisted in my chest. She was so mesmerizing. I'd given everything to keep her with me except for the one thing that finally ended up pushing her away.

Honesty.

"I should have told you about Will's plan from the start, but I was so messed up from what Aspen did to me. I couldn't afford to lose you." She stared back at me silently. Was she still angry about it? "You were so strong when everything got tough."

"No, I wasn't," she said finally. "I tried to leave you. You were the strong one. You'd just been through that horrible breakup with Aspen. You were going against your friends and family. All for me." She blinked like she'd just had an amazing realization. "All along you've been the strong one." Her face crumpled, and she whispered, "I've been so horrible to you." A lone silver tear ran down her cheek. "I'm so sorry," she said, her voice thick with emotion.

I did the only thing I could think to do. I took her in my arms and held her close to me. She leaned her head against my shoulder, and I buried my face in her curls, savoring the sweet smell of wildflowers.

Chapter 47

Call 911

Preston

I parked the truck and ran through the pounding rain. When I got inside, the restaurant was warm and dry, but extremely crowded. I flicked the water droplets from the sleeve of my leather jacket and pivoted around, looking for Destiny. She probably wasn't out of the bathroom yet. Two spots opened up on the bench behind me, and when no one else immediately sat down, I took a seat.

Right as I was starting to wonder if she'd fallen in, Dad called. Usually I didn't answer my phone on dates, but since Destiny wasn't around, I didn't see the harm in it.

"Hey, Dad, how's the basketball game?"

"Preston…" It was Brinlee. Dad must have forgotten his phone. Brinlee had stayed home to catch up on her favorite show, and Dad had taken the other kids to a basketball game with free tickets he'd gotten from work.

"What's wrong?" I barked. I didn't mean for it to sound so sharp, but the fear in my gut twisted into my words.

"Something's wrong with Mom. She won't wake up."

"Did you call 911?"

"This isn't supposed to happen," she stammered. "Her treatments were working. She was showing improvement. She was going to be okay."

"Brinlee, listen to me. Can you tell if she's breathing?"

"Yeah, she's breathing."

Thank goodness.

"Okay, where is she?"

"She's lying on the bathroom floor. I came in here to get a pair of tweezers because I lost mine and—"

"Brinlee, I want you to hang up and call 911 immediately. I'm going to find Destiny, and we're coming straight over there."

I hung up the phone and walked up to the hostess stand. One of the waitresses, a redhead with a name tag that read "Jessie," was dropping off a couple of menus. If it weren't for the scowl she was wearing, she would have been quite pretty. "Excuse me. I was wondering if one of you would be willing to help me."

The waitress named Jessie looked at me with a spark of recognition, and her scowl changed to a look of shocked revelation. "Oh my gosh! You're Preston, aren't you?"

"Do I know you?"

"Destiny and I used to hang out." She shrugged. "I don't really look the same. And the entire world can be grateful for that." She muttered the last part under her breath.

Jessie? I vaguely remembered her. Red, frizzy hair, braces, and glasses. She was annoying, even back then. "Could you help me find her? I'm having a family emergency, and I need to grab her so we can leave. She told me she was in the bathroom, but I can't exactly go in after her."

"Are y'all dating now?"

When I nodded, she said, "Adorable!" in a syrupy sweet voice. Honestly, she sounded a little too happy about it, and I couldn't for the life of me figure out why.

"Yep. I'm kind of in a huge hurry. Can you help me find her?"

"Well, she's definitely not in the bathroom," she said with a triumphant glint in her eye. "I just saw her. Come with me."

"You're a total lifesaver."

Why was she smiling like that?

Chapter 48

Fixed and Broken

Destiny

Somewhere, in a far-off corner of the restaurant, a mariachi band began playing a romantic song. I pulled away from Isaac and gazed into his eyes. They were so warm and beautiful. The lights were twinkling above, and, for that moment, we weren't in Tennessee anymore. We'd run away to some tropical village in Central America.

And he still wanted me, even after everything I'd done to him.

And just like he had done so many times before, he leaned forward and kissed me. But this time I didn't push him away. The smell of sandalwood enveloped and intoxicated me. I wrapped my hands around him and felt the muscles of his back through his shirt. He groaned and pulled me closer. At that one small gesture, I went wild. All the pain I'd felt suddenly changed into passion, and we were making up for lost time. I was back at my hammock spot with him, and it was like we'd never left each other.

Suddenly, I realized what I was doing, and I pushed away from Isaac in horror. How could I have allowed myself to take it this far? I was here with Preston!

"What's wrong?" he asked. "I…I'm sorry, Destiny."

"No, it's not you. I'm here with Preston."

Isaac's eyes drifted over my shoulder and widened. "You're not kidding."

I scrunched my brow. "What do you mean?"

Isaac pressed his lips together like he was about to deliver bad news. "Destiny…he's standing right over there."

I spun around, and the first person I saw was Jessie Larsen. My jaw fell open. She was wearing an apron and the same red Mexican shirt all the other waitresses wore, except hers clashed with her orange hair. How she'd gotten a job here as a waitress was beyond me, but whatever. She glared at me with a strange mixture of jealousy, disgust, and worst of all, triumph.

Behind her, Preston stood, feet planted firmly on either side of him. I'd never seen him look so haunted and grief-stricken, not even that day in the tree house when he'd found out his mom might be sick again.

He strode forward. "What the heck, Destiny? I don't get it." He shook his head. "I just don't."

I stared back at him, horrified. I had no idea how to give him a logical answer.

"I trusted you," he whispered.

Chapter 49

Chewed Up and Spit Out

Preston

This was no assault. He hadn't forced himself on her. She'd *chosen* him.

The annoying redheaded girl looked over at me and gave me a flirty smile. No, thank you. She looked like she would chew up and spit out any guy who came near her.

She chewed up and spit out her friends, too. If Destiny hadn't been betraying me, I might have felt bad for her.

"What's he doing here?" I asked, barely able to keep my voice from shaking.

"Preston, calm down," she said.

"Calm down? You're kidding, right?" Mom was passed out on the bathroom floor and my girlfriend was making out with her ex in the middle of what was supposed to be our date, and she wanted me to be calm?

"Have you been playing me, Destiny?" I said.

She opened her mouth to speak, but closed it again. "Of course not!"

"Oh sure. So sucking face with your supposed ex doesn't count?" How was I supposed to ever trust her again? She was just as bad as he was.

"Don't speak to her like that!" Isaac said.

"Don't put your hands where they don't belong!" My vision blurred at the edges.

"Maybe you should ask Destiny about that, because last time I checked, she seemed to think they belonged just fine."

Rage burned in my chest, and I slammed my fist into his gut. Destiny gasped, "Stop it." Before I could throw another punch, Destiny wedged herself between us, grabbing my arms.

I pushed her hands away. Our eyes met. "Preston. He doesn't deserve it. He didn't know." I couldn't stay and look at the sadness in her eyes one second longer. So, I turned and bolted for the door.

Chapter 50

Goodbye

Destiny

"Preston! Wait!"

He wove through the crowd and away from me quickly. Guilt and dread built up in the pit of my stomach. I finally caught up to him in the lobby. "Please. You have to wait. Don't just leave it like this," I said, my voice breaking.

He spun around to look at me, and the grief and torture in his eyes were too much to bear. "I have to go," he said.

He stepped out into the rain. "Preston!" I called after him and followed him into the downpour. The rain splashed against the puddles, distorting the reflection of the streetlights in the parking lot.

He didn't turn around.

"Are you just going to leave me here?" I called out.

He shoved his hands in his pockets, hunched his shoulders and disappeared behind a row of cars. I ran after him in the rain, but I couldn't tell what direction he'd gone in. I called for him, but he didn't answer.

I stepped between cars, finally catching up to him. "Listen. He kissed me unexpectedly. I just got caught up in the moment."

He looked at me with a calmness that sickened me. "I have somewhere I need to be." He stepped into his truck.

"No. Stay a minute and try to work this out with me."

"There's nothing to work out, Destiny. You've been flirting with him in seminary right in front of me all week. You kissed him in the middle of our date. It seems to me like you've made your mind up, so why don't you just go back in the restaurant and finish ruining your life with him?"

"No! If that was true, then why would I bother coming out here in the rain?"

"I don't know!" He threw his hands out, palm up. "Guilt?" His phone rang, and he fished it out of his pocket and swept it up to his face. "Brinlee? Did you call the ambulance? Okay, good. Hold on, I'm coming. Give me five minutes." He ended the call.

"What's going on?"

He crammed the phone back into his pocket. "I have to go. Family emergency."

I grabbed his arm frantically. "What do you mean? Is it your mom?"

His mouth hardened into a firm line, and he gave a short nod. "Brinlee found her lying unconscious on the floor."

"What?" I stepped away from him into the rain. "Is she going to be okay?"

"I don't know."

"When did you find this out?"

"While you were supposed to be in the bathroom."

I gasped, raising a hand to my mouth.

He shut the door and drove away, leaving me standing in the rain. My heart broke for him. He'd stood by me, sitting in the cold for days on end, watching me mope over another guy. He'd been scared to let go. His heart had been aching from his mom's illness. And then he'd opened himself to me, given me his fractured heart, tender and vulnerable. And what had I done? I'd smashed it thoughtlessly when I'd allowed myself one selfish, lustful moment.

And now Preston was suffering. I should be the one to help him. But it was too late. Maybe someday he'd learn to forgive me, but for now, he needed time away from me.

He had to be strong for Brinlee and the rest of his family while he was dying inside.

Chapter 51

Come Inside Where It's Warm

Isaac

I searched the parking lot in the pouring rain and finally found her to the far left, standing alone, staring listlessly at an empty parking space. She hadn't even bothered to put her jacket on. I took it from her arms and wrapped it around her shoulders.

"He left me." Behind her words there was a sorrow that made me shift from one foot to the other uncomfortably.

"Come inside and eat. I can give you a ride home."

She looked at me indecisively and then back toward the empty parking space for a long moment. "I'm sorry. I just can't."

"How are you going to get home then?"

"I'll call my mom."

If she made that phone call, any chance I had of getting her back would slip away. "It's just dinner," I said gently. "You don't have to make any sudden decisions tonight."

She released a long, shuddering breath and nodded. "Okay."

I brushed back a clump of wet hair stuck to her cheek. "We're going to figure this out," I promised. "It's going to be okay." She pulled up her hood, and we turned back to the restaurant.

When we got inside, Destiny stiffened. Jessie stood at the kiosk and greeted us with a sour expression. Destiny pulled the buzzer from her pocket and stood there, frozen, staring at Jessie.

There was no way I was letting Jessie antagonize Destiny anymore tonight. I reached for the buzzer, and Destiny hesitantly placed it in my palm. I walked up and handed it to Jessie. "Destiny doesn't need this anymore. You can cross her name off the list."

Jessie scowled and mumbled instructions to the overly-flirty Hispanic hostess who'd shown me my seat. "Okay." The hostess raised her eyebrows and hid a scandalized smile, but she took a pencil and marked a line through Destiny's name without a word.

How awkward. Maybe I should have just let her call her mom. If I'd realized Destiny was still dating Preston, I never would have kissed her. Heck, I wouldn't have even shown up. When I'd gotten her text, I was sure she'd already broken it off with him. And then when she'd responded so passionately to me holding and touching her, the idea had solidified in my mind. If I hadn't been so caught up in the moment, maybe I would have stopped to ask her about Preston. Sometimes you want something so intensely your mind refuses to accept that there might be serious consequences.

I led her back to my table and pulled out her chair for her. Once I was seated, my waitress appeared almost immediately. She must have been watching everything from the sidelines. Great. This wasn't the way I'd imagined the moment when I got back together with Destiny, if that's what this was.

After the waitress took Destiny's drink order and left to fill it, Destiny raised her eyes to mine. "I didn't mean to invite you here tonight."

I'd begun to suspect as much, but I still wasn't clear on how or why. "How do you accidentally ask someone out to dinner?"

She twisted a still-wet curl around one of her fingers and wouldn't meet my eye. "Remember how I insisted that we use those code names back in November? I kind of used Preston with a winkie face as your code name." She winced. "I figured that if anyone saw me texting you, they would think it was him, and it would convince them that I was over you."

"That makes sense," I said. I'd done the same thing when Aspen had asked to come over to sing with me. And it had totally thrown my dad off. "So did it work? Did anyone see you texting this fake Preston?"

She shook her head. "No, they never did."

"But it caused you trouble tonight."

She released a jagged breath. "I feel so bad about what happened to Preston."

"I have to say, I feel bad about that, too. I know what it's like to find your girlfriend in the arms of another guy. I never would have taken it that far if I'd realized you were still with him."

She looked away from me guiltily. "I think he hates me now, and I don't blame him. What I did…" She glanced at me warily and then back down at her lap.

"You regret kissing me." I stated it softly, with resignation.

"No!" Her eyes snapped back to my face. "Ugh. I don't know. I'm going to be honest with you, Isaac, because I care about you a lot."

"Okay," I said slowly.

"I still want him."

Ouch. I'd been hoping for something a bit less painful. I kept my face neutral. "But?"

"But…I can't stop thinking about you."

"Oh." I didn't know what else to say.

"I thought I was so happy with him. Everything seemed so perfect. But then, you kept showing up, and I couldn't think straight. Now I've messed everything up. If I date you, we're right back to where we started with the lies and hiding. I don't know if I can do it again." I braced myself for the words that would keep her away from me forever, but instead, she said, "But at the same time, I don't know how I can live without you."

"Then don't." I leaned forward eagerly in my chair.

"But if I stay with you, I'll hurt Preston."

"That shouldn't be the reason you stay with him. You don't owe him anything."

"How can you say that? He was there for me like I was there for you when Aspen dumped you."

"I didn't ask you to become my girlfriend that day in the barn because I felt obligated to. And I certainly didn't do it because I was trying to dig dirt up on the Mormons. At that point, it didn't matter what your religion was. I did it because I couldn't get you out of my head."

Her eyes glistened and her lips parted slightly, but she didn't speak.

"Here's what I'm trying to say. This is your life. These are your choices. You don't owe me because of our past differences. And you certainly don't owe him, either. Don't let guilt make the decision for you."

"I don't know what to do," she moaned, crossing her arms over the table and resting her head on them.

"You should be with the person who makes you the happiest. And if you decide that person is Preston, then you should be with him."

Her face clouded with mixed emotions. "I think I just need some time. And even though I hate to say this," she said, cringing. "You'd better not kiss me again until I figure this all out." It wasn't ideal, but it was certainly better than her saying she couldn't see me anymore. Or, worse yet, that she wanted to be with him.

I nodded. "I understand."

Chapter 52

Pills

Preston

I dashed across the lawn, and leapt up the porch steps, two at a time. I flung open the door. "Brinlee?"

"Back here."

I raced down the hall to Mom's bedroom. There were two paramedics crouched over Mom, checking her vitals. "How is she?" I asked, heart pounding.

"Are you her son?" The paramedic was tall and thin and had short, cropped, graying hair.

"Yes."

"She's unconscious, but stable. We're going to have to take her in."

I nodded. Brinlee was sitting on Mom's bed watching them with puffy eyes. I sat next to her and put an arm around her, grateful for someone to comfort. I was a hair away from losing my mind completely. "Do you guys know what happened?" They exchanged a glance, and the gray-haired one cleared his throat.

"She tried to kill herself," Brinlee said.

"What?"

The paramedics didn't look up to deny what she was saying.

"I saw them find her empty pill container on the ground next to her. They asked me how many she was supposed to have left."

I'd just bought her those pills with my savings last week. "She should have had another twenty pills in there." A normal reaction to this situation would have been sadness, and maybe, if she'd actually died, I would've felt that way. But she was still alive, and for some reason, all I could feel was fury. Toward Mom. Toward Destiny. They were the two women I'd sacrificed the most for, and on the same night, they'd both chosen to leave me.

Chapter 53

Intruder

Destiny

By the time we left the restaurant, the rain had come to a complete stop. The entire night had been so overwhelming. I didn't even stop to think that maybe getting a ride home with Isaac wasn't the brightest idea. It wasn't until he'd pulled into the driveway that I realized the idiocy of my decision.

Part of the reason riding home with Isaac was so weird was the fact that we didn't know where our relationship stood. Half of me wanted to grab the front of his shirt and pull him toward me, and the other half wanted to walk away and never speak to him again. The worst of all of it was how nice he'd been. If he'd been a selfish jerk or rude to Preston, it would have been easy to push him away. But no. Even when Preston had punched him in the stomach, Isaac hadn't retaliated. During every moment of the entire night, he'd been incredibly understanding and amazing.

Isaac brought the truck to a stop, and I popped off my seatbelt. "Thanks for the ride," I began awkwardly. I turned to see a figure on the opposite side of the front lawn moving cautiously in the shadows where the edge of the woods met the grass. "Is it just me, or is there someone out there?"

"Where?" Isaac asked, leaning toward me to get a better look out my window.

"On the other side of the grass, kind of where the woods start to go uphill," I said.

"Wait here, I'll go check it out," Isaac said.

I opened my mouth to protest, but before I could stop him, he was out of the truck and creeping in the shadows along the edge of the woods toward the mysterious figure. My heart flew into panic mode. I wasn't sure what worried me more: the chance of someone creepy sneaking around my home or Isaac being caught here with me.

Definitely the last of the two. I slipped out of the truck to stop Isaac from getting himself discovered. "Isaac," I whispered. "Wait." But he was too far away and couldn't hear me, and I didn't dare raise my voice any louder. I followed the tree line around the edge of the front yard as it curved over to the spot where I'd seen the intruder.

I crept up to Isaac's side. He put out a hand to slow me. Did he think I couldn't hold my own in the woods?

Just then the person began crossing the lawn to the corner of the house, and I could make out the outline of someone in a sweatshirt with the hood pulled up. Isaac called out. "Who's out there?"

Really? Did he *have* to speak up? If my family opened the front door to see who was yelling across the front lawn, I'd be busted big time.

The figure froze and turned toward us, the golden glow of the floodlights falling onto her features. Oh *shiz*. It was Olivia.

"I should be asking you the same question," she said, walking toward us. When she got closer, her eyes widened. "Isaac? What are you doing here?"

"I'm trying to make sure Destiny's safe."

Olivia snorted. "Destiny, I thought you learned your lesson about him."

"Wow. It's nice to see you, too," Isaac said. "You know, I think I'm going to head home. Text me if you need anything, Destiny." He crossed the lawn back to his truck.

When he was out of earshot, Olivia said, "Seriously? You are so stupid. He hates us. What are you doing with him?"

"He's not like that, Livie. You know we've been wrong about him."

"You're going to defend him after everything he did? Sure, Mom and Dad were nice to him at church, but that doesn't mean they actually trust him to date you."

"It's called forgiveness. You should try it sometime."

"There's a difference between forgiveness and outright disobedience, which is why I'm going straight into the house to tell Mom and Dad."

"No, you're not," I said.

"Oh yeah? How are you going to stop me?"

"What were you doing out in the woods just now?"

"I was taking out the compost for Mom," she said smoothly.

"Sure you were. Smelling like the Tahitian breeze. I know I always put on perfume before I dump the compost."

"Shut up."

"Come on. I know you were out with Hudson."

She stared at me with wide eyes. "Who told you?"

"Remember the day I answered Hudson's phone?"

"You had his phone?" she asked.

I explained how he'd left it in the pocket of his jacket and how Preston had read all the messages.

"Oh my gosh! Preston knows about this, too?"

"Yep."

"I can't believe this." She hugged her arms around her midsection with her chin tucked to her chest. She raised her head and said, "Hey, wait a second. Wasn't Preston supposed to be taking you on a date tonight?"

I twisted a curl around my finger uncomfortably. "Um. Yeah."

"So was all that a lie to have an excuse to go out with Isaac instead?"

"No, of course not. Something happened with Preston's mom while we were at the restaurant, and he had to leave early. Isaac just happened to be there, and he gave me a ride home."

She folded her arms and gave me a hard look. "I already know about Preston's mom. Brinlee texted me, freaking out. But there's no way you're telling me the whole story. Preston would never leave you alone with Isaac like that."

I stared back at her. What was I supposed to say? I opened my mouth to tell her my story, but the words wouldn't come. Finally, I managed in a low voice, "You're right. Something else happened tonight. I'll tell you, but you have to promise to keep quiet about Isaac and me."

She shook her head and re-crossed her arms. "No way! I'm telling on you for your own protection."

"Fine. You say a word about Isaac, and I'll tell them about Hudson."

"No! You can't tell them!"

"Oh yes. I can. Just watch me." I knew there was a reason I hadn't told on her…yet.

"Fine. I won't tell them."

"Won't tell them what?"

"About Isaac being here tonight."

"No. You won't tell them about Isaac being with me ever. From now on."

"Destiny! You can't be serious."

"I'm dead serious. You don't get to go sneaking around with Hudson and get away with it and then act all self-righteous when I want to have a nonmember boyfriend."

"Hudson's a Mormon," she said.

"Yeah, sure he is. I haven't seen him at church even once."

"He's working on it," she said defensively.

"The only thing he's working on is his longboarding skills," I said.

"How can you say that?"

"I'm sorry," I sighed. "That was uncalled for." I looked away. "I'm not here to judge you. I have my own set of problems. I just don't want you to think you can act all high and mighty with me when you're pretty much doing the same thing and totally getting away with it."

"Ugh. Okay, fine. I won't tell them anything about Isaac."

"Good. You'd better not. I need to figure this all out on my own without Mom and Dad being involved."

"So what happened anyway? How are you all of a sudden with Isaac instead of Preston?"

I told her the entire story. Somehow, knowing that Olivia had been sneaking out, too, made me feel more comfortable spilling. The more I told her, the guiltier I felt. Finally, as I finished my story I said, “I feel so terrible, Livie. I broke Preston’s heart. I don’t know what to do.”

“How could you?”

“I realized how constant Isaac’s been through all of this, even when I was united with my entire family in pushing him away.”

Olivia shook her head in disagreement. “So, he never stopped trying to get you. I have to admit that’s kinda sweet, but that doesn’t mean it’s a good idea for you to go back to him. I still think he’s bad news.”

“I’m not so sure. I feel so alive when I’m with him.”

“Yeah, but what does God have to say about it?”

“What does God have to say about you and Hudson?” I shot back.

“That’s between me and God,” she retorted.

“I guess I can say the same to you then.”

Chapter 54

Nightmares

Preston

Brinlee and I followed the ambulance to the hospital in my truck. A couple of hours later, Dad called. He'd just come home from the game when Megan plugged in her phone and saw our messages. As soon as he heard the news, he rushed to the hospital. When he arrived, he took my seat next to Mom's hospital bed.

"What have they done to help her?" he asked.

"They had to pump her stomach," I told him.

The doctor came into the room and explained that Mom's pills had put her in a deep coma-like sleep, but weren't strong enough to actually kill her. Since they could still make her very sick and damage her liver, they had to pump her stomach. Mom woke up, but didn't say much to any of us. Brinlee and I stayed the night, curled up in separate corners of the little sofa in Mom's room.

Since she was on suicide watch, her nurse checked on her every fifteen minutes. I probably should have taken Brinlee home, but neither one of us wanted to leave Mom just yet. I slept through most of the nurse's visits, but one of them woke me around four. After she left, the room was dark and quiet.

I should have been able to fall back asleep immediately since I was so tired, but I had a crick in my neck from trying to sleep in such a horrible position and my mind began to wander to Destiny. Her betrayal had been shoved to the back of my mind through Mom's crisis, but it was still there, festering. And every now and then when the hospital chaos would die down, it would resurface and I'd relive the scene of her in Isaac's arms like a reoccurring nightmare. Part of me felt guilty for leaving her in the parking lot like that, but it was a very small part.

When Brinlee and I walked into the basement the next morning, Megan was sitting on the couch watching an old black-and-white movie. She turned off the TV with a click of the remote.

Brinlee curled up next to her and put her head on Megan's shoulder for support. She looked so small and lost, much younger than the thirteen-year-old that she was. Megan reached around and comforted her in a motherly way. "Why did she do it, Meggie?" Brinlee asked in a tiny voice.

"I think she was tired of being a burden on the family," Megan said.

"That's no reason for her to try to kill herself!"

"Brin, she's been sick for a long time," I explained gently.

"I just don't understand it. She seemed like she was doing so well."

"She pretends she is." Megan smoothed the brown, fuzzy blanket draped across her lap. "But she's been broken inside for years."

"But why?"

Megan and I exchanged a glance over Brinlee's head. We were the only kids in the family who knew why Mom had started having all these issues. When she was a teenager, she'd suffered through a horrible tragedy. She had been babysitting for a family from church, when one of the kids snuck out and drowned in the pool on her watch. She'd had an awful time dealing with the guilt, and ended up partying with a rough group of friends for a few years, drowning all her pain in drugs and alcohol. By the time she met my dad, she'd gotten sober and clean, was working and going to school, and had started going back to church again. But she never talked about her rebellious days. It was her darkest secret.

I wouldn't have known a thing about it if Megan and I hadn't discovered it for ourselves. One day, not long after we'd moved to Tennessee, the two of us were playing hide-and-seek. Megan found a journal containing the entire story in the back of Mom's closet. When I found Megan, she had already read most of the story, and she showed me the journal entry. We never told Mom about it, but as time went on, we overheard bits and pieces of conversations between our parents that explained it. Dad had thrown around words like "PTSD" and "trauma from your past." After some thorough Internet research, Megan and I discovered that PTSD stood for Post-Traumatic Stress Disorder. The incident she'd experienced while babysitting was the trauma. It had been so life-shatteringly horrible that the stress it caused had changed the way her brain worked.

I looked back at Brinlee. I worried about her. Being thirteen was tough enough. Knowing about Mom's dark past was an added strain she didn't need.

"Why are you guys looking at each other like that?" Brinlee asked. "What aren't you telling me?"

"You don't need to worry about Mom," I said soothingly.

"Yes, I do!" she said. "Whether you like it or not, I'm going to worry about her. Just tell me what's going on. I'm tough. I can handle it"

While that may or may not be true, I wasn't at liberty to reveal Mom's secrets. "I think she was worried about Dad using our college funds to pay for her cancer treatments, and she wanted to save us the trouble." *But the stress from her cancer triggered her PTSD, and it made her so crazy she couldn't handle life anymore.* I knew that because I'd heard the doctor say as much when Dad had thought I'd dozed off in the corner.

Brinlee shook her head. "It's all so horrible."

I gave her a hug. "It's going to be okay, Brin. We're going to be strong for Mom because she needs us right now. Okay?"

She nodded. "Okay."

"And we're going to be strong for the twins and Anna," I said.

"Where are they?" Brinlee asked. "Do they even know what's going on?"

"They're playing upstairs. And no," Megan said. "They just think she had a bad reaction to her medicine."

"Well," Brinlee said, pushing up from the couch. "I'm going to go charge up my phone and see if I can get some more sleep."

"That's a good idea," I said. "That was probably the worst night's sleep I've ever had."

I went back to my room and climbed into bed, pulling the covers up over my shoulders. After I'd just begun to doze off, my bedroom door opened.

"Preston?" Brinlee's voice penetrated the haze of sleep I was slipping into.

"What?" I mumbled.

She came in and sat on the floor next to my nightstand. “What happened last night on your date with Destiny?”

“Nothing.” I rolled away from her.

“Don’t turn from me. I already know.”

I sat up and looked at her. “What do you know?” I growled.

“She kissed Isaac right in front of you.”

“Shut up, Brinlee.” I pulled my spare pillow over my head and moaned. “Why are you coming in here to tell me this?”

"Brinlee, what's going on?" Megan said from the doorway.

“Meggie, you have to read this.” They were silent for a moment. Megan must have been reading text messages from Brinlee’s phone, but I couldn’t be sure since I still had a pillow covering my head. Then came the gasps and Megan trying to comfort me, but I wasn’t in the mood for any of it.

“Just back off! Both of you! I don’t want to talk about it.”

“Brin, we’d better let him get some rest.”

Megan shut the door, and I fell asleep. But it was far from restful. From the moment my eyes closed, I was bombarded with alternating images of Destiny in Isaac’s arms, and Mom sprawled across the bathroom floor. Then Destiny was standing in the rain, and I was driving away, leaving her alone, followed by Mom in a hospital bed with a nurse changing yet another IV bag in an attempt to flush the drugs from her system. Then I was watching Mom’s listless eyes, not focusing on anything, after she’d woken up.

And that was the worst image of them all.

Chapter 55

Shifting

Destiny

I woke up Saturday morning with dread sitting in the pit of my stomach like a boulder. I checked my phone for messages from Preston, but I couldn't see any. Isaac's words rang in my mind over and over. *You should be with the person who makes you the happiest.* But who was that? They were both so incredible. How could I possibly choose between them?

At this point it didn't matter. I owed it to Preston to try to make things right. He hadn't done anything to deserve the way I'd treated him. He would probably just turn me away, but I had to try. I climbed out of bed and knocked on Michael's bedroom door.

"It's open."

I pushed open to door to see Michael, still tucked in his bed, staring at his phone.

"Hey, can I borrow your car in a couple of hours?"

He glanced up at me. "Why?"

I swallowed thickly. Had Preston already texted him about what happened last night? "I want to surprise Preston with some banana bread."

"Sure. My keys are on the dresser."

"Thanks." Avoiding his gaze, I walked to his dresser, scooped up his jangling keys, and made my way to the kitchen.

I knocked on the Nelsons' front door with two plastic-wrapped loaves of banana bread. While the bread had baked I showered and dressed in the blue shirt that Preston loved because it brought out my eyes. Then, I'd curled my hair and spent extra time on my makeup.

The door opened, and Anna's angelic face smiled up at me. "Hey, Destiny, come on in." She hugged me and stepped back, tucking a long, golden strand of hair behind her ear.

"Where is everyone?" I asked.

"Well, my dad's still at the hospital with my mom, and I think everyone else is trying to sleep. My mom had a bad reaction to her medicine, and they had to pump her stomach or something. I'm not sure about all the details," she said, waving her hand in a very adult-like manner. That was how Anna was though. When she wanted to be, she could be extremely mature. She reminded me a lot of Megan at that age. But I'd seen Anna have meltdowns plenty of times, too. Megan said it was Anna's way of dealing with her mom's illness. Sometimes the smallest thing could set her off. Usually, it was over some fight she'd gotten into with Brinlee or the twins. Preston called her his little land mine because he never knew who was going to step on her emotions to make her explode.

"That's horrible. I feel so bad." And I did. More than ever now. "Um. Do you know where Preston is?"

"I have no idea," Anna said. "I haven't seen him at all this morning."

"I'll go check downstairs," I said.

"Did you bake him that bread?"

"Yep," I said from over my shoulder. "It's banana."

"Yum!" I heard her say as I jogged down the staircase. I walked into the family room, and Megan was watching TV on the couch.

"Hey," I said. I hadn't talked to her about what had happened last night, but I had a pretty strong feeling that she knew everything.

She looked up at me, and her brow rose. "Peace offering?" she said, indicating the plastic-wrapped loaves. Okay, so she did know.

My cheeks burned. She probably thought I was such a bad person. Butterflies fluttered in my stomach. No, make that an angry swarm of hornets. This was going to be much harder than I'd thought. Maybe I should go back upstairs, drop the bread on the kitchen counter and leave. It wasn't too late.

No. I wasn't a coward. I made the mistake. I needed to face the consequences. I took a breath and clenched my shaking fists around the bread in my arms. "I need to talk to Preston."

Megan nodded. "You should. He needs a friend right now."

A sob caught in my throat. Could I be that friend for him? Would he even let me? "Where is he?"

Megan watched my face carefully, her sharp gaze no doubt catching my anguish. "He's in his room."

I passed Megan and Brinlee's room and saw Brinlee passed out on her bed through the cracked door. I chewed the inside corner of my bottom lip and faced Preston's closed bedroom door. With a trembling hand, I reached out and hesitantly knocked twice.

I listened closely, but there was no answer. My stomach clenched. Heart pounding, I rapped on the door again, this time more firmly.

"Who is it?" Preston's muffled voice came through the door, barely audible.

"Um. It's Destiny."

Preston was silent for a long time. Just as I was beginning to contemplate either leaving or barging in, I heard the sound of fabric rustling. Preston opened the door and leaned against the doorframe, running a hand through his hair. He was a total mess. He was still wearing the green plaid shirt he'd worn on our date last night, but it was crumpled. Dark shadows had settled under his eyes, which were red-rimmed like he'd been crying. Seeing him like that caused the boulder in my stomach to sink even deeper. I longed to kiss away his hurt.

To erase the past.

His brow furrowed slightly, and his eyes were emotionless like something had died inside of him.

"I'm so sorry."

He snickered, a wounded, angry sound. "You think a couple of loaves of banana bread and a flimsy apology is going to make it better?"

"No…" I said slowly.

"You made a choice to be with him. If you feel like he's the guy for you, whatever, good for you," he said bitterly. "But kissing him in the middle of our date? Come on, Destiny. Couldn't that have waited? The least you could have done was dump me after the date."

"I didn't mean for it to happen that way."

"No." He shook his head, looking away from me. "I saw you. You meant all of it."

I stared at his haunted eyes and bit my lip. I couldn't deny it. What I'd felt for Isaac was overwhelmingly genuine, but I was willing to push all that to the side to make things right with Preston. "I want this to work out between us. I choose you, Preston. Please forgive me."

He stared at my mouth, like the action of my lip being caught between my teeth had captured his attention. A small flicker of desire lit in his eyes. But he quickly extinguished it with the shake of his head. "You say you choose me, but how do I know you actually mean that? How do I know you won't go back to him next week or even next month? I can't trust you anymore, Destiny. Find a way to get him out of your system. Until then, stay the heck away from me."

He didn't mean that. He couldn't. "I can't lose you, Preston." My voice broke. "You're my rock, my anchor when times get tough. I will beg if I have to. Please take me back."

He stared at me with a stony expression. "Look, Destiny, I'm exhausted. I spent the entire night in the hospital with my mom. Right now I need to focus on taking care of my family. Now, if you don't mind. I'm going to get some much-needed rest." He stepped back and shut the door.

I stumbled backward, and the loaves tumbled from my arms. I gasped for breath like my air supply had been cut off. How could I breathe without him? He'd *always* been there.

"Are you okay?" Megan was beside me picking up the fallen loaves.

I couldn't even answer her. I shook my head and rushed past her. I had to get far away from this place. I was too close to him. There were too many memories here. I slipped out the back door so I wouldn't have to face Anna upstairs and circled around the house to Michael's Civic. I climbed in, started the engine, and pulled the door shut.

Was it really over?

I needed Preston to come out and take back the words he'd just said to me, to tell me he still cared about me enough to trust me. But he didn't come, and I knew I didn't deserve it. What I did was completely unforgiveable. His words echoed in my head. *Find a way to get him out of your system.* But how could I do that?

I put the car into drive. At first I was just going to go home to hide in the tree house, but as I drove, the trees parted and Walnut Ridge came into view. I pulled up to the stop sign, and instead of looking to the left and right for oncoming traffic, I kept my foot on the brake and stared up at the gap in the ridge that divided the mountain where Hudson's house was and Isaac's land. It was once my future, well, in my daydreams anyway. It seemed like years since I'd been up there stargazing with Isaac. Why of all places did it seem like I needed to be there? Maybe because it was a quiet, private place, where I'd once been blissfully happy. I couldn't be sure, but it was calling to me, pulling me like a magnet.

Although I'd only been to Isaac's land once in the dark, I'd noticed the turnoff as I'd passed it many times since then. I didn't have any problem finding it. I parked my car where the gravel disappeared into the dead grass. The mountaintop was scattered with boulders that nestled among the trees and tall, dry grass.

The view was overwhelmingly scenic, just as it had been from Hudson's house. I sat on a rock and drank it in. It was strange to see it from this side. The last time I'd gazed down on this valley I was looking out the windows in Hudson's house with Preston's arms around me. Living without him was like walking on a shifting foundation that might crumble at any moment.

And then the tears began to flow. He really was gone. Sure, I'd still see him, but he wouldn't belong to me anymore. Painful sobs burst from deep within me as I stared out at the vast world below me. I pulled my knees up to my chest and wrapped my arms around my shins. I rested my forehead on my knees and sat like that for a long time, rocking back and forth as I cried. I used my sleeve to wipe away the tears that had run down my cheeks. I lifted my head and took in a gulp of fresh mountain air. I stared at the wet spot my tears had made on my knees.

How could it be true that Preston wouldn't be there for me anymore? I'd taken him for granted all this time. *Find a way to get him out of your system.* He was right. I couldn't keep dating him as long as I was still daydreaming about Isaac.

But what did he mean by that? Did he want me to go back to Isaac as a trial? I shook my head. Surely he didn't mean that! On the other hand, what if I wasn't supposed to get Isaac out of my system? Maybe there was a reason I'd been so drawn to him all this time. Wasn't it possible that Isaac could become my new rock foundation if I learned to build a relationship, brick by brick, starting with the truth? Of course it was. I just wasn't so sure I was ready to say goodbye to Preston forever.

But as long as I had Isaac around, I didn't get that choice. Sure he could graduate and go off to college at the end of the semester. But he might stay here and go to the university across town where I'd taken my voice lessons with Sister Poff. If he joined the Church, he might *never* leave my life. As long as Isaac was hanging around, wanting me, Preston wouldn't come near me. That left me with two paths. Be miserable and alone with no one, or give Isaac another chance, starting fresh.

Somewhere down the hill, behind me, gravel crunched beneath tires, and the roar of a heavy-duty engine sounded through the trees. I twisted around on my rock to see Isaac's truck. I wiped at my eyes frantically and checked my reflection with my camera phone. Thank goodness for waterproof mascara. I rubbed the little bit that had still smudged, but there was no way to hide that I'd been crying.

The engine shut off and Isaac swung down from the cab. He walked toward me, shoving his hands in his jeans pockets. "I wasn't expecting to see you here," he said softly. "Did Hannah tell you I was coming?"

I shook my head. "I came here to think."

"That hammock spot not working for you anymore?"

I shook my head and blushed. "Every time I go there, all I can think about is you shoving me up against the oak tree. Not exactly the best place to clear my head."

Desire flashed in his eyes. Was he was reliving the memory? I certainly was. "And coming here doesn't remind you of stargazing with me?"

"Maybe if it was nighttime, but I've never been here during the day. Everything looks different."

His eyes held such compassion and love. "You've been crying." His voice was oh so tender.

"I tried to make things right with Preston today, but…"

"But he wouldn't take you back?"

"No. He wouldn't."

"I'm sorry I caused so much trouble for you. It wasn't the way I would have wanted it." Isaac was hardly the same person I knew last fall.

The cocky boy he'd been when we'd first begun dating had changed into someone thoughtful, selfless, loving, and mature.

"What's done is done. Now I have to go forward with life and make the best choices with the paths I have in front of me."

"And what have you decided to do after all your thinking?"

"I have no idea if this is going to work or not, but I want us to start over, to build a relationship based on honesty, loyalty, and trust."

Chapter 56

Waterfall

Isaac

Did I just hear her right? "You want a relationship with me?" I asked incredulously.

She bit her lip in a *very* distracting way. "As long as that's okay with you, that is."

"Are you kidding? Of course, it is!"

"But no lying. To anyone. If we do this, we have to be completely open about our relationship."

"I like the sound of that," I said, unable to restrain the wide smile tugging at the corners of my mouth. "You don't by chance have a date to the Valentine's Banquet, do you?"

"I told my family I was going with Preston, but I haven't asked him yet. How is it that you don't have a date already? I would have thought that you and Evelyn would be going together."

My smile dropped a bit. "I was hoping that somehow things might work out with you."

Her eyes widened. "Wow."

"So is that a yes or a no?"

"If we do this, it won't be easy to convince my parents that it's okay."

"If we're going to have the kind of relationship you're talking about then they need to know about it, and eventually be okay with it. The best way to start is by being honest with them."

"Okay," she decided. "I'll give it a try. I'll talk to my mom first. If I can get her on board, then together, we might be able to convince my dad. It does help that you've been coming to church. They won't be able to keep you from me for very long if you're seriously trying to learn more."

"That makes sense. They were a lot nicer to me the last time I came to church with you."

"How's that going anyway?"

"Church is great. I'm almost done with the Book of Mormon. It's really fascinating."

"That's so awesome, Isaac. I can't even tell you how happy that makes me. How is it that your dad is letting you do all of this?"

"I'm eighteen now. I told him he didn't have the right to tell me what church to attend. He threatened to kick me out, but my mom talked him out of it. She told him I'd be more likely to stay a Baptist if I lived under their roof."

"She has a good point, actually."

"I guess so."

"Well, if you're going to keep coming to a Mormon church, I think you should go with me instead of that other ward."

"Are you sure that's a good idea?" I asked. "What about Preston?"

She sighed as though the question was painful for her. Then she squared her shoulders and looked me in the eye. "Preston is part of my life. I can't hide you from him forever. We might as well get used to the idea that no matter where I go he's going to be somewhere nearby."

"Not at school."

"No, but at school your dad is always lurking around."

I laughed. "Lurking? You make him sound like the Bethel swamp monster."

"I swear he hates me. He was still giving me dirty looks last week, and we broke up last November."

"Don't worry about my dad. I won't let him hurt you."

She stepped closer to me and wrapped her arms around my waist, nuzzling her head against my chest. I breathed in the familiar smell of wildflowers. "The view is incredible up here." She led me over to the right and pointed to the mountain on the other side of the gap. "See that house over there?"

"That huge mansion?"

"Yep. That's Hudson's house."

How weird. I'd seen that house so many times before, but I'd never realized I actually knew the person who lived inside it. "How do you know?"

"A bunch of us walked up there not too long ago."

"From your house?"

"Yeah." She walked a little closer to the edge of the mountain. "When I was at his house, I looked across the gap and realized this was your land. It was really hard for me."

It broke my heart to hear about her being in pain, but I knew the feeling well. "See that brown roof peeking through the trees right up against the base of the mountain? That's your house."

"Oh my gosh. You're right. There it is. How'd you know?"

I studied the fallen leaves beneath my feet. “I came up here a lot after our breakup. My eyes couldn’t help but drift that way.”

“That sounds like torture.”

“It was,” I admitted. “You were so close, but so far away.”

“The breakup was horrible for me, too, Isaac.”

“I’m so sorry.”

“It’s in the past now.” Her eyes drifted back to the wide expanse before us.

“Want to see the creek?” I asked in an attempt to change the subject.

“You have a creek up here?”

“Yep. There’s a waterfall, too.”

I led her into the edge of the woods around some massive, rounded boulders. “The waterfall’s over this way.” And just as I said it, the sound of cascading water drifted through the trees.

I took her hand and led her down the path Josh and I had created as kids and had kept beaten down by our various visits over the years. The path wove between a few car-sized boulders, and the waterfall came into view. “There it is,” I announced. “It’s only about a five-foot drop, but it’s still pretty cool.” The waterfall was part of a stream that ran along the top of the ridge. Josh and I had spent many long, lazy summer afternoons splashing in the water after family picnics.

I sat on a nearby boulder, and she scooted next to me, our knees touching. My arms ached to hold her close to me, but I held back. If I rushed too much, it could scare her off, but somehow I had to show her how much I cared.

“It’s peaceful here.” She studied my face for a moment.

"What?"

She chewed her bottom lip. Oh, *man*. What a tease. My heart raced furiously as I took in her thick, dark hair tumbling down her shoulders, her luminous blue eyes, her creamy skin, and her deliciously kissable lips.

"Kiss me, Isaac." She spoke the words so softly I wouldn't have heard them if I hadn't been sitting so close.

I cupped her face in my hands, and tenderly brought my mouth to her sweet, soft lips. She melted against me and wrapped her hands around my triceps. I moved my lips over hers harder, more hungrily, and she sighed against my mouth, her warm breath tickling my skin. "You have no idea how much I've missed you."

"I've missed you, too," I whispered in between kisses.

We kissed for a while longer, and I savored each moment. Every kiss, every second I got with her was precious.

She told me about a dream she'd had where we were snuggled up in her hammock during springtime. She explained that she realized later that her heart was recognizing what her brain was refusing to admit. "So the only way you could acknowledge it to yourself was through your subconscious?"

"I guess. It sure confused me at the time. And then you showed up to seminary. By then, I didn't stand a chance."

I wrapped my arms around her waist, drawing the back of her shoulders toward my chest. "I think we should make this dream a reality sometime."

She placed her soft hands over mine and her voice was tender when she spoke. "I'd really like that, Isaac."

Chapter 57

Out in the Open

Destiny

The next time I saw Preston was Sunday morning. I caught his eye from across the room, but he looked away as though I was invisible. There were dark shadows under his eyes and their usual twinkle had faded.

When Isaac came in, Michael invited him to sit between him and the missionaries again, but Isaac politely declined. “Destiny asked me to sit with her today.” So far, no one from my family seemed to realize that we were more than friends, but I planned to tell them soon. I just hadn’t worked up the courage to do it yet.

Preston’s mom didn’t come to church. After he blessed the sacrament, he returned to sit with his family at the end of the pew, which happened to be directly in front of Isaac. Although he acted as though nothing was wrong, it was impossible to miss the rigid way he sat in the pew, not even helping Megan when the twins got out of hand at one point. It was like…he had just simply…shut down.

Isaac walked up to me in the hall at school and put his arm around me. Hannah’s eyes widened. “Are y’all back together? What about Preston?”

I was going to have to get used to that question. I had it coming to me. "It didn't work out between us."

I put on a confident face, but inside, I was trembling. I looked into the faces of the passing students and saw the shock registered there as they took in our renewed relationship status. By lunch, the gossip mill was churning full force. I passed Jessie's table and their discussion suddenly quieted as she and her snobby friends stared at me. It was only a matter of time before Dr. Robinson found out.

In Primus, Isaac and I performed together again, and we totally rocked it. Our rehearsals were starting to get longer and more intense, with practices after school as well. Isaac and I would be spending more time together than ever before. *This is a good thing.* I told myself. I didn't have time for a relationship with Preston anyway. Even if I had picked him over Isaac, I'd be spending all this time with Isaac at rehearsals, and it would eventually have driven a wedge between Preston and me.

Word of our reunion was flying around the school like wildfire. Just before lunch Michael stopped me in the hall with a furious look on his face. "What the heck, Destiny?"

"What?" I asked defensively.

"What are you doing with that jerk again?"

I took a deep breath. I deserved this. "Please, don't call him that."

"Have you completely lost your mind?"

"No, I've given this a lot of thought, actually."

"What's going on?" he said, pulling my arm to guide me to the side of the hall when he noticed some curious glances directed our way.

"Isaac and I are dating now." This is what I got for procrastinating. What did I think was going to happen when I didn't tell Michael ahead of time about Isaac and me? "I'm sorry. I should have told you before. I just knew you would be unhappy about it."

"When did it happen?"

"This weekend."

Understanding lit in his eyes. "So that's why Isaac said you'd invited him to sit with you during church."

"Yeah."

"I thought you were dating Preston." How did he not already know? Preston must have really retreated into himself if he hadn't even told Michael. How could I explain this to Michael without him just getting angrier? His anger didn't matter. I'd promised Isaac I was going to build our relationship on the truth, even when it was painful.

"Preston and I broke up. This is going to be hard for you to understand, but I want to be honest with you. Do you have some time to talk later on today?"

"After school?"

On the drive home, I told him the entire story. He didn't say much, but his hands tightened around the steering wheel during the most uncomfortable parts.

"I can't begin to understand what this is like for you. I just hope you're making the right choice."

"And if I'm not, I'll figure it out eventually, won't I?"

"Yeah, you will. I'd just hate to see you go through that kind of pain again."

He was *really* going to freak if he ever found out about Hudson and Olivia.

"When are you telling Mom and Dad?"

"I guess I'll tell them after school today. Isaac asked me to the Banquet and I still have to try to convince them to let me go."

"Good luck with that. You're going to need it."

"No kidding."

That night I approached Mom in the office where she was checking her email. "Can I talk to you for a minute?

"Sure."

She turned around and looked at me expectantly.

"Some stuff happened this weekend, and I want to be upfront and honest with you about it."

"Okay…" she said slowly.

"I decided to start dating Isaac again."

Her face remained impassive. "Oh really?"

"Yeah."

"And what about Preston? It seemed like the two of you have had something going on lately."

"Yeah. Well, I found out some stuff about Isaac. I was totally wrong about him. He's an amazing guy."

"I'm sure he is."

"All that stuff about him trying to dig up dirt on the Mormons was true at first, but he's different now. I changed him, Mom. I can't just walk away from that."

I braced myself for another lecture, but instead she said, "That makes sense."

There was an awkward pause as I waited for her to elaborate, but she never did. "So," I continued, mentally crossing my fingers that she would be receptive to what I was about to say next, "Isaac asked me to go to the Valentine's Banquet with him."

"Destiny, you know you're not allowed to date nonmembers," she said calmly, staring ahead at the computer screen.

"You know he's been investigating the Church and attending seminary, right?"

"I thought you'd already asked Preston to go with you. That's what your father told me."

I shook my head quickly. "I was going to, but I hadn't done it yet."

"Isaac has caused you a lot of grief. What makes you think that's not going to just happen all over again?"

"He told me he's in love with me. He would never do anything to hurt me now. I trust him."

"I don't understand how you can jump between guys so quickly."

"I don't understand it either... It's complicated." And it really was. My heart barely made any sense to me these days.

"He's graduating in a few months anyway, Destiny. Why can't you just wait it out?"

"Because I can't stop thinking about him. I can't even sleep without dreaming about him. Every time I close my eyes, he's there, smiling this gorgeous smile at me. Please let me go to the Banquet with him. It would mean so much to us if we could have your blessing."

"You know, even if you get my blessing, you'll have a much harder time trying to convince your father."

"I know." I said, breathing a sigh of relief. It wasn't a yes, but it wasn't a no either.

The rest of the week the drama grew steadily. Valentine's Day was on a Friday, and for the first time in years, Valentine's Day was the same day as the Banquet. Whenever we weren't in rehearsals, Isaac was with Aspen and Will and the other student body officers either getting ready for their Valentine's Day fundraiser, or preparing the decorations for the Banquet. He invited me to come help them in the student lounge during lunch on Thursday.

Before lunch Isaac met me at my locker with this totally gorgeous smile on his face. "You ready?" he said, taking his hand in mine.

"Yep," I said.

We walked to the student lounge, a room with ratty, old couches, a snack machine, and a pool table. Aspen and Will sat cross-legged on the floor with the other student body government officers. She was tying a red ribbon around a candle. She looked up when we came in, and her hands grew still. She looked back down at her work quickly, but her brows rose as though she were deep in thought.

"Okay guys, what have you done so far?" Isaac asked.

Aspen filled him in, and then Isaac said, "Awesome. Destiny's going to help us out as well."

"Great!" Aspen said in a fake, cheery voice. We worked together tying on ribbons and putting together centerpieces, but an awkward silence hung over the group.

"So, Destiny, how've you been feeling lately?" Aspen asked.

"I've been feeling just fine," I said. "How've you been feeling?"

She smiled at me like I was a little kid and ignored the question I shot back at her. "Good for you. I know sometimes people in your condition have a hard time of it."

I stared back at her.

"What's that supposed to mean, Aspen?" Isaac barked.

"What? I'm just asking a polite question," she said.

"No. You're trying to start something with my girlfriend."

"Oh!" Her eyebrows shot up. "You're dating her again?" her voice rose in pitch as she said it. It wasn't like she didn't already know. She was probably the first person the gossips would have told. "I would have thought you'd have learned your lesson by now," she sneered.

"Jealous much, Aspen?" Will said.

"Shut up, Will," she snapped.

Isaac gave Aspen a dirty look. "I'm sick of you attacking Destiny."

"I'm not attacking her," Aspen said defensively.

"Sure, you're not."

"I'm just trying to be her friend."

"Oh yeah, because accusing someone of being pregnant is a good way to make friends."

"I'm not accusing her."

"You sure sounded like you were."

"I'm just trying to make sure she's okay."

"And why wouldn't she be?" Isaac retorted.

"Isaac, you can't hide it anymore. Pretty much everyone knows what's going on by now."

"What are you talking about?"

I sat silently, tying ribbons around candles while keeping my eyes carefully trained on my work.

"I mean, look at her. She looks like she's been putting on weight."

Seriously? I hadn't gained a pound for the last six months.

"No, she doesn't," Isaac said. "This kind of garbage is what I'm talking about."

"She needs help. I'm just trying to be a good Christian here. It's the Godly thing to do."

My mouth twitched. For some reason this was so absurd I had to restrain myself from bursting out laughing. I never knew what ridiculous hypocrisy was going to come out of Aspen's mouth next. The sad thing is, she actually believed that her twisted lies were somehow valid. It blew my mind that she could lie to herself for so long that she would actually start believing it.

"Aspen, if you don't leave her alone, I'm going to tell everyone what I saw you and Will doing in the parking lot at Sophie's."

"Whoa, Robinson, leave me out of this." I glanced from Will to Isaac. If Isaac decided to go public with his knowledge of Will's drug use, he'd have every right to do so.

"You don't have any proof of anything," Aspen said. "And hurling a bunch of ridiculous accusations at us would just make you look desperate."

"Desperate? You mean the way you look every time you hurl accusations at Destiny?"

For once, Aspen didn't have a snappy comeback. She glared back at him defiantly.

"Do you really think people would believe you over me?" Isaac challenged.

"Yeah. I do."

"You're delusional then."

"No, Isaac. You're the one dating a Mormon."

Ugh. Not again. Why did these people always have to bring my religion up?

"And what's wrong with that?" he asked with a challenge in his voice.

She looked down at her work, her expression suddenly neutral.

"Tell me, Aspen. What's wrong with being a Mormon? Do you even have a clue what they believe?"

She kept her eyes lowered as she reached for a hot glue gun.

"I didn't think so. Well, let me tell you a little bit about Mormons. First of all, both you and Will were incredibly wrong about them. They're kind, hardworking, Christian people. They do a few things that I think are kind of weird. No offense, Destiny."

"None taken…I think."

Isaac chuckled. "Well, for one thing, they don't drink coffee. To me that's completely nuts, but I respect that about Destiny. She believes in something and she practices it, even when it's hard and people are making fun of her for it. That takes courage. I'm not so sure I could do it."

Will rolled his eyes. "Are you done, Robinson? When did you become such a Mormon lover? It's disturbing."

Isaac looked at me, and a slow, tender smile spread across his face. "I think it started the night of the retreat when you told me that Destiny had the hots for me."

Will made a noise of shocked disgust. "Are you for real? Robinson, you've let her completely brainwash you, dude."

Isaac didn't take his eyes off of me when he murmured, "If this is being brainwashed, then I'm totally okay with that."

I stared back into his fathomless brown eyes, and a tiny sigh escaped my lips.

Chapter 58

Daddy's Permission

Isaac

I stepped out of my truck and stood there in my tux, staring up at Destiny's house as I tried to cam my pounding heart. I gripped the plastic carton containing Destiny's corsage between my sweaty palms. I had no clue how this was going to go down. Destiny said she'd gotten her mom to finally agree to let me take her to the banquet. Her dad wasn't crazy about the idea, but after her relentless begging he'd finally given his permission for her to go on this one date with me but no more.

I walked up the sidewalk and pushed down the uneasiness in my stomach, praying that Destiny's parents would learn to accept us.

I knocked on the door, and Olivia answered it with a guarded expression. Behind her I heard raised voices. Ugh. This couldn't be good.

"Mom, this is nuts! How can you guys even say this?" Destiny said.

"How can we know for sure? You admitted yourself that you climbed out your window in the middle of the night to be with him, and the next thing we know you're lying to us about dating him. Michael said he'd heard rumors that you guys were sneaking out of class to meet each other under stairwells."

Whoa. How had he heard about that?

"And then Olivia tells us you'd been secretly texting Isaac with Preston's name. All that time you'd been spending with Preston. What was that actually about? A cover-up so we wouldn't realize you were dating Isaac? You and Preston were inseparable for months, and now all of a sudden you're not? Michael said you won't even talk about why you and Preston aren't ever together anymore."

"It's none of his business," she said in an acidic tone. Olivia stepped into the room, but since no one else had noticed my arrival, I stayed in the foyer. "Livie, how could you tell Mom and Dad?"

"What else was I supposed to do? This thing with Isaac has gone far enough."

"No, Olivia, you know what's gone far enough? You sneaking out to go see Hudson."

"Hudson?" Mr. Clark spoke for the first time. From where I stood, hidden in the foyer I could only see the side of his face. "Who's this Hudson guy?"

I couldn't see Olivia's face because her back was to me, but she stood very still with her back straight and stiff.

"Yeah, Olivia. Tell Dad who Hudson is," Destiny taunted.

Olivia screeched and put a hand over her mouth. "Shut up, Destiny! Shut up!"

"No, I won't shut up! You repeat some bogus rumors you heard at school, and now you've got Mom and Dad convinced it's all true. Well, it's not. It's a bunch of lies Aspen made up because she's jealous Isaac doesn't want her anymore."

"Who is Hudson?" Mr. Clark asked again, his voice growing louder.

I took a half step closer to the side, and my breath caught, but not because of the tension in the room. For the first time that night, I finally saw Destiny. She stood in the middle of the room wearing a floor-length dress that reminded me of the color of her eyes when the sunlight hit them. Across her torso were tiny, sparkling rhinestones. Her hair was pulled up partially with curls spilling down her back like a waterfall. Tiny curls framed her face. More than anything, I wanted to take her in my arms and treat her like the princess she looked like tonight.

How could her own family treat her so horribly? It had sounded like Olivia had overheard the rumors Aspen had spread about Destiny being pregnant and had repeated it to her parents. And they had believed it. It infuriated me to no end. How could they believe that? Didn't they know Destiny well enough to know she would never do that? She deserved better. I swore to myself then and there to never treat her that way.

"Answer me, Olivia!" her dad bellowed.

"He's a guy from school."

"Calm down, Ben, you're terrorizing her. I'm sure Olivia has a perfectly reasonable explanation for whatever Destiny's accusing her of."

Olivia's shoulders relaxed a bit. This really didn't look good for Destiny. Her parents already knew she'd been sneaking out with me, and now they suspected that she'd gotten herself pregnant. Destiny was cornered and desperate, and they'd assume she'd be willing to hurl false accusations toward Olivia to get the focus off herself. While she may have been pushed to reveal Olivia's secrets by her desperation, she would never be one to make up crazy stories to deflect negative attention.

But then Olivia did something unexpected. She said, "No, Mom. Destiny's telling the truth."

Her mom's mouth flopped open. "What?" she said, her brows pulling together in confusion as though she'd misunderstood something somehow.

Olivia sighed. "Hudson and I became friends after the paintball game, and we did sneak out together once. He's really crazy, and he likes to joke around all the time. This one night we kept daring each other to do crazy stuff, and he dared me to meet him in the woods. It was no big deal. We're just friends who like to one up each other on wild, crazy dares."

It sounded like a reasonable enough explanation to me, but the look of fury on Destiny's face said otherwise. She was about to explode, and it was going to ruin our night worse than it had already been ruined.

"Ahem," I said stepping into the doorway. Destiny's eyes fell on me, and she bit her lip.

Mrs. Clark turned around and said, "Isaac?"

Mr. Clark stood up from his chair and gave me a thin-lipped smile.

"Sorry to interrupt, but I'm here to pick up Destiny," I said formally.

"Yes," her mom said. "She's ready to go."

I stepped into the room and all eyes were on me. I turned to Mr. Clark and nodded. "It's good to see you, sir."

He stared at me for a long moment, and it took some effort to keep from shrinking back. Then he nodded, but he didn't smile.

The next five minutes stretched out for what seemed like an hour. I breathed a sigh of relief when Destiny was finally in my truck with me and we were on our way to the school.

"Well, that went much better than I'd expected," she said.

I clenched my jaw shut to hold back the biting remarks on the tip of my tongue. It could have gone much worse, but I was still furious with her parents for believing the rumors.

"What's wrong?"

"How could your parents talk to you like that?"

"They were just upset."

"But they believed those stupid rumors."

"So did you," she said softly.

"What?"

"When you saw me in Walmart with that test, you thought it was mine," she said.

"Destiny. I'm so sorry. I should have known better. I just saw it, and I freaked."

She turned away from me and stared out the window. This wasn't how I'd expected our night to go. It was a miracle her parents had allowed us to go out together. I should be focusing on how happy this moment was for us, not making it worse.

Chapter 59

Valentine's Banquet

Destiny

"Ready?" Isaac held his arm out in a gentlemanly manner.

I placed my hand on his arm. Together we walked into the large room that didn't look anything like the gym it had been yesterday. Tiny white lights embedded in black swaths of fabric twinkled overhead like hundreds of little stars in the night sky. The room glowed with a golden aura put off by candles in the center of each of the round tables that were scattered around the gym. Everything was black or gold except for the red ribbons on the candles and the wide red bows tied around the backs of the chairs.

"Whoa. Y'all did an amazing job decorating this place," I admitted.

Isaac shrugged. "Aspen may be annoying and deceitful, but she's a master at decorating."

"Isaac! You brought her!" A red streak flew past my peripheral vision and the next thing I knew, Hannah had her arms wrapped around Isaac in a gigantic bear hug.

"Hey," he said in a slightly strangled voice.

"Oh, sorry. I guess you might like to breathe," she said, stepping backwards sheepishly.

"Where's Evan?" I asked.

"He came down with a stomach bug last night, so I decided to still come by myself. It's probably for the best anyway. We've been fighting a lot lately." She waved a hand and said, "Enough about me." She grabbed both my hands and squealed. "I can't believe your parents let y'all come together."

"Michael was furious," I said, glancing across the room to where he and Megan were already sitting together at one of the round tables.

"Well, Michael can just get over it," Hannah declared.

Isaac watched Michael with a troubled expression on his face.

After we'd eaten, I decided I couldn't take it anymore, and I got up to go confront Michael about the dark looks he kept sending our way and tell him to cut it out. I stood up and walked past the area where people were in line getting their pictures taken when someone grabbed my arm.

"Hey!"

"Shhh." It was Hannah.

"What are you doing?"

"Come here," she whispered, waving me into some artificial rosebushes clustered in flowerpots blocking the north exit of the gym.

On the other side of the double doors, I heard the distinct southern drawl of Isaac's dad. "Bethel has a zero tolerance policy for pregnancy. We support Godly values at our school."

Hannah turned to me, her face white as a sheet. "Oh my gosh. My life is over."

"Hannah, calm down. No one knows it's you."

"I'm sorry, Dr. Robinson," said a high-pitched voice I recognized instantly. "This has to be so hard for you and your family. I'm pretty sure it's why they're back together. It's for the baby."

"My family? What do you mean by that?" Dr. Robinson asked in horror.

"You mean, you don't know? Destiny is pregnant with Isaac's baby. Think about it. Doesn't it sound like Isaac to stand by her side when she's in trouble? He's just trying to do the right thing."

"How can you prove that it's his? Has he admitted it himself?"

"Not exactly, but I heard them talking about it in the hall together. Why would he act all worried about it if it wasn't even his kid?"

Hannah pulled me away from the door and back to a darkened corner of the gym. "What's she talking about?" she hissed.

"She overheard Isaac and me talking about me buying the pregnancy test one day. She thinks it was mine."

Hannah's face drained of color. "How long have these rumors been going around?"

"A few weeks now."

"How is it that Dr. Robinson's just now hearing about it?" Hannah asked. "Or me for that matter. You should have told me!" Honestly, Hannah must have been lost in her own world to have not heard the rumors by now. Even Olivia had heard them.

"Aspen must not have cared that much about telling Dr. Robinson until she saw that Isaac and I had gotten back together."

"And you've just been taking the blame for it? It doesn't sound like you've been denying it very strongly."

"I'm doing it to protect you. I don't care what they think about me."

"You could get thrown out of the school for me! That's not cool, Destiny!"

"I'm not going to get thrown out of the school. All they have to do is give me a pregnancy test."

"How can you prove that you didn't just go have an abortion?"

Oh. I hadn't thought of that.

"I'm going to have to tell everyone the truth," Hannah decided.

"No, Hannah. You can't do that. Isaac and I will take care of it."

She crossed her arms and her eyes met mine with a determined glint in them. "This is my problem. You guys shouldn't have to deal with it."

"We want to help you. We can handle it. You have enough to deal with."

She sighed. "Okay, but if it doesn't go well for you, I'm speaking up."

"Thanks," I said with a relieved lift to my shoulders.

"You amaze me, Destiny," she said in a small voice. "I can't believe you're doing this for me."

I hugged her, and we went back into the gym to face the consequences of the conversation we'd just overheard.

Isaac walked toward us. "Where have you been, Destiny?"

"There's an issue," I said quietly, but before I could explain further, Dr. Robinson and Aspen strode toward us.

"Isaac, I'm disappointed in you, son," Dr. Robinson said.

"Why are you bringing this up again? I told you Destiny and I are back together. You can't tell me who to date. The only reason I ever stayed away from Destiny was because she asked me to leave. But now she finally wants me back, and I'll be by her side as long as she wants. This is my choice. Not yours."

Dr. Robinson frowned slightly. "I know the truth about what's going on now. I warned you about her, but you wouldn't listen to me. You've gotten yourself into a real mess this time. There are always consequences for our actions, son. I'm sure you're well aware of that now. I admire you for trying to make the best of a bad situation and for trying to do the honorable thing for your child."

"My…what? This is ridiculous!" Isaac said, rolling his eyes.

"Don't take that tone with me, son. What you two have gotten yourselves into is the result of a very serious sin."

"Dad," Isaac groaned. "Destiny isn't pregnant."

"I know you're just saying that to protect her," Aspen said. "But I heard you two talking about it with my own two ears. And Destiny doesn't even deny it."

"Destiny?" Dr. Robinson said. "Is what Aspen is saying the truth?"

I swallowed, my throat suddenly dry. "Um." I glanced at Hannah, who was wringing her hands nervously and then looked at Isaac's pleading eyes. How could I protect them both? "No, I'm not pregnant," I said.

"She's lying," Aspen said. "Look at the way she keeps shifting her eyes from Isaac to Hannah."

"No. I'm not. Aspen only thinks I'm pregnant because she overheard Isaac and me talking about me buying a pregnancy test for this girl from my church."

"Why would you buy a pregnancy test for someone else?" Aspen said. "That doesn't even make sense." She was talking rather loudly, probably on purpose, and had started to draw a crowd.

"She was too scared to buy it herself, so I went in to buy it for her." I hated how my voice trembled as I said it.

"Lies," Aspen said. "Nobody would do that."

"Take her to the school nurse and have her tested," Dr. Robinson said. "But try to be a bit more discreet. Don't forget this involves my son."

"I don't believe this. Can't this wait until Monday morning?" Isaac complained.

"No, son. It can't. Not when our family name is actively being tarnished."

"You've gotta be kidding me," Isaac complained.

Isaac and I followed Aspen to where Nurse Adams was seated at a table of chaperones. Aspen leaned down like she was going to whisper and said, once again, a bit too loudly for my liking, "Excuse me, Nurse Adams. We have a student here who needs some medical attention."

Nurse Adams turned around in her chair. "Destiny! Is everything okay?"

"Yeah, I'm fine."

"What's the matter?" she asked.

Aspen's eyes flitted around the table and leaned forward like she was trying to be discreet, but she only drew even more attention to us. "She needs a pregnancy test."

Nurse Adam's eyes grew wide, and her head whipped around in shock. "Oh. I see." Her mouth set into a firm line. "When do you want to get that taken care of, sweetheart?"

I was going to be sick. "Um. Right now, please."

Nurse Adams nodded curtly. "All right, then. Let's get this over with."

I turned around and almost bumped into Hannah. “Destiny,” she hissed. “I can’t let you go through with this.”

“It’s too late now, Hannah. I have to.”

“Is it okay if I come with her?” Hannah asked.

“That’s up to Destiny,” Nurse Adams said.

“Yeah,” I said. “I’d appreciate it if she came.”

Nurse Adams climbed out of her chair, and Isaac came up to us. “Destiny, this is horrible. I don’t feel right about it at all.”

“Maybe you should have thought about that before,” Aspen said snottily.

Isaac glared at her stormily, but I put a hand on his arm. “Isaac. Ignore her. She doesn’t know what she’s talking about.”

Aspen snorted. “I’m pretty sure I know how it works.”

“Yeah,” Hannah said. “You would.”

Aspen made a preppy sound of indignant shock. “No, I wouldn’t,” she said her voice raising an octave.

“Nurse Adams,” Isaac said. “This is just a big misunderstanding. Destiny isn’t…” he glanced around the hall. “It’s not what they’re saying it is.”

“Well, we can be sure of that in just a few minutes, hon,” she said, reaching into her bag and pulling out a set of keys to unlock the door to her office.

She walked into the small clinic and opened a cabinet. She pulled down a pregnancy test, similar to the one Hannah had taken in Walmart. “Do you know how to use this?” she asked.

I nodded, hating it that Aspen was still sneering at me from the doorway. “Can I get some privacy?” I asked.

"Of course," she said, shutting the door.

"We'll just wait for you out here," Hannah said.

"I'm not pregnant," I said to the nurse. "It's physically impossible. I was seen buying a test for my friend from church, and some of the students are starting rumors around the school."

"Well, if that's true then you don't have anything to worry about," she said.

I nodded. I took the test and came back out with the negative results.

"Well, you were right. You're definitely not pregnant."

I shrugged. "I was just doing it so Dr. Robinson would stop accusing me."

"What? Why would he do such a thing? That doesn't sound like him at all."

"He's worried that his son's involved."

"Ah. I see. That would change things a bit, I suppose. Parents do tend to go a bit nuts when their kids are possibly wrapped up in this kind of drama."

"I guess so," I said. "It's just annoying because it's a lie. Can you make sure Aspen knows it's false? I don't want her spreading any more rumors about me."

"Of course, sweetheart."

She opened the door for me to leave. As I passed through the doorway, she said. "Aspen, can I have a word with you?"

Aspen went inside and Nurse Adams shut the door.

"I'm glad that's over with," I said.

"This is all my fault. I feel so terrible I pulled you into this mess," Hannah wailed.

Isaac put his arm around her shoulders. "It's okay, Hannah. She wanted to do it for you."

I stepped toward Hannah, and we hugged each other. "You deserve it. You've been there for me so many times before."

We started heading back to the gym. "Let's just forget that ever happened," I said. "Want to get pictures with me, Isaac?" I asked.

A huge smile spread over his face. "More than anything."

And suddenly it seemed that by getting pictures together in front of the entire school it was our way of announcing that we were dating and we weren't ashamed of it. It felt strangely liberating to be able to look them in the eye and say, "Yes, I'm with Isaac Robinson. What are you going to do about it?"

Isaac and I got into the line for the pictures, and he wrapped his arms around my waist from behind. I sighed and leaned into him. For that moment everything was perfect. My stunningly beautiful boyfriend was wearing a tux and was holding me in his arms. Aspen had finally been proven wrong. Hannah's secret was safe, and I really didn't care what everyone else thought.

"Hey, Destiny," Megan said.

Oh man. I'd forgotten she was here. I twisted around in Isaac's arms to see Megan and Michael standing behind us in the line. How awkward. I released a puff of hot air.

"Hey, Megan," I said.

"You guys having fun?" she asked politely.

I tried to give her a genuine smile, but it came off feeling forced. "Yep."

"Hey, Michael," Isaac said.

Michael stared at Isaac's arms around me and frowned. Ugh. Why did he have to care so much? I knew exactly why, but I couldn't think about *him* right now.

"Did y'all like the salmon?" I asked lamely. What else could I say to them?

Megan nodded a little too emphatically. "Yeah, it was really good."

"How are you feeling about the *Les Mis* rehearsals?" Isaac asked Michael.

He shrugged. "It's coming along."

"He's doing amazing," I said. "Don't you think?"

"I agree." Isaac bobbed his head. "You make a fantastic Jean Valjean."

"Thanks," Michael mumbled and looked away.

Isaac continued to make an effort to chat politely with Michael, and by the time it was our turn to get our picture taken, Michael was giving him more than one-word answers. Isaac and I stepped in front of the back drop, and he held me close to his chest.

"You smell good," he murmured in my ear.

Thank you, Bath and Body Works. I smiled to myself just as the photographer took the picture.

Right as we stepped away from the photo area, I spotted Aspen talking to Dr. Robinson. He was staring intently at her face and then became visibly relieved. He must have really thought his son was about to make him a grandfather. The thought made me want to take turns laughing, screaming, and crying. But mostly I was just relieved that the rumors would be stopped. There was no way Dr. Robinson would want those kinds of lies spreading about his family. I could see that from the furious way he was listening to Aspen as she sheepishly explained herself to him.

Will came up to Isaac. "Hey, Robinson, can I talk to you for a minute?"

Isaac glanced over at me, a quizzical expression on his face. "Sure," he said. "What's up?"

"I meant privately," he said, shooting me an annoyed glare.

"Anything you have to say to me can be said in front of Destiny."

"Whatever, dude." Will shrugged. "Suit yourself. I just wanted to let you know the school board came up with a decision."

"What kind of decision?" Isaac's shoulders tensed.

"This kind of decision." Will pulled a folded piece of paper from his pocket and opened it.

Isaac took it from him. "What is this?"

I glanced over his shoulder and caught a glimpse of the paper. It looked like a list of basic Baptists beliefs. Nothing I hadn't seen before. Isaac sucked in a sharp, sudden breath. "No. They can't do this."

"What?" I asked.

I took another glance and caught the words: "Book of Mormon." *What the heck?* "Let me see that," I said.

Isaac didn't hand it to me.

"Isaac, what is that?"

He turned to me, and his brown eyes softened as his perfectly sculpted eyebrows drew together. He pressed his lips into a firm line and then spoke carefully as though he was terrified each word would cause me pain. "It's a Doctrinal Statement. The school board met this afternoon to set up the finishing touches on the new application process Dad's been working all year to implement. I'm so sorry, Destiny. I didn't know this was going to be a part of it."

The pit of my stomach fell away. "What does that mean for me?" I whispered.

"I'm not exactly sure. They may not make you sign it since you've been here for so many years."

"Sign it?" I still wasn't following him.

"This is my dad's way of getting back at me," Isaac said. "He knew I was going to the Mormon church and talking to the missionaries."

"You're not making any sense. What does he want me to sign?"

"Don't you get it? He's trying to get rid of the Mormons."

"By signing a stupid paper? How's that supposed to get rid of us?"

"Did you actually read this? You would have to sign at the bottom saying you believe everything on the list in order to attend Bethel next year."

"What?"

"Yeah, and they're specifically targeting Mormons. Look at number six. It says right here that you have to believe the Bible is the only Word of God and not any other book, including the Book of Mormon and all these other religious books."

I glanced at the paper, and sure enough, there was a long list, targeting religions from all around the world. "So, your dad isn't only targeting Mormons, but basically anyone who doesn't believe exactly like he does."

"Pretty much."

"That's horrible! How is that supposed to bring people to God?"

"What did you expect?" Will said. "You're a Mormon in a Baptist school. If you're going to attend Bethel, then you'd better believe like we do."

"So, if I want to stay at the only school I've ever known, I have to deny my faith?"

"This is so wrong," Isaac said.

Hannah came across the room to me. "What's the matter, Destiny?"

I opened my mouth to answer, but Michael and Megan walked up to us before I could speak.

"What's going on?" Michael asked, shooting a look at Isaac.

"It's happening," I said, a sick feeling of certain dread settling into my stomach. "They've finally found a way to get rid of us."

"What?" Michael said in a shocked voice.

"Let me see that," Hannah said, ripping the paper from Isaac's hands. "What is this?"

Isaac filled them in on the details and Hannah passed the paper on to Michael and Megan to look over.

"They can't do this. It has to be illegal somehow!" Hannah protested.

"Yes, they can," Will said. "And it's *going* to happen. They've been working on the Doctrinal Statement all year long."

"How did you know about this, and I didn't?" Isaac asked.

"Like we'd tell you," Will snorted. "I knew you were lost the minute I noticed you and Destiny had gone to see the horses at that practice at Aspen's house."

A corner of Isaac's mouth tugged upward as the memory of that amazing day flitted across his face. "I can't really deny it."

Michael looked away awkwardly, and Megan smiled a little, but it didn't reach her eyes. It was like she was grieving in place of Preston. I didn't want to think about the pain he was in this very moment, or what kind of questions he would ask Megan when she got home. Would he wonder what color dress I was wearing, or if I'd looked happy with Isaac? I worried about him so much. Somehow, I would make it up to him.

Michael returned his eyes to the paper, and as he read his jaw tightened.

"I'm really sorry, Michael," Isaac said.

"For what?" he asked. "You weren't the one who wrote this paper."

"I know," Isaac said. "But I still feel responsible. I don't regret a second of my time with Destiny, but I'm perfectly aware that it was a huge factor in the creation of the statement," Isaac said.

Michael nodded, and some of the hardness fell away from him. "I appreciate that. So what are we going to do?" Michael asked.

"We fight," Isaac said, his voice determined. "I won't stop until I've done everything possible to get this Doctrinal Statement overturned."

Chapter 60

Where's the Fight?

Preston

I tucked the blankets around Mom's shoulders and handed her the steaming cup of herbal tea from the bedside table. "You got it?"

"I'm sorry, Preston."

"You don't have to keep apologizing, Mom. I don't blame you for what happened. You're sick. But you're going to get the care you need, and everything's going to be fine."

She smiled, but her eyes had a faraway look in them. She was worrying about our college funds again. It didn't matter how many times I told her I could pay for my own college, she still worried.

Even though she'd apologized dozens of times since she'd come home from the hospital last weekend, it still felt good to hear it again. But there was no way I was letting her know how badly she'd hurt me by trying to leave. Showing her that pain would only make her feel more guilt, and that would only make her worse.

I flipped on the lamp and handed Mom her Kindle. Just as I walked toward her bedroom door and flipped off the overhead light, the front door opened. I turned around at the sound of high heels clicking against the ceramic tile of the entry way. Megan wore a floor length purple formal and had her hair all pinned up and curled.

My chest tightened painfully, and I averted my eyes. I was supposed to be going to that banquet tonight. Michael had told me weeks ago that Destiny had been planning to ask me to the Valentine's Banquet. The heart-shaped box of chocolates and book of poems I'd written for Destiny for Valentine's Day were buried deep in the back of my closet behind a dusty stack of comic books. I'd thought about ripping the poems up or burning them in the fire pit in the backyard, but I couldn't bring myself to do it.

I wasn't sure why. She hadn't even seemed the least bit heartbroken over me. As far as I could tell, she spent her every waking moment with Isaac, and if they were apart, she was thinking about him. They were constantly in my face. If I hadn't been so dedicated to going to seminary, I would have dropped out. It was sickening to see them sitting together every morning. They weren't holding hands or anything, but Michael told me they started dating pretty much immediately after our breakup. I always did my best to pretend they weren't in the room, but it never worked. I told myself a thousand times that she wasn't worth it, that I was better off without her.

But who was I kidding? Living without Destiny left a gaping hole in me. I was broken without her. Every time she crossed my mind, I ached so deeply it was hard to focus on even small, everyday tasks, like brushing my teeth or getting my books from my locker.

"How was your night?" I asked Megan, out of politeness more than anything.

"It was…interesting."

What did she mean? Did I really want to know the answer? What if she was just going to tell me how Isaac was all over Destiny the entire night? Michael told me a few days ago how shocked he'd been that his dad had given Destiny permission to go to the Banquet with Isaac.

If I didn't lighten up, I was going to lose it again. I'd shed enough tears over Destiny to last me a lifetime. I forced a smile and hid my heart-wrenching pain the same way I usually did. "How was it interesting? Did Michael put some moves on you or something?" I joked. Their relationship was no more romantic than that of a brother and sister.

She blushed. "None of your business."

"Wait. What? So you're saying he did?" I didn't see *that* one coming. What the crap did he do? Did he kiss my sister? Ugh. This was so weird. How did Michael deal so well with me dating his sister? And just as I wondered it, I understood how. He knew that as long as I dated Destiny, she was protected from Isaac, and that more than compensated for any weirdness that his best friend dating his sister would have caused.

"Like I said, none of your business." Megan spoke firmly. I repressed a slight shudder. I didn't have any kind of compensation to make up for the weirdness of him making out with my sister, or whatever it was they did. "That's not what I meant when I said interesting." She blushed again and cleared her throat. "Something unexpected happened."

Her words pulled me from the weird image of Michael kissing my sister, and I focused more closely on her words. She described the discovery Isaac made that the school was coming out with a Doctrinal Statement all the students had to sign in order to return the next year.

"So, does that mean the Clarks are going to Acorn Creek next year?" Hope gnawed inside me. If Destiny were to go to school with me next year, surely she'd forget about Isaac, wouldn't she? He'd be graduated and off to college by then. That would mean no more Isaac in seminary, no more *Les Mis*, and Isaac would be distracted by thousands of available college girls. For the first time in a week, I could breathe just a little more easily.

Megan shook her head. "Isaac said he was going to fight against it."

"Good for him, but why fight for Destiny to stay in a place where she isn't wanted? It's not like he's going to be there next year."

"I think it's a matter of principle to him. He doesn't want his school to become the kind of place that excludes others."

"It's a private school. That's what it's for."

Megan slumped down on the couch, kicking off her high heels and wiggling her toes with a sigh. "I don't know, Preston, maybe he's just trying to impress Destiny."

I clenched my jaw to hold back the biting remark on the tip of my tongue. Suddenly, I was furious. All the hurt I'd felt from Destiny's betrayal turned to white hot anger, and it was all aimed toward Isaac.

She glanced at me, and her face blanched. "Sorry, that was really insensitive of me."

"No. You're absolutely right. You know, none of this would have happened if he hadn't started creeping up on my girlfriend with his flashy smile and smooth talking." When I knew he was dating Destiny I gave them space. Well, that wasn't going to happen this time.

"He kind of does have a flashy smile," Brinlee agreed, coming up the stairs. "I can see how it was hard for her to resist it."

"That's not helpful," I said with an irritated frown.

"Sorry, I couldn't help myself. But just because he has a flashy smile doesn't mean he should get away with it," Brinlee said, putting a hand on her hip. "Where's the fight in you, Preston? You've been crying over her all week long." I opened my mouth to protest, but she kept chattering on. "Don't even try to deny it. My room's right next to yours and the walls are paper thin. If you care about her so much, why don't you just go after her?"

I closed my gaping jaw. I couldn't think of a single reason not to. Brinlee was absolutely right.

"You know her better than he does. Before this school year he never even talked to her. You've been friends with Destiny since you were building Lego empires with her on your bedroom floor. Don't let him win. You're a great guy, and eventually Destiny's going to realize what an idiot she's been. She's going to come crawling back to you begging for your forgiveness."

"Brinlee, she already did. You obviously didn't hear what he said to her when she brought that banana bread over. I'm not going to deny that she totally deserved it, but he was pretty harsh. It might not be so easy for him to convince her to come back."

"All he has to do is apologize and grovel a little bit."

"You don't get it, Brinlee. You didn't see them together tonight. They were practically inseparable." Megan darted her eyes toward me and clamped her lips together, like she'd just realized she'd said too much. "I just don't want to see Preston get hurt again."

It wasn't like I didn't already know, but it stung to hear it vocalized. But I was done with crying. "I don't care if my heart gets trampled on again," I said as I jogged down the stairs to get ready for bed. "She's worth it." It would be a long, hard fight to win her back properly, without her thinking of him every spare moment, but I was up for the challenge.

Right before I turned the corner into the family room I heard Brinlee squeal upstairs, "Oh my gosh! That's so freaking epic!"

Acknowledgements

Thank you…

Heavenly Father. Without Him, this wouldn't even be a book. So many tearful prayers went into the creation of this story, and I owe it to Him that it turned out the way it did.

My husband, Jared. You convinced me to return to writing, and you've been amazing and encouraging on the days that I thought I couldn't continue. Without your input, Preston would still be a skinny, awkward gamer nerd.

Mom and Dad for all your support as you watched your daughter become an author. Your excitement and approval of Destiny fueled me along as I wrote *Synchrony*. Mom, thanks for your editorial help. You found a lot of typos on your road trips with Christy and *Synchrony* is a better book because of it.

Melissa, for brainstorming storylines with me and coming up with some brilliant ideas. Your editorial skills are amazing. I was very impressed with how many things you found for me to fix.

Christy, you've always been here for me, even when you were far away. So much of this story was written for you. Thanks for helping to find all those pesky typos!

My beautiful kids, Rebecca, Ammon, Ethan, and Braedon. Thank you so much for your patience with me and the long hours I spend working to share my writing with the world. I'm so impressed with how much you have all grown up since I've become a writer.

A huge thank-you to all the young girls who have supported me by reading *Destiny* and *Synchrony* and giving feedback, passing out flyers and bookmarks, and telling their friends about *Destiny*. Andrea Monchecourt, Julia Monchecourt, Christine Monchecourt, Haeley van der Werf, Savannah van der Werf, Jaylyn Brown, Christianity White, Evelyn Hancock, Ashley Johnston, Kaylene Buchanan, Jeanette Dodge, Michaela Dodge, Jess Lashway, Emma Ellison, and Silje Ellison, you guys light up my life. Every time I hear any kind of feedback from you, it totally makes my day!

My amazing beta readers. I have no idea what I'd do without you guys! Soso Bassiouny, Janet Brown, Shaundra Warner, Bianca Smith, Katie Watkins, Kate McNicol, Sharon Wilt, Emily Mitchell, Emerald Barnes, Scott Ray, Melanie Valderrama.

My writing partner, Destiny Shackleford and her shoutout to *Destiny* in her book. I love brainstorming stuff with you!

My editors Anna Coy and Anissa Wall. You are both amazing. Thank you so much for all the hard work you did on *Synchrony*.

Deanne Monchecourt for showing up on my doorstep on the Destiny release day with dinner, balloons, and your sweet, little, die-hard Destiny fans. I was very deeply touched by your thoughtfulness that night. Thank you for your endless support, talking up my book to your friends, and buying stacks of paperbacks to ship to them.

Rachel Harris, Joanne Rock, Karen Rock, Ophelia London, Chantele Sedgwick, Casey Bond, Veronica Bartles, Megan Curd, Emerald Barnes, Carlyle Labuschagne, and Rachel Brownell for donating your books to be included in giveaways promoting my work.

Lola Verroen from Lola's Blog Tours for organizing the Destiny and Synchrony Blog Tours and going above and beyond in everything you do.

The Destiny Street Crew and all the awesome bloggers, Twitter followers, and Facebook friends who have shared posts about my books. You guys have helped more than you'll ever know.

My amazing photographer and business partner, Virginia Hodges of Virginia Rose Hodges Photography. You are my rock. Anytime I had a rough day while I was writing this book, you were there for me, rallying in my corner. Your pictures are stunning and are only getting better and better. I'm honestly speechless by how far you've gone to help me gain success. Thank you for finding the amazing cover models for Synchrony.

Selena Renteria and Christian Lopez, you two did such a great job at the Synchrony photo shoot. Christian, it was such an honor to meet you and to hear you sing. Your voice is amazing! You make such a great Preston. Selena, it's spooky how much you look like the character I see in my head. You're beautiful, talented, and hilariously funny. Keep up the good work and just see where it takes you in life!

Dear Reader,

I hope you enjoyed your stay in Destiny's world! If so, I would love it if you would consider leaving a review on Amazon.com or Goodreads.com. Every bit of support from my readers is appreciated. I'm always thrilled to hear from you guys, so please, feel free to connect with me online.

Cindy Ray Hale

About the Author

Cindy Ray Hale lives in a little slice of wooded heaven near Atlanta, Georgia with her husband and children. She spends way too much time following up-and-coming musicians on YouTube and dreams of joining their ranks one day. She's a bit of a health food nut and can't live without her daily green smoothies. She tries to stay sane as she juggles writing with four kids, staying active on social media, and keeping up her book blog at http://cinnamoncindy.blogspot.com/. In addition to writing and self-publishing two Young Adult Contemporary novels, she has also written articles for "New Era" magazine and The American Preppers Network.

For more information on The Destiny Trilogy and Cindy's upcoming books visit http://destinybycindyhale.blogspot.com/ or follow @CindyRayHale on Twitter.

28368841R00231

Made in the USA
Charleston, SC
10 April 2014